THE RIPPLE EFFECT

Praise for *The Ripple Effect*

'A joyous British romp – *The Ripple Effect* is an Ealing comedy for the 21st century'
Alan Coren

'There are some wonderfully funny set-pieces in this endearing study of English grit'
The Times

'Beautifully captures the devotion, passion and commitment of football fans, and the way the most unlikely things can happen on the pitch'
Irish News

'Packed with twists and turns, plus one final surprise, it's a great read'
Birmingham Post

'Great fun'
Choice

'Proof that Holland is a master of comedy'
Northern Echo

'Holland has done it again. Another comical gem from the new master of stand-up'
Western Mail

'Like finding two blobs of jam in your jammy doughnut, Dominic Holland's book makes you smile in a world sadly lacking in blobby jammy bits these days. Read it on a day when you wish the good guys could always win'
Fi Glover

'*Only in America* was a step in the right direction, but *The Ripple Effect* heralds Holland's emergence into the big time'
Sunday Times

'Expect odd looks on the train when you la
John Inverdale

'Football fans will love it. An old fashioned romp with a twist at the end as surprising as Seaman going to City'
Paul Hawksbee, 'The Hawksbee and Jacobs Show', *Talksport*

'Weird, witty and proof that Holland is a master of comedy'
Yorkshire Evening Press

'Packed with twists and turns, it's a great read even if all you know about football is that David Beckham plays it'
Irish Examiner

'Not every stand-up comedian manages to be as funny in print as they are on the stage. Dominic Holland is one of the few who is'
Liverpool Daily Post

Praise for *Only in America*

'An LA to London love story to rival Notting Hill'
Heat

'Laugh out loud and I couldn't put it down are two clichés that for *Only in America* really do apply'
Daily Express

'A hilarious modern day fairytale'
Hello!

'I read this book in one sitting and absolutely loved it. Funny, sweet and sharp with a wondeful story'
Graham Norton

'The characterisation is warm, the dialogue is witty, and the plot – friendly, feel-good fantasy . . . will make you smile'
Guardian

'A lively, funny read'
Sunday Mirror

'This book is so charming and funny. A genuine page turner, I read it on holiday and missed big chunks of Venice'
Sandy Toksvig

'It is the only book I have read in one sitting. Of all the books by comedians turning their hands to novel writing – including Stephen Fry, Alexei Sayle and Ade Edmonson – this is the funniest, most enjoyable and satisfying'
Simon Wilson, *Nottingham Post*

'Holland's novel is witty, warm, enjoyable, addictive, captivating and hilariously funny. Laughing out loud on your own can be an unnerving business, but laugh uncontrollably I did'
Katherine MacAlister, *Oxford Mail*

'Hilarious and touching novel'
Surrey Comet

'The kind of story where you know right from the beginning how it will come out, the pleasure being in how cleverly the ending can be contrived for greatest happiness'
Observer

'Farce meets fairytale as film writer Milly struggles to get her script noticed . . . Great fluff and nonsense'
Company

'As soon as you pick it up, you forget about everything that you have to do, and you read it from cover to cover and you laugh out loud and you love it'
Jenny Hanley, Saga Radio

Dominic Holland is an award-winning stand-up comedian and broadcaster who has made countless television appearances, and whose BBC Radio 4 Show *The Small World of Dominic Holland* won the Comic Heritage Award for best radio series. His first novel *Only in America*, a hilarious blend of Hollywood madness and London desperation, is available from Flame and is currently in development with BBC Films.

You can visit Dominic Holland at
www.dominicholland.com

Also by Dominic Holland

Only in America

DOMINIC HOLLAND

THE RIPPLE EFFECT

FLAME
Hodder & Stoughton

First published in Great Britain in 2003 by Hodder and Stoughton
A division of Hodder Headline

A Flame paperback

1 3 5 7 9 10 8 6 4 2

A CIP catalogue record for this title is available from the British Library

ISBN 0 340 81987 1

Typeset in Sabon by Phoenix Typesetting, Burley-in-Wharfedale, West Yorkshire

Printed and bound in Great Britain by
Mackays of Chatham plc, Chatham, Kent

Hodder and Stoughton
A division of Hodder Headline
338 Euston Road
London NW1 3BH

For my Mum and Dad

To all the AFC Wimbledons out there

ACKNOWLEDGEMENTS

A few people are anxious to see their names in print, so let me thank Gavin Style straight away. An avid Leeds fan, Gavin's infectious enthusiasm for early versions of *The Ripple Effect* helped me considerably.

Thanks to David Conn, the sports journalist, for writing *The Football Business*, the seminal work on football which helped me greatly in the writing of *The Ripple Effect*.

A big thank you to everyone at Supporters Direct and in particular to Brian Lomax for his time, even though his office was bloody freezing. Also, my thanks to Simon Binns and David Boyle for getting behind the book and inviting me to their conference at Highbury.

Of course, my thanks to my editor Mari Evans and my publicists Emma Longhurst and Ros Ellis and to everyone else at Hodder and Stoughton for their support.

I must acknowledge Andrew Frost who, as the real life doughnut terrorist, inspired this novel. When he recounted his funny anecdote over lunch that day, I shouldn't imagine he ever expected a novel to appear as a result.

I have met a great many real life Bill Baxters since *The Ripple Effect* has been published, who have been a tremendous help in getting the book talked about amongst football fans. Chief among them is Mike Harrison of City Gent fame. I am enormously grateful to Mike for all his enthusiasm and support for the book. I am always staggered by the passion of the Bill Baxters out there and I hope this book does them all justice.

Writing novels while being a stand-up and a dad requires a lot of tinkering with time and this book simply couldn't have happened without the energy and kindness of my wife, Nikki. Thank you.

As this is an acknowledgements page, I hereby accept the howling mistake in a passage midway through the book. I originally wrote the piece before he was sacked and although I did have time to change it, I decided not to both as a tribute to the man, who I regard very highly, and because I liked the passage in question and figured my readers could suspend reality for a few pages at least.

Finally, it has been enormously heartening for me to hear from so many readers of both my novels. In comparison with stand-up and its immediate feedback, writing books is a solitary business and so every e-mail I've received has been a great source of encouragement to me. Thank you very much.

THE RIPPLE EFFECT

CHAPTER 1

Bill glumly pushed his way through the Perspex apron door on to the floor of Beatty's Home Bakery. He was greeted by the familiar heat and permanent plume of chalk-white dust hanging thick in the air. The extractor fans had long since packed up, and Bill wondered what chance his lungs had if the industrial vacuum machines couldn't take it. Figures clad from head to toe in white overalls bustled around the two stunningly inefficient bakery lines, all with one eye permanently on the big wall clock, which appeared to be the only thing that was ever wiped clean. The bakery had just achieved its centenary and to celebrate had produced twenty thousand commemorative bloomers, which had been doled out free to everyone in the town of Middleton. One hundred glorious years marked by a loaf of bread, hardly inspirational stuff as Bill had mentioned at the time.

A wiry Indian lad stumbled past, pushing a carousel of crusty hot rolls. He must have been new to the job because Bill didn't recognise him. As a result of the shift work and the derisory rates of pay, the labour turnover was much higher than the financial one at the bakery. For most employees, Beatty's provided stopgap jobs, and only a few reluctantly accepted that this was their lives' lot. Bill was different, however. He was proud that he'd been there for twenty-five years and had never considered that there might be something better for him elsewhere. He'd bought his own house, raised a family, and had no problem with spending another twenty years diligently providing the surrounding community with bread. He was in a groove now, a well-worn smooth groove that fitted him perfectly. Curry might have taken over from fish'n'chips as the nation's favourite take-away, but bread's position in the English diet is unassailable. Every year, sunburnt Brits return home from their annual holidays determined to continue eating poncy Italian bread, but within days their resolve crumbles and they load their toasters with cardboard instead.

Baking bread is a job for life, Bill assured himself, and given his family circumstances, it seemed he might well have to work all of his. His wife, Mary, at the ripe old age of forty-four, had just given birth to their first son, some twenty-one years after their second daughter, Katherine, was born. It had been an accident, according to Mary, a mix-up with her dates and 'the change' that she had been preparing herself for. Bill had never questioned her about it, but he suspected that his son, future star centre forward of Middleton Edwardians Football Club, had in fact been a meticulously planned mistake, particularly as Mary had spent fifteen pounds on new underwear for the fertile night in question.

Bill couldn't believe how overcrowded their little house had suddenly become. No sooner had Tom arrived, complete with his rocker, cot, playpens and goodness knows what else, than Katherine announced that she too was moving back home with her baby because her gobshite of a husband had left, this time for good. Bill and Mary were still paying for her blasted wedding, hastily arranged before Katherine's bump began to show. Bill hadn't wanted to be a grandfather at little over forty, and his consternation at becoming a father again as well was tempered only by God proving his existence by granting him a son. His entire life had been dominated by females, but now in the Baxter household the male offensive had finally begun.

Space and money were both in stiflingly short supply, but Bill couldn't remember being happier. He was a shift supervisor at Beatty's and it seemed he had risen as far as he was ever going to. Production lines aside, if there was a fast track at the bakery, Bill had certainly never found it and the irony of his situation certainly wasn't lost on him. He needed more money and yet spent his entire working life surrounded by dough. At least, though, no one in his family would ever go hungry.

Smithy, the shift supervisor Bill was relieving, looked mightily pleased to see him. He pulled off his hat and wiped his face with a damp paper towel that was hanging from his waist.

'You all right, Bill?'

'What do you think?'

'So what the hell happened then?' Smithy asked, loosening his hairnet, and taking out his earplugs.

Middleton Edwardians FC had played at home earlier in the evening, and their dismal showing was the cause of Bill's mood.

'Don't ask. It's all too miserable.'

'Useless. Bloody useless. Only we could lose a soddin' two-nil lead. Eh, when have we ever come back from—'

'Sixty-one,' Bill butted in. He wasn't showing off. Showing off wasn't in Bill's nature; he just happened to know the answer. He could recall anything, however seemingly inconsequential, about his beloved Middleton football team. 'Against Kidderminster Town in the league. Two-nil down, we won four-two. Perry Jones got a hat trick.' He could also have described each goal in great detail but chose not to. That would have been showing off. Middleton Edwardians Football Club, founded 1902, gained professional league status exactly ninety-nine years later and had been teetering on the brink of financial oblivion ever since. This was only Middleton's second season in the English Third Division, and bookies weren't offering odds on the team remaining there come the end of the season.

'I don't know what's sadder,' Smithy chuckled, 'us losing, or you knowing so much useless information.'

'Probably both,' Bill laughed.

'You're bloody wasted working here, Billy boy.'

This was something that Bill had heard many times before. 'Ah well, too late for me now,' he replied loftily. 'Little Tom, though, he's going all the way.'

'Family well?'

'Were when I left 'em. Little'un's a bugger for sleeping, though. Mary is absolutely knackered – but still, that's what she wanted,' he added wryly.

Smithy grimaced at the idea of having kids again. Unlike Bill, his kids had all left home, and there was no chance of him having any more either, because his wife hadn't been long behind them in leaving.

'You're better off here at work, Bill. Although maybe not tonight.'

Bill groaned. 'Meaning?'

'Bloody short-staffed again, int we? Three no-shows. I've had to work the bloody line meself for most of the shift.'

Bill's hopes of a quiet night 'at mill' were fast receding.

'So what's going on to line one now?' Bill had a dull feeling that he already knew the answer. 'Ah no, it's not bloody jam doughnuts, is it?'

Smithy chuckled. 'I don't know why you bother askin' questions.'

Bill groaned. He'd just been watching a load of professional doughnuts and would now complete his day baking the bloody things.

While Americans like to adorn their doughnuts with all manner of sugars, syrups and chocolates, it is a strange fact that the English consider a doughnut needs nothing more than a healthy dollop of raspberry jam. It lurks within, ready to pounce upon the delighted owner within a few energetic and suspecting bites. Incredible though it may seem, each day the English brush the remnants of eight million jam doughnuts from their lips and shirt fronts, a thousand of which are proudly made at Beatty's Home Bakery, Middleton, Cheshire. By quirk of fate, a Beatty's doughnut carries much prestige and even a price premium, the only Beatty's product to do so. Today, with corporate consolidation, and mass-production lines reigning supreme, anything that can be determined as being made by hand carries a special kudos. Whether it be hand-cooked crisps or a hand-rolled pizza, it is a modern-day phenomenon that people are happy to part with more cash for products involving hands at some point in their manufacture.

In reality, this might only involve a hand switching on a machine, but in the case of a Beatty's doughnut, 'handmade' status really could be claimed. This was an unexpected yet fortuitous consequence of the chronic lack of investment in new machinery at Beatty's, where the only way a plain doughnut could be transformed into a jam doughnut was if some poor stupefied employee spent eight hours injecting them with jam. And when that employee happened to be Bill Baxter, shift supervisor no less, already in a bad mood because his team had squandered a two-goal lead, it was no wonder that the resulting doughnuts might not pass quality control. Not that Beatty's had a quality control, of course.

An hour into his shift, Bill was becoming increasingly irritated as he loaded each doughnut with jam and sent it on its way, to be instantly replaced by another one screaming for its fill like a hungry kid at tea time. Despite his obvious capabilities, Bill had seriously underachieved throughout his life, either through a total lack of ambition or an easy sense of contentment – it depended on one's interpretation. As a child he'd had two ambitions: to play for Middleton and to be as tall as his dad. Realistically, he'd never stood a chance with the former, and with his dad standing at a little over five feet six, the latter was hardly anything to aim for, and by the time he did see eye to eye with the great man, he'd forgotten about it anyway. Not that Bill ever considered himself an underachiever. On the contrary, being married with three kids, one grandchild and having more friends than John McCarthy at the height of his incarceration suited him just fine. It all depended by what yardstick success was measured, and if it happened to be a state of happiness, then Bill Baxter could claim that his life was as successful as Churchill's or Pelé's, his two all-time heroes. And no one who knew him would disagree either. People tended not to disagree with Bill anyway because, unlike the town's football team, in any discussion Bill was almost unbeatable.

He squeezed the jam trigger gently until another bun was fit to burst; it was instantly replaced by another sugary dough ball.

'. . . three points down the sodding drain,' he muttered to himself angrily. 'Could have gone twelfth tonight. Highest club position in the English football league . . . EVER.' He paused and recalled the ball trundling agonisingly over the goal line for the third time as the Middleton keeper floundered and instinctively prepared to hurl blame at whichever defender happened to be closest. Bill sighed at his lot – a Catholic who supported Middleton Edwardians FC, a particularly heavy and cumbersome cross to bear. Out of character and totally unexpectedly, Bill clenched his fist and, before he could stop himself, brought it smashing down on to the most recently filled doughnut. As the doughnut collapsed, jam jetted out and across the production line. Delighted with himself and feeling he was watching it happen in slow motion, Bill followed the jam's path as it snaked through the air like a cruise missile, albeit without any directional equipment. He followed the jam until it was stopped by the face of an unfortunate bakery colleague. Bill thought it might be the Indian lad from earlier, but he couldn't be sure, since his face was covered with jam. The lad stood statue still, seemingly not believing what had just happened to him.

'Sorry about that,' Bill offered immediately, if rather feebly. It was an apology hopelessly undermined by his stifled giggles.

It took a moment for the young man to register what had happened to him. He knew that he'd been hit by something, but with his face covered in a red liquid, he could have been forgiven for thinking that he might actually have been shot.

Bill could now see that it was indeed the Indian lad he hadn't yet met but felt sure he was about to. The lad licked his lips. If he was at all relieved that he'd been hit by jam rather than a bullet, then he wasn't showing it as he turned and glared at Bill, his face a study in fury.

'Ya fockin wanker. What are ya doin'?'

'Sorry, lad. It were an accident,' Bill offered, surprised that a youngster had just called him a wanker and yet, bizarrely, he had still felt the need to apologise.

'An accident?' the lad screamed above the constant hum of the bakery. He bent down, threateningly picked up the catering bucket of jam and seemed to have every intention of emptying the contents over Bill's balding head.

'Now come on, son. Don't be silly. You don't want to lose your job, do ya?'

'No, 'cos I've always wanted to work in a fockin bakery.'

'OK, now, calm down. It were an accident. I'm Billy Baxter, shift supervisor, or your boss, whichever you prefer. You can call me Bill – everyone else does.' He smiled broadly, his kind and handsome face persuading the young man to relent.

'What about twat? How does that sound?'

'Oi, that's Mr Twat, thank you,' Bill joked, and smiled for the last time. He'd now suffered a 'twat' and a 'wanker', and he hoped the lad might realise that he'd used up his insult quota. 'An odd way to meet, eh?' he said, holding out his hand. 'So I'm Bill. What's your name?'

'Vippin.'

'OK then, Vippin, good to meet ya.'

'You can call me Vip, although I prefer V.I.P.' It was a joke the lad had probably used all his life.

'Suits ya. Very Irate Person.'

They shook hands and Bill handed him a towel from his station desk.

'Sorry, Vip. Start today, did you?'

'Yeah, but I'll not be around long. I'm only here 'cos me mam made us get a job.'

Bill smiled. How many times had he heard that?

'I've heard about you anyway,' Vippin said.

'Oh?'

'People say you're alright – as a boss, I mean.'

'Oh yeah, as I've just proved, covering you in jam.'

Vippin laughed. 'People say you're smart as well.'

Bill instantly began brushing down his brilliant white coat. 'Well, I do try.'

Vippin laughed again. 'You know what I mean.'

Bill knew full well, but was suddenly bashful. 'You shouldn't believe everything you hear, especially not in here.'

'So what's with you and the jam then?' Vippin asked, a fair question, under the circumstances.

'I smashed a doughnut, didn't I?'

'Yeah, I can see that.' Vippin wiped a blob of jam from his nose. 'But why?'

Bill remembered the reason and suddenly felt a little bit embarrassed. Frantically, he tried to think of a more worthy reason for beating up a doughnut, but he couldn't.

'Middleton lost tonight,' he offered shyly. 'They were two-nil up,' he added, hoping it might strengthen his case. It didn't.

'Is that it?' Vippin was incredulous. Like most youngsters living in the shadows of Old Trafford, the fortunes of Middleton Edwardians weren't uppermost in his mind. 'Did you go? To the game, I mean,' he asked.

Bill nodded and smiled again. Did he go? In nearly forty

years, he'd only ever missed a handful of games. 'Yeah, I went. You follow football?' he asked innocently.

'Yeah, course. It's not just cricket with us lot, you know,' Vip spat out indignantly, suddenly becoming angry again.

'All right, lad. So, who's your team then?'

Vip tutted and rolled his eyes. What a stupid question. 'United, of course.'

Now it was Bill's turn to tut. What chance did his little club have these days? From Singapore to Mogadishu and everywhere in between, kids were supporting the famous but increasingly soulless Manchester United. Bill was pleased that he was different and had opted for Middleton – not that he'd ever really had a choice, mind. It would have been difficult explaining to his dad that he didn't want to support the team his old man had played for as centre forward. His mum used to take him to the matches each week and young Bill saw his dad score 46 of his 112 Middleton goals – and, being Bill, he could recall every one. A picture of Bill's dad in his baggy shorts and thick cotton shirt hung proudly in the club bar and Bill wished his old man had survived to see the proud moment when the club gained full professional league status. It would have been a worthy sendoff for the old bugger. Over the years, Manchester United had plundered the entire contents of a silver mine while Middleton's trophy cabinet was filled with a bunch of dried flowers that hadn't originally been dried, and even they hadn't been won.

'Do you go to Old Trafford, then, Vip?'

'Yeah, been a few times when I were a lad. Can't afford it now, though, even if I could get tickets.'

This was exactly what Bill meant about soul.

'You can always get in at our place.'

Vippin laughed. 'Yeah, wonder why. Are you even in the league?'

'Now careful, laddie. Personal insults I can take, but not the club, OK?'

'So what division are you in, then?'

Bill hoped the question might be another joke, but it wasn't and he sighed. 'Third division and we're still in the cup.'

'You draw United, maybe I'll come down.'

'It would be an honour to have you. Anyway, speaking of the reds,' Bill pointed at Vippin's overalls, 'you have my permission to go and get yourself smartened up.'

'Oh well, that's very generous of ya.'

Vippin made off towards the male locker room but stopped and turned round. 'Eh, Bill, some advice for ya . . .'

'I'll never support United.'

'No, not that. Go easy on the jam, eh?'

Vippin was rude and belligerent, but Bill liked him and hoped he wouldn't leave too soon. His break for the jam fight meant that a backlog of dough balls had built up, each clamouring for a jam fix.

' "Go easy on the jam, eh?" ' Bill chuckled to himself.

For the remainder of his shift, Bill barely filled a doughnut with its proper allocation of jam. Most got none at all; others were merely grazed with jam. Handmade premium jam doughnuts with no jam – what a fantastic idea. Suddenly, his shift began to pick up speed as he imagined hapless people raging at shopkeepers about the state of their jam-less dough-nuts. Of course, such a claim could only really be made once it had been eaten, swallowing the evidence, as it were, and so casting considerable doubt on the complaint. Bill didn't quite know why he was doing it, but it felt entirely the right thing to do. It was his little protest, his stand. Somehow, it all made perfect sense. Earlier in the evening, Middleton had squandered a two-goal lead, and it seemed only fair that other people, however unconnected and remote from Middleton, should also be made to suffer.

CHAPTER 2

PC Keith Waddle felt like a kid on Christmas Eve. He swallowed his last mouthful of wretched cottage cheese and barely chewed the remainder of his celery. That way, he didn't have to taste the wet string passing itself off as food, and as a bonus his system would have to expend even more calories trying to digest the stuff. At half-past eight, Waddle triumphantly consulted the diary pack that had come with his godforsaken American diet course. One more day to go; he could hardly wait.

He held his stomach in as best he could and looked at his huge reflection in the oven door. A definite improvement, he told himself, failing to see anything ironic in the fact that one of the two kitchen appliances largely responsible for his bulk was currently reflecting it. With both hands, he spanked his stomach to the tune of a football chant at the end of which he substituted 'Eng-er-land' with 'Treat Day', and proceeded to run around his kitchen with his arms aloft. Tomorrow was the day he had thought would never arrive. Tomorrow was 'Treat Day', whereby his fascist diet allowed him as a treat any culinary delight of his choosing. He opened his diary at 8 January, and looked at the self-adhesive Treat Day sticker he'd stuck there all those miserable weeks ago: 'Well done, calorie champ, you've done it. It's Treat Day.' With digital timing and as if it knew what it was due, Waddle's stomach rumbled loudly and he stroked it reassuringly. Not long now, he thought as he caressed his hairy dome fondly. The last eight weeks had been the most difficult of his life, but despite a faltering will, he had prevailed and now Treat Day was his prize. There was to be no deliberation; Waddle knew exactly what his treat was going to be. There was never any doubt about it. In fact, PC Waddle had stopped calling it Treat Day altogether. Tomorrow was Jam Doughnut day.

It was a bitterly cold morning, which felt even colder to Bill as he emerged from the warmth of the bakery. With the woolly hat that Mary had knitted for him pulled down over his ears, and his donkey jacket collar hitched up, his whiskered face could barely be seen.

'Morning, Ernie,' Bill said as cheerily as the bitter morning would allow, plonking his fifty-five pence on the counter as Ernie separated Bill's *Daily Mirror* and *Middleton Chronicle* from the various piles of newspapers. Bill always had the right change for his papers, keen as he was to get home after a night shift. 'Fresh this morning, eh?'

'Don't notice it any more,' Ernie replied, looking up briefly. 'Bloody shocking last night, weren't they? Should blinking well pay us to watch them.'

Bill smiled. How many football fans uttered those very words every week, only to find they screamed themselves hoarse at the next game and were still paying for the dubious privilege?

'Standing out there, freezing our wotsits off,' Ernie continued.

'I thought you didn't notice it.'

'Ya what?'

'Don't matter.'

'So, come on, Bill. What's the positive, then, from last

night?' Bill was often called upon to find a positive side to whatever scenario had befallen the club. It was becoming an increasingly irksome task.

'Er . . . well . . .' he began blindly, 'last night's collapse gets our season's collapse out of the way.'

'Ya what?'

Bill wasn't altogether sure himself. 'You know, every club collapses at least once a season . . .'

'And?'

'So we might have a good cup run.' As positives go, Bill knew this was particularly lacklustre. Not so much a silver lining, more a foil trim.

'Is that it?'

'Best I can do at the moment, I'm afraid.' Bill really wanted to get away now. 'Anyway, Ern—'

'D'you know, I was trying to think last night, when was the last time we came back from two down?'

Bill had no intention of answering this question again but, as it turned out, he wouldn't have to.

'Kidderminster, nineteen sixty-one,' Ernie announced, much to Bill's stunned delight.

'Bloody hell, Ernie, you're absolutely right. Do you remember, Jones got a hat trick?'

'No. Smithy told us last night over a pint. Bit worrying, mind, because I think I was bloody well at that game 'n'all.'

'Amazing what Smithy knows, eh?' Bill half-smiled.

'Isn't it?'

'OK, then, Ern.'

No doubt Mary had had another terrible night with little Pelé, as Bill often called his son, and he liked to get home before she was finally wrenched from her sleep for good. He walked up the high street, which had largely remained unchanged since he was a boy, apart from the shops, of course. It appeared that the current hot retail competition was for people's cast-off clothes. Help the Aged, Oxfam, the Imperial Cancer Fund and Sue Ryder all screamed out loudly for anything that people no longer wanted. In fact, there was no longer a first-hand clothes shop in the town, and it amused Bill to think that the local population was effectively sharing each other's rags, with the charity shops offering an intermediary ironing and laundry service.

Bill scanned the headlines of both newspapers as he trundled up the street.

'Calls for Beaumont to announce plans for Middleton FC,' yelled the headline in the *Chronicle*. Bill folded the newspaper, put it under his arm and quickened his pace, keen to get home and scrutinise the article.

At the brow of the hill, the cobbled street came to a faltering end. The rest of the cobbles had been stolen by an opportunist gang of gypsies. They would have pinched the lot if the suspension on their truck could have taken the weight, but they never did return for the rest. They were like rogue builders, only in reverse.

At this point, Bill's eye was always drawn to the Middleton Edwardians FC ground, which now came gloriously into view. Bill would have liked to say that the ground loomed large in the distance, towering grandly over its founding town. Sadly, though, even the most die-hard and deluded fan couldn't describe it so. It loomed pathetically, if at all. One stand had been closed for two seasons because it was deemed unsafe, another required essential repairs, and the remaining two were only half covered. But a struggling team with pretty dire facilities aside, Middleton was a wonderful football club, and each week, up to five thousand supporters faithfully turned up, silently resigned to settle for a draw. However, like all football fans, every last one of them had secret lofty ambitions for their club – dreams of Premiership status, an FA Cup win even – but realistic ambitions for the club were rather muted, and league and commercial survival were the current preoccupations. Promotions and silverware would have to wait. Of course, this wasn't anything to sing about from the terraces, and while visiting fans frequently chanted 'Going up', the Middleton terraces had more dignity than to break out into 'Staying Alive'.

Supporting Middleton was like being a parent to a problem teenager – a constant cause of worry. Indeed, the club was the only thing in Bill's life that he ever really needed to worry about, and he did, constantly. The article in the *Chronicle* referred to the club's new owner, Mr Conran Beaumont. Every Middleton fan understood that the only thing the club needed more than league points was pounds sterling, but it wasn't until the recent death of the long-time owner, local philanthropist Milton Thorpe, that the true extent of the club's perilous financial position came to light. The club had been founded by Thorpe's late father, who had made his fortune from the cotton industry, and the first Middleton team that ever turned out had been his mill side, with the current stadium eventually being built on the site of the old mill.

Six months after Milton Thorpe's death, the club and its surrounding land had been bought by Mr Conran Beaumont, a London-based businessmen with no connection to, nor, it appeared, any interest in, football. Excitement had spread through the town at the news that a sugar daddy was going to make the club great – not again as the cliché went, but great for the first time. But Bill stood almost alone in being highly sceptical about the new chairman and his intentions. Bill's initial and most ill thought-out objection to the man had been never trust a man with a surname for a first name. Ernie had used Lloyd George as an example to undermine this facile point and Bill couldn't be bothered to correct him.

Bill suspected that Beaumont was much more interested in the twelve acres of land the club stood on, or more accurately leant on. From football club to luxury flats with concierge and gym in the blink of an eye. This was becoming a sad and depressing reality throughout Britain and one which Bill had always figured would eventually confront his club. He hoped that he might be wrong but suspected he wasn't. Since Beaumont's takeover, Bill's suspicions had grown. The man hadn't made any announcements and nor had he visited the club, and so Bill had begun to prepare for the inevitable. Over the years, he'd collated newspaper cuttings on the closure of similar small clubs along with planning reports and statements. They were turgid and depressing documents that Bill had never really read, but now, though, seeing the *Chronicle*'s headline, he felt that he should.

Indeed, Bill might have been an underachiever all his life, but perhaps it was preordained that this was his time to deliver. He hadn't known it, but perhaps he had been saving his energies for something much more important than a career. And, if his suspicions were correct, then Mr Chairman Beaumont hadn't reckoned on his opponents, the passionate people of Middleton, ably led by a shift supervisor of the local bakery with a point to prove.

Bill had decided that a pre-emptive strike was the best policy against his probable foe. Churchill himself – the greatest Briton ever – would have applauded his strategy but perhaps not his method.

'Dear Mr Beaumont,' Bill had written one evening last week, having lost all patience with the man's silence, especially since the rumours of development deals had become rife.

Firstly, let me take this opportunity to welcome you to Middleton Edwardians Football Club. No doubt, you will be aware what a fabulous club it is, with a history closely linked with the mill town of Middleton and its people. That is why the club has such committed support (fourth highest in the division). Now, I am sure you've heard the rumours that you bought the club for re-development purposes, this would be a tragedy for our town and would probably end up with you being shot, and therefore what would be the point? Please don't be alarmed. This is not a threat in any way, no one here wants to shoot you and I'm sure that you in turn don't want to be shot. Also, there are many other reasons why the land shouldn't be developed, but I won't bore you with them here, because you being shot is the main one anyway.

That said, I and the thousands of people of Middleton welcome you warmly to our town and to our club. Sorry if a part of this letter has come as a shock to you, but we feel that honesty is best for everyone.

On behalf of the thousands of Middleton fans, you have our sincere best wishes.

'Dad!' Katherine had screeched, as she'd read the letter.
'What?'
She'd looked at Bill fondly. 'Dad, do you want me to write this out properly?'
'No. I'm not bothered about the grammar.'

'I wasn't meaning the grammar.'

'Well, what then?'

'Like, making the same point, but without threatening to kill him.'

Bill had hurriedly retrieved an envelope from the dining-room drawer.

Bill turned off the high street into Hazel Close, where he had been born nearly forty-two years ago. Again, it hadn't changed much, apart from the array of ugly satellite dishes plastered on to almost every house front, including his own. His home looked quiet. There were no lights on and the bed-room curtains were still drawn. He carefully opened the gate and let himself in, mindful not to let any of the accumulated heat escape. Ideally, he would get a half-hour with his papers before little Tom woke up. Quietly, he stood for a moment on the door mat, listening intently, and smiled to himself as he heard a faint gurgle from Tom's bedroom. It wouldn't remain faint for long and so he quickly retrieved his son before he woke his mum.

Bill popped the one remaining bottle of made-up formula milk into the microwave, taking care to stop it before the machine pinged because Mary had banned it for heating baby food, having read some article or other. Tom gurgled as he sucked urgently on the teat, oblivious to his dad kissing him gently on his forehead. Bill hoped that Tom might inherit his granddad's sporting genes, but even if he didn't, he reasoned that with his son's renowned lung capacity, he could still serve the club remarkably well from the terraces, which with luck might be completely covered by the time he reached his teens. Tom settled in the same rocker that his sisters had rocked in and Bill went about making himself a cup of tea.

'Bill, have you got Tom?' Mary called out half an hour later.

'Yep,' he responded, self-satisfied.

'You're an angel.'

'I know,' he muttered.

'I'll be down in a sec, love.'

Bill put the kettle on again and slung a tea bag in a mug for her and another in his. Mary entered their tiny living room wearing an enormous bathrobe that Katherine had stolen from a London hotel and made straight for Tom, who was starting to cry.

'Thanks, love. You been back long?' she asked as they kissed each other good morning.

'About an hour. How was your night?'

'Fantastic. Buster here was only up five times, weren't ya?' She nuzzled her nose into his chest.

'Mary, that's ridiculous. You're going to have to leave him to bloody well cry.'

'Bill,' Mary snapped.

'Oh, he can't understand that.'

'Yes he can. It all goes in. I've read about it.'

Bill tutted. 'You and your magazines.'

Bill couldn't really grasp what it was about bad language that Mary found so heinous, particularly as she was Irish, a race surely in a league of its own when it came to swearing.

'How was work?'

'Not great. I spent the whole night filling doughnuts with—'

Mary held up her finger, sensing another unacceptable word about to surface.

'Jam. Filling them with jam. Or not, actually.'

'What do you mean?'

'Oh, nothing. It's not important.'

Bill was absolutely right on almost every count. Conran Beaumont had no interest in Middleton Edwardians FC as a football club, but actually didn't much care for its development opportunities either. Conran was completely disinterested in the whole scheme, which had been entirely conceived by his rather desperate business partner, Marcus Howell. In London, the two men were having a leisurely late breakfast at Claridge's. Marcus laughed nervously as he put Bill's letter back down on the table.

'Well, it's to the point, at least,' Conran joked.

Marcus was relieved that Conran didn't seem at all ruffled by Bill's crude threat. He'd warned Conran that there would be vociferous opposition to their plans but he hadn't mentioned death threats, and this was before their plans had even been officially announced. Conran was proving to be the ideal business partner for the venture Marcus was about to launch him on. He was obscenely wealthy, and so really did have more money than sense, but the cliché would still have applied had he been absolutely flat broke because Conran was also profoundly stupid.

'Actually, I think it's bloody funny. All friendly at the beginning, and then he's going to kill me.' Conran grinned defiantly, his tiny yellow teeth made prominent thanks to his almost complete absence of a lower jaw. The importance of a chin is rather overlooked until one is missing. It gives the impression that the person is permanently unimpressed with everything, although given Conran's means and his profligate lifestyle this was in fact fairly accurate. He had once tried growing a beard but shaved it off when a girlfriend pointed out that it was more of a throatie than a goatie.

Marcus read the letter again. 'Yes, you're probably right. Nothing to worry about.'

'Absolutely.'

Marcus wanted to share his confidence but reassured himself that at least it wasn't his life being threatened. He congratulated himself on having the foresight to keep his name out of the frame.

He produced a copy of the *Middleton Chronicle*, and Conran's eyes immediately widened. At last, a reaction, Marcus thought.

'Bloody hell, that photo of me is awful. Marcus, you really must arrange for me to have some decent photos taken.'

Marcus forced himself to smile. Yeah, like I'm your secretary, and, anyway, there's only so much a photographer can do. Marcus had a problem with power, more specifically his lack of it, save over his secretary at work and occasionally his wife. And no one took him seriously either – that was another thing that blighted his life but was also about to change.

Conran scrutinised the article, which portrayed him rather negatively.

'Hah, Marcus, listen to this: "Conran Beaumont, the millionaire playboy". Oh, I do like that. Perhaps I should have that on my card.'

He snorted with laughter and Marcus felt obliged to join in. Marcus never laughed much these days, at least not genuinely. He was altogether too stressed.

'Millionaire playboy! Do you know what, Mark, I might get this framed. Shame it's not a national.'

Marcus hated being called Mark and wondered whether

Conran did it deliberately, to remind him of his origins. He had been christened plain old Mark Howell, but chose to become Marcus shortly before starting his career in law. As a result he lost touch with practically everyone from his Mark days, even his family, who said he might as well add arsehole as a middle name. It was quite a sacrifice to make, but one he had felt sure was worth making. Marcus Howell was the sort of wanky name that suited senior partners of major law firms.

'Can I keep this?' Conran asked, with the newspaper already in his bag. 'Dad'll think it's a scream.'

Marcus forced yet another false laugh, surely the most exhausting thing known to man after taking kids swimming. Conran Beaumont didn't suffer any insecurity about his background and why should he? In monetary terms at least, he was only a few down from royalty, and with the exception of looks, he had everything in life that Marcus wanted. Unimaginable wealth and yet he hadn't needed to bother with anything as mundane as a career. Being born was all he had needed to do, and given the size and shape of his head, that must have been a piece of piss as well. Conran was in his early forties but he looked older and, although he'd lived most of his life in South Africa, he spoke with the invaluable plummy English accent that comes with an Eton education. His grandfather had made a dubious fortune from various African mineral mines but latterly his father had gone semi-legitimate and founded a property development company that currently spanned the globe. Unfortunately for Conran, they built properties not chins.

Marcus and Conran had met twenty years ago on their respective world travels when they'd been on a bid to find themselves or, more accurately, women to sleep with. No surprise then that they had both gravitated to Bangkok. Marcus had been working his way round the globe, suffering the indignity of youth hostels, and had been delighted to hook up with Conran, who was swiping his credit card on a route that coincided with his father's hotel empire. Marcus Howell was intelligent, handsome and ruthlessly ambitious and Conran Beaumont was ugly and rich with no need for ambition. It was a devastating combination and they instantly became good friends, dependent on each other for the pleasures that life has to offer.

After twenty years of sacrifice and effort, Marcus had made salaried partner at McCormick and Laing, one of Manchester's largest law firms, but he had long since realised that his career had plateaued. He hadn't been told as much, but other lawyers with less experience had been promoted above him and that spoke volumes. It was a combination of the lack-of-respect thing again, and his lower second-class red-brick degree. What chance did he have up against a limit-less supply of Oxbridge bastards? At forty-one, his career had effectively ended, at least from a salary perspective, and if desiring untold wealth is considered crude then Marcus was as vulgar as a Benidorm beach on a summer's day.

What Marcus wanted most was more money than he could possibly spend, but crucially with enough time to at least try. He also wanted respect, of course, but he figured respect is just a factor of wealth anyway. Marcus needed either a lottery win or a lucky business opportunity and so he was near tearful with delight when Milton Thorpe, owner of Middleton Edwardians Football Club, had had the good manners and timing to finally croak. And having physically clung on to life for so long, by the time he died, Thorpe's once powerful mind had long since turned to mush and his vast estate and affairs had been left in total chaos. This had suited his lawyer, Marcus Howell, perfectly. Thorpe had bequeathed his entire estate to his two absent sons, to inject, snort and generally squander as they wished after they had settled an impressive inheritance tax bill with Her Majesty's Inland Revenue. To settle the tax liability, property had to be sold and this was how Marcus planned to forge his invitation to the rich club. Marcus suggested that one particular property on Middleton Avenue was the best prospect for the brothers to sell and, remarkably, he had already lined up an eager buyer, willing to pay an amount for the property that coincidentally matched the tax liability exactly. The brothers had readily agreed and a hastily convened company called Table Top Management had become the new and proud owner of Middleton Edwardians Football Club, quite literally a steal at £1.8 million. Everyone was delighted, but especially the two directors of Table Top, Marcus Howell and Conran Beaumont. Marcus, though, had needed to raise half a million pounds himself and it hadn't been easy. He'd remortgaged his house, and sold off his two investment flats and his beloved Porsche to raise the money, while Conran had simply made a phone call. To support his disproportionate borrowings, Marcus had been forced to work harder than ever before, and neither his wife nor his mistress seemed to understand the meaning of economic restraint.

'I quite like the idea of owning a footie team, you know,' Conran chortled glibly.

Marcus glared at him. They'd had this conversation before. Marcus could ill afford a long-drawn-out affair with the club limping on for years. On the contrary, this had to be Middleton's last season in action. That was a certainty.

'Hey, I've got some pals over from Jo'burg, and they've hooked up with some cracking totty.'

Marcus wasn't listening any more. His mind was distracted by the pressure he was under. He was in the big time now. Finally, after years of not being taken seriously, he was playing at the main table and, like a real player, he'd committed everything. But it was worth it. A two-million-pound investment for twelve acres of land with a developed value conservatively estimated at some thirty million pounds. Unlike most trains in the country, this particular gravy train was bang on time, and as it eased itself up against the buffers, there were only two men waiting to board it. Marcus could almost taste the success. The plan was foolproof. It was perfect. He'd thought of everything; nothing could go wrong.

PC Waddle didn't need his alarm clock this morning. Today was jam doughnut day and he was already shaving when his alarm began rattling. He dragged his blunt razor painfully across his fat pink cheek. As a blob of blood appeared on his chin, he realised he should have changed the blade after all. Well, if the darn blades weren't so expensive . . . he muttered to himself, but soon began laughing at how appropriate it was as he wiped the blood away. Later this morning his chin was going to be covered in jam anyway. This was his special day. It was Treat Day, jam doughnut day, and nothing was going to ruin it.

CHAPTER 3

Some things have become almost synonymous with each other: apples and pears, strawberries and cream, and now football and money. Seth Meyer was a football agent, a new breed of professional that hadn't existed twenty years previously but had since helped football quietly nudge itself up to the abyss of financial ruin. England had more registered football agents than any other country in Europe and a sad number of football clubs currently had their noses pushed right up against the wall.

Seth's job was to extract as much money as possible from the football clubs for his playing and, more often these days, non-playing clients. Seth's star client was none other than Lee Robson, a loyal Tottenham Hotspur servant approaching the end of his contract – or 'name your price time', as it's affectionately known.

Seth was not having a good morning and was currently having a telephone conversation with Lee, trying to persuade him that he should re-sign with Tottenham.

'Two grand! Is that it?' Lee barked angrily in his phone. He was in an 'exclusive' clothes 'boutique' on the Kings Road, buying that week's latest fashions, and would have phoned Seth back but for the fact that he rather fancied the beautiful shop assistant and wanted to impress her.

Seth sighed. On the wall of his Wardour Street office was

a full-length photo of a more youthful Lee Robson playing for West Ham before he joined Spurs five years ago.

'Yes, Lee, that's it.'

'Well then, no, 'cos it ain't enough.'

Seth took his feet off his desk and sat up straight in his big leather chair. 'Lee, are you sure about this? An extra two grand a week, over two years—'

'My suits cost two grand.' The assistant blushed and smiled as Lee winked at her. I might be in here, he thought to himself. 'So, great, I retire in five years' time with nothing more than a pile of clothes.'

Seth's eyes wandered. He'd heard all this crap before. Posturing – it was the same at every negotiation.

'It'll take you to nearly twenty grand a week, at a club you're happy with, in London.'

Lee was admiring himself in a full-length mirror and wasn't listening.

'Lee . . .'

'Have you got this in blue?'

'What?' Seth was confused.

Lee watched the assistant sidle off to the stock room, giving him the privacy he needed.

'Seth, do you wanna know why this is happening?' It was a rhetorical question.

'Go on.'

'It's 'cos of that wop Bertoni. Apparently, he's on forty fucking gees a week and he's playing like a wanker.'

Seth winced. Not at his client's greed, but because he didn't have any players on his books earning that kind of money, and he didn't like to be reminded of it.

The assistant returned smiling and held aloft the blue suit.

'Thanks, love.' Lee gestured that his phone call was irksome but it was one he just had to take. Business, eh? The business of him trying on clothes while trying to get hers off. He moved into a changing room.

'Well, what about me moving to Chelsea?'

'Yep, I've made contact and I'm speaking with them this afternoon,' Seth lied. He hadn't bothered calling any other clubs because both he and Lee knew full well that Tottenham would be retaining his services. It was just bravado and modern-day football parlance. This particular charade, though, was into its fifth month and Seth was now thoroughly bored. Of course, he'd put feelers out to other clubs and he'd tried for a lot more money because, after all, he stood to benefit as well, but at almost thirty Lee wasn't a long-term prospect for another club and Tottenham knew as much.

Lee emerged from the dressing room with his shirt open and noted the assistant's eyes admiring his rippled stomach. 'So what are you saying, Seth?'

'I'm saying it's a good deal and I think you should sign. Look, I'm going to keep pushing for more anyway.'

'Good.'

'But, Lee, Tottenham's your home. OK, the money could be a little higher; I could probably get you more elsewhere—'

'Where?' Lee interrupted, a question Seth hadn't been expecting but it didn't faze him. He knew exactly how to deal with this situation.

'Yesterday I spoke with Aberdeen.'

'Aberdeen,' Lee screeched through gritted teeth. Seth might as well have said Kabul FC. 'I am not fucking going to Aber-fucking-deen.' He darted back into the dressing room and this time completely closed the curtain. He would have no choice but to buy the suit now because his outburst had cleared the shop of all the customers who had been browsing and he wanted to keep the assistant interested in him.

'Exactly, which is why I think another two years at Tottenham is right for you. Plus you'll get your testimonial there.'

'Yeah, fat lot of good that'll be now that St Niall bloody Quinn's done his bit.'

'You won't have to do that.'

'No. Don't worry, I won't. So, you're saying Spurs again?'

'Yes, Lee, I really am.'

Lee emerged from the dressing room and nonchalantly carried a pile of clothes over to the till.

'Think about it for today at least. I haven't signed anything with them yet. London is where you belong; you've got your modelling here, and that reminds me, the ad agency's been on the phone. They need to film next week, so I've pencilled Tuesday morning after training.'

'Fine.' Lee slid his black Amex card over the counter to the assistant. It wasn't the only thing he was going to give her.

Seth put the phone down triumphantly. Twenty per cent of an extra two grand a week, lovely.

Just along from the Strand in London's West End, PC Keith Waddle pulled his car door shut and gingerly placed the paper bag on the seat next to him so as not to knock any sugar from his prized possession. He checked that his radio was off, opened his flask and poured himself a large cup of Earl Grey tea, or piss, as he often wittily called it to himself. Actually, he was almost used to it by now and had conceded that he even quite liked it, which wasn't something he could ever admit to the lads in the canteen. His saliva glands on full alert, he was dribbling like Pavlov's dog as he carefully drew out his jam doughnut delight. Eight weeks of misery were about to become worth it and he plunged his head into the doughnut like it was an air bag saving his life. He shut his eyes to heighten his sense of taste, lay his head back slowly against the head rest and began to chew delicately, moaning loudly as he did so. His tongue was on a search mission for any jam and quickly reported none present, which Waddle decided was a good thing: it gave him something wonderful to look forward to. His stomach was equally excited at the prospect of finally getting hold of some decent scoff, and was churning and screaming for the mouth to finally swallow. As he swallowed, Waddle was careful to brush his lower lip, making sure that not one grain of sugar was lost. He wanted to absorb every calorie the doughnut had to offer.

He opened his beady little eyes and looked greedily at his doughnut. It was still there, it wasn't a dream and it hadn't been stolen. He was surprised, though, that there wasn't yet any hint of the jam lurking within. He turned it round, hunting for the telltale indentation where it had been inserted. Reassuringly, he quickly spotted it, although worryingly there didn't appear to be the usual accompanying red trail. PC Waddle took another huge mouthful and sat back once again with his eyes closed and waited for the jam explosion. Nothing.

In horror, his eyes shot open again. There was no jam in his mouth; there was only one bite left of his doughnut and that didn't look promising either. Suddenly, his Treat Day was becoming a nightmare.

Urgently, he went back in his mind. He'd definitely asked for a jam doughnut – of course he had. He'd hardly slept last night for those two words bombarding his mind and, yes, the girl who'd served him had definitely filled the bag from the jam pile. In a brilliant and clear blue sky, a menacing black cloud appeared directly above him.

'So where's the fucking jam?' he shouted, bashing his free fist heavily on to the steering wheel, probably causing the air bag to at least think about making an appearance. Rather pathetically, he still held out hope that some jam still awaited him and, needing to see it, he pulled the last piece of dough apart. And there it was. He needn't have worried about it exploding out of the bun and missing his mouth altogether. There was barely a scraping of jam. Weeks and weeks of fucking bird seed and cabbage, and this was his reward.

An attractive couple walked across the road in front of Waddle's squad car, so wrapped up in each other, they didn't even notice him. They were both slim, young and attractive, and they looked as happy as PC Waddle felt miserable. Was this some kind of sick joke? 'OK, and cue, attractive couple crossing the road, lovely . . . and stand by Mr Kipling cake lorry ready for drive-by. Are the people dressed as celery ready?'

The world is certainly a cruel place, PC Waddle thought to himself as a tear formed in his eye. Vanquished and thoroughly dejected, he felt anger stirring within: why am I the shape I am? Look at that skinny bastard over there, probably doesn't even realise how lucky he is. Waddle was sick of it all. It wasn't his fault, anyway. There was nothing wrong with his size. It was only a problem because other people made him feel that way. It was society's problem, not his.

PC Waddle was now seething with rage, and tremendously

grateful that he was a policeman, because today someone was going to pay for his miserable jamless lot.

Bill sat at a table in the Middleton club bar directly below a picture of his dad. Team photographs adorned the walls alongside two commemorative boards in honour of the players and members who had died in the two World Wars. In truth, it was a bar no one would choose to drink in unless they were a Middleton fan. 'Grimy' and 'earthy' would be an estate agent's way of describing the place, or 'in need of some modernisation'. Bill was trying to make the best of a ploughman's lunch that had to be almost a season past its sell-by date.

He was joined by his oldest friend and Middleton's general manager, George Harris. George had responsibility for all things commercial at the club, which currently meant keeping creditors at bay. It was a full-time job offering part-time wages, demanding managerial and economic wizardry way beyond any human's ability, let alone George's. He spent his time dashing from financial catastrophes and dodging increasingly irate creditors, like utilities and the Inland Revenue. To George, it felt more like fire containment than fire fighting because the extinguishers were all empty and he only had a fire blanket left.

Bill pushed another limp bit of lettuce to the side of his plate and consulted his menu.

'Bloody hell, George, the menu says "crisp lettuce", look.'

'I bring a packed lunch,' George answered.

'Don't blame ya. Might as well serve Stilton cheese; least that's s'posed to be mouldy. Here, look at that,' Bill complained, holding up with his fork the offending bit of

Cheddar in various shades of yellow and with one conspicuous green spot.

George chuckled, although it was no laughing matter.
Middleton needed all their supporters and could ill afford to
poison and kill any of them.

Bill could sense George's anxiety. 'Things not picked up,
George?'

'Oh yeah they have. Since we last spoke things have totally
turned around. I'm getting quotes for two new stands.
Thought we'd go with a hotel attached to one of them – you
know, like they have at Chelsea.'

'All right. But it's never been any different, has it?'

George shook his head. 'Never been as bad as this. Had
two cheques bounce last week. Players cheques, 'n'll.'

The first rule of any professional football club wanting to
remain professional was to keep the players well fed and
watered.

'Which ones?'

'Claydon and Thomson.'

'Ah well, Thomson, now fair enough. Those last two goals
he let in were as soft as shit,' Bill chuckled, trying to make
light of the situation.

'Did us a favour actually.'

'Oh?'

'We couldn't have paid out the players' win bonus
anyway.'

Bill laughed. 'Oh that's great, that is. I now support a team
that actually can't afford to win.'

George didn't laugh. 'I've got the electric people threatening me with turning off the power. Can you imagine if they
did it during a game?'

Bill was non-plussed. 'So?'

'A flood-lit match, Bill.'

'Oh right. They couldn't do that, could they?'

'I expect they can do what they like.'

'No, but they wouldn't, not during a game.'

'Whatever, Bill, they want paying. And then I've got the bloody tax people chasing me. The accountants are threatening us, and I'm struggling with me VAT.'

'Nonsense, Georgie boy. There's not an ounce on ya,' Bill joked again, but still George didn't laugh.

'The VAT people aren't laughing, Bill. They'll close us down. This club can't make it on what's coming in. It's as simple as that and we haven't got any famous old players who'll come and help us out.'

'And football's booming, eh?' Bill scoffed. 'Five thousand paying punters and we can't make it? So then where's our new owner, eh? Where's he and all his promises?'

'Had some suits with hard hats snooping around again the other day,' George announced.

'What? Who were they?' Bill demanded.

'Dunno, never asked.'

'Shit, George, why the hell not? What were they doing?'

'I don't know, measuring.'

'Measuring! Fockin' hell, man, you should have stopped 'em.'

'What? How? I can't stop people measuring.'

Bill finished his pint and slammed his glass down on the table. 'I'll give him something to measure. How much do we need?' he asked purposefully.

'What d'you mean? What for?'

'To pay people off. The electric, the gas, the tax people?'

'Jesus, Bill. Loads.'

'Well, go on, how much exactly?'

'I don't know exactly, millions, how's that?'

Bill felt winded. 'Right, well, we'll just have to make savings.'

George looked around at the state of the bar and at the closed stand outside. 'Where?'

'I dunno – the players, pay them less.'

George looked at his friend in exasperation. Media speculation was rife about players taking cuts but it was easier to write about than actually to implement. The only cuts football players were known for were haircuts.

'What?' Bill demanded.

'I can just see their agents buying that. We'd be fielding our youth team within a week.'

'But we can only pay them what we've got coming in,' Bill protested.

'No, Bill, we pay them what other clubs would pay them, otherwise they leave – which means, like most clubs, our wage bill exceeds our income.'

'But that's ridiculous.'

'Welcome to professional football.'

Bill laughed at the hopelessness of it all. 'Why do we do it? My team can't afford to win or lose.'

George didn't disagree.

Finally a sufficient space appeared for Daryl to overtake safely. He edged his truck out into the right-hand lane and gently drew level with the Fiat Multipla that had been holding him up for the best part of a mile. Out of curiosity, he turned to see who could be driving so slowly and was surprised to find that it wasn't an old lady but a pretty young woman who must have passed her test that very morning to be driving so cautiously. He smiled at her as he carefully eased his truck back into the correct lane. It was probably nerves or relief that the truck had finally overtaken her, but she definitely appeared to smile back at him. Anyway, whatever the reason, Daryl was thrilled. Politely, he held his hand aloft to say thank you. He didn't know what for; she hadn't done anything apart from be attractive and that hardly warranted a thank you, just as ugly people don't deserve a good telling off.

Daryl casually peered in his rear-view mirror, anxious to get a better look at her, but, alarmingly, she and her Fiat had been replaced by a police car hard up on his bumper. His worry soon turned to horror as his cab was suddenly filled with blue beams of light, enveloping and giving his heart a firm squeeze. The siren followed, just a quick burst, in case there was any doubt that the policeman hadn't made his presence felt. This was a situation familiar to Daryl but still not one he was ever likely to be comfortable with.

'Fuck,' he muttered to himself. What was he being stopped for? He looked at his speedometer. Thirty-five, so no, not speeding. Brake lights; possibly, but that'll just be a warning, surely. Unlike Middleton, with nine points Daryl didn't want any more on his licence. His mouth instantly dried and he quickly swigged his Coke, turned off his radio and hit his left-hand indicator to let the police officer know that his presence had been registered and that he intended to pull over. He yanked his handbrake and cursed his laziness. He'd been meaning to strip his cab of the centrefolds that were stuck all over the place but had never quite got round to it. The truth was, he'd grown attached to them; it was as though he actually knew them all and couldn't bear to say goodbye to them. The central part of his steering wheel was definitely a mistake. It was just a pair of breasts, and surgically distorted ones at that, not the most politically correct sight to greet the officer. One thing was certain: if this was a woman copper, Daryl wouldn't have a prayer.

He looked in his side mirror and was momentarily relieved to see a male officer approaching. However, Daryl could see that, for whatever reason, this copper was seriously pissed off and his heart sank.

PC Waddle had been angry an hour ago, he was now incandescent with rage. His experience earlier this morning had unleashed a monster in him that he hadn't known he was harbouring. What he should have done after his doughnut disappointment was to have a good old-fashioned shout, to exorcise some of his rage, but PC Waddle had been way beyond such a measure. Instead, he had stomped back to the offending baker's shop, but not to complain – that would have been fine. No, he had returned to buy more doughnuts, the worst possible option available to him. He hadn't been able to help himself; it was as if he'd been compelled by a higher force.

'A dozen jam doughnuts, please,' he had quivered, before scarpering back to his car, or 'jam jar', where he had gorged himself, stuffing doughnuts into his face as sugar sprayed and jam dribbled everywhere. It was a feeding frenzy worthy of any great predator, only in this instance there would be unbearable guilt and remorse post-feeding. The inevitable despair had indeed crept up on him, but was held in abeyance whilst he'd devoured doughnut after doughnut. And then, finally, with the box lying empty on his enormous thighs, it had consumed him entirely. The day when he might want to see his nude reflection now seemed more distant than ever.

His diet had been shattered and he'd wondered whether he could actually feel his belt tightening as he sat there covered in sugar. All that effort, diligence and sacrifice ruined by one, or, more accurately, twelve moments of madness. And why had this happened? Because some bastard in some fucking doughnut factory hadn't filled a fucking doughnut with jam.

Daryl and PC Waddle eyed each other warily. Daryl was highly alarmed. What could he possibly have done to make this officer so incredibly angry? Had he been daydreaming and unwittingly wiped out an entire family on a zebra crossing? Surely he would have remembered that.

'Hello, officer. Can I help?' Daryl asked with a half-smile in an attempt to diffuse the situation.

'In a hurry, are we?' PC Waddle asked.

Daryl looked at him blankly. He was confused. He hadn't been speeding and didn't know how to answer the question.

'Erm . . .' he faltered, 'no, not especially. Why?'

'Why? Then, how do you explain the speed?'

Daryl fumbled for something to say, something that might placate this nutter who was still staring at him madly.

'What speed?' Probably not the best response Daryl might have come up with.

'Thirty-four miles an hour. That speed.'

Daryl stood on the pavement and watched as the policeman completed a fairly comprehensive inspection of the truck. He had wondered whether the whole thing wasn't a piss-take, some sort of elaborate wind-up. However, the copper looked genuine enough and Daryl couldn't see any television cameras or dodgy characters lurking. He had never imagined wanting to meet Beadle but now he was almost praying for him to materialise as some dodgy traffic warden or something. Daryl passed the mandatory breath test, but knew he was about to fail the anger test. Officer Fat Chops was poking around in the back of the truck, presumably, looking for the rocket launcher Daryl was planning to fire at Whitehall, or maybe he'd been tipped off about the three barrels of raw opium concealed under the floor or even the three Peruvian asylum-seeking pygmies stashed in the glove compartment. Daryl told himself this was just a copper having a power surge and, like all surges, it would pass, leaving Daryl with nothing more than a warning. Daryl had plenty of warnings of his own for him – like lay off the pies, for a start – but his hopes of escaping with a warning evaporated when the officer suddenly produced his charge pad and began noting down the vehicle's registration.

'You ain't booking me,' Daryl shouted angrily, approaching Officer Waddle.

Without even looking up or turning his head, PC Waddle continued writing, expertly playing the deaf routine taught to all police officers on their first day at Hendon.

'No. Not for thirty-four miles an hour. Fuck sake.'

Waddle didn't approve of such language and looked at Daryl the way a headmaster would at a schoolboy.

'Yeah, while you're at it, you might wanna do me for swearing as well.'

PC Waddle returned to his pad and began writing again.

'This is bullshit.' Daryl slammed his boot hard into the passenger door of his van, making a rather large and ugly dent. 'Shit!' he yelled, although it didn't matter, seeing as he'd lost his job now anyway.

PC Waddle tutted to himself sanctimoniously and handed Daryl the ticket that would render him unemployable. Ex-cons found it hard to get work as it was, and those without driving licences found it almost impossible. Certainly his days as a wheel clamper would be over, anyway.

'This'll cost me me job, you know.'

'Well, then, you should have thought about that before you broke the speed limit, shouldn't you?'

'You don't give a shit, do ya?'

'See that over there,' Waddle said, pointing. 'That's a school full of kids. Protecting them, that's what I give a shit about.'

'Oh well, aren't you the regular super hero,' Daryl screamed in protest. 'See these.' He pointed to his feet. Waddle was confused as he looked down at Daryl's boots.

'In case you was wondering what they are, they're feet. I don't suppose you've ever seen yours.'

Waddle flinched at the insult.

'Your problem, son—' Waddle began, aware that while he held all the official power, he was losing out on the unofficial confrontation.

'Scuze me,' Daryl interrupted, 'but you fink I've got a problem.'

'Yes, I'd say so,' Waddle faltered, now slightly unsure of himself.

'Well, tonight, when you get undressed – and you'll be alone, I expect – think of me and then ask yourself, who's the one wiv the fuckin' problem?'

PC Waddle had turned crimson with rage and was weighing up whether he might be able to get the little shit on something more sinister. His right eye was twitching and a bead of sweat had formed on his brow.

It was an impressive show of anger, impressive enough for Daryl at least to stand down. He couldn't recall ever seeing anyone quite this angry before and it surely wouldn't be long before the copper turned into a huge green bodybuilder with hopelessly ill-fitting clothes. PC Waddle glared a while longer at Daryl before suddenly turning on his heel, muttering to himself as he went. Daryl couldn't quite work out what he was saying, but thought it sounded like 'doughnut'.

CHAPTER 4

Collection tins for football and social clubs are now a familiar sight across the country, but given the scale of Middleton FC's debts, the buckets were hopelessly inadequate. In reality, collection skips would probably have been insufficient and so the collections served the purpose only of making the townspeople feel as if they were trying to help.

Typically, Bill was the driving force behind the team currently working the high street and train station, and, in the process, was breaking any number of council and national regulations on charitable collections. Bill hadn't bothered applying for either permission or a licence, though that wasn't laziness or anarchy on his part, more an acceptance that he wouldn't have been granted permission anyway. Each registered charity eagerly awaits its turn on a strict rota to be evaluated by the relevant subcommittees. That was another thing counting against Bill: Middleton Edwardians weren't registered as a charity. Even though it would probably benefit them to do so, the people of Middleton were proud of their club and didn't much like the idea of it being in the same league as a donkey refuge.

'Come on now, anything you can spare. Anything at all,' Bill yelled loudly over the din of his bucket, which he was shaking rigorously, thereby contravening yet more regulations concerning soliciting for donations.

'Hello, madam, we even take euros now. It's our club's only way of getting into Europe.' Bill was no slouch when it came to collecting money, his humour and kind face usually winning over anyone unfortunate or foolish enough to catch his eye. An attractive and smartly dressed lady was one such victim and she smiled back at him, knowing that she would now have to cough up at least some shrapnel. Much to Bill's surprise and delight, the lady threw a crisp new fiver into his bucket. Bill always thought it ironic that a handful of coppers amounts to nothing and yet makes a huge commotion as they crash into the bucket and yet the highly valuable notes make no noise at all, almost as if they are secure in their own innate value. Bill thought the lady deserved a fanfare of some sort and gave her one of his very special thank you smiles. The woman blushed, sending a shimmer of excitement through Bill's body.

Resisting the urge to turn round and see the woman again, Bill gently squeezed one of his son's ankles, which was peeping out from his baby sling. 'I've still got it, Tom lad, and with your looks you'll have it too, son.'

Bill had taken Tom with him, primarily so that Mary could have a break, but it had also occurred to him that the presence of a child could tip a wavering donor in his favour. A technique pioneered by the Romanians, it was another form of child benefit, so to speak. Bill knew all the tricks and would rarely shout about the cause he was collecting for. People feel obliged to hand over cash when confronted with blindness, sick children or some hideous disease. It makes them feel better about themselves, but people certainly feel less inclined to shell out for a football club that is struggling to pay its already overpaid players, who are crap in the first place and can't win anyway. Bill always found it much more effective to keep things ambiguous and let people decide for themselves whether the cause was a worthy one.

'All this change is terribly heavy. I do accept notes,' Bill called out, shaking his bucket to emphasise his little quip. Two local lads, one of whom worked at the bakery, winked at Bill as they passed.

With a keen sense for the pitfalls and dangers that come with illegal collections, Bill spotted a rapidly approaching problem out of the corner of his eye. An elderly woman was moving purposefully towards him, brandishing a collection tin in one hand and violently waving a walking stick in the other. Bill was in the shit and for a split second, he wondered whether he shouldn't just scarper, but such was her passion and spring, he wasn't altogether sure that he could outrun her.

'Have you got a licence?' she fumed.

Pointlessly, Bill smiled, but he knew he would have to do a lot better than that.

'What are you doing here? This is our day, we have the whole day.' She whipped the appropriate documentation from her woollen coat, a task made more difficult by the fluorescent green vest she was also wearing emblazoned with the words: 'The Cheshire Cats Hostelry'.

Bill knew that he was faced with a Herculean task. Old-aged cat fanatics are unquestionably the most vociferous collectors and are almost impossible to placate.

'What are you collecting for?' she asked. Another perfectly reasonable question and one that Bill couldn't bring himself to answer, although he did feel a sense of superiority, having decided his cause was far more deserving than a load of homeless cats. 'The council said that we would be the only ones collecting.'

Rather unhelpfully, a man emptied his pockets full of

change into Bill's bucket and grinned broadly at him. It was Smithy, who'd been collecting at the station before another rampant cat pilgrim had seen him off.

'You shouldn't be giving that to him,' the old lady charged. 'Who's it for?' she demanded to know again.

'The Tigers,' Bill blurted out in a blind panic. It was an inspired fluke, which he would later claim as a piece of cunning ingenuity.

'Oh.' She immediately calmed down. Bill was evidently collecting for cats as well. She looked up at the child on his back, who by sheer good fortune, was holding his favourite cuddly toy, Tigger. Tom was also clad in the colours of Middleton, a rather unattractive black and yellow stripe, which was absolutely perfect for Bill's tiger story. 'Tigers,' the old lady barked, seeming to approve.

'And others. Other cats, you know. All the big ones really.'

'Lions?' the old woman asked.

'Yep. We do lions.'

'Don't like lions. They're cruel. Sometimes they kill their young.'

'Well, we're more tiger-based than lions, to be fair. But I didn't realise it was your day. It is the ninth today, isn't it?'

She eyed him suspiciously. 'No. It's the eighth.'

Bill smiled broadly at his mistake. It seemed to have the desired effect on his rabid interrogator. They'd gone from being enemies to almost being team-mates, both on the side of cats the world over.

'You should be here tomorrow.'

'Yes, I realise that now. I am so sorry.'

'Strange, though, that the council would give us consecutive days. Ridiculous, really. I'm going to speak to them first thing in the morning.'

It wouldn't take the council long to realise what had gone on and who the likely culprit might be. Bill headed a long list of suspects assumed to have masterminded financial scams to benefit the club at the council's expense. The most infamous one to date was the illegal rigging of the floodlights at the Middleton youth pitch adjoining the stadium to run free of charge from a nearby electrical substation. The situation was exacerbated when the council discovered that they were providing cash subsidies for lighting that was already being scammed for free.

'It's not just tigers and lions that need help, you know. We've got cats in this country needing help,' the old lady went on, quoting the tired argument used against overseas charities.

'Yes, you're right, and I feel terrible. Why don't I let you have what I've collected? It's only fair,' Bill said, anxious to head off any trouble with the council.

'Not at all, but I would appreciate it if we could continue on alone.'

'Absolutely, you carry on,' Bill said, backing away hurriedly as he spoke.

Daryl drove along Knightsbridge, past Harrods and on into Chelsea before pulling his truck over. He was so angry that he couldn't drive any longer, at least not without being a danger to other road-users. He was numb with anger as he stared at the speeding ticket once again. He banged his head repeatedly against the steering wheel and finally left it there, resting against the photograph of the enormous silicone bags posing as breasts. If only they were real, he thought, in more ways than one. He'd checked his driver's licence again, in case he'd made a mistake, but of course he hadn't. He was going to be banned from driving. 'Thirty-fucking-four,' he whimpered to himself.

A brand-new yellow Porsche Boxster was parking on the opposite side of the road outside a suitably expensive-looking restaurant. With its extra skirting and vents, it was a car just like its owner: screaming to be noticed. A handsome young man emerged from the driver's seat as a tall attractive blonde woman unfolded from the passenger side. No back seat, no boot, just enough space for him, his bird and his ego. Both were expensively dressed and she waited as the man fed a ravenous parking meter and placed the ticket on the dash rather than sticking it to one of his tinted windows. Apart from himself, Lee Robson, centre forward for Tottenham Hotspur, loved his car more than anything else in the world. In descending order, cars, women and football were his passions. Lee was the unofficial patron saint of men's magazine *culcha*. Like his women, Lee loved his cars when they were new but quickly tired of them, and by the time a new model was launched, Lee was always ready for a change. Lee's wife had long since left him, fed up with his philandering. It had been inevitable. She pre-dated his fame and so the marriage had always been doomed in the long term.

Lee's current live-in lover was Kelly, an ex-glamour model who, in car terms, would shortly be in need of a private registration plate to hide her age and mileage. Today, though, Lee was having lunch with Carmen, his very latest squeeze, who was not only incredibly attractive but, much to Lee's delight, was more than happy to indulge his sexual fantasies and games.

As he approached the restaurant, Lee allowed himself a glance back at his beloved car. It bleeped loudly as he locked it, letting everyone know that they could look and covet, but in no circumstances could anyone even think of touching.

The sound of the alarm roused Daryl from his misery and he looked up just in time to see the back of a beautiful woman disappear into the restaurant. Daryl sat in his scruffy clamping wagon staring at the four-wheeled sports erection and quickly became overwhelmed with self-pity. As a child, he'd often dropped off to sleep dreaming of owning a car like that. The man was probably a footballer, Daryl mused bitterly, remembering the glittering career he had once been destined for. As an England schoolboy he had been signed to Charlton Athletic and played two seasons in the reserves before they let him go. Now, the closest he was ever likely to get to a car like that was when he fixed a clamp to one of its wheels, which in fact at this very moment seemed like a perfectly logical thing to do. He was going to lose his job anyway, so why not sign off in style, and put a rich person's nose out of joint in the process?

CHAPTER 5

George's desk was covered in money, and although there were a few notes and several pound coins, mostly it was shrapnel piled to varying heights.

'Eleven hundred and ninety-nine pounds and fifty pence,' George announced, as Bill and his team began applauding themselves. Bill reached into his pocket, theatrically produced a fifty pence and casually threw the coin on to the table. It smashed over a few of the pound piles but it didn't matter.

'Make that twelve hundred,' he said, as if he were some big-league poker player.

'Good work, lads,' George said, although he didn't sound exactly excited.

'What will that get us?' Smithy asked.

'Well, not a new player but it's half the win bonus for the weekend.'

'If we need it, that is,' Bill joked. Middleton were visiting Gillingham this weekend, who were currently top of the league and would most likely remain there come Sunday.

'Right, who's going to get this lot down to the bank, then?' George asked. 'Come on, lads. I can't do it, it'd look well dodgy. The council are bound to do one of their investigations.'

'Why do we have to pay it into the bank?' Smithy asked.

'No one's paying it in. We're getting it changed.'

'Into what?'

'Into notes, Smithy. There isn't a lot I can do with coins. We've got enough trouble with cash payments without paying players in loose change.'

'Well, I can't do it,' Bill said.

'No, certainly not, Bill,' George agreed. 'Smithy, you should do it. Best off going to Altrincham, eh. Young Sam's the new manager there, you know.'

'Seriously?'

'Yeah, I was talking with his mum yesterday. Done well, int he?'

'Bloody has. George, get on to him for a loan,' Bill joked. 'Anyway, FA Cup draw today.' He rubbed his hands together enthusiastically. 'Big away fixture coming up; I can feel it.'

'And then it'll be Europe next season,' George chirped.

Bill chuckled. 'What? On a booze run?'

Although Lee and Carmen had been served a veritable feast, Lee hadn't much enjoyed his meal. There wasn't a problem with the food as such, but rather the fact that nobody in the restaurant had recognised him. Lee positively basked in the trappings of fame, and not being recognised reminded him that his glory days would inevitably have to end – and, unlike Mr Lineker, he had no prospect of a cosy media job on the agenda. On this occasion, however, Lee put his anonymity down to restaurant policy: 'Don't bother the celebrities. They like to be treated just like everybody else.' What a load of bollocks. Not being treated like everybody else was the whole point of being a celebrity. And so Lee was delighted towards the end of the meal when a young waiter who hadn't served their table finally caved in under the pressure of being in the presence of one of his heroes.

'Excusa me, Missta Lee Robsona, no?'

Lee tutted and smiled wryly at Carmen as though this was a minor inconvenience he had to suffer everywhere he went.

'That's right, yes . . . Alessandro,' Lee replied loftily, reading the man's name badge, delighted with himself and his reconfirmed status. Excuse me, Carmen, while I make someone's day. 'Do you have a pen?' Lee asked.

'Scuza . . . er, itsa not policy, buta . . .'

'Don't worry about policy. How many rules have I ever broken?' Lee laughed. 'I played against Del Piero, you know. What would you like me to sign?'

'No, it'sa not—'

Lee read the *Sun* cover to cover every morning but by his own admission hadn't read a book since *Peter and Jane*, and so it wasn't really a surprise that he couldn't read body language either. Before Alessandro could make himself properly understood, Lee had scrawled his flamboyant signature on the menu with a dedication to the young man.

Alessandro held up the menu. 'Yessa, thank you, signor, butta I really wanted to aska yoo about Signor Bertoni. 'Ee'sa my favourite player . . .'

'Oh.'

Carmen lowered her head as Lee grimaced.

'Bertoni?'

'Yes, I lova him.'

'Well, you might be in wiv a chance, 'cos he's a closet poof. Just the bill, please, waiter.'

Alessandro scuttled away.

'Bloody Italians. The Italians, I tell ya, all mouth and no trousers that lot. You know about their tanks, don't ya . . . ?'

By the time the bill arrived, Lee was eager to get out of the restaurant. The bunch of Italians by the bar were all laughing hysterically and Lee sensed that he might be the cause of their fun. Cheeky bastards had even left his Amex chit blank in case he felt inclined to add to the fifteen per cent he'd already been hit for. While Carmen was still being helped into her jacket by a salivating waiter, Lee was already sitting in his car, having been humiliated quite enough for one day. 'Fucking foreigners and most likely Arsenal fans 'n'all.'

With his hands on the little racing wheel, he straightened out his arms. Hugged by his leather seat, he breathed in the new smell of his car and immediately began to calm down, hoping that the foreign food servers had noted his wheels. Well, they certainly would when he pulled away, because he intended to leave most of his back tyres outside their grotty café. Finally, Carmen, the *svelte* beauty, emerged from the restaurant and nonchalantly sauntered her way round to the passenger side. God, she was sexy, even if she did take her time. Lee finally smiled. This afternoon she could take all the time she wanted. She smiled back at him wickedly and he adjusted his trousers.

However, as she got round to the passenger side of the Porsche, her face turned ashen with shock.

'Fuck sake, Carmen. It wasn't that embarrassing. Get in the car, will you?' Lee yelled out at her as he lowered her window.

'You've been clamped,' she mumbled.

He looked at her oddly, as if he hadn't heard her correctly.

'Clamped – they've clamped you.'

If this was a joke, then it wasn't funny. Granted she was sexy, but no woman was fit enough to joke about a bloke's *mowta*.

'Someone's clamped you.'

Lee calmly stroked his chin, weighing up the possible

alternatives in his mind. He couldn't have been clamped – for one thing, there was no notice stuck on his car. He was legally parked, for God's sake; he couldn't be clamped. There had to be another explanation.

He ripped the keys out of the ignition and pounced athletically out of his car, which was so low to the ground that he fleetingly wondered whether Porsche provided hoists for older drivers. He looked down at his front passenger wheel aghast. A disgusting hunk of yellow metal had been attached to his beloved car, and what rankled most was that the colour matched.

'Oh well, this is just fucking great,' he yelled. 'Just fucking superb.'

An elderly couple walking past had no idea what he was referring to and so clutched their valuables and quickened their step.

Lee shook his head in disbelief and squeezed his eyes shut. After a few seconds, he opened them again, but the clamp was still there.

'FUCK . . . FUCK . . . FUCK. FUCK.' He crouched down and peered at it a moment before gingerly touching it. 'They've clamped my CUNTING car.'

It was an odd use of English, but under the circumstances perfectly understandable. A crowd instantly began to gather and so far no one disagreed. Lee was arguably more famous for his temper than he was for scoring goals and after today that would no longer be in any doubt whatsoever.

'Right. OK, OK . . .' He paced back and forth, mumbling to himself, to make some sense of what had happened. He scanned up and down the street, hoping that the road clampers might have had a death wish and hung around to meet the owner of the legally parked car they'd clamped.

Pushing his hands through his hair once again, he barely managed to stop himself from kicking the clamp and settled instead for kicking a nearby bin. Angrily, he marched up to the parking meter and began studying it again. He looked at his watch and it was clear that his temper restraints were finally about to shatter.

'It's still got twenty minutes to fucking run,' he screeched at the top of his voice.

In anguish, Lee beckoned passers-by to study the meter for themselves, as if somehow they were going to make it all OK.

Daryl was standing a good forty yards away from the fast-growing and increasingly enthralled audience. He recognised Lee now and was grinning like a kid who'd found a porn magazine on a train. Although he'd had the good sense to return his truck to the yard and report a clamp stolen, he figured that he might have to admit his guilt now anyway. As a committed Arsenal fan there was no greater service he could do for his club than to clamp the Tottenham centre forward. Respect was due; they might even make a brass bust of him for the Arsenal club bar. Daryl no longer hated the fat copper. In fact, he reckoned that he owed him a pint and probably a pie as well.

'This is utter bollocks,' Lee bellowed, as he gave up trying for the second time to remove the clamp with the screwdriver Porsche had kindly provided in their wheel changing kit, and turned instead to his mobile phone.

At that very moment, Seth had his phone pressed to his ear. He was lying on his desk with his pants and trousers around his ankles, listening to a woman in Swindon breathing various sexual obscenities down the line. It had taken him nearly twelve minutes or, more importantly, over eighteen quid to get to this point and he wasn't interrupting his call now for whoever it was trying to get through.

'The person you are calling knows you are waiting,' Lee heard in his mobile phone.

'Yes, I fucking know that,' he seethed. 'Pick up the phone, Seth.'

A few moments later, Lee was politely told by the robotic woman that he might like to try again later. This was something Lee wouldn't be able to do, not with his phone, anyway, having just hurled it on to the pavement with quite literally shattering force. Without saying a word, Lee held out his hand and Carmen duly handed her phone over. Lee had a thing about mobiles and got through about one a month.

Seth was relieved that the other call had finally been cut off. 'Now, carry on, you horny bitch . . .' he pleaded.

'That's it, right there, oh yes, yes, you big monster . . .' the bored housewife moaned into her receiver while Seth's imagination and right hand ran riot.

He was just about to get his money's worth when the familiar beep filled his earpiece once more, ruining his expensive and tawdry moment. It had to be an important call.

'I want it all . . .'

Seth moaned but not in lust. 'Er, excuse me, lady,' he said, taking her by surprise. Up until now, he'd been pretending to be a male gigolo and 'excuse me' was certainly not in character. 'Can you hold on? I need to take another call.'

In line with their role play, it would have been better if the lady had said something like, 'Oh no, baby, do you have to? I need you. Hurry back.' But she didn't. Instead she opted for, 'Yeah, whatever.'

Angrily Seth sat up and hit the appropriate button. 'Yes, hello, who is this?'

'It's me, for fuck's sake. You've been on the phone for ages.'

'Yes, getting you more money. Now what do you want?' Seth barked.

'I've been clamped.'

'What?'

'You heard. I've been clamped.'

Seth hadn't ever been picked for a football team in his life, and yet had managed to become a millionaire from the game, but none the less he still resented the extent to which his clients abused his services. He hung up his original call. He couldn't bear the thought of paying for a service he wasn't receiving, and the romance of the moment had passed anyway.

'You've been clamped!' Seth exclaimed.

'Yes.'

'Well, what are you phoning me for? What can I do about it? Try and get the money up.' Seth had entirely underestimated Lee's situation, not to mention his fury.

'Listen, you ungrateful little shit, do you have any idea how much money you make out of me—'

'OK, Lee. Listen. I'm not sure what you think I can do about it. Where you park is your business, and if you park illegally—'

To preserve his ear drum, Seth instinctively held the phone a foot away from his ear. If Lee's reply was loud in Seth's office, then he could only imagine the scene his client was causing in the street, and Seth hoped that there were no press present. Inevitably, though, they would have been called and were no doubt en route chasing down their story.

*

The crowd surrounding Lee's car had swelled now to some twenty people, all of whom had been shown the meter and the clamp. Outrageous, everyone agreed. Maddening, infuriating – they all had complete empathy for Lee, they all understood his anger, but as yet, none of them had been able to help and none had dared ask for an autograph.

'I'm serious. He's tried pulling it off with his hands, and now he's bellowing into his mobile,' Daryl said excitedly into his phone. 'Here, listen . . .' Daryl held up his mobile phone. 'D'you hear that? That bloke shouting . . . that is Lee Robson.'

Shopkeepers started to emerge to see what all the commotion was and office windows began to fill up with prying eyes. Everyone within range wanted to know what the hell was happening, and once they saw, asked themselves: bloody hell, is that Lee Robson?'

'There isn't any sticker on the car with any fucking phone number – why do you think I'm calling you, you wanker?' An appropriate choice of expletive, as Seth was still sitting on his desk with no pants on.

'What about signs?' Seth protested.

'Seth, you're not listening, are you? There are no signs. There is nothing except a big yellow clamp on my fucking car.'

'Well, Lee, I don't know what to—'

He didn't manage to finish his sentence because Lee ended the call in his typically unorthodox way, this time by hurling the phone against a wall, narrowly missing an innocent bystander as it was obliterated.

'Lee,' Carmen protested, but Lee didn't hear her. He was now bent double at the waist with his head buried in his hands, the classic striker's 'how did I miss from there?' position, the only difference today being that the onlookers didn't dare jeer and use hand gestures to suggest he was sexually relieving himself. Lee rubbed his eyeballs, at a complete loss as to what to do next.

The only person who could end his misery was Daryl, but he had absolutely no intention of doing so, particularly as he was busy phoning everyone in his mobile's address book.

Daryl's eye was suddenly drawn away from the commotion to a spot further down the street. He smiled broadly, hung up his phone, and looked to the heavens to give praise to a God that, until today, he had never known existed. The Nigerian traffic warden parked his moped and began ambling over towards the fragile football star. He kept his helmet on, which in the circumstances would turn out to be an inspired move.

'What is going on here?' the warden asked.

Lee perked up as soon as he saw him. A parking official, someone in uniform at least, someone who could help. He was so relieved to see him that he kept shaking his hand and then beckoned him over to the meter. Lee urgently recounted his story, which seemed to be entirely lost on the official.

'Whose car is this?' he asked.

It dawned on Lee that the warden hadn't in fact arrived with a set of keys and an apology. Quite the opposite, in fact.

'Whose car?' Lee asked incredulously. 'It's mine, innit?'

'Well, you cannot park it here. The meter has run out. You must move it at once.'

Now there was a hushed 'a player has been seriously injured' silence from the crowd.

Lee gawped at the warden in utter disbelief. 'What d'you want me to do? Fucking carry it?'

Carmen took the more pragmatic approach and began ferreting in her bag for any loose change she might have to refeed the meter. 'I'll sort the meter out, Lee.'

'No, you cannot do that. This is a non-returning bay. You must please move your car, or I will give you a ticket.'

'Are you blind or deaf?'

'I beg your pardon?'

'It's fucking clamped. How can I move it? That's the problem.'

'Yes, it is your problem, not mine.'

The crowd murmured as the warden repositioned himself in order to get a look at the numberplate. Had he recognised Lee, he would have stood a reasonable chance of guessing the registration: 'Lee2'. To ensure that his registration plate was truly noticeable, Lee had had it made especially small – to go with his mind, one might presume.

Lee pointed at the traffic warden. 'Do not even think about giving me a fucking ticket.'

Daryl knew exactly how he felt, having suffered a similar fate earlier in the day at the hands of PC Waddle.

On television, the 'what happened next' round is everyone's favourite in the nation's favourite quiz, *A Question of Sport*. It is always something unexpected, hopefully outlandish and usually funny. No one, though, could have guessed what Lee was about to do. Exasperated, he'd tried being polite, or as polite as he could be, but it hadn't worked, and now he saw no alternative. His mind clouded in blind rage and a surge of white-hot anger coursed through every channel in his body. Something was going to give. Lee was going to explode. He took a few steps back and steadied himself to charge. He grimaced and launched himself at his car, swinging his right foot as hard as he could at the offending wheel clamp. Ironically, having built a career on kicking things, Lee Robson would be forever remembered for this kick. There was never any contest. The human foot coated in a soft Italian moccasin versus tempered steel. It would have been the greatest giant-killing ever, had Lee prevailed. Everyone winced as Lee crumpled to the floor, joining the two mobile phones. Sadly Lee's right foot was in nearly as many pieces as the phones, making Beckham's broken metatarsal look like a bruise.

Lee's moaning and writhing on the ground seemed hardly even to register with the warden. The lengths that people will go to to avoid getting a ticket these days, he thought to himself, as he diligently stuck the plastic envelope to the windscreen.

A siren pierced the din. Members of the crowd suspected it was probably an ambulance sensing that a glory job was on hand because a multimillion-pound toe was at least broken. Only it wasn't an ambulance at all, but a police car, responding to complaints of noise and excessive use of profane language. It was like being at a football match, one resident had complained. The car came to a stop, and a portly officer got out and rolled over to the chaos on the pavement.

'Scuze me. Stand back now, please,' PC Waddle said. This was always his favourite moment of being a policeman: the sense of power he got from telling people that they should stand back and that there was nothing to see. With his years of experience, Waddle make a quick assessment of the situation, and came to entirely the wrong conclusion. Man down next to a sports car. It was either a failed carjacking or a mugging with an outside chance of being a hit-and-park.

'OK, could everyone move back now, please? There really is nothing to see here,' Waddle intoned with as much gravity as his high-pitched voice would allow. No one budged an inch. Nothing to see, you're joking mate, this is better than the movies.

'Officer, oh, thank God, please, you have to help me,' Lee pleaded.

Waddle looked down and recognised him straight away. 'Lee Robson. You're Lee Robson.'

Yes, finally he'd been recognised. Good old copper. A sense of relief drifted over him. Can you please make my car driveable again, and I want this traffic warden deported.

'What's happened, Mr Robson? Are you hurt?'

'This twat has just given me a parking ticket for not moving my car because it's been clamped.'

Waddle's face fell a little. He had been hoping for something a little more exciting.

'And?' he asked.

How and why Lee came to be prostrate on the floor was quickly explained to Officer Waddle. Finally, Lee managed to get himself upright but needed to be supported by his garish car and girlfriend. It was suddenly all too much for him and he began to weep openly. It hadn't done Gascoigne any harm and he noted that David Seaman had played a similar card at the last World Cup. An ambulance was now snaking its way down towards the restaurant.

'OK, if we could give Mr Robson some room now, please . . .' Waddle announced, and this time the crowd did shuffle backwards, seeing as how the star was crying.

'Your ambulance is here now, sir. I'll sort out the car situation for you.'

'Thank you,' Lee croaked, barely able to speak. As a rule,

he didn't much care for police, but this officer was thoughtful and also English.

'Before you go, Mr Robson . . .' Waddle began.

Lee allowed himself a smile. Terrible timing, but, yes, he would sign an autograph.

'You were in the driving seat when your girlfriend noticed the clamp?'

'Yes,' Lee whimpered.

'Have you been drinking, sir?'

CHAPTER 6

The FA Cup, the greatest knockout competition in the world, offers a chance for every English football club to have its moment of glory and, perhaps more importantly these days, to generate some much-needed cash. The Middleton club bar was thronging with fans eagerly awaiting the draw for the third round. This was the glory round, where the glamour clubs added their illustrious names to the competition. It was only the second time in their history that Middleton had made it this far and already people were talking about winning the cup. More chance of nicking the bloody thing, Bill reckoned. He was due at work in an hour, the last of his night shifts for a while. The excitement at the bar was increased by the presence of a few reserve team players and the club's manager, Joe Burke. All were devoutly praying for a lucrative away tie.

'Number Forty-Three, Manchester United . . .' the radio crackled.

This was the big one, Manchester United at Old Trafford – without question, the tie of the round – and a reverent silence descended on the room. Were Middleton to draw United, then everyone would be a winner, including, most obviously and literally, Manchester United themselves. It would be a day out for the fans, the club's biggest ever payday, and an audition for the Middleton players to finally get themselves noticed and be plucked from football obscurity.

'. . . will play . . .'

The bar was stiff with anticipation. Everyone's breath was held and everything crossable was crossed.

'. . . Number Eighteen, Preston North End.'

A moan rang out. 'Lucky bastards.'

Manchester United, everyone hates them and everyone wants them, the greatest paradox of the English game. Middleton would have to wait another year, if they could survive that long. The disappointment, though, was short-lived. Middleton fans, like all football fans and especially fans of England, had come to live with continual disappointment and managed to bear the burden with surprising optimism. There were plenty of other gravy ties left for Middleton.

'OK. Come on, Liverpool, let's be havin' ya,' Bill shouted out, to everyone's approval.

Every time a club was announced, a sigh of relief rang out. Given Middleton's limited ground capacity, the last thing they wanted was a home tie because in the FA Cup all gate receipts are still halved, as they used to be in the league. And so should Middleton draw a Liverpool or an Arsenal at home, half the proceeds of five thousand punters would really be a lost opportunity, and certainly wouldn't keep the Chancellor of the Exchequer happy. Soon, though, Liverpool, Arsenal and Newcastle had all been announced and the mood in the bar was beginning to droop. Only Bill remained optimistic. He had a peculiar feeling that things might be about to change for his club. He didn't know why, and nor could he explain it. He just had a feeling.

'Number Twenty-Six, Tottenham Hotspur . . .'

Another big club.

'. . . will play . . . Number Sixty-Two, Middleton Edwardians.'

Instantly, the bar erupted with cries of joy. It was as if they had actually won the cup, but in reality they were celebrating the fact that they were about to be knocked out of it. Grown men, lifelong Middleton fans, hugged each other with happiness. Years of non-league football and their recent wretched troubles as a professional club had suddenly become worth it. A cup tie against Tottenham Hotspur. OK, not a Liverpool or a United, but a big club none the less. Everyone was ecstatic at the prospect of facing the likes of Lee Robson and Claudio Bertoni. What a relief. Perhaps even Hoddle himself might fancy this tie and don his boots one last time.

There was equal relief, albeit for different reasons, in the White Hart, the Spurs fans' local pub in North London. The few Tottenham fans gathered had long since given up any hopes of ever winning the league again, and had reluctantly conceded that the domestic cups were their only realistic chance of glory. Drawing Middleton suited Tottenham perfectly. It was the closest thing to a buy. Tottenham could march on towards the final, and Middleton would bow out, but in the process clear some of their debts. As is often said in sport, everyone's a winner.

Marcus Howell lived not ten miles from Middleton and he too was incredibly excited about the local football club, but not because they had just drawn Tottenham in the cup. Indeed, he hadn't listened to the draw and wasn't even aware that Middleton Edwardians were still in the competition.

It was his plans for the club that so excited him and they

were simplicity itself. Marcus planned to secure planning permission on the land and then sell it on at an obscene profit to a large property developing company. The latest valuation of the land with planning permission was estimated at between twenty-eight and thirty million pounds, and Marcus had agreed that provisional fee with the international developer Spelthorne PLC. Thirty million pounds! The thought of it alone made him shudder.

Such high returns are commensurate with risk, and Marcus stood to become either scandalously wealthy or financially and professionally ruined. 'Who dares wins' is the motto of our most celebrated soldiers, but can equally be applied to the brave ventures of Marcus Howell. He too was putting his very life on the line, and with so much at stake, he had been ruthless and pedantic in his planning.

His cunning strategy had finally become complete once he had recruited the services of Brother O'Dowd, Grand Master of the Cheshire Masonic Lodge, better known as Councillor O'Dowd, head of Middleton District Council. Councillor O'Dowd was the Chubb key to the door marked 'Planning Permission'. After ten years of suffering the stupefying boredom of being a mason, it appeared that Marcus's membership was about to bear fruit. So many pointless meetings in cold halls in ludicrous costumes – he loathed almost everything about Freemasonry: the pomp, the ceremony, but above all he despised the deceit. No sane man would ever suffer such preposterous crap if somehow it wasn't going to serve his own purpose.

What was wrong with the motto 'I'll scratch your back, you scratch mine', or even preferably, 'I'll scratch yours, you give mine a rub'? In essence, that was what it came down to.

Why did they insist on dressing it up into some worthier cause? What cause could be more worthy than oneself? Marcus was sick of swearing his allegiance to God and the Queen and of getting roped into a plethora of half-baked charity ideas, wasting his money at silly auctions, bidding for some rugby player's signed jockstrap to raise money for sick kids. Shit, he didn't even have any kids. To Marcus, Masonry seemed nothing more than an adult swap shop for professional favours.

And, as a lawyer, Marcus felt very much in favour deficit amongst the Masonic membership when it came to professional services rendered. How much free advice had he dispensed over the years, and for what? One conservatory on the back of his house that was apparently twelve inches too high. Big deal! He would have to give up the house anyway when he eventually got round to leaving his wife. But now, at last, it was harvest festival time for Marcus, and he fully intended to gorge himself.

In the lounge of the Grand Temple, Brother O'Dowd reclined in a leather chair, with his feet dangling akimbo, his legs being too short to reach the floor.

'So you've submitted the plans then?' O'Dowd asked.

Marcus nodded. 'This morning. Registered mail. It'll be there tomorrow.'

O'Dowd sniffed the air, his nostrils flaring as he processed what he'd heard without bothering to look at Marcus, like he was some mafia don receiving word from a foot soldier eager to please. Marcus wanted to punch his lights out. O'Dowd drew the remnants of his brandy around his glass, before tipping the glass back and finishing it off.

'Another one?' Marcus asked.

O'Dowd smiled. 'Why not?'

Tight bastard. I'll get them in again, shall I, you corrupt little worm? Marcus resented O'Dowd even more than he did Conran Beaumont. At least Conran brought his money to the equation. O'Dowd had nothing to offer, apart from his pathetic little job – and his greed, of course. He wasn't taking any risks at all and yet he stood to gain handsomely. That was what irritated Marcus most. It was thanks only to his foresight and endeavour that this parasite was being gifted with such a fabulous opportunity and yet he didn't seem in the least bit grateful. O'Dowd even gave the impression that he was the one doing Marcus a favour, which brought to mind a tapeworm taking the credit for weight loss. Marcus decided that O'Dowd was exactly like a tapeworm, and in this instance had more than secured his pound of flesh in return for guaranteeing his planning approval. A penthouse apartment in a new development on the Western Algarve to be exact. Marcus had offered him the permanent use of an apartment in a new complex being built by Conran's father, but O'Dowd had sensed that he was more valuable than that. And he was right. Under special negotiations, O'Dowd had been allowed to purchase the half-million-pound apartment at cost price and had even insisted that Marcus act as his lawyer – free of charge, of course.

Marcus returned from the bar and placed the brandy in front of the bloated worm.

'How's the apartment coming on?' O'Dowd enquired.

'Fine, I think. I haven't checked. How do you think the application will be received?' Marcus asked through gritted teeth.

'Not well, but then what do you expect? It's not every day we get an application to rip the heart out of a town . . .'

Marcus didn't care for his turn of phrase.

'. . . but don't worry, that's progress. As soon as the planners get through with it, it gets passed on to me. Planners just make recommendations, no actual power.' O'Dowd smiled greedily. Marcus was risking everything on the patronage of a man he loathed. 'Who dares . . .'

'. . . Brother Howell, stop looking so worried. You're in safe hands here.'

Marcus absolutely hated being patronised; it was all part of his lack-of-respect hang-up.

'You just relax and let things take their course. Our little development is as good as done.' O'Dowd leant over and rested his hand on Marcus's shoulder. In the body language dictionary of patronising gestures, this was only one down from messing his hair up or squeezing his cheek.

Marcus flinched. So it's 'our' development now, is it, you sanctimonious turd, and who said anything about it being 'little'?

'When will I be able to choose the interior for the place in Spain?'

'Portugal.'

'Oh yes, Portugal. The Spanish place is another deal I've got going through.'

Marcus glared at him.

'I'm joking.' O'Dowd laughed, but Marcus didn't join him. He couldn't be arsed with false laughter any more. It was too exhausting. Marcus hadn't laughed genuinely for ages, probably not since Milton Thorpe had died.

*

A large gathering of photographers stood outside the Chelsea and Westminster Hospital. It was a hospital well used to media attention. Positioned as it was in such a wealthy part of town, it almost continuously tended to someone rich or famous and usually both. Lee Robson had been whisked here by ambulance with the press in hot pursuit, purely in their capacity of serving the public interest, naturally. They already had a great tabloid story for their editors but nobody felt that the story was finished. It had 'to be continued' emblazoned all over it. In an ideal world, Lee would oblige them by punching whichever poor doctor was assigned to his mangled foot and then, in true celebrity fashion, seek solace in a blow-job from some star-struck nurse. Potentially this story had every detail that journalism increasingly exists for, and because it was played out so publicly it was set to dominate the press for a few days at least.

Seth Meyer drove anxiously along the Euston Road, listening to Radio 5 Live, his misery now complete.

'Our top story this hour: in an amazing chain of events, the Tottenham Hotspur star Lee Robson has been admitted to hospital with a suspected broken right foot after attempting to kick a wheel clamp off his eighty-thousand-pound Porsche car. There are also unconfirmed reports that he has been charged with drink driving and he might yet be arrested for assaulting a traffic warden, who was trying to issue him with a parking ticket . . .'

Seth couldn't take any more. He turned the radio off and, even though he was in a London traffic jam, cracked open his window. No matter how laden with fumes and lead it was, Seth needed the air.

*

Similarly, Lee was seeking some noxious gas because he desperately needed sedating – his anger rather than his pain getting the better of him. How could he be lying prostrate and utterly helpless in a hospital bed with multiple injuries from a parking incident! Unsurprisingly, his foot had come a distant second to the wheel clamp and his hand hadn't faired much better against the warden's crash helmet. And even in hospital, the place of healing, Lee had managed to pick up another injury. His girlfriend, Kelly, had rushed to the hospital as soon as she'd heard the news that her baby had been injured. Her sympathy and concern had evaporated, though, when a mischievous hack explained that Lee had been having lunch with a younger, more beautiful and blonder model than she. Kelly did what any proud ex-glamour model would do in the circumstances: crashed her shoe into the bastard's face and set off posthaste, presumably to a hairdresser's, at least.

Everything hurt, including his pride and ego, as Lee lay in bed alone apart from his thoughts of revenge. He was a passionate believer in conspiracy theories. He was convinced that Princess Diana was murdered, that Maxwell didn't die and that the Americans never went to the moon. Now added to this list was the Lee Robson conspiracy theory – perhaps the greatest conspiracy of them all, because one thing was certain: this was no ordinary chain of events. This hadn't just happened by chance. Someone was behind it. Some cunning bastard had set this up. The drugs were starting to kick in now, keeping the various pains at bay, but they were powerless to cope with his anger. Over and over in his mind, Lee pictured finding the bastard and then consoled himself by imagining just exactly what he would do to him, which always involved a rolling pin or bog brush at some point.

But who could have done it? That was the burning question. It had to be someone with power. Only a person with connections would have a traffic warden and the old bill on his payroll. It had to be a right clever bastard. Not many people would have the connections and nous, and that narrowed the search down considerably. But then, it also had to be someone who didn't like Lee Robson, which opened it right up again. Whoever this criminal mastermind was, Lee was going to find him, and Lee was going to kill him.

'Have you just put Viennese whirls in there?' Bill asked somewhat angrily.

Vippin didn't have the answer he figured his boss was looking for. After the excitement of drawing Tottenham in the cup, the night shift was flying by and, as a result, crusty rolls had been overlooked.

'We've got no bloody crusty rolls.'

Vippin feigned a look of sheer horror. 'My God, Bill, how are we going to cope?'

'Ya cheeky little . . .'

Vippin wasn't paid enough to worry about a shortage of crusty rolls. Actually, nor was Bill, but he did anyway. As supervisor, Bill bore responsibility for providing the people of Middleton and beyond with sufficient crusty rolls each day.

'Shit, Vippin, right after those whirls, it's just crusties in both ovens, OK?'

'Yes sir.' Vippin saluted his bakery mentor. Even he was

caught up with the excitement of the impending glamour cup tie.

'Are you going down to London, then, Bill, for the match?'

'No. I thought I'd listen to it on the radio, ya daft bugger. I went to Norfolk once to see them play Cromer, but I can't be arsed going to Spurs.'

'All right. Perhaps I'll come with ya.'

'And you'll be very welcome, son. If you can get a ticket, that is.'

Vippin looked disappointed.

'Don't worry, I'll sort you out, and your mates as well. The more the merrier. Have you ever been to London?' Bill asked innocently.

'Course I fockin have. What d'you think I am, man?'

'Eh now, Vippin, listen. Remember what I said about the anger thing. You need to calm down, son. No one's havin' a go at ya.'

'Yeah, no, sorry. It's just that I have been to London.'

'Well, good, then. You can show us round.'

'I think I will come, ya know.'

'By the end of this season, you'll be a season ticket holder.'

Vippin chuckled at the thought as he moved off towards the second oven.

Smithy, eager as ever to please Bill, rushed over with momentous news. ''Ere, Billy, Billy, have you heard about Tottenham?' he blurted out, hoping that Bill didn't already know. The most exciting thing about spectacular news is being able to tell other people about it.

'Bloody hell, Smithy, course I have. I was there at the draw, wasn't I?'

'No, not that. About Lee Robson.'

'What about him?'

Smithy could barely contain himself. He knew something football-related that Bill didn't.

'He's out – out for two months at least.'

'No, seriously?'

'Yeah, he's bust his foot.'

'What, in training?'

'No, something to do with his car.'

'What, a crash?'

'Yeah, think so. I heard something about him losing it. Must have been going too fast.'

'Did he hit something?'

'Yeah, think so,' Smithy answered blindly.

'Anyone else hurt?'

'Just him, I think.'

'What, not seriously?'

'No, he's not dying or anything. But he's out of football for a while.'

Bill beamed. What tremendous news. Now even he was beginning to believe the ridiculous. Middleton go down to London and silence White Hart Lane, get featured on *Match of the Day*, and get discussed by Messrs Lineker, Brooking and Lawrenson. What would Hansen make of our stout defence? How far did they feel we could proceed? Could we win it? Bill didn't honestly think for one moment that Middleton could win any cup let alone the FA's, but he did passionately want to beat Tottenham. Bill had never liked the chairman of Tottenham Hotspur, famous for his electronics and miserable little dishes. Now, Bill and Middleton had their chance to serve him up a dish of their own.

'Bill, oven number two's gone and blown again,' Vip called over to him.

With the impending crusty roll shortage, this would normally have been a disaster, but tonight nobody was too concerned. Minds were elsewhere – in North London, to be precise – and nothing could dent Bill's mood, not even if he had to fill a load of jam doughnuts.

Seth paced frantically up and down in front of Lee's bed, agitated and angry. In contrast, Lee, now heavily sedated, had calmed down considerably.

'I always said your temper would get the better of you.'

'Oh, Seth, shut up, will you? Just shut up. Doesn't it look like I've been through enough? I'm trying to think positive here, so I don't need you—'

'Positive?' Seth protested. 'How can this be positive? The only positive thing is your fucking drink driving test? What were you thinking?'

'Yeah, all right, don't go on about it. I've only just got that motor, remember.'

Seth stared at his client. Was he being serious? 'I wasn't meaning not being able to drive the bloody thing.'

'Well, what then? I mean, it ain't like I'm a fucking racing car driver, is it?'

'I don't mean that either,' Seth exploded. 'I mean the press. They're going to have a field day with this. Shit, they already are.'

'Scuze me, but aren't you s'posed to be cheering me up? And bollocks to the press. They ain't ever liked me since I hit that photographer. And, anyway, all publicity is good. That's what they say, ain't it?'

'Oh, yeah. This is great.'

'So then, get out there and turn this round to my advantage.'

'Are you serious?'

'Yeah, course.'

'Do I look like Paul fucking Daniels?'

'Look at Tony Adams. He gets pissed and smashes his car up. Suddenly he's a hero with a book out.'

Seth didn't bother responding that there was enormous goodwill towards Adams throughout the country, which certainly wasn't there for Lee. 'And the assault charge?' he asked wearily.

'They'll have to drop that. I hit his helmet, for Christ's sake. Hurt me more than him,' Lee pleaded, holding up his injured hand. 'Anyway, Seth, I've got some good news for ya.'

'What? That this has all been a dream, or nightmare more like.'

'While I've been lying here, I've been thinking—'

'Forgive me, Lee. And the good news is?'

'That you was right all along. I'm gonna stay at Tottenham.'

Oh, whoopee. Tottenham will be thrilled. A player out for two months at least, facing a driving ban and a possible jail term for assault, and he chooses this very moment to decide that he wants to renew his contract. If his foot didn't heal properly, Lee might even struggle to get into the Wormwood Scrubs team. Lee's value had just plummeted, and it was questionable whether he was worth anything at all, although this clearly hadn't yet dawned on the man himself. He was either in denial or he simply didn't understand how grave his situation was. Seth wondered what drugs he'd been given. One hundred milligrams of Delusional Optimism, he suspected.

'You brought me anything, then? What's in the bag?' Lee chirped.

Seth had almost forgotten. 'Got you a couple of doughnuts.'

'Oh, nice one. Jam, I hope.'

CHAPTER 7

Bill skipped enthusiastically along the high street on his way home from work, stopping briefly to chat with a milkman. No one had bothered to explain to the people of Middleton that the FA Cup had apparently lost its cachet. Even at this unearthly hour of the morning, the FA Cup tie was uppermost in people's minds. Bill hopped into Ernie's paper shop, hoping to signal that he was in a rush and didn't have time for a chat. Ernie was delighted to see him.

'Well then, Billy boy, you were right again.'

'You can depend on me, Ern.' Bill plonked the correct money down on the counter for his papers and his pools coupon.

'Don't know why you bother with this pools nonsense, Bill. The lottery's odds are much better.'

'Fourteen million to one, aren't they?' Bill asked defiantly.

'Someone's gotta win, though.'

Bill didn't like the lottery. Working-class, desperate people handing over their cash each week to prop up some opera house or art gallery. And what the hell was Billy Connolly doing advertising it?

'Have you heard about Robson then?' Ernie asked eagerly, desperate to talk to someone about it. He'd tried discussing it with his wife but she wasn't interested.

'Yeah, Smithy said. Done his foot, hasn't he?'

'Not just his foot,' Ernie chuckled, as he unfolded the

Mirror. 'ROBSON CLAMPED', bellowed the headline above a picture of a man crumpled on a pavement with an inset picture of a man kicking the car. A strapline below assured the potential reader that more incredible pictures and the full story could be found inside on pages three, four and five.

'Bloody hell. What, was he mugged?'

'Busted his foot, didn't he? You ain't going to believe this. He parks his flash car up, right—'

'Ernie, I'd love to stop and chat, but you know . . .'

Bill turned to leave because once Ernie got started on a subject he might never get away.

'He got arrested as well, Bill,' Ernie protested, his face a picture of disappointment.

Bill rushed off home as quickly as he could, scanning the papers for an explanation about the demise of poor old Lee Robson. He'd bought the *Daily Telegraph* as well, because Lee had even made their front page and Bill was hoping that they might give Middleton a mention. Nationals hardly ever featured Middleton, and never on the front page.

'Hello,' he called as he shut the front door.

Mary and Tom were already up. Tom looked ready for the day and Mary looked ready for bed.

'Another bad night, love?' he asked, kissing her.

'I might as well work nights with you,' she sighed.

'You're a little monster, that's what you are. Come here, champ.' Bill picked up Tom, who was destined for a career in security or minicab driving if his sleep pattern didn't change soon.

'Where's Katherine?' Bill asked.

'Poor thing's back at work.'

'What, already?' Bill looked at his watch.

'Yeah, and she was working late last night.'

'Are we picking up Tess from nursery, then?'

'Yeah, eleven o'clock.'

'Right, fine. I'll do that. Why don't you go and grab an hour, love?'

Mary looked relieved. 'Love you, Bill.'

'I wanna watch the telly, anyway. Have you heard what's happened to Lee Robson?'

'Who?'

Bill turned on the television and instantly Lee's sorry story was being recounted in all its gory detail. The newspaper stills must have come from a video camera because it seemed that Lee's entire downfall had been preserved for ever on tape and was now being played continually on every news channel. It wasn't earth shattering news – and, indeed, not even that important – but because the whole thing had been captured on film and was so comical, combined with it being a slow news week, anyway, the Lee Robson story was big news. Like most people in the country that morning, Bill and Mary stood in front of the television, transfixed by what they were seeing. A reporter narrated the story, although it was fairly self-explanatory.

'. . . Lee Robson, having already failed his breath test, is now being charged by Officer Waddle, but watch the traffic warden here in the corner of your screens. You can't see it very well from this camera angle – remember, this is all amateur video footage – but the warden is now processing a parking ticket for Lee Robson and it is now that Robson attacks him . . .'

On television, Lee could clearly be seen hobbling towards the traffic warden and then launching himself at him, with flailing fists. One fist crashed on to the helmet, followed by a desperately thrown right upper cut, which might have had more success had Lee not lost his balance and crashed back down to the pavement. The warden was no fool and clearly knew an opportunity when he saw one, or felt one, albeit with the helmet's protection. Like an honours graduate in Compensation Culture from Litigious State University, he instantly held his face and began stumbling back and forth as if concussed. Rivaldo himself would have been proud of his performance, and, likewise, 'no win, no fee' lawyers were probably prostrating themselves in front of him now with their offers of legal help. If a lawyer could get this personal injury charge to stick, imagine then the legitimate claim they might have against the manufacturer of the warden's crash helmet.

The report finished for the umpteenth time and Eamonn Holmes was back on screen, his rotund face doing its best to look earnest. His female co-presenter looked equally crest-fallen and disgusted.

'Thank you, Rob. Well, well, well, what is it all coming to?' Eamonn asked. 'Perhaps the best person to speak to is the officer closely involved with the case, PC Keith Waddle, the officer who arrested Lee Robson. He joins us now outside a central London police station. Officer Waddle, thank you for joining us.'

'My pleasure,' Waddle said, as casually as he could, hoping to give the impression that this television interview was a little irksome, an intrusion into his busy schedule of fighting crime and making London's streets safer for all the pretty ladies out there. What a load of horseshit. This was possibly the proudest moment of his career and he wouldn't have missed it for all the jam doughnuts in the world. In actual fact, today was his day off, but nothing could keep him at home with his gnat's-piss soup whilst some shitty superintendent took all his glory. Already that morning he'd had his hair cut and had used almost half a tube of hideously expensive whitening toothpaste. Women like men in uniform, that was a given, so imagine then what a man in a uniform on telly did for them. Waddle was praying that he was about to find out.

'Officer Waddle, can you tell us exactly what happened?'

'Well, I was notified of a potentially violent incident taking place and straight away I responded . . .' Waddle began his carefully rehearsed statement, with its subtext of 'large desperate man keen to meet any female whatsoever'.

Bill flicked the television over to BBC1. They were still covering the story, as journalists desperately tried to stick a more sinister spin to it. The ghastly behaviour of Lee Robson was surely just one symptom of a much greater problem. This demonstrates the malaise of our celebrity-obsessed, artistically bereft and, above all, avaricious culture. More questions were being asked than were being answered, and up and down the country anyone remotely connected with psychology, football or, ideally, both, was being hastily chauffeur-driven to various television studios. The BBC had literally wiped the sleep out of Emlyn Hughes's eyes and he was thrust on set.

'Well, in my day there were a lot of shenanigans going on too,' Emlyn began.

'Yes, but, Mr Hughes, with respect,' the interviewer butted in, BBC speak for *don't give me that shit*, 'I accept that, but it wasn't anything like it is today. I mean, here is a young man, role model to many thousands of kids, drink driving, causing a disturbance of the peace and attacking a traffic warden. You can't say that this sort of thing took place in your day?'

'Well . . .'

'Did you ever do this kind of thing?'

'Erm . . .' Emlyn started to laugh. Golden Rule Number One for a sports star on television: when in doubt, just laugh – a strategy Emlyn himself had devised and handed on so expertly to Kriss Akabusi.

Bill was now in a remote-control frenzy. GMTV were replaying the whole video again, but this time with a graphic caption in the bottom corner of the screen reading, 'Your Say. Why are our sports stars behaving like this?' complete with a Web address and telephone number. Bill even toyed with the idea of phoning in himself, putting the record straight once and for all. He knew exactly what had caused Lee's calamitous outburst.

PC Waddle now appeared on the screen again, the perfect person to fill the space.

'And you want our Tom to be a football player? Disgusting, the lot of 'em,' Mary stated emphatically, and Bill didn't feel inclined to disagree.

'It's money that's caused this, you know. What those players earn these days. It's not right. It's corrupting to even want that much money, let alone have it.'

'So how come you do the pools then?' Mary asked.

'Huh?'

'You heard.'

'It's not the same,' Bill answered, slightly irritated.

'How so?'

'Because I'll never win, that's why?'

'So why play?'

As this was another question he couldn't answer, Bill decided to answer an entirely different one altogether.

'All I'm saying is what I've said all along. Money eventually ruins everything. Heavyweight boxing . . .'

Mary kissed her impassioned husband on the cheek. She'd heard this speech over and over, and was too tired anyway. 'Well then, we could do with being a little bit more ruined, Billy Boy.'

Bill laughed.

'Don't tell me. Stanley Matthews would turn in his grave. I'm going to go and grab half an hour, then. Tom's been fed.'

'Ah, no, Mary, hang on. He's filled his pants here, love,' Bill called out, holding Tom aloft to his nose, but Mary had gone.

'Oh no . . . I can't do pooh . . . Mary.' Bill was mightily relieved to see his flustered wife reappear.

'God's sake, Bill.' Mary picked up the child.

'Eh now, language. Not in front of Tom.'

She returned briefly a few moments later with a baby complete with a brand-new nappy for him to punish at will. Bill was still absorbed in the morning's media bonanza and was using a well-timed advert break to rifle through his various newspapers. The *Daily Telegraph* had hastily put together a graph showing how players' earnings had grown over the last twenty years both in real terms and against inflation.

This is exactly what I was talking about, Bill thought proudly, congratulating himself on having the same ideas as the *Daily Telegraph*, no less. It was a shame that Mary had gone to bed. He'd show her later.

'Look at that, son. I was right all along. They should have

me on the news. Your old man, they should have asked me.
I could have told 'em what's caused all this.'

As far as Bill and his love of facts were concerned, football
was the most popular game on earth and also the best thing
ever to have come out of an English public school. The
professional football league was formed in 1880, and its co-
operative status allowed each club to flourish. All gate
receipts were halved between the clubs, ensuring teams with
remote populations could compete with the clubs fortunate
to have homes in cities. Finance was evenly distributed
throughout football, the principle being to preserve competition and the broader health of the game. However, such
wholesome and sensible ideas couldn't possibly withstand
the tidal wave of Thatcherism that swept the country,
destroying much in its path and making a few people very
wealthy indeed.

Bill's other favourite football fact was a little more
contentious, namely that English football was officially
sentenced to death in 1992 with the birth of the Premier
League. The big clubs hadn't much cared for the co-operative
way in which football was run and had effectively voted to
keep the lion's share of football's finances for themselves.
The sport conceived out of amateurism had become Football
PLC, a business sitting alongside oil companies on the Stock
Exchange. Individuals made personal fortunes from selling
off century-old clubs they should never have been allowed to
own in the first place. Clubs founded and loyally supported
by their local communities were sold to the City of London,
whose criterion for success was fiscal and not sporting.
Players were now earning one hundred thousand pounds a
week, and ordinary fans shunned in favour of corporate

hospitality boxes – for the betterment of football, it was argued; so that we can compete in Europe. 'Bloody nonsense,' Bill argued. 'So that pockets could be lined, more like.'

According to Bill, football's soul had perished at the highest level. Manchester United beat Bayern Munich at Old Trafford and thirty thousand businessmen thank their suppliers for inviting them along. And meanwhile, many famous old football clubs struggle to survive, and if they go bust, so what? It doesn't matter, because we've got the Premiership.

Lee hadn't had a good night at all. A combination of the drugs wearing off and listening to the radio had propelled the hapless star into a deep and possibly incurable depression. Lee and his story dominated all the sports and most of the news coverage, with the general conclusion being that his career in the top flight of football was probably over. It was unimaginable, but Lee's misery had really only just begun.

Alongside its obvious victims, 'Clampgate' had thrown up a few prominent winners as well, chief among them Carmen, now the subject of a frenzied tabloid bidding war for her story. After considering each offer and carefully counting and comparing the number of noughts, Carmen opted for the *Sun*. In a vain attempt to placate his girlfriend Kelly, Lee had dumped Carmen, which actually was a spectacularly stupid thing to do. Dating Lee, and eventually marrying him, had been Carmen's planned escape route from her previous life as a high-class call girl. Now though, Guy Vincent, the PR executive who'd managed to stick himself to Carmen first, firmly advised her to opt for maximum exposure and financial gain while the going was good. The *Sun*'s story had been printed this morning, complete with a pictorial of the lovely Carmen in various states of undress. No one quite knew what the people of Mogadishu would make of the story, but it was still called a 'world exclusive'. On Page Three, Carmen appeared topless, sitting on a wheel clamp, and revealed the irony that Lee liked nothing more than clamping her to the bed along with the inevitable claims of marathon bonking sessions that she found exhausting. Four pages appeared in all, with more salacious revelations promised for tomorrow and, indeed, for as long as Carmen could keep making them up.

Like Lee, Seth had barely slept a wink either. Sitting at his breakfast table with a bowl of soggy cereals and a copy of the *Sun*, he couldn't face either of them. Damage limitation was the phrase bombarding his already clouded mind. He'd spoken briefly with Tottenham yesterday, who would say nothing more than that they were reviewing the situation. It sounded ominous, as though they were about to offer Lee a job at the club shop.

Seth's mobile phone rang again: another journalist no doubt. What was it now? What had Lee done this time? Been caught running amok in a kid's ward with a packet of sweets and an erection?

Like Marcus, Conran Beaumont hadn't listened to the FA Cup draw. At the time, he had been literally tied up in a business meeting in a Mayfair establishment with two frightfully friendly and attractive hostesses.

Conran had recently reached a watershed in his life. After years of denial, he had reluctantly accepted the fact that women would only ever find him attractive once they established how wealthy he was, and then they would almost immediately want to get married to him or at the very least sire his heir. It wasn't a particularly happy realisation for him, but it did clear the way for a much less complicated, if more expensive sex life, because prostitution provided the perfect solution to his sexual needs and wants. And it was nothing to be ashamed of either, he decided. It was simply a fact that in the hand that he'd been dealt, he didn't have any picture cards and there wasn't anything he could do about it. Simply put, women only ever wanted him for his money, which meant that any girlfriends he had were prostitutes in everything but name. And any beautiful woman with an ugly and rich husband is really little more than a lady of the night but with just one client. Of course prostitutes weren't cheap, but he figured that they were still a darn sight cheaper than getting divorced.

Now, he stepped out of his en suite sauna and went naked to the kitchen he hardly ever used to fix himself a green tea, which someone had told him was good for his skin. He drank the tea looking out from his veranda, with its magnificent views over Regent's Park, then, turning to his mobile phone, Conran noticed that he had a message waiting for him.

'You have thirty new messages,' said the mechanical, emotionless Orange woman, an apt description of either of the prostitutes from earlier on, in fact.

'Jesus, thirty . . .'

'To listen to your messages—'

Conran's phone beeped: another call was trying to get through, which he decided to take. Not a good move, as it turned out.

'Hello.'

'Mr Beaumont?'

'Yes, hello.'

'Hello. I'm calling from the *Sunday Express*.'

'Oh right.'

'Got a piece going in on giant killing. Wondered if you'd like to comment.'

Conran looked at his phone. Had the man said giant killing? 'I beg your pardon?'

'What are your feelings about giant killers? Could you be one this year?'

'Could I be a giant killer?' Conran asked.

'Yes.'

'Are you trying to be amusing?'

'No, sir.'

'Well, I suggest you try again. Good day.'

No sooner had Conran ended the call than the phone was ringing again.

'Hello,' he answered tentatively.

'Mr Beaumont?'

'Have you just called me?'

'No, sir.'

'Oh good. Who are you?'

'Gerald Harper, Associated Press. Wanted to get a line from you about playing Spurs, especially now with the Robson story.'

Conran was confused again. 'I'm sorry but I have no idea what you're talking about.'

'The FA Cup draw. Middleton, Tottenham – without Lee Robson, of course.'

Over the next hour or so, Conran managed to assimilate most of the facts as he conducted painfully embarrassing press interviews with anyone who happened to get through to his mobile phone. God knows how they had got hold of his number, but Conran was delighted that they had. This was the kind of attention an international playboy deserved and he got rather caught up in the excitement of it all.

'And so you think Middleton can go all the way?'

'Yes, of course I believe that Middleton can win, that's why I took them on. I have big plans for this club . . . And yes, come May, I wouldn't be at all surprised if my lads don't get to walk out at Wembley.'

A journalist laughed. 'You won't be as surprised as the builders. It'll be Cardiff—'

'Please, please. One game at a time. We've got to beat Tottenham first and then we'll prepare for Cardiff . . .'

Marcus finally managed to get through to his moronic partner after filling his message box with increasingly irate messages pleading with him not to talk to the press. It was too late, of course, and the story had already changed from a giant-killing story, to a generic one on businessmen who know absolutely nothing about football taking over small clubs. Anyway, it was hardly the public relations scoop Marcus had planned.

'Fuck, thank God, Conran, I've been trying to get hold of you all morning.'

'About the Spurs draw? Isn't it exciting?'

Marcus sighed. 'No it isn't. Frankly, it's a pain in the arse. We could do without the bloody attention.'

'What's the name of our manager, by the way?' Conran asked.

'What? I don't know. Burke. Joe Burke.'

'Shit. I knew it was something like that. I called him Pratt, damn.'

'Who've you been talking to?' Marcus demanded.

'Oh, you know, just some chums.'

'Not journalists?'

'What?'

'Journalists? Have you spoken to any journalists?'

'They've been trying to get through, leaving messages—'

'But you haven't spoken to them?'

Conran grimaced. 'No, why?'

'Good. Just don't speak to any journalists. In fact, no, scrub that. Don't speak to anyone about the club. Have you got that?'

Conran gulped. He'd been answering questions all morning and he suspected that he probably hadn't fared too well. The pools panel would have given him a resounding home defeat.

'Loud and clear.'

'Good. Thank God I got to you. Now, I've submitted the plans to the council, which means the shit is about to hit the fan up here, so you might as well come up and face it.'

'Absolutely.'

'Where are you now?'

'At the flat.'

'Well, you'd better get up here.'

'To Manchester?' Conran asked.

'Yes, where else? I'm going to set up a meeting with the Club.'

'Why?'

'Shit, Conran, we've discussed this already. See if we can't get them on board.'

'Yes, of course.'

'This is going to work, Conran,' Marcus said excitedly.

'Great.'

Conran didn't seem excited at all. Either he didn't know what was going on, or he wasn't excited by the prospect of becoming even wealthier. Whichever it was, Marcus thought he could at least try to sound interested and also just a tiny bit grateful.

Bill hurried to his front door, hoping the bell hadn't woken Mary. Must be the postman with a package, he thought, and so he was a little surprised to see George standing there.

'George, come in, come in.'

'Hello, little Tom.' George twinkled the baby's nose as he stepped into the tiny house.

'Tea, George?'

'Erm . . . yeah, go on then.'

Bill filled the kettle again and retrieved a clean mug from a cupboard in the spotlessly clean kitchen.

'Tottenham away, eh? God, I'd love to knock them out. Did you know it was—'

'Bill . . .'

Bill looked at his friend, sensing he hadn't come to celebrate. It was half-eight in the morning, after all.

'Bloody hell, George, what's up? It's not Susan, is it?'

George shook his head. 'You were right all along. Beaumont's made his first move. I've just had a phone call from the *Chronicle*.'

Bill sat down on a PVC stool that really needed throwing out. 'Go on.'

'It's like you said, flats or something. He's proposing we do a ground share with another club, most likely Altrincham.'

This was what Bill had known all along would eventually befall his town and club. It was simply inevitable that a businessman was going to come along and fall in love with Middleton Edwardians but for all the wrong reasons. And, strangely, Bill actually felt some relief now that it had happened. At least now the enemy had officially declared himself and had given him something to work at.

'Ding ding, seconds out,' Bill murmured.

'He's going to chuck loads of money at it, Bill. I shouldn't wonder if he hasn't already bought someone up at the council. I don't trust that lot meself.'

'There's no way on God's earth that he's turning our club into a supermarket.'

'Luxury flats,' George corrected him.

'Luxury flats,' Bill spat. 'It's always luxury flats, isn't it? Never ordinary homes for ordinary people, always bloody luxury ones. Well, not at our club. When's it being announced?'

'Today's press.'

Bill sighed and handed George the tea he didn't want in the first place.

'Ta.'

When George had left, Bill sat in front of his telly again. The Lee Robson debate was still raging, but suddenly it wasn't entertaining any more. Bill no longer had time for such trivialities. He had more pressing things on his mind.

CHAPTER 8

Seth put the phone down slowly. He looked at his watch and wondered whether his client was still sedated. He hoped he was. As expected, Tottenham were not altogether backing their erstwhile employee. Ten years ago, they would have already appointed counsel rigorously to defend their valuable asset. Now, though, the best Lee could hope for was a pay-and-play deal, and even that was looking doubtful. The club would want to follow his progress back to full fitness and, more importantly, wanted to know as soon as possible whether or not Her Majesty would grant him his liberty to grace their field at all. Tottenham's only commitment to Lee at this stage was to honour the rest of his contract. All three weeks of it. Seth gulped.

Of the three people who had caused 'Clampgate', only Daryl the wheel clamper knew that he was involved. Bill didn't have a clue and nor did PC Waddle, busy as he was trying to remain in the public eye. Meanwhile, the national debate surrounding Lee rumbled on. Lee Robson had never been such big news. Over the week following the incident, without question Lee had the most column inches, something the *Sun* happily agreed with in yet another world exclusive according to Carmen. On television, Robert Kilroy-Silk stared at the camera intently before asking with almost no gravitas whatsoever, 'What causes extreme anger such as this?' after which the familiar images of Lee Robson filled the screen. And then Kilroy was back in shot again, leaping around his hastily arranged studio audience of people with anger problems, complete with a couple of half-respectable-looking people in the front, no doubt experts in anger management.

Lee was now a broken man and sat up in bed sobbing. Seth held his hand. He hadn't taken the news about his employment prospects very well at all. Shattered glass covered the floor where his bottle of Highland Spring had hit the telly. Nurses and orderlies quickly came scurrying from all directions, not to help their famous patient, but more in the hope of witnessing another gossipy titbit to sell to the hacks still clogging up the waiting rooms with their cheque books and ambition. Seth valiantly fended them all off.

'It's going to be OK, Lee.'

Lee wiped away a tear. 'I know. All I need is a name, and I'll have him fucking shot.'

Seth tenderly put his arm around his client. It's what Jerry McGuire would have done. 'Come on, Lee, you have to let that go. It's not helping,' he pleaded anxiously. 'You have to concentrate on getting better, getting fit and proving these bastards wrong.'

'I will. I fucking will. I'll show 'em,' Lee blubbed, now with his head plastered to his agent's bosom. Football players are famous for embracing each other, but after fifteen years in the game, this was Seth's first cuddle. 'Why is this happening, Seth? I mean, why me? It's not fair.'

'I know, I know . . .'

Lee wiped his nose. 'I'm gonna . . . I'm gonna . . .'

'Get fit,' Seth prompted him.

'. . . gonna fucking kill him.'

Seth looked like a very worried man indeed. Even taking the best possible scenario, his personal situation looked increasingly desperate.

'And what happens before then?' Lee asked.

'What do you mean?'

'Between my contract running out and me playing again.'

It was an excellent and expensive question and one that Lee had every right to ask, only Seth, his agent, the manager of his affairs, couldn't really answer it.

'Let's not even think about that, eh?'

'And what about the assault charge? He was wearing a helmet – it's not like I hurt him.'

'Exactly. I've already spoken to my lawyers. The charge will be dropped, so it'll just be the driving ban, and it's like you said: you're not a racing driver.'

Seth got up to leave. He felt almost faint with anxiety. His hands were wet with perspiration. He needed to get out of there, think a few things through, make a few phone calls. He had other clients to take care of, clients who were able to play and therefore able to earn, and Seth had to make sure that they remained in his fold.

'OK then, Lee, you leave it to me,' he managed to say, as he got to the door. A porter had come in and was busy sweeping up the glass.

'Seth, you know the bit between me getting fit again and my contract running out?'

Seth grunted and barely managed an 'Uh huh.'

'I'm insured, right?'

'Yeah, course,' Seth mumbled, hoping Lee wouldn't notice him shaking. No, Lee, you haven't got any insurance because I haven't paid your premiums. That would have been the honest answer, but it was too hideous even to contemplate.

*

A truly great news story is one that feeds itself. Every day, something else is thrown up, another victim is implicated and the whole story can be told again. Jeremy Davidson, MP was one such quaking victim, sitting directly in the path of the 'Clampgate' tornado. Jeremy was the new face of New Labour, the face that had got them elected but was still despised by its old guard for changing them. Public school, Oxbridge, the bar, exactly like the party's great leader himself, whose career pattern Jeremy dreamt of emulating one day. Already, he had been noticed in the highest political circles and was marked out as a future player. And with so much at stake, so much to lose, Jeremy followed 'Clampgate' with juddering trepidation, wondering whether it might cruelly curtail his glittering career if the link between himself and Carmen was ever made.

Her fame and cachet increased daily with every new tawdry revelation and further pictures of her clad in nothing more than a pearl choker. How long would it be before she realised that some of her previous clients might offer her some worthier news coverage than a football player?

Jeremy pushed aside the day's newspapers. He hadn't been mentioned – another day's reprieve at least. With every passing day, his chances of survival increased, but he didn't feel confident, not yet, anyway. What Carmen had on him meant that he might never be able to appear in public again. Jeremy clamped his eyes shut at such a thought. This was awful, not just for him, but for everyone. Damn it, this country needs me, he moaned into his hands. And what blasted awful timing as well, just when things were starting to move ahead for him politically.

Jeremy firmly laid the blame for his situation at his blasted mother's door. The wretched woman, it was clearly her fault, packing him off to prep school, then boarding school, and hardly ever even acknowledging her only son. Was it any wonder that now as an adult he craved the attention of a mother figure? Childhood had been denied him and so was it so peculiar that he wanted to be a child now? That he liked nothing more than pulling on a big nappy, donning a bonnet and paying women to let him suckle them. Jeremy had just been invited on to a subcommittee dealing with MPs' ethics and outside interests, his first inexorable move towards junior ministerial ranks, and now he might have to decline the invitation. Scrutinising the behaviour of other Members of Parliament wouldn't be easy if ever his sexual proclivity were revealed. It was so unfair. Other MPs happily hit the bottle every night and that was fine, but he hits the bottle of milk and he'd be the one not fit to govern and lead. The MP with the flex and the orange in his mouth would finally be forgotten if this ever got out and at least he'd had the good sense to make it his final act, so that he didn't have to suffer the cruel jibes himself.

Jeremy rubbed his eyes slowly. He could feel a panic attack welling within as he tried to reassure himself that the odds were still in his favour. It was so long ago and he was certain that Carmen didn't know his real name and nor did she know what he did for a living. She'd known him by a variety of names, most often Munchkins, as she undid his 'all in one' and reached for the wipes. Jeremy came over all faint just thinking about it and had to snap himself out of it. His only hope of surviving the probable crisis would be to lie low for a while, perhaps taking some sick leave up at his family home in Perthshire until this tornado had blown itself out.

Jeremy breathed in heavily through his nose, assuring himself that everything was going to be fine. He looked at himself in the mirror. He was strong and handsome with, crucially for political office these days, a full head of hair. He clenched his jaw defiantly, and looked as manly as any man can look while sucking on a dummy or, as Jeremy preferred to call it, a soother.

For a man travelling to a town he was about to ruin, Conran Beaumont was remarkably at ease with himself. This wasn't because he was callous and unfeeling, but more because he was almost completely unaware of the harm he might be causing. He'd been bamboozled into the whole scheme by a rampant Marcus, and hadn't really given it much thought. And why should he? He trusted Marcus absolutely, and liked the idea of being able to help out his old friend. Conran cheerily entered the Loughton Hall Hotel on the outskirts of Knutsford. The drive up from London had been problem free. He'd even given his driver a break and driven some of the way himself. The speed cameras had flashed him a few times, but it didn't matter because his chauffeur would cop the tickets if they ever materialised. Isn't that what chauffeurs were for these days? Life was good to Conran and he embraced it with both arms.

He noticed the young lady behind the hotel reception was very attractive.

'Can I help you, sir?'

'Oh, I hope so.' Conran peered at her name tag so tantalisingly attached to her young breast. 'It's no secret why they've got you on reception.'

The young woman's lower jaw fell open like a trap as her eyes rolled upwards. It was unmistakable body language that Conran had seen a thousand times before but it no longer worried him, safe as he was in the knowledge that one look at his bank statement and her mouth would be agape for a very different and altogether more pleasurable reason.

'The bar?' he asked, moving off in its obvious direction, pointing as he went.

The receptionist didn't bother to answer him. She'd figured he was loaded. With his looks and that level of confidence, there couldn't be any other explanation. Money didn't do it for her. She couldn't imagine anyone happier than her mum and dad, and they had bugger all money between them and a new little baby boy to cope with.

Conran burst into the bar, his confidence fully restored, and looking forward to seeing his old chum Marcus. Marcus, in contrast, looked like a man who was about to go into battle.

'Marcus, how the hell are you?' Conran bellowed from across the bar, leading with his outstretched hand. Marcus leapt up to meet him, trying to quieten him down in the process.

'So, what are you having?' Conran boomed.

'Keep it down, eh?'

'What?'

Marcus didn't want a drink. 'I'll just have an orange juice,' he said quietly, his eyes darting back and forth on the lookout for a possible sniper.

'An orange juice!' Conran bellowed in mock masculine disgust. 'Have a drink, man.'

'No, really. I'm driving,' Marcus insisted, now aware of the attention that Conran was drawing to himself. His looks and accent would make him stand out in a crowded Cheshire hotel anyway, even before his face was plastered over the front of the local newspaper.

Conran tutted. 'How many times have I told you? Get yourself a driver.'

It was typical of Conran to be utterly unaware that not everyone was a millionaire who could afford to be driven about planet earth.

'I would do, but I just like driving too much.'

'Have you still got that little Porsche?'

'In the garage at the moment,' Marcus lied. He didn't want Conran to know just how stretched he was. It might encourage him to push ahead with the plans without him. Marcus didn't trust anyone.

'My driver's very reasonable. Two hundred a day. So just an orange juice, then?'

Marcus nodded.

'Well, I'm afraid you'll have to get that yourself; it'll ruin my image. Up here, I'm a playboy millionaire, remember. And while you're up, I'll have a brandy.'

By the time Conran had finished his brandy, they still hadn't started discussing their plans and Marcus was becoming very agitated.

'I like it here, you know,' Conran said, looking around the large open-plan lounge area.

'What, this hotel?'

'No, up here. The North! Haven't spent much time up here, actually, but it's true what they say: the people are so much friendlier, don't you find? Lovely girl on reception, did you see her?'

Marcus's temper was about to snap. 'No I didn't. Now can we please discuss the club?'

'Yes, of course. So do you think we can beat Spurs?'

'I couldn't give a shit.'

'No, me neither. Have you heard from the council yet?' At last, a sensible question.

'No, not yet. But the word's out, you know, with the locals.'

'How've they taken it?'

'Not well, I should imagine. I expect the local press will probably lead with it tonight.'

'I hope they don't use that same ruddy picture of me.'

Marcus decided to ignore the comment. 'The planners are almost certain to reject it.'

'But we've got a man on the inside, right, at the council?' Conran said, taking Marcus by surprise. So he did listen sometimes. Some things did go in, after all. Occasionally, Marcus wondered if Conran's stupid persona wasn't merely an elaborate act to lure in potential deal makers like Marcus, only to cut them loose at the end.

'Yes. We've got someone on the inside.' Someone I got to. Someone I fingered and someone I sorted out, while you sat on your fat arse doing bugger all.

'Splendid. Well then, it doesn't matter what the planners decide,' Conran beamed.

'And you'll have to visit the club now.'

Marcus had expected the grin to vanish from his partner's face but it didn't. If anything, it just got bigger.

'Great. What, for a meet and greet?'

Duck and dive more like. There was no way this was an act. The man was stupid.

'Well, it won't be canapés on the lawn, Conran.'

'That's fine. We'll just have to remember to eat beforehand then,' he joked.

'Now, of course, I'll attend any meetings with you, but only as your lawyer.'

'Right.'

'Not as your partner.'

'Right.'

Marcus needed more assurance than a 'right'. He needed to know absolutely that this buffoon understood how important it was that Marcus couldn't be associated with the deal.

'My equity involvement in the business cannot come to light.'

'Absolutely.'

'That's just between you and me.'

'No prob-a-lemo.'

Marcus bit his lip.

Jeremy Davidson, MP's plan to lie low had just been obliterated in spectacular style. Davina, his political assistant, was delivering what should have been wonderful news, news that all MPs wait for, and she couldn't understand her boss's limp response.

'But why me?' Jeremy demanded to know.

'What do you mean, why you? What the hell's wrong with you? This is your break. It's what we discussed. You always said that you wanted to get on to *Question Time*. That was one of our goals for the year.'

'Yes, I know, but not now, that's all.'

'Why?'

'Because I'm not ready, that's why.'

The BBC's *Question Time* programme is to politicians what *This Is Your Life* is to luvvies. It signals their arrival on to the main stage after years of pissing around on the fringe. No doubt it's a frightening proposition, but not one an ambitious young MP could afford to pass on.

'Not ready! Jeremy, what nonsense.'

'Look, I just didn't think it would come round this soon, that's all.'

'What's wrong?'Davina demanded.

'What do you mean? Nothing.'

'Yes there is. Something's happened.'

'No. Nothing's happened,' Jeremy insisted.

'Jeremy, this is why we've hired a bloody PR person. Of course you're ready.'

'No, I can't, I just can't.'

'Look, this isn't *Have I Got News for You*. No one's going to make you look like a twat.'

'But why me, though?' he quivered.

Davina considered whether it was worth telling him the truth and decided that it was. 'Oh, all right. They've been after Gordon for ages, and his office has suggested you. Don't you get it? They see you as a safe pair of hands. Isn't that great?'

'Yes, it is, but not at the moment. I'm not feeling well – tell them I don't feel well. God, my back.'

'Oh, don't be so bloody pathetic. I'm not telling them anything of the sort. You're doing that programme.'

'No, I'm not. Look, Davina, can't you see . . . can't you see that I'm just plain scared?'

Davina smiled. 'So is everyone.'

Jeremy looked terrified. Not faring well on the programme was the least of his worries, considerable though they were.

'But what if I'm the panellist who doesn't get any rounds of applause? There's always one . . .'

'Don't be ridiculous. You'll be fine, and they'll brief you on everything. Since Dawn Primarolo was on, they haven't taken any chances. They practise scenarios with you, the lot.'

Jeremy started to feel faint. If that tart Carmen saw him on television, he was finished. He thrust a hand in his pocket so that he could at least hold his dummy.

'When is it?'

'Next week.'

'What?' he screamed. 'No, I can't do it. I'll need weeks to prepare. Tell them I can't do it.'

Suddenly a head popped around the door. 'Knock knock.' A young, stern-looking woman stared at them both. Her name was Cas Harper, and she was special adviser to the Chancellor. 'Jeremy Davidson?'

'Yes.'

'Am I dead?' Cas asked.

'I'm sorry?' Jeremy jibbered.

'You look like you've seen a ghost.' Cas laughed briefly. 'Congratulations. We've got three hours for you this afternoon at number eleven. Two o'clock, please.' It wasn't a question.

The 'Clampgate' tornado had just changed direction and now directly in its path was Jeremy Davidson, MP.

CHAPTER 9

While the Middleton players were busy with their agents, planning their various moves away to other clubs more likely to pay them their uneconomic wages, the fans and people of the town under the energetic stewardship of Bill Baxter were mobilising themselves to ensure that the football club indeed remained local. Perhaps rather predictably, their first course of action had been a vociferous and relentless letter-writing campaign to the council's planning department, making their feelings about the club perfectly clear. Postmen are not on commission. They aren't on piece rates. However many letters they deliver makes no odds to what they earn and it follows then that Christmas is their least favourite time of the year, but there was no resentment from the postmen as they heaved about all the mail destined for the planners.

Everyone wanted to help. The club wasn't just a ramshackle professional outfit. It was a club that had grown out of Thorpe's cotton mill, which had employed three thousand people in its heyday, and therefore practically all the local people felt an affiliation with the club. It provided an affectionate link to Middleton's glorious industrial past and no one much liked the idea of that being broken.

Without realising it, Bill was standing directly beneath the picture of his late dad as he addressed his assembled war cabinet for the battle against Table Top Management. Here was a crack team of specialists, highly trained individuals, each with a particular skill; all experts in commercial warfare. At the head was Bill Baxter himself, energetic under-achiever with a point to prove. George Harris, general pessimist with a unique talent for pouring cold water on almost any suggestion; Reggie Hill, a Middleton fan who has infiltrated the district council, role not yet determined but sure to come in handy; Sean Mills, Head of Human Resources at the council and the official eyes and ears of the football club faction; Michael Abbott, local solicitor reluc-tantly drafted in to head up the legal division; Bruce Wakes, *Chronicle* sub-editor and therefore the team's head of communications and propaganda; Harry Tomlinson, local bank manager and the man saddled with the guilt of having to refuse the club credit; and finally Smithy, no discernible talent or role but always keen to get involved anyway. Here, then, was Bill's hastily convened *Great Escape* cast and any fool would realise there was a glaring lack of Steve McQueens and a surplus of Donald Pleasences.

The team digested the ominous information that George had for them. Beaumont's lawyer, some little shit called Marcus something-or-other, had called the club yesterday to set up a meeting between Beaumont and the club. It was Bill's idea that some of the fans should be at the club to greet them. To provide a warm welcome, as it were.

'If everyone here tells and brings five people, and they in turn do the same, then there's no reason why we shouldn't have thousands here,' Bill stated defiantly, producing a sheet of paper that he'd retrieved from his archive. 'Because let me tell ya, lads –' he began reading out a list of names – 'Guildford City, Wealdstone Town, Morpeth Town, Bridlington Rovers, South Shields United . . .' Bill stopped and showed the sheet of A4 to his cabinet. 'And, lads, this is just in the last twenty years. Hundreds of clubs like ours are now car parks, shops or whatever, but no longer football clubs.'

Smithy was disgusted. 'We should treat this meeting of theirs like a bloody home game.'

'That's a fantastic idea, Smithy,' Bill enthused.

Smithy was delighted with himself, sensing that his role within the team was developing. He quite liked the sound of 'tactical strategist and scenario title inventor', but didn't know whether Bill would let him have it.

'Come Wednesday we have to show these two twats that we aren't going to roll over, and we ain't gonna let 'em flog off our club. Smithy's right: this is a home game, but one we can't afford to lose.'

The cabinet and various hangers-on immediately cheered and started to clap. The meeting was over. What now, Bill?

When Marcus had contacted the club to set up the meeting, he had done so with a grand sense of self-importance. After suffering years of mediocrity and lack of respect, things were about to change. His application form to join the million-aires' club was neatly filled out. Proposed, seconded and signed. It was just a formality now.

'. . . so, George, would you like to come here for the meeting?' Marcus suggested confidently on the phone.

'Er, no, not really. I was thinking that you and Mr Chairman might like to come here. Seeing as how it's this club you're looking to shut down.'

Marcus grinned. He was expecting this kind of cheeky belligerence. He'd left nothing to chance. Every possible scenario had been played out in his mind and he had contin-gencies for them all. His exhaustive planning had firmly removed the element of surprise from his enemy's arsenal.

'Very well, George, we'd be happy to meet at the club—'

'I take it you know where it is?' George asked sarcastically.

'I think we can find it. And who can we expect at the meeting?'

George hadn't thought about it. 'I dunno; me and a few others. Why?'

'No reason. So, Wednesday afternoon, then. Looking forward to it.'

Marcus had put the phone down triumphantly. Everything was going exactly to plan. Of course, it wouldn't be an easy meeting, but he felt confident that he could handle it. After all, how difficult could it be? Three or four irate officials with not five O levels between them, more at home with a team sheet than a balance sheet and with nothing to show for themselves but a load of shite about passion and history. Not easy, but for a highly skilled lawyer, a piece of piss. Everything was under control. Marcus had planned for everything.

The Chelsea and Westminster Hospital was leaking like a cheap flat roof. Lee was being released today and the pack of photographers had gathered once again, tipped off, no doubt, by a nurse or a porter. Given the treatment the press had meted out to Lee over the last few days, Seth was anxious that his client shouldn't indulge them any further and had arranged for Lee's exit through the trade door of the hospital.

In actual fact, Lee had been enjoying Carmen's sexual revelations about him. He'd been buoyed to read about his insatiable sexual appetite and stamina, but her disclosures today had taken a nasty turn. The advice of Guy Vincent, her

PR 'expert', was that Carmen needed to up the ante because public interest in her was beginning to wane. After careful consideration for a few seconds, Carmen had agreed, and so this morning the great British public was reliably informed that Lee was in fact a film buff, although not in the Barry Norman sense of the words. Lee was much more than that. Apparently, his home was a regular and busy little film studio, turning out hundreds of amateur films that Lee directed and starred in himself, mostly without the permission of his various co-stars or, more accurately, ex-girlfriends.

Modern-day celebrity is a phenomenon for which the public has an unquenchable appetite. Newstands bulge with glossy magazines that are bursting with nothing and yet sell millions of copies. Paul Weller said that, 'The public gets what the public wants . . .' and right now the public wanted to read about and see pictures of the rather forlorn Lee Robson.

A blue Jaguar drove quietly down the alley alongside the hospital, pulling up outside an innocuous-looking door. The young photographer felt a surge of adrenalin. He'd been sitting next to a festering wheelie bin since the hospital employee who'd organised Lee's exit with Seth had first called him, the deal being that they would split the proceeds. Anxiously, the photographer looked at the door. Two years out of college and not a single picture sold to the national press, but he could sense that this was about to change.

The door opened slowly and, after a moment or two, Seth emerged and checked that all was clear. He opened the back door of the Jag, checked for the all-clear and beckoned towards the hospital door. Suddenly a forlorn-looking figure appeared. Unmistakably, it was Lee Robson, shuffling along on crutches, hardly the athlete or even the express train that the papers were full of. Nervously at first, the photographer clicked away. Pictures of a star getting into a car guaranteed publication on the inside pages and the start of a possible career. He didn't know why he was being so cautious. It wasn't as though Lee was in any state to chase him and rip out his valuable film, and nor, for that matter, was his fat, balding companion.

'Oi, Lee, how are you feeling?' the photographer called out, his confidence growing because he'd already bagged some printable shots and now he was after the action shot, the front-page bonanza.

Lee had delivered right from the start of this story and dutifully he wasn't about to disappoint now. He turned angrily in the photographer's direction, firing off a stream of expletives and shaking his crutch. Gleefully, his tormentor reeled through his film, every frame worth more than all his photographer's equipment put together. Without realising it, Lee was transforming people's lives.

Traffic warden Emmanuel Undago sat in a chair, smiling hopefully. Sitting opposite him was his new best friend, lawyer Joel Reed. On viewing the tapes several times, Joel had advised Emmanuel that the concussion route was unlikely to prove successful, although all was not lost because he certainly had a claim for emotional trauma. Already, Joel had arranged that Emmanuel was seen by two expert doctors, each of whom had agreed that the traffic warden was suffering from trauma, and had provided their damning testimonials to substantiate as much, as well as their substantial invoices for services rendered.

Joel checked through his writ once more. The writ that he

was about to serve on Lee Robson. He smiled. It was perfect, like a cheque waiting to be cashed.

'So, Emmanuel, you have to remain off work.'

'No problem,' he beamed.

'Less of the smiling. You're an emotional wreck, remember.'

'Oh, yes, sorry.'

'Don't apologise. You've got nothing to be sorry for. You were attacked, remember.'

'No, I can't, my memory's gone.'

Joel laughed. 'That's the spirit, although don't go too far. So, if you just sign here – not too neatly though, your hand's a little shaky.'

'Two hundred thousand pounds!' Emmanuel exclaimed as he peered at the document for the first time.

'Oh, don't worry about that. This won't ever get to court. They pay us off, so we go in high. It gives us all something to work with. It's only fair. It allows us some leeway and, besides, this won't come from Robson himself.'

'It won't?'

'No, he'll be insured.'

Marcus sat behind his desk in his cramped office, barely able to see daylight for the mountain of work that was amassing before him. The firm's senior partners must have been busy on the lunch circuit, getting fatter and richer as Marcus processed the work they brought in. What an incentive for him to leave all this drudgery behind. He could feel his life expectancy shorten with every document he drafted and, looking at his burgeoning in-tray, he reckoned he might only live another ten years. Without any sense of irony, Marcus decided to sacrifice another fifteen precious minutes of his life and lit up a fag, despite the new nonsmoking policy the company had implemented.

Conran's assurances that he hadn't spoken to any journalists had turned out to be utterly hollow. Some of the nationals and all of the locals had featured the impromptu telephone interviews his moron had given.

'Chairman doesn't know who team manager is', 'Chairman's big plans for Middleton: Luxury Flats' – the copy was even uglier than the same photo of Conran that they'd all used before. And later today they were meeting the club to try to get them on board. Marcus kicked his desk in fury.

A town on match day has an unmistakable feel to it. An air of excitement and expectation reigns. The streets are busy and the pubs crowded, packed with fans, each of whom knows more about football than the other and sets about trying to prove it. Today, though, wasn't a match day; today was the meeting day. A meeting between Mr Conran Beaumont, club chairman, his lawyer, Marcus Howell, and three thousand or so angry Middleton fans. The whole town had been galvanised into action. Bill was overwhelmed by the response to his call to arms. In fairness, not everyone present was a football fan because local people had many different reasons for opposing the development plans, but the net result was the same. A bandwagon had been set in motion, that many had been delighted to hop aboard. Collection buckets were being rattled noisily, war had been declared and it seemed the people of Middleton were up for it.

The gates to the ground were wide open and the north stand was slowly filling up, becoming a blur of yellow and black. Marcus and Conran should be proud indeed. For their meeting this afternoon, they had drawn a crowd nearly as large as any home game this year.

Conran's driver was back in London ferrying his mother in and out of shops on New Bond Street and Marcus had sold his car, so they were reduced to using a local minicab to take them to the meeting. It was a grubby old Nissan something or other, which Marcus decided was ideal because they didn't want to appear to be ostentatious. The atmosphere in the cab was, to say the least, tense because Marcus hadn't long finished scolding Conran over his current press disaster. Conran had tried to make light of it, which only made Marcus even angrier and now he was sulking. He hadn't really wanted to buy the bloody club in the bloody first bloody place.

'Busy today, isn't it?' Conran remarked, as a way to break their silence as the stale-smelling minicab approached Middleton town centre.

Marcus ignored him.

'Do you think there's something going on?' Conran asked.

Still Marcus said nothing. He was quiet, curiously studying the scene before him and beginning to think the unthinkable. So much for his airtight planning; it might just have sprung its first leak.

'Who are all these people?'

'Is there a market in the town today?' Marcus asked their Bangladeshi cab driver.

'No, sa. Market on Tuesday.'

As the car proceeded through the pretty little market town, the streets became busier still – morons all clad in the same yellow and black colours that Marcus assumed were the colours of Middleton. But there couldn't be a match today, not on a Wednesday afternoon.

'Is there a match today?' Conran asked.

'No, sa. There is a meeting, I think.'

'What?' Marcus shrieked.

Only two things were definitely airtight now and they were the sphincters of the men in the back of the cab. They hadn't even arrived yet and already Marcus's plans seemed hopelessly deficient.

'Shit.' Marcus thought he'd covered every eventuality, but not this one. He didn't have any contingencies for crowd control.

'Bloody hell, do you think they're all here for us?' Conran asked.

Marcus didn't bother to respond, although he was quietly heartened that at least his stupid partner understood the gravity of their situation.

'We could always cry off,' Conran suggested. Under the circumstances, it was a very reasonable idea and, in fact, it was exactly what Marcus was thinking himself. Turn this smelly cab round and get the hell out of here. But that wasn't really an option. It would only delay things and delays were something he certainly couldn't afford. Marcus and Conran both shifted awkwardly in their seats and the cab driver politely cracked open his window.

'This might be a little rougher than we'd expected.' Marcus braced himself as the floodlights reared up in front of them and the car turned into Mercer Street.

Not a hundred yards from the ground, the car's progress was made difficult by fans walking casually in the street. Now, they were totally surrounded by the enemy. It felt as if they were in a Trojan horse whose head had fallen off just short of its target, but fortunately nobody knew who they were. Not yet, anyway.

Conran was now regretting having his blasted photograph appear in the newspaper. He dipped his head and brought up his newspaper to cover his profile because his total absence of chin was a dead giveaway.

'Marcus, this looks like it could be bloody awful.'

'It was never going to be pleasant,' Marcus said, his knuckles snow-white as he gripped the door handle, which he'd already made sure was locked. 'Just think of the money, Conran.'

'But I don't need any more money.'

Well I do, you lucky bastard. 'You'll be a millionaire in your own right. That'll make your dad so proud.'

Conran grunted.

'Just keep calm and I'll do the talking.'

'Don't worry, I'm not going to say a bloody word.'

The cab hadn't smelt very pleasant when they'd got into it, but it was now unbearable, filled with the pungent odour of pure fear, and understandably the driver now had both front windows down and had speeded up considerably. Cold air blasted into the back of the car, and neither of the passengers felt he could complain. The car swung through the gates of the ground with Marcus and Conran eager to get out and run for the safety of the office block that faced them. At least, they assumed the meeting was taking place in there and not on the pitch. A small party had gathered to welcome the two dark knights in rusty armour.

'Here they are – Mr chinless and his little gimp,' one man shouted as they emerged from the car.

Marcus fixed his gaze on the ground to avoid getting

involved in a pointless slanging match. Conran, however, didn't see it that way. After all, Marcus had only been called a gimp.

'Now just a moment—' Conran began, wagging his finger, before Marcus wrestled his arm down and led him firmly through a door that looked like an official entrance. An old lady with a mop in her hand barely looked up as the pair of terrified-looking suits burst through the door.

'Ah, hello, would you mind showing us where the offices are, please?' Conran blubbed, an odd question really, given that he owned the whole place.

Bemused, the old lady pointed and they hurriedly made for a flight of stairs.

The meeting should have taken place in the room laughably known as the boardroom. But it was quiet and as far away from the north stand as possible and therefore entirely inappropriate. Much better to use meeting room B, where the 'B' stood for bar. The club bar stood directly opposite the north stand and significantly was in full view of the noisy ranks of fans that had gathered. For the purposes of intimidation, it was perfect.

'Mr Beaumont, Mr Howell . . .' George greeted the two men at the top of the stairs. 'This is Joe Burke, the team manager.'

'Rather more people here than we expected,' Marcus said, attempting to lighten the mood, referring to the packed stand now in full voice.

'Well, it's not everyday that someone comes along and tries to rip the heart out of a town, is it?' George said aggressively. It was a line that he and Bill had been rehearsing. In fact Bill had been winding George up all morning and he was now almost as fired up as his dear friend, who was currently singing himself hoarse just a few feet away.

Marcus counselled himself not to panic. 'Who dares wins', and all that. This was never going to be a stroll in the park. He'd been expecting a frank exchange of views and a little heat, but, he had to admit, not so early on, and not from thousands of the buggers.

'I wouldn't quite put it that way,' Marcus smiled as best he could.

'Well, how would you put it?' George asked, seizing the initiative.

'Well. Erm, an opportunity for us all, might be more appropriate.'

George and Joe both scoffed.

'Yes, well, shall we sit down somewhere and discuss it or do you want to stand here and argue like schoolboys?' Marcus added as sanctimoniously as he could. His assumption of the intellectual high ground was only fair and reasonable.

George looked at him contemptuously before shuffling off in the direction of meeting room B. He'd worked out a special convoluted route for his guests that took them outside and literally within spitting distance of the amassed throng.

'Who's the wanker with no chin?' the crowd sang beautifully as the two men hurried by. 'Who's the wan – an – ker with no chin, who's the wanker, who's the wanker . . .' And so on. There were no other words to the song.

Conran had suffered such comments all his life but never from so many and never in the form of a song before. Understandably, he was seething. 'This is quite insufferable,' he said, fighting his urge to remonstrate with them.

'Just ignore them,' Marcus pleaded, his eyes fixed forward, trying to visualise the money that was going to make all this worthwhile. Conran was proud of his ancestry. The Beaumont chin was like the Roman nose, and certainly nothing to be ashamed of. In an act of defiance, Conran forced his shoulders back and held his head high to accentuate his jawline while the insults rained down. For the first time since Marcus had come to him with his plans, Conran felt a deep desire to show them just how wealthy and powerful he was and to rub each of their common little faces in it. By the time George had opened the door to the bar, 'You're going to get your fucking heads kicked in' rang out loudly from the crowd and both men were desperately relieved finally to get inside.

'This is bloody intolerable,' Conran continued.

'Conran, please . . .'

Marcus theatrically brushed himself down as if he had been somehow contaminated. He was acutely aware that here was a situation he needed to take control of. He was a highly qualified, highly skilled and intelligent lawyer sitting in a bar that he part owned, facing two men who most likely couldn't count beyond eleven.

'I suppose you think this is funny?' Marcus began.

George paused and thought about it for a second before nodding. 'Yeah, I do actually.'

'And this is where we're going to discuss things, is it?' Marcus asked.

'Yeah. If it gets a bit hot in here, don't worry 'cos I can always open a window,' George smiled. The bar wasn't heated during the day and even in the evening, the radiators were sadly underwhelming and the place only ever really warmed up by sucking the heat out of its occupants.

'Can I just say that I think what is happening here today is quite intolerable,' Conran began once more.

'I couldn't agree with you more,' George responded. 'And all these people out here today, they feel the same too because what you're planning to do with this club is quite intolerable.'

'Let me handle this, Conran.' Marcus was rising now to his challenge. He'd taken enough shit.

'You seem to be missing some harsh realities here.'

'Oh?'

'Yes. Would you like me to explain some of them?'

George gestured that he would.

'First of all, this is a business, and business isn't necessarily—'

'No it's not. This is a football club. It's people like you who've made it a business.'

'Yes, and because of that, football in this country is booming.'

George took a moment to look around theatrically at his 'booming' surroundings. 'And you bought us 'cos we're a booming club, did you?'

'I could sue them all for slander, you know,' Conran hissed, seething because the crowd were once again thrashing out the chinless song.

'Well then, you'll have to offer a lot of writs. Your lawyer will love you.' George stared at Marcus, who was realising that he might have underestimated George as well as being aware that he hadn't yet exerted any authority over proceedings whatsoever.

'Look, I think we've all got off—'

'And, anyway, in law surely slander has to be a lie?' George was now looking at the jaw in question. Bill would have been proud of him as Marcus continued to flounder for some solid ground.

'Perhaps we might be able to talk about this in an adult fashion?' Marcus appealed.

'OK then. Why have you bought our club?'

'Erm . . .'

'Been a fan long, have you? Who's your favourite player?'

'Look, this is all utterly irrelevant.'

'Exactly, 'cos you're not interested in the club. It's just the land that you want.'

Marcus took a moment. 'Look, whether Mr Beaumont is a fan or not has got nothing to do with it.'

George tried to interject again but Marcus wouldn't let him by raising his voice. 'THE FACT IS . . . is that this club has no future on its own and you should be bloody grateful that Mr Beaumont stepped in when he did.'

'Oh God, how rude of me. I've not said thank you, have I?'

'Well then, why don't you buy it back from us?' Marcus screamed, his patience finally shattering as the petty points against him steadily mounted.

Now at last it was George's turn to squirm. Buying the club back was hardly an option and suddenly George felt impotent and Marcus sensed that it was his turn now.

'That's right. Give us the money and we'll walk away. How does that sound to you both?'

'How much?'

'Just short of two million pounds.' Marcus added smugly, 'Which doesn't include your rather impressive debt, which continues to mount as we speak.' Marcus gestured, put up or shut up. He'd made his point.

'Look. Neither Mr Beaumont nor myself want this to be a fight. And it needn't be. You might not believe it, but we want to work with you on this, because there is only one solution here that suits us both. I have to live in this area as well, you know,' Marcus joked in reference to the crowd outside, still singing, although it was now a little ditty about them going home in a 'fucking ambulance'.

'. . . and so you see, it's not just a football club, it's the town itself – and for all those reasons, we all want and need this club to stay here, where it's always been.'

For nearly twenty minutes, George had pleaded the case of the club. Not a brilliant performance but certainly an emotional one. It was largely predictable yawn, yawn stuff that could equally be applied to hundreds of clubs up and down the country, and Marcus hadn't bothered listening to a word and barely even noticed when George had finished.

'. . . and that is exactly the kind of commitment that we want to build on. And yes, that lot out there as well, we need their support also.'

'So, you're doing this for the club?' George snorted.

Marcus couldn't quite bring himself to say yes.

'You see, we figured you're doing this for the forty million quid.'

Marcus smiled calmly. At last all of his rehearsals were about to pay dividends.

'Firstly, let me say that those figures in the press are total nonsense, and second, you have to be realistic here. Yes, we are business people. No, we are not impassioned football fans. But we are not asset strippers,' Marcus lied effortlessly. 'This club as it stands is simply not financially viable but we are offering you a way to survive and that is a fact.'

George scoffed.

'What alternative do you have? Continue as you are, haemorrhaging money until you go bust? Do you not think that other developers won't come along after us? They'll be queuing up, and none of them will give a sod about your football club.'

George didn't respond.

'How many developers do you think would be sitting here with you even discussing things like this? None. How many would be trying to secure the interests and future of the club at all? None.' Marcus was now in full flow and enjoying himself.

'So why are you shutting us down, then?' George asked rather pathetically.

'We're not shutting anything down. If anything is shutting this club down, it's bloody football itself. Your players' wage bill alone is more than your income. How long can any business survive like that? Shit, George, two-thirds of the Premiership clubs aren't making money – how long do you think you can go on for? None of the utilities have been paid for six months, and what about the Customs and Excise?'

George looked shocked.

'Yes, George, I've seen the accounts and they make grim reading. Yes, we're moving the club, but at least that way there will still be a club.'

Given the start that he'd had, this was a brilliant speech from Marcus. Conran was convinced, anyway. He listened intently, rubbing his face where his chin should have been, congratulating himself on being the man responsible for saving this 'great' club.

'The only way this club can survive is to raise money, and that means selling off an asset.'

'Like the ground.'

'Needs must. How many players have you got worth two million quid?'

George looked resigned. Marcus was absolutely right.

Common sense was now prevailing, Marcus sensed the tidal change and he wanted to continue until the club was totally beached. On his feet, walking up and down like a courtroom lawyer charming the pants off a jury, he could see the end of his gold-laden rainbow. Even the gathered ranks outside the bar had finally gone silent, as if quelled by his rhetoric. The meeting was already over two hours old and many of the supporters had left for other matters that needed their urgent attention. The key to the whole deal as it stood at the moment was Marcus being in a position to finance his loans and that meant he needed the planning permission sealed as soon as possible. That was the whole point of setting up this meeting. If Marcus could somehow get the support of the club, it was a done deal. Marcus would be home.

'And if we agree to it all, I'd want assurances for the club,' George pointed out.

Welcome aboard. Marcus could have kissed him. 'I guarantee you that Middleton will remain in football.'

'I'd want a commitment in writing,' George said reluctantly. Bill would do his nut.

'I'll draw up a contract as soon as I'm back at the office.'

George looked pensive.

'If you're honest with yourself, George, then you'll know that it's the only way. We bought this club for development purposes, that I grant you, but look at what we're offering as well. A future! This is win win.' Marcus normally hated American management speak but here it seemed entirely apposite.

'I'll need to speak to my people.'

'Of course, but time is against us all. I have a meeting with the VAT people on Monday and they aren't famous for extending their payment terms.' Marcus held out his hand by way of concluding the meeting. 'Let's make this work, George.' Let's make me stinking rich.

CHAPTER 10

Seth sat slumped in his office with the *Racing Post* open on his desk. It was the only paper he could face since 'Clampgate' had happened and, more worryingly, gambling was the only solution he could see to his mounting problems. Seth's gambling addiction had led him into a classic spiral of debt, trying to bet his way out in the search for an elusive, problem-solving big win. Only Seth's wins were never quite big enough and were always hopelessly outnumbered by his losses.

It had not been a good morning. The 1.30 at Lingfield had just cost him two grand when the second post had arrived. Hadn't they done away with the second post? Seth read the writ from Emmanuel Undago, the stricken traffic warden. Seth groaned; this whole escapade was becoming surreal. A week ago, things had been OK, not good but still OK, manageable at least. He'd still had his problems, but Lee was going to re-sign and he hadn't been unduly concerned. Now, though, everything was fucked and all because one of his clients had been wheel-clamped. Lee was due half his wages from his insurance policy, which Seth would have to find himself and where was he going to find nearly ten grand a week?

He was throwing the writ in the bin when his phone rang. More bad news, he expected. He was on a steep black run of bad luck and could come up with nothing more than a feeble snow plough to try to slow himself down.

'Hello.'

'Seth, it's Sylvie.'

Sylvie sounded cold. She worked at the advertising agency that handled the campaigns for Ford Cars UK, which Lee had been starring in.

'Sylvie, hi. I was about to call you. Don't worry about Lee; he'll be fine for next week. As long as he's just seen in the car . . .'

'Seth,' she was definitely irritated, 'there is no next week. I would have thought that was obvious. I'm calling out of courtesy.'

'Why?'

'Oh, for God's sake, are you serious?'

No, desperate actually. 'Aren't you being a little rash?'

Sylvie now quite rightly lost her temper. 'Rash! First up, he's the face of Ford, and now he's all over the telly with a bloody Porsche.'

'But he did kick it, didn't he?'

'Oh, shut up. Then there's the assault charge—'

'We're fighting that.'

'Oh, great. So it's just the drink driving charge then? Can you imagine anyone less suited to a car ad?'

Seth thought about it for a second. Stevie Wonder, perhaps, but he didn't bother saying it. 'OK, poor old Lee. Another boot goes in good and hard—'

'Oh, don't sound so hard done by; we're going to honour his contract.'

'You are?'

'Yes. We're buying him out of the next two ads.'

'Oh, that's great. Thank you.' Seth gushed a little too much. He needn't have sounded so appreciative. Sylvie's instructions from the client were to 'dump Lee at whatever cost, just get rid of him'.

'You'll invoice us then?'

You bettya.

'Sylvie, thank you. Perhaps we might be able to get something else off the ground a little later, when this has all died down.'

'I doubt it.'

This was the first piece of good news Seth had received all week. The snow plough was having some effect, it was just a question of how long his thighs could hold out. Ordinarily, he would have told Lee that he'd forced the ad agency to honour their contract, that he'd got rough with them and made them cough up, but these were extraordinary times. Now it suited him better to say that the agency had in fact reneged on the deal so that Seth could use the money to pay Lee's wages. A quick calculation and he reasoned that he'd just been given a six-week reprieve.

With a surge of adrenalin, Seth picked up the *Racing Post*. He was feeling lucky.

Lee lay on his sofa while his girlfriend, Kelly, gathered the rest of her things and a few things of his that she fancied as well. Still in plaster, he couldn't stop her.

'Kelly, I've said sorry. What more can I do?' he said angrily.

She ignored him.

Since Lee had apologised and, more importantly, dumped Carmen, Kelly had intended to forgive him, but that was before the *Sport* newspaper had tastefully published a still from one of Lee's home videos of her being taken from behind. God knows where they'd got it from, and Lee feared more pictures would follow.

Two removal men were helping the humiliated damsel

out with her stuff. Kelly unplugged the fifteen-grand television.

'Oi, what are you doing? You ain't taking the telly.'

Calling it a telly was to do it an injustice. It was a cinema screen. A tasteful, seventy-two-inch, plasma monstrosity with more speakers than a Dixons back wall.

'Yes I am, Lee, and d'you know why? Because it's mine. You bought it for me, d'you remember?'

Lee pinched the bridge of his nose, trying to remain calm. She was right, the cinema belonged to her. Lee had bought it for her after her modelling contract was cancelled, which had signalled the death knell of their relationship anyway. It had been a present to cheer her up. Actually, she would have preferred a holiday or some clothes and she had taken some persuading that he hadn't just bought it for himself. Words which Lee was now choking on.

'Go on then, take it, you callous bitch. Tellies are like girl-friends . . . I'll get another one.'

Kelly popped her head back through the front door. 'You might wanna get a smaller one this time, though, Lee. You being unemployed and all that.'

Bill sat in disbelief as George recounted what had happened at the meeting.

'And you agreed to it?'

'No, I haven't agreed to anything. Bill, you've not been listening.'

'Well, it sounds to me like you've agreed it.'

'Listen, will ya—'

'All right, go on, then.'

'Bill, the sad fact is, that he has got a point.'

'Yeah, I know that. That's obvious. To make as much

money as they bloody well can. Did you tell them about the club and the town?'

'Yeah, yeah. They know all that anyway from the turnout.'

Bill sat quietly for a moment. 'So you think he's got a point?' He needed confirmation, such was his dismay.

'Yes, Bill, I do. Look, I don't like it any more than you do, but I work here, remember, and we're on the bones of our arse. Even before ITV pissed off, we were going bust and in . . .'

'But, we've managed before.'

George just shook his head.

'So, all football clubs will eventually have to shut down, then?' Bill spat.

Sadly, this wasn't too far from the truth. The big shake-up that steers the bankrupt sport on to a more realistic economic parabola was coming but it would scythe through the game, taking enormous casualties with it. Bill welcomed such a change but he didn't want Middleton included on the RIP list.

'But, Bill, I've got them to agree to fund the new club.'

Bill laughed. 'You don't believe that, do you? Why the hell would they do that?'

George had no answer for him.

'And so a ground share. That's the only way we can survive?' Bill asked.

'Unless you've got a few million quid.'

'And what did he say when you suggested that Altrincham move to our ground? Share our ground?'

George's eyes narrowed and he bit his lip. He knew there was something he'd missed. He looked like the school kid caught holding the aerosol can.

'Shit, George, I told you I should have been there.'

*

Ten days after the plans of Table Top Management were submitted, the planning committee formally rejected them, which suited Marcus perfectly. The faster they could be resubmitted and rejected again, the sooner they would bypass the planners altogether and land straight on the desk of Councillor O'Dowd, who was currently in Portugal choosing tiles and other fittings for his apartment.

No such luxury jaunts for Marcus, though, who was holed up in his office chipping away at the mountain of legal work that was sustaining his massive borrowings.

'Marcus, that's the bank manager on the phone again,' Jane, his secretary, whispered as she appeared at his door. Marcus rapidly drew his finger back and forth across his neck. That man was the last person he wanted to speak to. He was new at the branch and clearly eager to make an impression. How dare he call me at work anyway? Marcus thought. He didn't like the manager at all. Harry Tomlinson was too young, for a start. In fact, he didn't look long out of university and most likely had a degree in snowboarding or breadmaking.

'Jane, whatever you do, don't arrange a meeting with him.'

'But, he—'

'Tell him I'm abroad. Get him to write to me. I take it he can write. Anything else?'

'Yes, Middleton Edwardians have called regarding Mr Beaumont and Table Top.'

'Yes, yes.'

'They want to meet with you on Tuesday.'

'Not there again.'

'No, here.'

'Great.'

'They said they were waiting for a fax from you, putting in writing what you agreed.'

Suddenly a surge of excitement took hold of Marcus. He'd be seeing his ambitious little bank manager soon enough, to shift his account to the Caymans. Marcus handed her a three-page document that he'd typed himself.

'Here it is. Did they say that they'd agreed?'

'No, they didn't.'

'But they didn't say they hadn't?'

'No.'

'Fantastic. Are they bringing a lawyer with them?'

'They didn't say. A Mr George Harris is coming and a Mr Bill Baxter, head of the supporters' club.'

'Excellent.'

Marcus clapped his hands together. He couldn't wait.

It had taken an awful lot of soul-searching and courage for Conran to make the appointment, but he reasoned that his problem couldn't be ignored any longer. For all his blustering and bravado about links with the past, the truth was that he was thoroughly fed up with looking the way he did.

'Yes, we could certainly do something for you, but I should explain that what you need is a very extensive and complicated surgical procedure which can't all be done at once,' the Harley Street plastic surgeon explained.

'OK, that's fine. So what's involved then?'

'Well, first I would have to graft some bone on to your jaw, which would take up to eight weeks to heal and—'

'Bone graft?'

'Yes, I would literally fix a piece of bone on to your lower jaw.'

Conran's nostrils flared at the thought. 'But where would you get it from?'

'What, the bone? Well, there are a few options, but most likely we would get it from one of your ribs.'

Conran turned puce. 'My ribs! I'd have to provide the bone as well?'

'Well, yes.' The surgeon was accustomed to dealing with rich and spoilt people, but before now, all his patients had understood that they would have to provide their own body parts.

'Oh dear, this is all very complicated. I thought you might be able to get it from someone else, like a donor. You know, one hears about bone-marrow donors. Aren't there people who donate ribs? I'd happily pay.'

The surgeon was aghast but keen not to appear so and possibly lose this lucrative gig. 'Er, not that I know of.'

'Well, what if I knew someone willing to do it?'

'Do you?'

'Erm, well, I haven't asked him yet, but I'm fairly sure he'd say yes.'

'It's highly unusual, and it would be much better with your own bone, because there would be less chance of it being rejected, but yes, another person's bone might be an alternative.'

'Great. So what's after that then?'

'Once the graft is firm, I would take cartilage and some fat from . . . either you or your donor, and build you a chin.'

'Marvellous.' Conran pulled at his chin in anticipation. 'And do you think I might be able to have one with a dimple?'

'Yes, I'm sure I could manage that.'

'Bloody hell. That'd be great.'

Conran hadn't decided yet whether he was going to go through with it or not, but he was pleased that he had at least broached the subject. A load off his mind then, and hopefully eventually a similar load on to his lower jaw.

The BBC television programme *Question Time* is filmed live and this evening was being broadcast from the Imperial War Museum in Lambeth. It seemed an appropriate venue as the gladiators appearing on tonight's show gathered in the makeshift green room before commencing battle with each other on screen. A saccharine and false air of support and politeness reigned, but no one was fooled. Everyone realised that once out there, it was pleasantries over and gloves off. They were mostly quiet, going over their thoughts, and making a considerable effort to appear calm rather than terrified. No one wanted to show any sign of weakness to his or her fellow panellists. All were largely succeeding in their quest with the exception of Jeremy Davidson. He was failing badly. Jeremy looked as if he were on death row. And in some ways he was, because his entire life and career were on the line. He'd spent the whole afternoon being briefed and schooled in how to respond to the inevitable questions and accusations that would be levelled at him, but he hadn't absorbed any of it. His mind was utterly fixated on the terrible consequences should Carmen recognise him. Jeremy had decided that somehow he should try to disguise his appearance. He'd got rid of his trademark shock of curly hair by having it cut very short. This had been a good idea, but then in a moment of sheer madness, he'd also decided to go with an eye patch. What had possessed him? It was a calamitous mistake but one he had realised a fraction too late and there was nothing he could do about it now. With his patch, only the parrot on Jeremy's shoulder was missing. It instantly brought attention to him, the very thing it was designed to avoid. Naturally, everyone wanted to know what had happened.

'It's infected,' Jeremy lied, the first of many porkies that he was going to have to keep track of.

'Sorry to hear that,' Michael Howard said, his ingrained smirk irking Jeremy. 'Is this your first time on the programme?'

Jeremy suspected that he knew full well it was. 'Yes. I'm looking forward to it.' Second lie and counting.

'I'm sure you are. Still, not the best way to appear on *Question Time*. With something covered up,' Howard joked coolly.

Smug bastard, the show hadn't even begun and he was already scoring points. What would he be like when the cameras were rolling? It was a good joke, though, and broke the tension in the room. Everyone laughed except Jeremy, who was concentrating all his efforts on remaining upright and conscious. If he'd been given a little more notice, Jeremy would have grown a beard despite the disastrous implication facial hair spells for political careers these days. Frank Dobson's career stumbled with his beard and Mandelson's had only bloomed, albeit briefly, once he lost the tash. Only Blunkett had successfully managed to combine the two but only because he had a good excuse for not shaving.

A man wearing headphones popped his head around the door.

'Is everyone ready?'

Jeremy closed his good eye and took a deep breath. It felt like it might be his last.

*

Katherine wasn't happy that she'd had to watch *EastEnders* on the black-and-white portable because Bill had convened an impromptu war cabinet meeting in their lounge. The lads had left now, and strewn about Bill were newspaper cuttings, law reports and planning documents, all relating to the eighty-four football grounds that had been shut down in Britain over the last ten years.

'Dad, you should have your meetings in the pub, so Mum and me can watch telly.'

'They just popped round.'

'Yeah, right.' Katherine began flicking through a report and quickly shut it again, having read a paragraph or two.

Bill looked disappointed by her reaction. 'I was hoping you might help me with these, love.'

'Joking, aren't ya? Mum's reading one upstairs, though.'

'Is she?' Bill looked hopeful.

At that moment, Mary came into the lounge to collect the various mugs and plates. She looked flustered and added another document to Bill's pile. Wealdstone Football Club, founded 1906, now a gleaming supermarket.

'I'm sorry, love, but this is all nonsense.'

Katherine howled. 'Why can't they just use normal English?'

'So we can't understand it, most likely. Does it say anything about how the planning points were argued?' Bill asked Mary.

She looked blank.

'OK, I'll have a look at it.'

'How did it go today, anyway?' Mary asked.

'Ah, who knows? Apparently, they've got a point about this ground-share thing.'

'But then why can't Altrincham come and share with us?'

Bill smiled at his wife fondly. 'You should be general manager, love. Can you believe that George missed that point?'

'Now, you leave George alone. He's not been himself since Susan got ill, and you know he gets nervous.'

'But the good news is, they've offered the supporters the chance of buying the club back.'

It was both typical and sad that Bill would clutch at such a short straw.

'How much?'

'Just over two million quid.'

'Oh right, I'll just fetch me purse,' Katherine joked.

Bill laughed. 'We did some sums here, me and the lads. It's twenty-five of our houses.'

Mary glared at him, unsure whether he was joking or not.

'But young Harry Tomlinson doesn't reckon our banks would go for the remortgages.'

'Oh well, God bless Mr Barclay and Mrs NatWest, because us wives would have just rolled over and allowed you bozos to make us all homeless.'

'We weren't serious about it.'

'No, but you worked it out, didn't ya?'

Bill was stumped. 'Yeah, but only for a laugh.'

'Well, I never heard any laughing.'

'No, well, it weren't that funny after all,' Bill conceded.

At half-past ten, Katherine had gone to bed and Bill hadn't moved from his chair, still studying each report as closely as his untrained eye and mind would allow.

'You gonna read them all night then, Bill, or what?'

'I'll have to get Michael to look at them. I know they earn loads but I couldn't be a lawyer.

'No, but you could have been.'

Bill huffed. 'I'd sooner work in a bakery. What does "incumbent" mean?'

'Dunno.'

'Actually, I might have found something here.'

'Oh?' Mary was tired but she feigned interest for Bill's sake.

'The more the club represents to the town, the harder it is to close down. See, there's a replacement clause in local planning law.'

'Meaning?'

'Whatever's lost to the town, the local authority has to make provisions for it to be replaced.'

Mary looked thoughtful.

'So, we lose our football club, but there's a provision for us at Altrincham.'

'But what about the kids' football? They can't go all the way to Altrincham?' Mary reasoned.

Bill laughed. He must have been too close to things because he had forgotten about the youth football team entirely.

'Mary, you're a bloody marvel.'

'Sssh, Bill, you'll wake Tom.'

'Sorry.'

'No, carry on praising me, just do it quietly.'

Bill chuckled again. God, he loved his wife. What would happen to the youth football in the town if the club was shut? That was a belter of a question and Bill wrote it down immediately, more for effect than anything else because he was hardly likely to forget it now. Two local teams used the club's facilities, fielding six youth sides in total, and, impressively, two alumni were currently plying their trade as professional football players, although sadly not for Middleton.

'That's how we've got to think about it,' Bill enthused. 'It's called lateral thinking.'

'Ya what?'

'Which brings me back to the point I was going to make originally, before you brilliantly interrupted, and bless you for it.'

Mary blushed. 'Oi, give over.'

'Do you think you could get a women's league going?' Bill asked. Mary just looked at him. 'No, perhaps not. But what if the club was even more than just a football club, eh?' Bill asked triumphantly.

'But it's not.'

'Exactly. Not now it isn't. But it will be.'

Bill was delighted with himself. Mary too was pleased for him, but she dreaded whatever scheme might be germinating in his expansive mind. She was also keen to discuss anything other than planning law and football with her beloved husband.

'What's on the telly, love?' Bill asked, as he finally put his reports aside.

Bloody charming, Mary thought, as she flicked the television on.

David Dimbleby briefly filled the screen before the camera cut quickly to another more unfamiliar face.

'Who's he?'

'Dunno. Funny-looking bugger, though, isn't he?'

'I wonder what's happened to his eye?'

The panel on *Question Time* had just been introduced and was receiving a cordial collective round of applause. Even though it was a very distinguished panel, all eyes in the audience were on Jeremy and he could feel every one of them boring into him. He slurped another mouthful of water. His glass was already half empty, it was never going to be enough, and how would it look if he asked for more? He might as well tell the audience aloud that he was drying.

'Now our first question comes from a Mr Alistair McVey, who is a social worker. Mr McVey, your question, please?'

'Does the panel think that we are now heading towards a two-tier health system in this country, much like we have with our education system?'

'Right, are we heading for a two-tier health authority? I take it you mean public and private? Right, well, perhaps I should let Jeremy Davidson start with this one, as he so clearly has had call for recent medical assistance.'

A slight ripple of laughter spread through the audience, giving Jeremy a brief moment to compose himself. He needed a good start to the show to address his massive confidence deficit and this was a question he was well prepared for. This was his best chance of getting that all-important round of applause and having first crack at the subject was a huge advantage. Perhaps the patch had been a good idea after all.

'. . . before you begin, Jeremy, perhaps we can ask if you were treated by the National Health Service?' Dimbleby asked cheekily.

Jeremy hesitated while lie number three was loaded into the chamber ready for firing.

'Yes, I was. I was treated by my local GP who referred me to the local hospital, and very good treatment it was too, and thank you to all the doctors and nurses who cared for me. Now, in answer to the question, no, I don't believe that we have a two-tier health system operating in this country. Of course, there will always be individuals who wish to pay to have things done privately and this is their business and likewise the business of the professionals who carry out those services. That is good and proper and we the Government have nothing against such free enterprise. But, what we must do as Government is provide a first-class health service . . . free of charge . . . and at points of need throughout the country . . . and most crucially for everyone who WANTS and NEEDS it.'

Jeremy sat back, his one eye scanning the audience for any hand movements. One person clapped but quickly stopped when it became apparent he was alone. Jeremy had missed out a crucial part of his speech. He'd meant to say the Government 'must CONTINUE' to provide such a service, something which had no doubt been noted by the four government aides scrutinising Jeremy's performance. They weren't the only ones to note the omission. Jeremy had teed up an opportunity quite beautifully and Michael Howard, a *Question Time* veteran, eagerly pulled the fluffy cover off his enormous titanium driver.

'I agree with Jeremy, but my question to him is simply, then WHY don't you?'

The audience not only laughed but the bastards clapped as well. Shit, what an awful start. Two minutes in and Jeremy was already a laugh and a clap down. And, anyway, he thought, is it protocol for panellists to ask each other questions? Isn't that the audience's job, you bastard?

Everyone was waiting for Jeremy's response and it needed to be good.

'Well, Michael,' he faltered nervously, 'I for one believe that our National Health Service does in fact give a first-class service.'

Not good enough. An audible scoff could be heard from the audience, as hands waved in the air, people no doubt eager to recount their personal disastrous treatment and trolley stories. Appropriately for the subject matter, first blood had been drawn and it was Jeremy's.

'Well, which country do you live in then, and if it's this one, which health service do you use?' Howard fired back instantly to more approval from the hopelessly biased Tory audience. 'Because, quite frankly, I am tired of this Government offering nothing of any substance. Since this administration came to power, with promises galore, taxes have gone up in real terms . . . in real terms by twenty per cent, and our standard of health care has got worse. Waiting times in Jeremy's own constituency are up by fifteen per cent . . .'

Howard's offensive was hurting but not as much as the cameras' attention – all lenses were trained on Jeremy, broadcasting his panicked expression to the nation. His glass, like his mouth, was bone dry.

'Bottle's gone,' one of the government aides noted down neatly in her performance book.

'. . . what has to happen here is that the Government has to open its eyes,' Howard carped, pointing at the one-eyed Jeremy. A cheap shot, but one that the audience seemed to enjoy none the less. Cunts, all of them, Jeremy thought. He was reeling and, like a boxing referee coming to his rescue, Dimbleby decided to intervene.

'Professor Bloom, what's your take?'

Finally the light above Jeremy's camera went off. Thank the Lord. He was off air, out of the firing line, but he couldn't relax. Professor Bloom had been a late addition to the show.

'Well, I have to say, what Michael Howard has just said is largely a lot of nonsense.'

What a relief, an ally.

'Hear, hear,' Jeremy said loudly, overjoyed that someone else might argue his case for him, thereby keeping him off the blasted telly.

'We continually hear all these disaster stories: people on trollies and what have you, which, of course, are regrettable, but they are highly isolated instances and in such a large organisation they are sadly unavoidable . . .'

Again from off camera Jeremy uttered his total and un-equivocal support. Well said, Professor. I couldn't agree more – and do, for God's sake, man, carry on.

'All we hear about is chronic underinvestment, which is simply not fair. To illustrate my point,' the professor continued, 'might I ask you, Jeremy, which hospital treated your eye?'

Instantly Jeremy's camera was fired up again and he was back on screen, looking shocked, his one good eye opened wide. What the hell was Bloom playing at? Jeremy had already lied enough. This is *Question Time*; they ask the questions, not you. Will panellists stop asking me fucking questions?

'The Chelsea and Westminster.'

'There. My point exactly,' Professor Bloom beamed. 'The last time I visited the Chelsea and Westminster, they didn't even have an eye unit but if they treated Jeremy, one must have opened.'

Jeremy whimpered. Could things get any worse? The patch was definitely a mistake. The camera loved it. So far, Jeremy had been on screen more than bloody Dimbleby.

An aide wrote in her book, 'Professor Bloom a godsend for hapless Davidson. Excellent points scored with the flagging up of the new eye unit at the Chelsea.'

For Jeremy's sake, if only it were true.

CHAPTER 11

Early Saturday morning and Middleton was already busy. Exeter City FC was visiting today, the only team in the division with a worse away record than Middleton, and so there was a realistic chance of three points on the board for the home team. Every shop window, with the exception of the estate agents, displayed posters against the development plans. The petition was getting longer, and a large banner floating above the high street read, 'Welcome to Middleton, home of Middleton Edwardians FC since 1902.'

Due to his ever increasing workload, Marcus had spent the night in his office. Eighteen-hour days were very much the working pattern of a lawyer with hideously overstretched borrowings. He was barely asleep on his sofa when the phone shrilled at him very early on Saturday morning.

'Hello.'

Speaking of things he'd be leaving behind, it was his wife understandably wanting to know where he'd been all night. In the course of their tempestuous marriage, Marcus had had three affairs, two of which he'd managed to be forgiven for, and one which was ongoing since his wife hadn't found out about it yet.

'Marcus, where've you been? I've been worried sick.'

No you haven't, you've only just noticed. 'I've been here.'

'Where?'

'What do you mean, where? Here, in the office, working.'
To keep you in Prada.

'I've booked the holiday.'

Marcus sighed. 'Penny, I thought we'd decided—'

'No, you decided. Look, Marcus, I need to have something
to look forward to, and anyway, the nurse said it wouldn't
happen until I'm relaxed.'

Marcus pressed his sore eyes. The reason why they hadn't
conceived yet was because Marcus had been surreptitiously
masturbating five minutes before Penny demanded his dose.

'So, it's booked.'

'Right, OK.'

'Aren't you going to ask me where we're going then?'

'Yes, of course, where?'

'The Seychelles. I've booked us one of those villas on stilts.'

Oh great, that sounds nice and cheap.

'Three weeks in August.'

'Three weeks . . .'

'Well, we might as well. You'll need the break.'

'How much?'

'I knew you'd ask that,' Penny snapped. 'It's OK you
paying for golf membership you never use—'

'Penny, how much?'

'Seven thousand, but that's all in, everything.'

Oh, bollocks. It's never everything.

'Not up front?'

'No, twenty per cent now, balance in July.'

With luck by then everything might be in place and she
could go to the Seychelles on her own and, for all he cared,
she could stay there.

*

The early February sun was doing its best to brighten the day, but it was still freezing cold and Middleton had just conceded their third goal to Exeter. The few Exeter fans demented enough to have made the long journey north were raucously celebrating their first away win.

'Bring on the Spurs,' Bill shouted.

Today was the biggest home gate of the season, thanks to a display of solidarity towards the club, but not even the big gate receipts could coax a smile out of George. One of the four floodlights flickered a little and began to buzz. George wondered whether it was the electricity people showing them exactly who had the power and how easily it could be taken away. Exeter hit the Middleton post. It was poignant, somehow, that the noisy floodlights weren't merely illuminating the grim match below but also the mounting problems the club faced. The entire Middleton council had been invited to the game, an idea of Bill's that he was now regretting, especially since the Middleton players looked as though they couldn't be arsed even to try to compete.

'If they play like this next Saturday, Tottenham'll score ten,' Smithy said.

'In which half?'

'Perhaps they're saving themselves.'

'It's us who need saving,' sighed Bill. 'It's a good job Lee Robson's out.'

'They reckon he might be finished for good, you know.'

'Stupid bugger. Still, I don't feel sorry for him. He's bloody loaded.'

'Never mind his money. I wouldn't mind having that lass to keep me warm at night. Did you see the papers this morning?'

Everyone was agreed. '. . . fit as hell, that one.'

'And dirty as well,' Smithy added. 'I've always fancied it in an outdoor Jacuzzi meself.'

Everyone laughed, imagining Smithy and his girlfriend getting it on in an outdoor bath in the garden filled with a hose and a few futile kettle runs, being gawped at by the neighbours.

'And his old lady's left him as well.'

'Lucky bastard.'

More laughter. Their conversation was more entertaining than the match.

'Who saw that programme last night?' Smith asked. 'Robson was on it.'

'Which one?'

'Ah, you know, the funny show, what's it called? With the little posh fellah and the grumpy bloke . . .'

'What, *Frasier*?'

'No, for God's sake. It's English. You know . . . oh, what's it called? It's got the smug fellah in the middle.'

'*Have I Got News for You.*'

'That's the one. Did anyone see it?'

None of them had.

'Bloody funny.'

It was late on Saturday evening and Bill was tired, having been to the match and shared the post mortem with his mates. He slumped in his chair. Mary was now furiously knitting Tom something or other, but Bill couldn't tell what it was yet.

'What you making, love?'

'A cardie.'

'Bit of a dodgy colour, isn't it?'

'I like it. He looks good in green, and this is top-quality wool.'

Bill wasn't convinced that Mary liked the colour either. The wool had that classic end-of-line feel to him and must have been sitting in some bargain basket when Mary stumbled across it. Bill wasn't sure whether Mary liked knitting Tom clothes or whether she felt she had to for economic reasons. She certainly hadn't knitted anything for the girls and so he reluctantly concluded that it was to save money. Not that she would ever admit to it. Anyway, it wasn't as if Bill was ever going to get another job.

'It'll look lovely on him. Make it plenty big.'

Mary smiled at him affectionately. 'Well, I've got plenty of wool.'

That confirmed it then: it was definitely end-of-line. They were probably giving the stuff away.

'I could make you one as well, Bill.'

'No thanks, love. Not with these teeth; it'll clash,' Bill smiled as he flicked the television on.

Angus Deayton was laughing at some comment or other made by Paul Merton, who was looking characteristically as sullen and quizzical as he could.

'Oh, Mary, this is what Smithy was on about. Apparently, they slaughter Lee Robson. I hope I haven't missed it.'

'Ian and Boris, what's happening here?' Angus asked.

The footage of the hapless Lee Robson appeared. The studio audience laughed immediately. Hislop wasted no time, laying in as the film played.

'Here he is, kicking something very hard and then rolling around, just another day at work for him. That'll be fifty thousand pounds, please. Ah, now he's applying his fist to a helmet – he doesn't learn, does he? . . . And that's him failing his breath test and being arrested by a fat policeman . . . called Waddle.' Ian Hislop was now back on screen pulling his customary face of scorn at the state of our nation.

'Er . . . yes, and who is HE?' Angus asked.

'Lee Robson – a footballer, I believe, an ex-Tottenham football player, or "star", as some of the press call them,' Hislop announced, deliberately playing up his disdain for the beautiful game.

'Boris, did you see this story?'

'I did, yes. He was frightfully angry, wasn't he?'

'Well, can you imagine what he's like now then?' Ian scoffed.

'I'd say much the same,' Merton chipped in from the other side. Angus looked over at Merton for his inevitable explanation of the interruption. 'I mean it only happened a few weeks ago, he can't have changed that much,' Merton went on. 'It takes ages for people to change. I mean he might have had a shave or a haircut, but you'd still recognise him.'

The audience roared their approval. Hislop and Deayton both chuckled along, politely waiting for their colleague to finish.

'Boris, do you know what made him so "frightfully" angry?'

'Yes, he was parked quite legally, and some utter cad thought to clamp his motor car.'

The audience laughed both at his accent and the use of the word 'cad'. Over its many series, the programme had endured hundreds of guests who had failed to deliver, but Boris was considered a safe booking, able as he was to get laughs by pomposity alone.

Bill and Mary laughed along too.

'Blimey, what's he like?' Mary asked incredulously.

'He sounds even worse than Beaumont.'

'He's funny, though. I like him.'

'Ya what?'

'He looks like he could do with a good cuddle.'

Bill laughed to himself.

'And "Clampgate" has made quite a few people famous,' Angus prompted.

'His girlfriend,' Hislop said disapprovingly. 'Carmen. What a classy girl she's turned out to be.'

'Do you think?' Boris asked Ian. 'Gosh, I wouldn't say that. I would have said quite the opposite, in fact.'

Good old Boris. The audience laughed again, as much because he'd scored a rare point off Hislop.

'Er, I was being sarcastic, Boris.'

'Maybe he's had a tattoo,' Merton suddenly announced. 'That'd change him.'

Angus waited for the applause to subside for Merton's back-reference, always a guaranteed laugh.

'I don't think Ian was meaning that Lee Robson had changed physically, Paul.'

Paul looked confused. 'Well, what does Ian mean? No one can understand him tonight. First I can't, now Boris can't.'

Angus had heard enough and turned to camera expertly to reel off his pithy remarks on the débâcle.

'You are, of course, correct. That was Lee Robson self-destructing before the eyes of practically everyone in Britain. Lee now faces charges of drink driving and assault, which means if his broken foot does heel, he will still have excellent prospects as a professional football player. A media frenzy followed with all sorts of facts coming to light. The restaurateur announced that Lee had eaten lean pork well done.

Ironic then that five minutes later Lee should be well done himself, this time by a fat pig.'

A still of the rotund PC Waddle suddenly appeared on the screen. Bill roared with laughter, on his way to the kitchen with his mug.

The ramifications of Bill's empty doughnut were still ongoing. Jeremy Davidson was mightily relieved, having scanned the last of Sunday's tabloids. It seemed that he might just have got away with his calamitous appearance on *Question Time*. Carmen was heavily featured in her loveliness, but she had made no mention of her previous liaisons. Jeremy was in Perthshire to escape the media attention and political fallout that his eye had provoked, and was steadfastly refusing to answer his mobile phone. The Sunday broadsheets had covered his television débâcle with some glee, but mostly in the diary and review sections and crucially with only small accompanying pictures. He'd suffered political damage, but surely it wasn't irrevocable. People can forgive a bad performance on television; it shows a human side, he thought. Jeremy wrote that down. Anyway, it could have been so much worse. The best PR guru in the world couldn't have fashioned a comeback if it had been revealed that Jeremy was a Pampers fan. By tomorrow, he assured himself, it would all be over. He would need lots of rest and pampering but a full recovery was to be expected.

This, however, was hopelessly naïve. Jeremy's secret proclivity for wearing Babygros was about to become the least of his worries because his fictitious medical treatment had taken on a life of its own. Intrigued journalists had quickly established that the Chelsea and Westminster Hospital doesn't have a brand-new eye unit, and nor did they have any record of treating Mr Davidson. Obvious questions began to emerge like, why had he lied? Where was he treated? And was he treated privately? And any number of circumspect answers were being fawned over.

The story had been scheduled to run this Sunday but deadlines had been missed as journalists hunted in vain for the private clinic that the editors of the Tory press were praying Davidson had used. Unless something calamitous happened in the next six hours, three broadsheets were leading with the story of Jeremy's eye tomorrow morning. Like crossing the road, Jeremy was so obsessed with avoiding the oncoming milk float, he'd failed to look anywhere else and hadn't spotted the forty-foot articulated lorry bearing down on him.

Jeremy stayed in bed until late the next morning. He didn't have anything to do apart from drive to London and he was going to take the journey easy. What with the stress of the last few days, no one was more deserving of a relaxing day than he.

'Hello, Mr Davidson.' The housekeeper shuffled along the corridor. 'What can I get you?'

'Do you think that I might be able to have a full English breakfast?

'I can do you a Scottish one.'

Jeremy laughed heartily. 'That would be wonderful.'

'Cereals are there on the counter. Just help yourself.'

'Ah? Could I bother you for some warm milk for my cereals? It goes back to my childhood, I'm afraid.'

'Not at all. Would you like a newspaper as well?'

'That would be wonderful. Any of the large ones.'

'Right you are.'

*

It took a while for Lee to get to the front door.

'Oh, it's you.'

Charming. Seth entered the vast house, a case study in bad taste. A marble entrance hall giving way to an enormous fanning staircase complete with cut-crystal football newel post finials. The walls provided a gallery for Lee's career history, photographs showed him ascending from England schoolboy to full England international either scoring or celebrating his goals. Seth couldn't see beyond the staircase gallery, but suspected there wasn't a picture of Lee lying next to his Porsche clutching his foot. He looked dreadful; tired and desperate. He hadn't slept properly for days, kept awake by sheer rage.

'You look well, Lee.'

'Do I? I don't feel it. Have you spoken to Tottenham yet?'

'Yes,' Seth lied. 'They want you fit again. How's the foot?'

'Fucked.'

'Oh.'

'Actually, no, it don't hurt as much any more. This three months stuff in the press is all bollocks.'

'Good for you, Lee. That's the spirit.'

'Doc said I might even get the plaster off in a month or so and then I'll start training. I'll show 'em. Week-by-week contract my arse.'

This was good news. Seth needed Lee back playing again more than anyone.

'Where's Kelly?'

'I told ya, she's gone.'

'What, still?'

'Yeah, stupid cow. That blasted Carmen, Jesus. Every day, it's som'ing else. Me and 'er in the pool. Me and 'er and a mate. Makes me sick.'

'I wouldn't worry about it. No one believes the crap they read in the papers.

'Nah, it's all true, but that ain't the point.'

'Exactly. My point exactly.'

Seth couldn't help feeling jealous. Her and a mate! This was the very stuff of Seth's wildest dreams and, sadly, his sordid phone calls. He took twenty per cent of Lee's wages but would happily settle for one per cent of his sexual income instead, especially now that his wages had dried up altogether.

'You just concentrate on getting well again and ignore the papers. And stay off that foot.'

CHAPTER 12

Jane showed George and Bill into Marcus's office.

'Hello, gentlemen.'

'Mr Howell. Here is Mr Harris and this is Mr Baxter. Would anyone like a drink?' she asked.

Bill and George declined politely.

'Bill is head of our supporters' association at the club.' George might equally have said, 'our secret weapon'.

Marcus smiled warmly and offered his outstretched hand. Bill waited a moment, deciding whether or not to take it. He did eventually, but it made a point that wasn't lost on Marcus. This was not a friendly visit. It was already one-nil to Baxter.

'So, gentlemen, have we come to a decision?'

'Yes. We'd like to buy the club back,' Bill announced flatly as he began fumbling in his bag.

For an instant, the colour drained entirely from Marcus's face, until he realised that Bill's bag didn't contain a huge stash of cash or one of those enormous charity cheques. It was a joke and Marcus was annoyed at himself for not spotting it immediately.

'Yes, we'd like to buy it back.'

Bill fixed his determined gaze on Marcus, who was starting to feel distinctly uncomfortable. His offer for them to buy the club back had merely been a gesture to highlight their impotence because he knew they couldn't raise anything like the kind of money they'd need. Not unless they all re-mortgaged their little homes.

Marcus's eyes momentarily widened with alarm. 'Gentlemen, I'm quite convinced that you haven't come here with two million pounds.'

'I see your plans have been rejected, though,' George stated with some misplaced satisfaction.

'Yes, that's right.'

Bill didn't appreciate Marcus's smug reaction. 'But you expected that, didn't you? It's what you wanted, isn't it? I take it you've already resubmitted the plans, with some minor adjustments, of course.'

Marcus shuffled awkwardly in his chair. Bill spoke fluently and with a degree of unnerving confidence.

'Well?' Bill insisted.

'Yes, that's right.'

'And you'll be hoping they get rejected quickly again. Did you put something outlandish in the plans so they'd get thrown out immediately and go straight to the council?'

Marcus had taken an immediate dislike to Bill. For a head of the supporters' club, he was remarkably well informed. He gave the impression that he was just another lad, one of the boys, just another footie fan, but it was apparent that he was much more than this. Bill, the great underachiever, was now fully mobilised and making up for lost ground.

Bill had spent hours poring over the soporific planning reports and both he and Michael Abbott, the team lawyer, had established a pattern whereby developers deliberately circumvent planning departments. It had happened at Wealdstone in London, at Rochester in Kent and Chorley in Lancashire, but it wasn't going to happen in Middleton.

'Are you telling me the law?'

'Why? Do you need to be told, because that is procedure, isn't it? But you're the lawyer, you tell me.'

George was mightily impressed. It had definitely been a mistake not having Bill along for their first meeting.

'Yes, in actual fact, it is.'

'And so the question is, why would you want to by-pass the planners?'

'I hope you're not suggesting—'

'Makes me wonder whether you haven't got a friend at the council.'

'I beg your pardon?'

'Hey up, George. One for the record, a lawyer begging. Not paying you enough, are they?'

Bill didn't realise quite how hard he'd struck a nerve with his quip, but Marcus was shell-shocked. He couldn't just sit there and suffer such slanderous accusations, even if they did happen to be absolutely on the money.

'If you're insinuating—'

'Eh now, go easy with the big words.'

'I think you know perfectly well what I mean.'

'OK then, and you haven't answered me question.'

'Which one?' Marcus shifted awkwardly.

'Why are you so keen to by-pass the planners?'

'How dare you? Now you listen to me. Mr Beaumont is acting correctly and wholly within the law.' Marcus had to establish some initiative here, but he was mindful not to lose his temper because that implied guilt. Tempers are only ever lost in arguments, and lawyers don't have arguments, they have disputes or disagreements.

'So have you, then?'

'What?'

'Bought anyone on the council?'

Marcus crashed his fists on to his desk, the strait-jacket that had contained his temper finally busting its seams. He had taken quite enough insults from a lager-swilling sports fan. 'How dare you come in to my office and make such scurrilous accusations? Repeat them again, and I will sue you, do you understand?'

The pumping veins on his neck were a good indication that he was serious. Somewhat reluctantly, Bill backed down and nodded that he understood.

'Good. Well, I'm glad that we've got that cleared up.'

Marcus had been right to call Bill's bluff. He didn't have anything on him, he was just pissing in the wind and Marcus had just equalised, so it was one-all now. But it served as a useful warning for Marcus. If supporters of the club were looking out for any councillors who might be on the take, he would have to ensure that Councillor O'Dowd didn't get carried away with his ownership of a Portuguese penthouse. He could just imagine him boasting to some tart in his office about his pad in the sun and how it had a lounger with her name on it.

'This hasn't cost me anything, has it?' Bill said.

'What?'

'That advice. I know what you lawyers are like.'

Marcus didn't even bother to laugh sarcastically. Like most wizened lawyers, he'd heard all the jokes before and they'd long since worn thin.

'I take it from your attitude that you're still opposed to our plans then?' he said.

'How perceptive of you. And don't expect your application to get rejected quickly.'

'Oh?'

'No. We get twenty-eight days to appeal, and believe me, we're going to take them all. And then the planners have to consider any points that we might raise. We're going to be like Man United . . .'

Any football fan would have got the inference there and then. Marcus, though, wasn't a football fan, as he was about to prove.

'Meaning?'

'That we'll have loads of points.'

George laughed heartily. Top corner, keeper had no chance. Two-one, Baxter.

A bead of sweat formed on Marcus's brow. Who the hell was this bloke, this knight in shining armour they'd suddenly found? Where were the cloth-cap-wearing ferret strokers that he had been expecting?

'OK then, Marcus, so now we all know where we stand. It's been lovely chatting with you.' This time, it was Bill holding out his hand warmly. 'Are you and Conran looking forward to Saturday then?'

Marcus looked confused.

'You probably don't know – I expect you're a rugby man – but we're playing Tottenham in the FA Cup. That's Middleton, by the way.'

Full time, three-one, Baxter. What Bill wouldn't give for that against Spurs.

The Middleton District Council convened for its fortnightly meeting to discuss whichever resolutions had been put before it from the numerous sub-committees and council departments. It was a bitterly cold morning and people arrived clad in anything remotely warm, no matter if their clothes clashed.

Even a bright green home-knitted woollen cardigan wouldn't have raised derogatory comments on a morning like this. The assembled team drained the two catering flasks of warmish coffee that had been left for them and huddled around their battered board table. Ten pasty-faced, miserable-looking people who looked as though they'd never ever seen the sun, and Councillor O'Dowd, who, in contrast, looked like the life-giving orb itself. Having just returned from his jolly in the sun, O'Dowd was tanned and relaxed, almost a picture of health. His trip to the Algarve, though, hadn't been all the fun he was hoping for. In actual fact it had been quite fraught, mainly because his wife had insisted on accompanying him, and when it came to choosing the fittings for the apartment they couldn't agree on anything. Although when she hinted that she was thinking of taking up golf herself so that they could play together, suddenly she was given free rein with the interiors of his villa. Pastels, potpourri and borders it was, then.

O'Dowd was due to retire next year and the villa was his little present to himself in return for a career dedicated to serving the people of Middleton. It was a crying shame that he would have to keep it quiet, as Marcus had urgently reminded him twice since he'd got back. He felt sad and cheated that such a magnificent career of public service like his was having to end with so much subterfuge and secrecy. Far better if he could be publicly presented with the keys to the villa for services rendered. God, it wasn't as though he didn't deserve it. For starters, there were forty years of his scandalous underpayment in the public sector, without even considering what he could have earned elsewhere had he not been born with such a sense of civic duty. And he did regret that his final decision would see the closure of the old football club. He knew it wouldn't be a popular course of action. Hell, he didn't want to see it close, but crucially his desire to save the club wasn't as great as his need for a villa on a golf course with its own pool, even if the bedroom walls would be covered in shell stencils with matching duvet covers.

In the meeting, it quickly became evident that there was a broad opposition to the ground being closed and re-developed. This was exactly what O'Dowd had expected, and he wasn't worried. All contentious developments start out this way, with passionate and vociferous opposition, but it rarely lasts. Eventually, the opponents see the light, getting picked off individually, until a majority is in favour. O'Dowd had no doubt that he would eventually preside over a majority. It might take a little effort on his part, but for half a million quids worth of villa, it was worth it. O'Dowd was going to do whatever it took. As the opposition lined up against him, he kept quiet, happy to listen to opinions, arguments, points of view, and in his mind to construct a three-column chart of who was with him, who would never be with him and, most importantly of all, who was dithering and open to persuasion.

'What gets me is the way that Beaumont is pretending to be interested in the club. What a complete load of nonsense.' Sean Mills, trusted confidant of Bill and a member of Middleton war cabinet, opened the batting for the opposition.

'It's absolutely transparent. The only motivation for Table Top Management is to make money and to make as much as they possibly can.'

'Absolutely.'

O'Dowd mentally scribbled more names down under the opponents column with a caveat to remind Marcus to ease up on his bullshit concerns for the club.

'No concern whatsoever for the town . . .'

More sanctimonious drivel, another opponent.

'Well, I'm sorry, but I have to disagree,' a young woman called Martha dared to venture.

'What?'

'Well, at least in part . . .'

O'Dowd's ears pricked up. At last, an ally, and an attractive one as well.

'It's too simple to write off these plans from an emotional perspective. I mean, OK, yes, we'll be losing a great sporting facility . . .'

'And part of the town's history.'

'. . . yes, OK, but we must also consider what the town will be gaining.'

'Like what?'

'Well, housing for a start. We do have a chronic shortage, remember. And then there's the inward investment that will inevitably follow on from a prestigious development in Middleton. Have you read their report on the retailers they're already in discussions with?'

'But that isn't as important as the football club.'

'Nonsense. Not everyone in Middleton is a football fan, because if they were, the club wouldn't be in the financial state it's in, would it?'

Martha made perfect sense and was absolutely correct. O'Dowd was thrilled by her timely intervention, which paved a way for him, and he was equally excited at the prospect of coming to her rescue. Her opponents looked at him furtively, appealing to him for his support. Which way was the boss going to go? These were the moments O'Dowd had spent an entire career thriving on.

'Well . . . having listened to all the arguments, I have to say . . . that I'm with Martha.'

The room gasped.

'Now, hang on. I'm not saying that I approve of the plans either, but Martha is right.' O'Dowd glanced over at her as though she was a stricken bird that had fallen out of the nest. He would certainly enjoy nursing her back to health. 'I realise that it won't be an easy or perhaps popular decision to take, but we have to move beyond gesture politics here. It's not about being popular. Our decision here can't be based on emotion. As Martha said, we represent all the people of Middleton, not just the ones who love football. The long-term prospects of the town! That is what we have to concern ourselves with. No doubt, the club is an integral part of that town. That is something we can all agree on, but no one is suggesting that the club is going to fold. In modern-day sport now, ground-shares are a reality. Look at Wimbledon, Crystal Palace and Fulham. If Premiership clubs can share grounds, why not Middleton? Different sports altogether are now sharing grounds. I'm afraid it's a reality. And there's also an argument that it will benefit the club by guaranteeing that it actually has a future.'

Sean Mills sighed.

'And, so yes, Martha might well be right. We should give the plans careful and measured consideration.'

Martha blushed. O'Dowd eyed her hungrily. She was the newest member of the council team and until now he'd always thought her too young and attractive for him. Now, though, he began to wonder. Perhaps he was doing himself down. She was married to a copper so maybe it was a power thing with her. And if it was, then what would a Portuguese villa do for her?

A lively discussion followed in which O'Dowd coolly and authoritatively responded to all the protests. The genuine grievance in the whole affair was the amount Table Top Management had paid for the club. The two-million-pound fee pretty much amounted to theft, but as this wasn't the concern of the council, it made O'Dowd's job of defending the developers easier still. With a combination of the facts he had to hand, and his considerable political skill, it made for a brilliant performance. He certainly wasn't lacking any ability and might indeed have achieved greatness in the private sector if only he'd had an engine. Laziness had been his great undoing and it followed that he hadn't had the energy to do anything about it.

O'Dowd allowed himself a little smile. Suddenly, it seemed even more likely that he would be getting the keys to his villa. The opposition was already showing signs of crumbling. The economic facts were indisputable. Small clubs had to make way for a tiny minority. All over Europe, the football malaise had set in and, like a fungus, the leagues sustaining the top clubs were rotting. Purported top players were demanding scandalous wages and if smaller clubs had to perish to pay for them as a result, then that was deemed progress. Most of the arguments in the club's favour were emotional ones and although they were stirring and powerful, they amounted to little more than blank bullets; noisy but harmless. Emotional strength doesn't figure on a balance sheet, no matter how heavy it is. O'Dowd wasn't overly concerned. In his political career, he'd learnt that there was nothing quite as persuasive as the patronage of a boss. He counted three in favour of the plans, six against and three undecided. With his casting vote he was safe. He smiled as his mind drifted off to warmer climes.

CHAPTER 13

For a government obsessed with its image and presentation, it was still scandalously underrepresented by the newsprint media. Predictably, of all the broadsheets, only the *Guardian* was not feasting on the minor health scandal that Jeremy Davidson had caused and which had now enveloped the Health Secretary as well. He'd been caught off guard over the weekend by an opportunistic journalist asking him about the new eye unit at the Chelsea and Westminster.

'Something we can all be proud of,' the secretary of state had said, and suddenly it wasn't just Jeremy stewing in the media hot pot. Downing Street had other more pressing concerns than the eye of a lowly MP, but typically the press had forced it on to its agenda.

'This is fucking ri-dic-ul-ous.' The Prime Minister's press secretary was seething at what the morning papers had to say about the Government. The Prime Minister himself was equally angry and had sought assurances that the whole débâcle would be dealt with by lunchtime. It was a bullshit story that he wanted cleaned up quickly without any lingering smells.

'Where's Davidson?' the press secretary barked at a junior civil servant.

'Can't get hold of him, sir.'

'Stupid bloody fool, have you checked Beachy Head? As soon as he surfaces, he speaks to this office, then makes a statement, explains why he lied and then this thing's over.

'What if it turns out he was treated privately?'

'Oh, so what? He'll lose his seat at the next election. And have we heard from the Health Secretary yet?'

'He's on his way to see the Prime Minister now, sir.'

'Either confirm to me that Jeremy Davidson is dead or get him to clear this nonsense up.'

'Yes sir.'

Jeremy pressed his hands gently against his wet eyeballs as he tried to weigh up the options available to him. A traditional press conference was totally out of the question. He wouldn't last five minutes.

No, I was not treated by a private doctor. Well, where then? Actually I wasn't treated at all. There was nothing wrong with my eye. So, why wear the patch? It was meant to be a disguise. From what? I didn't want someone to recognise me. Who? A professional hostess called Carmen. You see, I like to get dressed up as a baby and have my bottom smacked and because this usually puts girlfriends off, I find myself in a position of having to pay for sex. So, I hope that's cleared everything up. Now, are there any more questions? Oh, all of you . . . They'd have a bloody field day.

Although the people of Middleton were absolutely supportive and steadfast in their opposition to Table Top's plans, few felt quite as passionate about it as Bill. People felt comfortable writing letters, rattling buckets, sponsoring this or that, but persuading them to run around a dilapidated running track on a freezing February night was proving far more difficult.

Middleton Edwardians was no longer just a creaking

football club: thanks to the running track that surrounded the pitch and Bill's inspiration, Middleton Athletics Club had been hastily founded. It was all part of Bill's strategy to exaggerate the loss to the town, thereby making it more difficult to lose the club.

However, the running track was in a similar state to the rest of the facilities at the ground. Clumps of grass and weeds had sprung up everywhere and it undulated like a slide in a water park. And yet it was arguably in a better state than the few athletes Bill and Smithy had managed to round up for the town's inaugural athletics meeting. Bruce Wakes from the *Chronicle* liked the idea and had sent along a photographer to record twenty or so athletes sporting ill-fitting tracksuits and trainers, designed more for shopping centres than race tracks.

'This is bloody ridiculous, Bill. We can't afford to run the floodlights for proper fixtures, let alone running races,' George complained. 'And it's bloody freezing.'

'We'll be all right once you get running.'

'If we get running.'

No one was running anywhere until the photographer was ready to catch them. There was no point burning themselves out before then, which made good sense because realistically no one looked as if they had more than a few sprints in them at best. A cloud of exhaust fumes hung in the car park above the parked cars with their engines still running. Proper athletes warmed themselves up on the track; Middleton athletes did so in their cars.

Bill was particularly pleased that Vippin had bothered to turn up and, because he was young and athletic, Bill had given him the starring role of the evening.

'That young lad over there, that's Vippin, the one you'll be photographing.'

'Right you are, Bill. I'll just get set up,' said the *Chronicle* snapper.

Vippin was rather enjoying his star status and sauntered over towards Bill.

'Hello, son, I'm glad you could come.'

'So am I now. Look at the tits on that.'

Bill followed Vippin's eye line to Katherine and frowned. 'That's Katherine. My daughter.'

Vip's face fell, but Bill's laugh dragged it into a relieved smile once again.

'I'll tell her that, shall I?'

'I'm sorry, Bill.'

'Don't be. I want you to chase her anyway.'

Vip's eyes widened.

'Round the track, I mean. Go on then, go and get your trackie off.'

Bill walked over towards Katherine.

'Heya, Dad.'

'That top you're wearing . . .'

'What about it?' she answered defensively.

'Is it your Tessa's, because it'd probably fit her.'

'It's fashion, Dad.'

'Is it? Well, it wasn't lost on my star athlete.'

Vippin was now in position. In order to capture this charade in a vaguely realistic manner, the photographer was using a very broad stroke of artistic licence and tonight he needed his camera to lie. Vippin squeezed the butt of the pole into his stomach and held it up at length as the photographer began snapping pictures of the first pole vault the stadium had ever seen. It would have been more convincing and powerful to have a shot of Vippin arching his back over the bar, but that wouldn't be possible. Vippin had never done the pole vault before, and even if he had, they only had the pole and no bar, let alone a crash mat.

'Shit. Hurry up, will ya? This thing's heavy,' Vippin begged, as the pole came crashing down to the ground.

'Don't worry, that's fine. I've got plenty of shots there.'

Bill suddenly came charging over in their direction, waving his arms. 'They're coming, they're coming. Get running, everyone, get running.'

'What? Who?'

'The council people. I've just had a call from Sean at the council. O'Dowd's coming down to see the meeting. We have to get running. Vip, get that lot out of those cars. Smithy, fuck sake, put the fag out.'

Within seconds, the track was a hive of strenuous activity and not a second too soon.

'O'Dowd, Martha and two other councillors hitched up the collars on their coats and walked briskly over to the north stand. The only impressive thing about the sight that greeted them was the turnout, although its quality was highly questionable. Portly men and their kids dragged from their televisions and Play Stations could be seen hobbling around the track.

'Good turnout. They must be keen.'

'Desperate, more like. Look at that one over there,' O'Dowd laughed.

'What, the one in jeans?'

'No, the one with the purple tracksuit . . .'

Smithy was taking the running a lot more seriously than the pack of runners he'd already left behind. At school, he'd once finished second in a cross-country race, which had been his sporting zenith until tonight. By the time he reached the stand where the spectators stood, he had lost all sense of reality. In his mind, he was now an Olympian being roared on by the crowd of sceptical council officials. Because he wasn't going fast enough for any of the track's glamour events, Smithy decided that he was heading the field in the marathon in the glory lap in the Olympic stadium. Twenty-six gruelling miles in the searing heat were behind him, and with a hundred metres to go, like all great athletes, Smithy found just enough juice in his energy reservoir for that exciting kick finish. Leaving the trailing pack even further behind, surely now the gold was his . . .

Unfortunately, the chasing pack wasn't chasing at all; if anything it was grinding to a halt.

'Does Smithy think this is a race or what?'

'Daft bastard's gonna kill himself.'

'Bill, I can't do another lap, mate. This is me at the end here. I'll die otherwise.'

By the time the pack had crossed the finishing line, Smithy was already looking for his imaginary family in the crowd to share his golden moment. Only Bill and two others continued on for a third lap of sheer torture. The other 'athletes' had all given up and were currently in various states of collapse. Above and beyond the call of duty, Bill and the others completed their third lap, whereupon their lungs steadfastly refused to allow any more running.

Bill sank to his haunches, sucking in huge gulps of freezing air. How the hell those bastards on the telly could do victory laps was beyond him. He wanted to curl up into a little ball and die; but that wasn't the impression he was looking to recreate for the councillors. Four other 'athletes' were still lying on the tarmac, hoping it seemed they were stretching muscles and not just the realms of possibility. This was the kind of commitment that the bloody players should be showing for their club. The current team lose three-nil to Exeter and they run off at full time. Run off! Bill and his mates were so exhausted it was doubtful whether they could crawl anywhere for the moment.

'This is the kind of commitment that will save the club, lads,' Bill panted, but there was no answer. None of the others could speak yet.

O'Dowd looked down at the pathetic sight.

'. . . it will be a shame if the town loses those kinds of athletes.'

'They're not much worse than the professional ones who play here.'

'Exactly. No loss at all then.'

It had now been two days since Jeremy's face had been plastered over every newspaper and news bulletin and still he hadn't broken his silence nor come out of hiding, though he knew that he would have to soon. This situation wasn't just going to blow over and the longer he left it, the worse it would become. Understandably, Davina was furious with him and demanded to know what the hell was going on, until Jeremy finally caved in and told her the truth, the whole truth and nothing but the truth. Immediately, Davina was ashen-faced and wished that he hadn't.

'So I'll have to make a statement,' Jeremy moaned.

'But why?'

'What do you mean, why? Because the press are all over me, that's why.'

'No, I mean the baby thing.'

Jeremy huffed. He'd never told anyone about his obsession before, and this was exactly why, because no one was ever going to get it.

'Oh, I just do, that's all. It goes back to my childhood.'

Davina stared at him, weighing up whether she should resign now, because if this ever got out, there certainly wouldn't be any illuminated exit signs or inflatable slides. Jeremy would be finished and, by association, so might she.

'I'll have to make a statement,' he reiterated.

'Not about the baby thing,' Davina shrilled.

'No, of course not.'

'But what then? What are you going to say?'

'I don't know, I'll think of something.'

'But what? I mean, what can—'

'Oh, Davina, shut up. I'll think of something. That's what politicians do. We get out of things and we make things happen. That's our skill.'

'Right then. I'll set it up. I'll get you on the news tonight.'

'No, not on telly. I'm not going on telly.'

'Why?'

'Shit. Haven't you been listening? Because she might see me.'

Davina knew now that she really did have no option but to look for employment elsewhere. In this age of telepolitics, she was working for an MP who couldn't ever appear on television again.

'It'll have to be radio.'

'They're gonna want you on telly.'

'I don't care what they want. It's radio or nothing.'

'Well, it'll have to be high profile.'

'Fine.'

'*Today* programme.'

Jeremy gulped.

The financial thumbscrew that Marcus was wearing had just been tightened because his wretched little bank manager had finally caught up with him. Their meeting had started off cordially enough, but it soon became tetchy and ended on a very ugly note indeed. 'Overstretched' was the word that he kept using. How dare he? How dare he call me over-stretched. Have I missed a payment? No. Well until I do, he can fuck off. That sentiment hadn't gone down well at all. It seemed Marcus's borrowings against his assets made him an adverse risk and this little shit didn't like taking risks. Wimp!

He also wanted to know what the money was for, some-thing that Marcus wasn't inclined to enlighten him about, and this hadn't gone down well either. To reduce their risk the Bank decided to reduce the term of Marcus's loan, thereby ratcheting up his repayments a few notches. Marcus was furious, but his threats to take his business elsewhere didn't appear to be of any particular concern to the Bank.

When Marcus left the bank he was incandescent with anger. Across the road he spotted a familiar face. He couldn't immediately place him but then it came to him. It was Bill Baxter, the pain in the arse from the football club. He was limping quite badly and looked to be in considerable dis-comfort. Marcus was glad. It wasn't enough to cheer him up but it was certainly better than nothing.

White Hart Lane was only two-thirds full for Tottenham's first foray into this year's FA Cup, and not many Tottenham fans had bothered to turn up. Not so the Middleton fans. This fixture was their very own FA Cup final and was without doubt the most prestigious game in their history. Eight thousand Middletonians had travelled down to London to get lost on the underground and remark on the price of its houses and how unfriendly its people were. As the game got underway, it was only the Middleton faithful creating any kind of atmosphere in the stadium.

'. . . and now you're gonna bee-lee-heave us . . . we're gonna win the cup.'

Giant killing is the very romance of the FA Cup, where a small team manages to dump out a giant team against all the odds. Like a featherweight connecting with a lucky punch and sending a middleweight or even a heavy sprawling to the canvas. However, in this game, it quickly dawned on everyone that no such upset was likely. To give them credit, the Middleton players were all playing their hearts out, but today it was only the Middleton goalkeeper, Thomson, who would have the opportunity to distinguish himself.

There was a huge gulf between the teams, and after ten minutes Bill was thrilled that Tottenham hadn't already scored. Bill's hopes for a win now seemed ridiculous, and he hastily downgraded his best-case scenario for the match to a draw and a nil-nil draw at that, because it seemed highly unlikely that Middleton were ever going to score. Could they hang on for another eighty minutes? That was the question. Joe Burke, their team manager, set about achieving just that, jettisoning the traditional formation of four–four–two, for the unorthodox formation of one–ten: the old, 'one goalkeeper, ten defenders, let's try and get ourselves a home replay' formation.

*

Also watching the game today in the directors' box high up in the west stand was a very sullen-looking Lee Robson. It was his first visit to a match since his injury and this wasn't a good game for him to attend because Tottenham were certain to win, not something an injured player ever likes to see. It makes them feel dispensable.

'*Bertoni is in space on the left. Will Garcia spot him? Yes he does. It's Bertoni in space on the left with just the keeper to beat. One-nil Tottenham.*'

The Tottenham fans didn't share the enthusiasm of the commentator on Radio 5 Live and barely managed a cheer. It was all so predictable, like American sprinters racing against the best Scandinavians and Indians in the heats of the Olympic Games. Lee wasn't best pleased either. The last thing he wanted to see was Bertoni getting a hatful. Couldn't one of the Middleton players do the right thing and chop him down? That would cheer Lee up no end and add impetus to his recovery.

Instantly the deluded Middleton faithful started to belt out a song of encouragement to their team. Lee looked over at them scornfully. If he'd only known that standing not a few hundred yards from him was Bill Baxter, the unwitting mastermind behind his downfall.

Bill too was becoming angry. Middleton needed to score and to do that they would have to at least get the frigging ball.

'*Here come Tottenham again. They're enjoying themselves out there today but they want more goals. Ridges to Garcia – he's been all over the place today – back to Ridges. Oh, a lovely turn, finding space down the left. This looks promising for Tottenham. Bertoni is in the middle, where else would he be? The ball's crossed in high, but too close to the keeper . . .*'

*oh no, he's fumbled it; can Bertoni gather? Yes he can.
Bertoni must score. Two-nil. Thank you very much. Poor old
Mike Thomson in the Middleton goal.'*

Now Lee had seen quite enough. They'd only played
twenty minutes and the wop was on a hat trick. He shuffled
out of his seat with his crutches, knocking over a glass of
wine in the process. He didn't care. The bloke it belonged to
was no doubt there on a jolly and wouldn't have paid for it
anyway.

'Sorry about that, mate,' Lee mumbled with as much
sincerity as an air hostess saying she hoped to see her passengers again soon.

'Don't worry. I didn't pay for it anyway,' the man joked
but Lee didn't laugh. 'Broken your leg, have you?'

'Yeah.'

'How did you do it?'

Lee looked at the man oddly. This must be the only man
in Britain who didn't know how Lee had broken his foot.
Even worse than that, this twat clearly didn't know who Lee
was either, even though he was sitting in the Tottenham
Hotspur directors' box. What was football coming to these
days?

As Lee shuffled off, another roar bellowed up from around
the ground. Tottenham must have scored again, and
knowing Lee's luck, it was probably that bastard Bertoni.
Lee picked the pace up a little. He just had to get out. The
man's wine glass was refilled by a waiter.

'Thank you very much.'

'You know who that was, don't you? The bloke with the
crutches.'

'No.'

'Lee Robson.'

'Who?'

Marcus sighed. 'Plays for Tottenham. You must have seen him on the news recently? Bloke who kicked his car.'

'Oh yes. Do you know, I thought I recognised him. Oh, and all that stuff about his sex life, poor chap.'

'Well, that's what you get if you go out with tarts.'

Conran looked at him. 'Believe me, they have their advantages.'

A shaft of fear suddenly took hold of Marcus. 'You haven't been with her, have you?'

'Who?'

'This Carmen. The one in the papers.'

'No, but I wouldn't mind.'

'Er, Conran, no. The last thing we need at the moment is you getting mixed up with anything unsavoury, anything that might rock the boat.'

'*The whistle goes for half-time and that looked oh so easy for Tottenham. Three up at the interval but it could have been so many more. Middleton, well, you have to feel a little bit sorry for the Cheshire minnows up against these London giants, but in truth, they might as well not have turned up today and I expect they'll be dreading the second half. Tottenham three, Middleton nil.*'

There was no way back for Middleton now, nothing left for them to achieve this season, apart from survive, but if they were kind enough not to, all the better for Marcus and Conran.

On the train heading back to Cheshire, the atmosphere was jubilant in spite of the drubbing that Middleton had received. The game had quickly become something of a joke, which the away fans had decided they should enjoy as much as anyone else. Every Tottenham goal in the second half was celebrated as if it were their own, and by the time the score reached thirteen nil, the Middleton fans were in a near frenzy. Middleton Edwardians were finally in the record books once and for all. Even the Tottenham fans almost came alive, and cheered when Tottenham conceded a last-minute own goal, a genuine consolation gift for the visitors on a par with a soggy piece of cake wrapped in tissue that kids get to take home from parties.

'Enjoy the match then, Vip?'

Vippin laughed. 'I did actually. That Bertoni's some player, eh?'

'Certainly is. We're making a bid for him, you know,' Bill joked. 'Sixty quid a week and all the bread rolls he can eat.'

'They reckon he's on forty grand a week, you know.'

'Which is disgusting, son. Ruining the game . . .'

Bill was immediately groaned out by all those around him.

'Not this one again, Billy boy.'

'All right, all right. So, you gonna come along again then, Vip?'

'What, to a match?'

'Why not? Fourteen goals of pure contentment.' Bill smiled wryly. How could any youngster be expected to support a little club these days? If things continued this way, it would just leave Manchester United and Arsenal in business, which would suit Sky TV and the City of London perfectly. In the hallowed Premiership, finishing as a runner-up would be the worst either club could do, giving them automatic qualification for Europe, and both teams would also contest the domestic cup finals as well. Perfect.

CHAPTER 14

'You're listening to *Today* on Radio Four. The time is twenty-nine minutes past seven, and after the news summary we will be talking with the Labour MP Jeremy Davidson, who is on the line from Israel.'

Jeremy's impending phone interview had rendered the subsequent Radio 4 news bulletin obsolete because he was about to become this morning's lead story. Jeremy gulped at his glass of water and immediately filled it up again, fishing out the two chunks of ice that had fallen in his glass. He paced up and down, looking out over a bustling Tel Aviv, but he couldn't enjoy the view, and nor could he listen to the news being piped down the phone line from London. He was the bloody news and for all the wrong reasons.

With everything at stake, Jeremy had decided upon a daring and treacherous strategy with which to try to extricate himself from the waist-high and rising shit that he was in. Telling the truth simply wasn't an option, so Jeremy intended to actually admit to his earlier lies, or falsehoods as he preferred to call them, but crucially he intended to make a virtue out of them. American politicians have made this an art form, but like metal detectors at school entrances, it was something from the States that hadn't come over here yet.

'Mr Davidson, we're coming to you now. Five seconds . . .'

Jeremy drained his water and stretched his mouth. He'd

role-played this interview over and over with Davina, and now he just had to think straight.

'Well, over the last week or so, perhaps one of the most peculiar political stories for some time has been the eye of a certain MP and where it was treated. There's been conjecture and speculation in the media, and I am delighted to say that to shed some light on the subject is the man who owns the eye in question, Jeremy Davidson. He joins me on the line from Israel. Mr Davidson, thank you very much for joining us.'

'Not at all, John. It's my pleasure.'

'Well, so many questions, I suppose the first of which should be, how is the eye?'

Jeremy laughed nervously. 'Absolutely fine, thank you. If I—'

'Now, on the *Question Time* programme on which you appeared, you said that you were treated at the Chelsea—'

'Er, no.'

'You didn't?'

'I did, yes I did, but it was a mistake.'

'Oh, so you weren't treated at the Chelsea and Westminster?'

'No.'

John Humphrys sounded a little bit disappointed because he liked to work for his political admissions. This one came on a silver salver and was hardly a victory for journalism.

'So where were you treated?'

'I wasn't treated anywhere.'

Now John Humphrys added confusion to his disappointment. 'What? Well then, that begs the question—'

'Then, why the patch?' Jeremy interrupted, hoping to give off an air of openness and confidence.

'Quite.'

'It was covering up a black eye.'

'Oh, I see, and I assume you didn't want people asking you how you'd come to get this black eye?'

'Exactly.'

Amusement for disappointment, it was all change in the BBC studio.

'And how did you?'

Jeremy laughed briefly. 'This is exactly the question I was hoping to avoid.'

'And I have to tell you that you failed quite spectacularly in doing so.'

'Yes, quite.'

There was a brief pause from both sides. Jeremy hoping that he might have forgotten the question, Humphrys thinking he had enough rope to hang himself already.

'So how did it happen then?'

'Well, it's all terribly embarrassing. Basically I'd had a rather strained argument with my partner in which a hair-brush was thrown and, unfortunately, it caught me in the eye.'

Humphrys chuckled inwardly but loud enough so that his rapt listeners could hear. '. . . and so, all the hospital treat-ment was a lie.'

'Yes, I'm afraid it was, which of course, I deeply regret, but it felt like a better alternative than to expose my girlfriend to any unnecessary publicity or embarrassment.' Protecting his girlfriend, you see, there was a reason for this harmless little lie.

Humphrys seemed utterly sceptical. 'Mr Davidson, not that I'm condoning lies, you understand, but wouldn't it have been a better lie if you'd not bothered with the patch and just said that you'd fallen over?'

'Absolutely, yes, but hindsight is a wonderful thing.'

'Pardon me, but I don't think hindsight is relevant here. It's common sense surely.'

Jeremy winced. 'Yes, I expect you're right and can I just take this opportunity to apologise humbly to anyone who might have been hurt or offended by anything that I might have done.' Jeremy here was drawing attention to the fact that no harm whatsoever had been done to anyone and this was Part Two of his master plan. This wasn't a bloke on the make or covering anything up. Here was a fellah doing the right thing, looking out for his 'missus', and, what's more, compromising himself in the process. The bloke's a hero. A very reluctant female friend of Jeremy's had already been lined up to assume the role of phantom girlfriend and hairbrush chucker. Jeremy explained that she probably wouldn't even be called upon but if she was, hers was a new BMW.

'Well, Mr Davidson, it seems that all this health scandal and general furore has been over nothing.'

'Yes, quite.' Jeremy punched the air with delight and relief. Humphrys himself, the great interrogator, feared by all, had said it. This was all 'nothing'. Jeremy was well ahead and hadn't even played his charity card yet.

'One thing confuses me, though?' Humphrys reloaded his gun.

'Oh?'

'Yes, why didn't you clear all this up as soon as it happened?'

'Of course, I would have done, but I've been away.' Flying to Israel only two days ago was where the ice over Jeremy's career thinned most dramatically. It was fortunate that Jeremy had lain so low since his televisual disaster. Davina had covered it with the guest house keeper but Jeremy was still gambling on airline staff not recognising him under his second possibly calamitous disguise.

'You're in Israel now?'

'Yes, on a kibbutz, working for one of the charities that I support.'

'And, you didn't get a phone call?'

'Not on this kibbutz. The first I heard about it was an hour ago whereupon I immediately arranged to contact your programme and put the record straight.'

'And now I expect you hope the matter is now closed?'

'I certainly hope so.'

'Might I ask, are you and your girlfriend . . . ?' Humphrys' cheeky question was a sure sign that the interview was over and Jeremy had survived.

'. . . back together? Yes and we're very happy.'

'Right, well I dare say your party and perhaps your constituents might have some further questions for you, but Mr Davidson, thank you very much indeed.'

George was sitting in the club bar nursing pints with Reggie Hill. George's general depressing state wasn't being lightened by anything that Reggie had to say. As an ancillary member of staff at Middleton District Council, Reggie was now a very senior member of Bill's war cabinet but what he'd managed to gleam from other council staff about the plans wasn't at all encouraging.

'You know, Bill raised the points about the kiddies football?'

'Yeah,' George moaned.

'They've covered themselves.'

'What? How?'

'Apparently, they've promised to turn the waste ground over by the canal into a footie pitch. They're even talking about a pavilion as well.'

'But that land's sodden with diesel from the old aerospace place.'

'Said they're gonna clean it up. They've got all the answers, I tell ya.'

George thought for a moment. 'But if they're gonna build a pitch, why can't they just move us out there; put some stands up and we're all happy?'

That wasn't bad reasoning on George's part, but it was hopelessly naïve.

'Yeah, not a bad idea. I never thought of that.'

In a high state of excitement, Bill entered the bar. 'Sorry I'm late, lads.'

'Usual, Bill?' Reg asked, getting up with his glass.

'Just a half thanks, Reggie. Got lots to do.'

George drained the remnants of his pint and handed his glass over.

'Bloody hell, George, what's up with you?

'Reggie reckons they're planning to built a pitch for the kids by the canal.'

'But that land's polluted.'

'That's what I said. But they're gonna clean it up.'

'Ah, bollocks they will. They'll not build a pitch, either. It's all bullshit. These developers, they make promises and then just forget about them because they know that the council can't afford to sue 'em. I've been reading about it. It happens all over the place.'

George nodded wryly at Bill and hastily decided not to bring up his master plan of relocating Middleton FC to the canal site.

Reggie placed the drinks on the table with a selection of crisps.

'George, have you told Bill your idea?'

George looked a little awkward. 'Don't be stupid, Reggie. I was joking.'

'Were ya?'

'Course I was. They're not going to build even a kiddy pitch, let alone a stadium for us.'

Bill was as confused as Reggie.

'Anyway, never mind that for now,' said Bill. 'You're not going to believe what I've found out.'

Both men looked up at him hopefully.

'Me and Katherine, we've been at the records office, and read the deeds that Thorpe left on the land.'

George admired Bill and his great energy. Not for a second had he conceded that their club was doomed, which most people, at least privately, had already done.

'Milton Thorpe, all-round good egg, yeah? Well, seems that years back, he wanted to protect his textile workers should anything happen to him or his firm – you know, like if it ever got taken over . . .'

George and Reggie didn't look at all excited because neither of them could see what Bill was getting at.

'. . . and he's done it with the land as well!' Bill exclaimed, as if it were marvellous news. 'See, he's written into the land deeds that the custodians of the land, i.e., his mill workers, have the right to buy back the land up to twelve months after it is sold. I've had it checked by Michael and he's confirmed it.' Bill held out his hands in utter delight.

Reg hadn't followed at all and just stared at his good friend. George thought that he'd got the gist of it, but he couldn't see how it could be even remotely good news. Together, their reactions were wholly underwhelming.

'Don't you see? We're the workers now. The Club is now the custodians of the land.'

'So?'

Bill was now exasperated. 'Bloody hell, you two, what are ya like? Legally we can buy the club back.'

This was what George thought it had all meant and this was why he wasn't excited.

'Bloody hell, Bill, what a find?'

'Yeah, isn't it?'

'So, all we have to do is come up with a few million quid,' George added sarcastically.

'But don't you see, it's now an official target?'

'But it always was. That was always Howell's offer.'

'Oh, George, he wasn't serious. He was probably just sussing out whether we had that kind of dosh. But now we can, legally – we can buy it back.'

Both George and Reggie just stared at him. Well, whoopee. What are we waiting for? Let's get the buckets out. Bill knew exactly what their next question was going to be, but he didn't want to pre-empt them. He wanted them to ask him.

'Not wanting to sound too down on you, Bill,' George began.

'Yeah, go on.'

'Where are we going to find nearly two million quid?'

Bill smiled mischievously. 'I have had a fantastic idea.'

Lee gingerly pushed himself off from the side of the pool with his good leg while Seth watched anxiously from the side with Tottenham's team physio and doctor. A combination of

Lee's natural good health and, more crucially, his constant whinging at the medics and it had finally been agreed that the plaster could come off, exactly five weeks after the incident. The foot could bear his weight but running was out of the question, and so swimming was Lee's route back to the top. He wanted to play football again and Seth wanted him earning again.

'How does it feel, Lee?'

Lee didn't answer. He probably hadn't heard the question as his arms crashed about, dragging his deliberately redundant legs after him. No sooner had he touched the end of the pool than he turned around and was pounding the water once again. He had a point to prove. To journalists, fans, his ex-girlfriend, his club, everyone. Indeed, the entire British public had written him off, and he was going to prove them all wrong. The 'Rocky' soundtrack was playing in Lee's mind. This was going to be one of the greatest sporting comebacks of all time.

Marcus arranged another meeting with Councillor O'Dowd for a much-needed update. He wanted assurances that things were progressing as fast as possible, although he was mindful not to look desperate. He certainly didn't want O'Dowd knowing how financially stretched he was because that would only increase the councillor's position of power. Marcus found O'Dowd insufferable at the best of times but it pained him now that he seemed to be so aware of just how powerful he was in this particular equation and, what's more, he was beginning to flex his corrupt muscles. O'Dowd insisted that their meeting take place well away from Middleton, which was probably prudent, given the circumstances, but he had also decided that London was the best venue and that Marcus should stump up for his first-class train fare and his hotel.

They sat in a quiet corner of the stunning atrium of the Landmark Hotel on London's Marylebone Road, drinking hideously overpriced coffee. 'It is just hot water and coffee beans?' Marcus wanted to ask the waiter.

'My end is ready to go. Just waiting on you now.' Marcus pulled at the skin on his throat, hoping that O'Dowd might volunteer how things were proceeding at his end because he didn't want to ask him.

'Good. Lovely hotel this, isn't it?'

'Yes . . . and your end?' Marcus blurted out angrily.

'Oh, you know, tootling along. You know how it is, these things take time.'

Marcus forced himself to smile. Time was exactly what he didn't have. 'No, not really. You must have a time-frame . . . ?'

'Well, it's very difficult to say. Like I said right at the beginning, these things have to take their natural course, otherwise they start to look suspicious, and I take it, that's the last thing you want.'

'But it's with the planners now?'

'Yes, and until they're finished with it, I can't do anything.'

'Fine. Well, how long do they need?'

'Thing is, you see, the club has raised an awful lot of points. Do you know Bill Baxter?'

Just the mention of the man's name made Marcus flinch. 'Well, can't you hurry them along? You must have someone on the planning team.'

Marcus was starting to appear a little desperate now, which amused O'Dowd in a sadistic fashion, and intrigued him also. Perhaps, he was undervaluing himself with just a villa on the Algarve. O'Dowd frowned at him.

'Look, if I start bullying planners, people are going to get suspicious. All it will do is flag up my vested interest. You see, Marcus, what you need to understand is that politics is a game of cunning and our position isn't served by giving ourselves away. Do you see?'

Marcus's nostrils flared as he quietly counted down from five to one. O'Dowd was entirely right, but he hated having it spelt out for him.

'The best thing you can do—'

'Don't you fucking patronise me.' Marcus pointed his finger angrily at his fellow mason. 'I know damn well what we have to do here. Who do you think put this whole deal together? I just want assurances that you're doing all you physically can.'

'Marcus, calm down, please. It's like I said—'

'Yes, I heard. But you need to understand that your golf handicap isn't coming down unless you come through, and that means it all happens this season.'

Far from being frightened by his sudden anger, O'Dowd was delighted. He knew now exactly how desperate his partner was. Each time he met Marcus, he could feel himself getting stronger. It was like going to the gym without the effort.

'Yes, I'm doing all I can. And yes, it will happen.

'This season?'

O'Dowd nodded. Marcus was disappointed that he'd lost his temper but he did take some solace from O'Dowd's assurances.

'Anyway, enough about work. Shall we eat?' O'Dowd looked across the dining room and specifically at a wonderful meal that had just been placed before a couple of Arabs to their left.

'No,' Marcus said tersely.

'Oh.'

'But don't let me stop you, you go right ahead. It's probably well worth it. I've got another meeting to get to.'

O'Dowd's face fell. He'd been looking forward to five courses followed by a night in the bar chasing rich totty about the place and hopefully eventually upstairs. Marcus had since decided otherwise. O'Dowd had already had enough jollies off his back. Marcus stood up to leave.

'Am I staying here?' O'Dowd asked rather pathetically.

'Yes, if you want to. You'll have to ask at reception to see if they've got a spare room.'

Marcus had taken enough shit from O'Dowd and he figured that from now on he should be the one throwing the punches. On his way out, he passed by the reception to cancel O'Dowd's room booking.

CHAPTER 15

When Michael had confirmed that the lease technically allowed the Club to buy back the land from Beaumont, Bill was so excited that he refused to let the small matter of raising the money dent his joy. His 'fantastic' idea was to raise the money by selling off some players and George was understandably unimpressed.

'But, Bill, two million pounds ¬ we'll not have a bloody team left.'

His point being that the entire Middleton side wasn't worth two million quid. They hadn't won for six games, and, in league terms, were currently the third worst professional team in England, and bets were off that they would still be a professional club come the end of the season in three months' time.

'No, but what if we raise half by selling players, and then we get on with raising the other half ourselves.'

'What, and enter a five-a-side league?' Reggie joked.

'But we'd still need to raise a million,' George whined.

'Ah, shit, George, a million quid is nothing these days. Houses in Knutsford cost that these days. This is our club. It's got to be worth a million bloody quid.'

'But how, though? How can we raise that kind of money?'

'I don't know. Government grants . . . bank loans . . . supporters' association. That kind of stuff. Smithy had a good idea. He reckons we should write to Thorpe's sons, see if they're interested, and Michael suggested that some other property companies might like to get involved.'

'Does he know any?' George asked.

'No, but I've asked him to look into it.'

What really excited Bill most about his plan was the prospect of raising the entire sum by selling off a single player. All it required was some creative selling because the value of a football player was so arbitrary. They weren't like jam doughnuts or bread rolls. They couldn't be valued by what they cost to produce. Even though George and Reggie were correct about Middleton not having any outstanding players worth millions of pounds, this was just a minor setback. The 'paper' value of a player is exactly that – how the player is discussed in the newspapers – and this was why Bill was so excited.

'Who's our most valuable player?' Bill asked.

George thought for a moment. 'Ronnie O'Mara.'

'And he's worth three, four hundred, absolute tops,' Reggie said.

'Right, so we just have to think of ways of getting his value up.'

'What, to a million quid?'

'Yeah, or more.'

'Have you gone mad? You can't just go making players better. What are you, some sort of wonder coach?'

'Oh, come on, lads, you know what I mean. We just have to hype him up a little, that's all.'

Now George and Reggie looked genuinely worried for their friend. It was hardly surprising. He'd been under huge strain of late and it was finally taking its toll. Bill had gone mad.

'But, Bill, he's only scored nine goals this season and three of them were penalties.'

Bill had thought of starting the hype by adding a 'one' before this to make it nineteen, before he realised that Middleton hadn't scored nineteen goals this season.

'But the press do hype players up,' Reg conceded.

'Course they do. I shouldn't be surprised if they're not on a cut. Look at bloody Rio Ferdinand. Thirty million quid, do me a favour.'

George was aghast. 'Rio bloody Ferdinand! Bloody hell, Bill. Number one, he plays for England, and number two, our players don't get written about in the press – not in the national press, anyway.'

Bill rubbed his eyes. 'Look, I haven't got all the answers. I'm not saying it's easy, lads, but you have to admit, it could be a way out. It's happened in the past.'

'When?'

'Look at that lad who said he was George Weah's cousin, said he'd played for Liberia. Do you remember, Souness bought him, didn't he? Turned out he was shit – and what about Arsenal? They bought the wrong Chinese lad, didn't they? Mix-up with the names and them all looking the same.'

'I can't see anyone getting Ronnie mixed up with a Chinese lad.'

Bill had to admit that his plan wasn't straightforward, not straightforward at all, but it was still worth a go. Anything was worth trying.

'Besides winning the bloody lottery, what do you suggest then?'

Neither of them had anything to say.

'No, exactly. So we just have to give it some thought. Ronnie's a good lad. You know how it is with pro footballers, a lot of it's just luck. Our Ronnie is capable of good football; somehow we just have to persuade another club that he's a bit better than he really is.'

Bill couldn't really sleep as his mind thrashed about with his imponderable problem. He felt as if he were on *Countdown* and had selected eight consonants and couldn't get past a three-letter word. Not surprisingly, Mary had been no help and had long since fallen asleep with Tom's cardigan nearing completion still lying next to her.

George was right: Rio Ferdinand was easy to hype up. A few half-decent games in a poor England World Cup side was enough even without his having a cool name, because in the image-obsessed world of today, a name is all important. What foresight Mr and Mrs Ferdinand had when they'd plumped for Rio, because had they named him Brian, Malcolm or Colin, it would have cost them dear. Ronnie O'Mara wasn't a sexy name. Ronald, Ronnie, Ron – however it was said, Ronnie O'Mara was never going to get anyone excited and Bill eventually drifted off to sleep still wrestling with his problem.

Within an hour, though, Bill was sitting bolt upright in bed, staring ahead, his mind processing as fast as it could. It was totally unrealistic to expect an English club to come in for Ronnie. None of them had got any money anyway, and besides, even if they could generate some hype around Ronnie, no English club would buy it. Every home-grown player is already well known to clubs and scouts alike. A great English footballing find these days is a six-year-old with an ambitious dad. Twenty-three-year-old wonder players can't just materialise unless they've been made in a laboratory somewhere.

Far from giving up, though, Bill could now see a solution

starting to take shape. What if they were to offer Ronnie to a club on the Continent, where they'd never heard of him? This would allow them to say whatever they wanted about their prodigy.

Suddenly Bill was entirely energised, his body forgetting that it was exhausted. Their bedroom was freezing but he either didn't care or hadn't noticed. His mind was already racing, imagining the fictitious *Chronicle* headlines they could run off and send over to Italian and Spanish scouts: 'Ronnie O'Mara: goal machine.' They could make video tapes on the training ground of Ronnie scoring as many goals as they needed. Free kicks, volleys, headers – sod it, overhead kicks, the lot.

What a scam it would be! Bill gave up hunting in the dark for his other slipper and sat down on the end of the bed. He knew, though, that something else was missing. It felt as though he had a six-letter word for Mr Whiteley, although somehow he knew that there was an unassailable eight-letter word waiting to be discovered.

Now in his equally cold kitchen, but with a mug of steaming tea, for no reason Bill scribbled on his pad, 'Ronnie O'Mara, Goal Sensation'. It didn't exactly sound convincing. Bill stared at what he had written and then a dark and mischievous thought occurred to him. He wrote out the name again, but his time with Ronald instead of Ronnie. 'Ronald O'Mara.' A glint appeared in Bill's eye and a smile cracked and spread across his face. A possible solution to all his problems stared back at him from the page – *the elusive eight-letter word*. It felt fatalistic, as if he was meant to prevail all along. First he'd discovered about the clause on the land and how he'd realised something incredible about Ronald O'Mara. What if Ronald O'Mara, with an innocent typographical error, were to become Ronaldo Mara? No longer from County Cork, Ireland, but a kid from the slums of Rio de Janeiro, a refugee from the great Brazil who had arrived in Britain with nothing more than his God-given talent for playing football.

It was only half-past three in the morning, but Bill rushed back upstairs to tell Mary. He simply had to tell someone.

Marcus was grateful O'Dowd had telephoned him with the news that the Club had somehow found out about Milton Thorpe's buy-back clause. It was irksome news and a little worrying, but certainly not catastrophic, Marcus assured himself. Indeed, this was the Achilles heel of his whole plan, but he'd already established that they couldn't raise the money themselves and, anyway, time was rapidly running out on the clause.

Marcus counselled himself not to panic. That, though, was easier said than done. Marcus had swallowed hard and rubbed at his sagging face. He felt that he'd aged more in the last three months than he had done in the last ten years. He'd long had a few grey hairs spouting by his ears but suddenly they outnumbered the black ones and he decided that he should dye them before it was too late.

'But what if they go to another developer with it?' O'Dowd asked.

Instantly, a few more hairs on Marcus's head turned white as a chill descended down his spine. So much for not panicking.

'After all, they'd get much more than you paid. Possibly ten times as much, especially with planning permission about to be approved,' O'Dowd smiled.

Marcus shuddered as he imagined his plans collapsing

about his ears. Now his victory over O'Dowd's hotel booking seemed particularly hollow and the saving he'd made was going to pale against what he suspected this call was going to cost him. O'Dowd wasn't calling to warn him at all. He was flexing his fucking muscles again. The greedy bastard was coming back for more. Marcus decided to play it dumb. O'Dowd would have to spell out his greed.

'Well, thanks for the warning, but I've got all that covered. Like I said, there are no leaks.'

'Oh?' O'Dowd pushed him gently.

'OK, then, but thanks for letting me know.'

'I must say, you're being remarkably calm about this.' O'Dowd nudged him again.

'Yes, well, I've been planning it for a long time and I'm not about to let it slip away.' Marcus spat, his toes now curling over the edge of the plank O'Dowd was making him walk.

'Exactly, Marcus. My point exactly.'

'And, anyway, there isn't time now to set up a deal with another developer.'

O'Dowd was tired of their shadow boxing and decided they needed to move their conversation on a little.

'Oh, I don't know. There are plenty of cash-rich developers the Club could hook up with. They'd snap their hands off.'

Marcus flinched angrily. 'Listen to me, O'Dowd. Exactly what are you suggesting here?'

'I'm suggesting how valuable I am to you,' O'Dowd answered, fully squared up for a fight.

'And how valuable is that?' Marcus seethed.

'Well, more than a villa in Portugal, that's for sure.'

'You greedy bastard. This is blackmail.'

O'Dowd shrugged. Not a term, he liked but he couldn't disagree with it, all the same.

'You utter fucking bastard.' Marcus was shattered. He hated being held to ransom but he couldn't see that he had any other option. That was what really rankled. 'What do you want?' He nearly choked on the words.

'First of all, I don't want us to fall out. We've known each other now . . .'

'Oh, fuck off with your friends bullshit. We're not friends and let's not pretend that we even like each other, because I certainly don't like you. So, why don't you just cut the shit and tell me what do you want?'

O'Dowd wasn't worried by this outburst because it was perfectly understandable. He would have felt exactly the same way.

'Two million. Half now—'

'No way. No fu—'

'Yes fucking way, because you don't have me, you don't have anything.'

Marcus's glass paperweight shattered as it hit his office wall and, holding his head in his hands, he growled angrily like a wild dog.

Now O'Dowd was worried.

'One million and only after the planning permission has been signed.'

'Half now.'

'No, no way, and do you know why? Because I haven't got it. You see, putting this thing together, I've put absolutely everything I own on the line already. Do you understand that? Do you even know what it is to take a risk in life, Mr Councillor?'

O'Dowd thought about it for a second. This had already been a very valuable phone call. He hadn't been expecting anything. He'd thought that Marcus would blind him with some legal jargon, and, anyway, he didn't have the energy to find another developer and put them in touch with the Club.

'OK then, a million,' he said as if he were making a worthy concession. 'And I'll want it in the Isle of Man account, like the property.'

Marcus grunted. 'O'Dowd, now you listen to me. I'm not a man to make idle threats, but let me make one thing clear: this deal has got to go through, and if you ask for a penny more, I'll see to it that you never swing a fucking golf club again. And I mean that.'

Marcus slammed his phone down and instantly with both hands grabbed a handful of hair and squeezed until it hurt. His brain throbbed and felt as though it were about to burst out of his head.

Bill's inner sanctum looked circumspect. It certainly was an ingenious idea. From Ronald O'Mara to Ronaldo Mara – bloody inspired even – but it wasn't without its difficulties, or even legal, according to Michael.

'Bill, I'm sorry, but I can't sanction this,' Michael began. In his career as a solicitor, Michael hadn't so much as exaggerated his lunch expenses and so a million-pound fraud was always going to be a struggle for him.

'Why?'

'Are you being serious?'

Everyone nodded their heads.

'I'm sorry, but I can't be involved.'

'Why not?' Bill asked.

'Why? Because I'm a lawyer and it's illegal. It's fraud.'

'No, it's not.'

Everyone in the room now sat up to attention. It wasn't often any of them had seen Bill lose an argument but this appeared to be one that even he couldn't possibly win.

'Of course it is. You've changed his name and nationality. That's fraud.'

'No, you see, we're not saying that. We're going to let them conclude that for themselves.'

'But, Bill, you've changed his name,' Michael screamed.

'No. It's just a typo, that's all.'

Michael got up to leave. 'Bill, can you call me in the office, please? We need to have a little chat.'

It seemed that everyone else had problems with Bill's scam too, but not from a legal perspective.

'But Ronnie's got ginger hair,' Reggie stated.

'So?'

'Brazilians haven't got ginger hair.'

'Yes they have. What about Socrates?' Smithy answered, so far the only loyal servant to stand behind Bill.

'He didn't have ginger hair. He had a sort of black man's ginger.'

'Socrates wasn't black.'

'No, but he wasn't totally white either. Not like our Ronnie. He's got a carrot top and skin like lard. We'll never pass him off as Brazilian.'

'Maybe he's an albino.'

'Yeah, thank you, Smithy.'

'And let's not forget that he isn't a shit-hot footballer either.'

Bill looked disappointed. Where was their sense of spirit, their sense of daring? 'What about the lad passing himself off as George Weah's nephew?'

'Well, at least he was bloody black.'

'Fuckin' 'ell, lads, we can get him tanned. It's not a problem.'

'I don't reckon Ronnie tans much.'

'He'd have to go white before he tans.'

Bill held up his hands in exasperation. 'Bloody hell. Will everyone shut up about his skin for a minute? Bruce is well up for it at the *Chronicle* and says he'll run some special editions just for us, with some useful banner headlines and stories. And listen to this, then. You know the lad who works for me? Vippin?'

'The pole vaulter.' The room laughed.

'Yeah, it only turns out that his uncle is a big noise in Bollywood and he's coming over here for a holiday. Apparently, he loves football, and Vippin reckons he could run us off a promotional video of our Ronnie.'

People pondered what Bill was proposing. This wasn't just a laugh then. Bill was serious. Well, it was certainly exciting, if nothing else.

'Come on, lads, we can bloody well do this. Ronnie's a bloody good player. He had a run out for Ireland as a kid. With a bit of luck he might have made it by now.'

'He's got a great left peg,' Smithy added.

'Smithy, he's right-footed.'

'Are you sure?'

'Shut up, you two. We can dress it up,' Bill enthused. 'The only problem might be in getting his agent on board, because he'll have to be up for it as well. George, who's his agent?'

'Seth Meyer.'

'Right, get him on the phone.

Lee pleaded guilty and the whole thing was over inside three minutes. The eighteen-month driving ban was a little difficult to stomach but the two-thousand-pound fine was a piece of piss for a man on ten grand a week, even though it was money provided by his agent and not some insurance giant.

Lee walked powerfully out of the court room. His foot was healing well and after nearly two weeks of training, Seth was already in negotiations with Tottenham for his new contract. They were still being a little obstinate: arguing that a pay-and-play contract suited them better than even a one-year extension. It seemed that the fallout from Lee's recent media exposure had yet to settle, and, a little worryingly, no other clubs had made any approaches for Lee.

Lee purposefully pushed through the first set of double doors at Bow Street Magistrates' Court, to face the hordes of waiting journalists and photographers, who all had their fingers crossed for another Lee Robson bonanza. Perhaps this time he might break his right hand on a post box that was staring at him strangely. But they were to be disappointed. Lee was the picture of calm as he emerged with his lawyer, who looked delighted to be in the momentary limelight as he read out a prepared statement to the effect that his client wasn't taking any questions.

'Lee, what are your future plans?'

'I said no questions.'

'Lee, how fit are you?'

'No comment. I said, no comment.'

Lee held his hands aloft and, like a Messiah, immediately quelled the masses before him. His solicitor seemed worried that Lee was going to speak, but not as worried as Seth.

'What happened to me this year – the injury and the press coverage – has been the worst episode of my life, but it's all behind me now and I just wanna get back to playing football again.'

'Have you settled with the warden?'

Lee shot a gruesome look in the direction of the questioner, pointed a finger and snarled, 'That warden is a—'

Seth dived to intercept the line of fire. 'Er, that charge has been dropped entirely, and Lee has nothing more to add.'

'No further comments,' his lawyer added, not wanting to be outdone by an agent.

'Lee, have you paid your parking fine?'

Lee stared down a section of the pack, but he couldn't determine who had actually asked the question. It was just as well because the journalist would have had his nose broken and Lee would certainly be facing an assault charge this time. It was clear that Lee Robson was still very raw and absolutely raging inside at what had happened to him.

The only thing Lee wanted more than to play football again was to find the bastard who'd set him up but, maddeningly, the detective he'd hired had produced nothing so far apart from an invoice. Lee was trying to put it all behind him, but it was difficult. His right foot, which still throbbed after each training session, was a constant reminder of the nightmare he'd been through. And so the last thing he needed was a journalist – or any one else, for that matter – taking the piss out of him. How, then, would he cope when he finally got in front of thousands of opposing fans?

CHAPTER 16

Marcus could have done without another jaunt down to London but he had needed to tie up a few loose ends with Spelthorne PLC, the company that was lined up to buy the land once planning permission had been approved. Conran had been unusually excited on hearing of his visit to London and had insisted that they have lunch together and that afterwards Marcus should come back to see his new place.

His apartment had proved magnificent, and Marcus felt that it alone was worth the entire trip down south. With this place, and at least three others just like it, Conran's lack of interest in the money he was going to make from the Spelthorne sale was hardly surprising.

'You look whacked, Marcus, really tired.'

Instinctively, Marcus brushed his hair which was now almost entirely grey, back over his ears.

'Yes, well, it's been quite a stressful time of late.'

'Then you put your bloody feet up, old boy. What do you want to drink? Beer, wine, Scotch?'

'A beer would be great.'

'You know you're very welcome to stay. I've got bags of room.'

'No, really, I've got to get back.'

'OK then, but my man's driving you.'

'But, I've already got a train ticket.'

'I insist. Have a drink, wait till the traffic's died down

and he'll run you back up north in no time. It's no trouble.'

'Thanks.' Marcus was grateful for the offer because he couldn't stand the prospect of four hours on a train opposite some spotty youth with a Walkman and a hearing problem, but he was also just a tad suspicious. Over lunch, he'd continually had the feeling that Conran wanted to ask him something, and after his recent bout with O'Dowd, he was highly sceptical of kindness in any form.

Marcus slumped into a ridiculously soft and comfortable leather sofa. This cow must have used moisturiser, he thought. His eyes were painful as he rubbed them and his nerves were more frayed than ever. He hadn't slept properly for weeks and no matter how hard he tried, he just couldn't relax. Conran handed him a beer.

'Thanks, Conran.'

He felt a little sense of guilt creep up on him. Conran had never been anything other than honourable and he suddenly wasn't proud of how he'd come to regard him as a rich buffoon, exploiting his company rather than enjoying it. Without Conran, there wouldn't have been any hope of a deal in the first place, and it occurred to Marcus, looking around his magnificent house, that Conran had probably only agreed to do this because he liked the idea of helping out his old friend.

'Cheers.'

'Marcus, there's something I've been wanting to ask you,' Conran said, somewhat sheepishly.

Marcus eyed him nervously. Not you as well, please God.

'How's it all going with the club?' Conran asked as nonchalantly as he could, but the question jarred all the same. It just didn't fit, like a Volvo waiting for a Mini to pull out of a parking space. This was the first time Conran had ever brought the subject up. What was next? Can we discuss our share?

'Good – you know, few small glitches but nothing to worry about,' Marcus sighed, trying to head off any demands.

'What about the decision from the council, are we any closer to that?'

Marcus sat up as straight as he could. Not an easy thing to do on a filleted cow. He was highly alarmed. Conspiracy theories flashed through his mind. O'Dowd had got to Conran. They had been gay lovers for years and were about to freeze him out. Murderous fantasies flashed through his brain; his life would be over anyway if the deal didn't happen, so he might as well have the satisfaction of killing them both. He was going to boil O'Dowd.

'It's due to be handed over to the council any time now and then it'll be green lit.'

'What, straight away?'

'No, not straight away, that might look suspicious. There's a four-week cooling off period as well, which is good because we'll need to make a few adjustments to the plans anyway. You seem remarkably interested all of a sudden.'

'Yes, well, it's a lot of money. And Spelthorne, they're happy with it all?'

Marcus was now shit scared. What the hell was going on here? He even knew the name of the company buying the club. It seemed that O'Dowd was merely first in the queue of little Olivers clutching their bowls and asking for more.

'Yes, they're happy. Why shouldn't they be?'

'No, no reason . . .'

'Because as with everything else in this deal so far, I have attended to every eventuality,' Marcus said emphatically.

'Good, and you're happy as well? Happy with everything?' Conran asked.

'Yes.'

'Good. That's good.' He smiled and Marcus thought how ugly he looked.

'Conran, is there anything on your mind?'

'Well, it's funny you should ask, because I was hoping that we might be able to have a little talk.'

'This is unbelievable.'

'There's no easy way of saying this, but I need to ask a pretty big favour of you.'

'Why can't you just come out and say it?'

'Well, it's a lot to ask.'

'Oh, is it?' Marcus looked about him at the palatial surroundings. 'Like you haven't got enough already.' First O'Dowd and now you. 'All right, come on, how much?'

Conran looked puzzled. 'What?'

'You people are all the same. How much do you want?'

'I don't want money. Why would I want money?'

Marcus was mightily relieved but equally embarrassed. 'Oh, I'm sorry. I thought maybe you wanted—'

'Bloody hell, no.'

'I am so sorry, Conran. It's just that I've been under enormous strain recently.'

'Yes, I can imagine.'

'So, please, how can I help?'

'Well, I was wondering whether you might be able to do something for me.'

'Sure, what, legal advice?'

'No, I've decided to have an operation.'

'Oh.'

'I'm finally going to get myself a lower jaw.'

Marcus looked bemused. 'Well, good for you. I mean, personally, I think you look fine, but if it makes you feel better about yourself . . .'

'It would.'

'Well, good then. Go for it. What, do you want my support?'

'A little bit more than that, I'm afraid.'

Marcus searched Conran's face for clues but none was forthcoming. 'What?'

'I was wondering whether you might be able to give me a couple of your ribs.'

Appropriately enough, Marcus's jaw fell open.

'My ribs?'

'For the operation. Cher's had hers removed, you know.'

Marcus stared at his business partner in disbelief. How much more was he going to have to go through? Yesterday O'Dowd had fleeced him for a million quid, and today he was being taken for the cage around his vital organs.

A disconsolate-looking Carmen sat in the West End office of the public relations company that had masterminded her fifteen lucrative minutes of fame. Guy Vincent of Vincent, Handley Associates, the PR genius behind her rampant rise to fame, sat opposite her, looking thoroughly bored. The offices of Vincent, Handley were predictably modern, decorated in black and grey, complete with chairs specifically designed for PR and advertising professionals only; in other words, uncomfortable and hideously expensive. Every inch of available wall space was crammed with the framed front pages of various red tops, which recounted the former media coups of Vincent, Handley Associates. All were 'exclusives' and generally involved notable persons doing something they shouldn't have done and usually with their loins. A space directly above Guy's bleached head had been made for Carmen's sexual *coup d'état* with Lee Robson and it would be hung as soon as the framers delivered it. However, Carmen and her story were very much old news now. The world had moved on and Guy had been reluctant even to take a meeting with her. No one was buying any further revelations about the sex life of the hapless football star. It had been over a month since Guy had managed to place a Carmen sex story in the press and that had been the shamelessly lame banana story, which, rather tellingly, had only been picked up by the *Sport*, a sure sign that Carmen's gravy train had finally hit the buffers.

However, Carmen seemed very reluctant to accept that she had used up her fame quotient. For four nights in a row this week, she'd been clubbing her tail off and had even snogged an old toothless guy with a turban but hadn't once appeared in any of the tabloids. This was why she'd demanded to see Guy. She wanted to know what he was doing for her.

Guy sighed. With the advent of reality television, it seemed that Warhol's fifteen minutes was no longer enough for some people. People now expected a half-hour at least. Guy recalled his job being a lot easier when his clients, satisfied with their brush of notoriety, would happily return to obscurity armed with a wodge of cash and a great scrapbook. Now, though, after even fleeting exposure, they somehow expected a career.

'What about the *FHM* shoot?' Carmen asked.

'Yep, I'm still pushing for that. I've got it pencilled for July and I'm quite hopeful for the cover. It'll depend on how the shoot turns out and what you take off.'

'I'll take it all off.'

'That's my girl. That'll certainly help. I'll give them a call.' Guy clapped his hands together. Now, I'm busy, you're old news, so if you wouldn't mind pissing off, how's that sound?

'And presenting work, Guy. What about that?'

He didn't even try to disguise his annoyance this time and breathed out heavily. Presenting work? What about it? Are you a journalist now? 'Yep, we're working on that. I've got some calls out with a few of the cable channels.'

Like so many before her, Carmen was finding that the fame pill she'd swallowed had a particularly bitter aftertaste. OK, so she'd managed to pay off her flat, big deal. But what else was there now? People just regarded her as a kiss-and-tell tart and she couldn't imagine ever being trusted by another rich young man again. She had a foreboding that she'd cashed in all her chips and was still short. Guy certainly seemed to agree and he would know – he was a public relations professional, after all. Carmen's fifteen minutes were long gone.

Guy looked at his watch and shifted forward in his seat, willing her out of his office. Her story was up, they'd each made a tonne of money and they'd slept together. There was nothing more for them to discuss, until such time as she managed to bag another celebrity, which was unlikely, considering what she'd done to Lee.

'There's no presenting work, is there?'

Carmen had changed tack, but the sympathy angle wasn't going to work either.

Guy shrugged. 'Look, if I'm being honest, you'll need to get very lucky. But I'm quite hopeful. You're a beautiful girl and I've got all the contacts. Now, if you'll just excuse me, I've got a lot of calls to make, chief among them *FHM*.'

Guy stood up. So, if you could get out of my office and get

your ass out there and back to work, like bait on a fisherman's line, I'll be happy. You've done sports stars, so try another pond; politicians are always good mileage.

Elsewhere in Guy's office were piles of newspapers that should have been filed long ago. Shortly, Guy would be celebrating his loathing of filing.

Carmen and Guy kissed each other the requisite three times and made for his door, whereupon she came across a pile of newspapers. A face she thought she recognised was staring out at her from the top one.

Guy opened the door. 'I'm only ever a phone call away.'

'Who's this?' she asked, holding up an old copy of *The Times*.

Guy was about to shove her into reception. He looked irritated and snatched a glance at the paper.

'Oh, some dickhead Labour MP. It turned out to be a bullshit story, but the Tory press are so desperate these days.'

Carmen looked at the caption for his name but it didn't mean anything to her.

'What's up with his eye?'

'Nothing, that was just it. Stupid twat. Now there's an example of bad PR. And people slag off our profession.'

'Do you have any other photos of him?'

'Carmen, look, I'm very busy.'

'One with his curly hair.'

Guy stopped talking instantly. His highly trained public relations antenna started to hum, as it always did when he sensed an exclusive.

'Do you know him?' he asked, rushing back from his desk to a pile of broadsheets by his window. He began ripping through them, looking for an old *Telegraph* he seemed to remember from a couple of months ago. Suddenly, he had it.

His adrenalin surged. 'Here, what about that?' He held it up.

Carmen stared at the face intently. There were two pictures of Jeremy, pre- and post-'Clampgate', showing how much he'd changed. Carmen concentrated on the pre-Clampgate Jeremy. It was a long time since Carmen had seen him, but she was pretty damn sure it was the kinky client.

'Do you know him?' Guy repeated frantically.

Carmen smiled and nodded imperceptibly.

'Jeremy Davidson, MP for Rainborough. Do you know him?'

'That's not what I called him.'

A klaxon was now sounding in Guy's head and he imagined sirens ringing out in the offices of Vincent, Handley Associates. Carmen was a bloody natural, a public relations godsend.

'Professionally, you know him professionally? Please tell me he was a client of yours.'

Carmen chewed the inside of her mouth. 'Pretty sure, yeah.'

Guy punched the air. 'You are a beautiful woman. What was he, a boyfriend or a client? Tell me he was a client, please a client, please, please, please, please.' A boyfriend would be good, but a client would be incredible.

Carmen was quite put out that Guy would even consider he could have been anything other than a client. 'What do you think I am?'

'What?'

'A client, of course.'

Guy held up his hands, to give thanks to God.

'And if he's who I think he is, then it was baby sex.'

Guy closed his eyes in sheer joy. Days just didn't get any better than this. He would have to clear a whole wall now for Carmen's impending exclusives. This might even make world news. With literally seconds to go, the clock on Carmen's fifteen minutes of fame had jammed. In fact, better still, it had been put back an hour, and not for British Summer Time either.

Guy set about fixing Carmen a drink, telling her to take a seat and put her feet up. He always had time for Carmen.

Seth was absolutely cock-a-hoop and skipped around his office. It was magnificent news. Tottenham's star striker, Claudio Bertoni, had only gone and broken his leg. This was exactly the kind of lucky break Seth figured he was well overdue. First he checked that it was true and when he confirmed that Lee hadn't been involved in breaking it, he really did start to celebrate.

'Let's see if Tottenham still want a pay-and-play contract now, eh?' Seth laughed to himself. They'd be begging for his signature and that meant it was going to cost them a fortune. Right on cue, his phone started to ring. 'That'll be Tottenham.' Seth cracked his knuckles and picked it up.

'Seth, it's me.'

'Lee, I was just thinking about you.'

'Have you heard about Bertoni?' Lee was breathless with excitement and could hardly speak.

'It wasn't you, was it?' Seth joked.

'I thought about it, though. Isn't it fantastic news? I couldn't believe it. I tell ya, there must be a God, you know, 'cos I've been praying this might happen. I reckon he might give up the clamper next.'

'How's the foot?'

'Fantastic. I've just done a run and I can't feel a thing. Two weeks and I'm as fit as ever.'

Seth heard his call-waiting alert.

'Good lad, good lad. Lee, listen, I've got another call coming. It's probably Tottenham. I'll call you back.'

'Nail 'em to the floor, Seth.'

'Oh, don't worry.'

Seth took the new call. 'Seth Meyer, hello.'

'Mr Meyer.'

'Yes?' It wasn't a voice he recognised.

'Hello, it's George Harris here.'

'Who?'

'Er, George Harris, we have met. I'm from Middleton Edwardians Football Club.'

'Right, is it important because I'm expecting a call.' Seth was irritated that it wasn't Tottenham.

'Well, you know that you've got Ronnie O'Mara at our club.'

'And?'

'We've got a slightly awkward proposition for you.'

Seth didn't bother responding.

'As you know, Ronnie's contract is about to run out with us, and—'

'He's not taking a pay cut, no way,' Seth said flatly. 'You don't want to believe all this crap about players taking pay cuts.'

'Actually, we want to let Ronnie go, but we wanted to see whether you might be interested in talking him up.'

Seth's eyes twinkled. 'What hyping him up, you mean?'

'Sort of.'

'How much were you thinking of?' Seth asked.

'As much as we can get.'

Seth smiled. What a day this was turning out to be. 'Can I call you back?'

'So, you're interested then?'

'Yes, of course I am. Look, I've got another call coming through.'

'Right, of course, OK, can I leave you my number?'

'Hold the line. Just hang on, will ya . . . Hello, Seth Meyer.'

It was Tottenham calling. 'Seth, we need to talk about Lee . . .'

Seth couldn't grin any more without splitting his mouth. He had been to the edge of the abyss but now he could feel that he was on his way back.

CHAPTER 17

Jeremy Davidson was reclining languidly in his office. His confidence had returned and it seemed that his career was back on track. Yesterday, he'd asked a pithy question in the House of Commons and two diarists had highlighted it in their daily columns and, what's more, only one made reference to his recent nadir. He'd had an awkward meeting with his constituency party chairman and two party whips but everyone agreed that no harm had been done and a slap on the hand was all that was due. He would have preferred a slapped bottom, but he didn't want to push his luck.

After his revelations on the *Today* programme, the press wouldn't leave him alone until they'd snapped him and his 'happy' girlfriend together, which, true to his word, had cost him a bloody BMW and which Molly Constantine had insisted on being metallic black with all sorts of sports options as extras. Molly's father was Lord Simons and that had been something else for the press to get excited about, and she had rather enjoyed the attention while it lasted anyway, so everyone was happy.

'You see, Davina, talent will always out.'

Davina, though, didn't share Jeremy's confidence. As far as she was concerned, his ship had all the hallmarks of the *Titanic*. She'd already put feelers out with other departments in the party and her curriculum vitae was currently been scanned by prospective employers.

'The interview for the ethics committee is tomorrow. What do you think Jeremy?'

'I think I should go for it. Why not?'

Davina looked uneasy, which he immediately picked up on.

'Look, that is a part of my life I've left behind now. Portillo did the gay episode and it wasn't a problem, was it?'

Davina thought for a moment. Wasn't it? Well, he didn't become leader of the opposition, did he? So yes, I would say that it probably was a problem for him after all.

'And, anyway, it would have come out by now. I've been all over the bloody press, so it's been a good thing. It's proved that I'm in the clear. This Carmen woman, she must have seen me by now and she clearly doesn't remember me.'

That was the problem for Davina. She figured that Carmen might have forgotten many of her former clients over the years but it was unlikely that Jeremy would ever be one of them.

'And you're not doing it now?' Davina didn't like asking such a personal question, but as her career was also in jeopardy she felt well within her rights to do so.

'Doing what?' he asked.

'You know.'

'No. It was just a phase I went through, that's all. A dark period of my life. I'm sorry that you had to find out about it.'

So am I. Believe me, so am I. 'And the ethics committee?'

Jeremy thought for a moment. 'I'm going to go for it.'

Davina gulped.

George, Bill, and Joe Burke, the team manager, sipped at cups of coffee while waiting for Seth in the communal reception area that he shared with two other sports agents. Pictures of illustrious sports stars were hanging on the walls and so none of the men bothered with any of the glossy magazines spread out on the low tables.

'Did Mr Meyer look after Gazza then?' Bill asked the pretty girl behind a desk as he pointed to the picture of the maestro on the wall.

'No.'

'Oh,' said Bill slightly disappointed. 'Could have been as good as any of them, that lad.'

George grunted his agreement. He still couldn't quite believe where they were sitting and what they were proposing to do. It was bloody madness. How on earth had he let Bill talk him into it? Michael had been on to them again, this time to warn them officially that what they were doing was one hundred per cent illegal. Bill looked at his watch.

'Mr Meyer, shouldn't be long now.'

'You're all right, love, no hurry. He's probably busy.'

Seth's door suddenly opened a crack and a tall athletic-looking man appeared in the doorway. Although, he still had his back to them, all three visitors from Middleton recognised him instantly. It was only Lee Bloody Robson.

Bill hopped nervously from foot to foot, grabbing at George's jacket and pointing at the doorway. 'That's Lee Robson,' Bill whispered.

'I know.'

Bill wondered what the protocol was with autographs.

Lee turned around and looked at the three men standing in front of him, staring. Unbeknownst to him, the architect of his humiliation was amongst them, the faceless person he'd imagined killing every night as he drifted off into another shallow sleep.

'Who are you lot? The bailiffs, come to turf the old sod out?' Lee joked. He could afford to joke now. The Tottenham deal had come through. He was back in the big time, and there was even a possibility that he might get a run out this Saturday against Arsenal, no less.

'Pleased to meet you, Lee. Bill Baxter, always been a fan of yours.'

'So you're the one, eh?' Everyone laughed and they all shook hands. 'If you're looking for an agent, lads, I wouldn't sign up with this one. Right old shyster,' Lee joked.

'Thank you, Lee.' Seth emerged from behind his client. 'Gentlemen, hello, I'm Seth Meyer. Thank you so much for coming down, do come in. Lee, we'll talk on the phone. Well done, lad, I told ya, didn't I?'

Seth was intrigued and bemused by Bill's proposal but equally delighted. The name thing was ingenious, and although, realistically, it was a long shot, as a betting man Seth relished just such an opportunity. Also, Ronnie was small beer for him anyway, and he wasn't too hopeful of getting him placed with another club once Middleton folded, so it was certainly worth a punt. Besides, the way in which things had picked up for him of late, Seth was feeling lucky.

'I think it's bloody brilliant,' Seth said, as he flicked through the mocked-up articles that Bruce had run off at the *Chronicle*.

'But is it ethical?' George asked.

Seth looked at him oddly. This is football mate.

'We've been advised that it isn't legal.'

Bill looked at the ceiling, but Seth didn't seem too worried.

'I wouldn't worry about that.'

'You wouldn't?'

'No, we're not telling any lies, are we?' Seth said. 'These are more extensions of the truth and, of course, a little typing error. Just can't get the secretarial staff these days.'

Bill laughed heartily. As far as he was concerned, Seth was a top bloke.

'What about the goals, though?' George insisted.

'As Bill here says, it'll be the video that gets them interested. The name, Ronaldo and the Brazilian thing will get 'em curious, but it's the video that'll do the job, and it'll be Ronnie on the video I take it?'

'Er, Ronaldo,' Bill joked.

'Oh, excuse me. It will be my Ronaldo on the video?'

'Absolutely,' Bill confirmed.

'Nothing to worry about then.'

'The action won't be in context, that's all,' Bill added.

'Well then, that'll be fine.'

'And will they buy him, just like that?' Bill asked.

'It's happened in the past but not nowadays. Clubs are very cautious. Seeing as he isn't known, they're definitely going to want to see him play.' Seth could sense Bill's disappointment. 'Eh, young Ronnie's a good lad. He'll be fine. As long as he doesn't have a 'mare. Now, has anyone discussed this with Ronnie himself?' Seth asked.

'No. We thought we should come to you first.'

'Quite right. Leave that to me. However, I do have one problem with the whole thing.'

Bill's heart sank. Just when it seemed things might be going their way.

'It's not time, is it, because—' Bill began.

'No, no, it's the fee.'

'Well, we can't pay you because—'

'No, you misunderstand.'

'Well, what then?' Bill asked.

'It's just that a million pounds – that's what you're asking for, yeah?'

Bill nodded.

'Doesn't seem realistic to me.'

'Well, we need as much as we can get because—'

'If you're going to all this trouble, making a video and doing all this stuff with the press, you should go for more.'

George nearly passed out. 'More?'

'Yeah, may as well go for two or three mill at least.'

Seth grinned greedily. George was terrified. What if he did get picked by an Italian club? After Ronnie's debut, Middleton would be crawling with men in dark glasses and black suits asking where they could find Billy Baxter and George Harris.

'Ya reckon?' Bill asked.

'Bill!' George screeched.

'Nothing to lose.' Seth smiled again. 'Good, OK then. You've got a film to make and let's hope Ronnie bangs a few in on Saturday. Leave the rest to me.'

Jeremy Davidson's face appeared on the television screen and the newsreader, Peter Sissons, took a moment before launching into the story.

'The Labour MP Jeremy Davidson, who six weeks ago caused a minor health scandal for the Government, is today involved in another scandal of a much more personal nature and one which threatens to end his political career. He stands accused by celebrity call girl Carmen, who shot to fame with her sexual revelations about the football player Lee Robson, of having sex with her while dressed as a baby. It seems a remarkable story and we can now cross to Mr Davidson's home where our political correspondent Drew Turner is. Drew . . .'

'Thank you, Peter. As you can see behind me, a whole posse of press and photographers has gathered outside the MP's home and they have been here all morning in the hope of getting a statement from Mr Davidson, or at least some sort of reaction to the stories that appeared in some of this morning's newspapers.'

'Drew, has there been any response from Mr Davidson's office?'

'No, nothing at all. Not even to deny the allegations that have been sadly laid at his door. We do believe that Mr Davidson is at home behind me, but as you can see, the curtains are drawn and it doesn't appear that he wants to make a statement at the moment.'

'Drew, can you tell us what exactly it is that Mr Davidson is accused of having done?'

The correspondent shook his head slowly. 'Well, Peter, it's a sorry tale indeed. The celebrity call girl Carmen is accusing Mr Davidson not only of being one of her ex-clients but also claims that he indulged in what is known as baby sex. Clearly, this is all very embarrassing for the MP, who was considered a high-flyer until six weeks ago, when he appeared on *Question Time*, and since that appearance everything has gone catastrophically wrong for him.'

'Thank you, Drew. I'm joined in the studio now by Dr Ditta Harman, who is the country's leading authority on sexual motivations . . .'

Unlike Jeremy, Carmen was not so camera-shy as she sat in the Thames Room at the Savoy Hotel, soaking up the incessant flashes from the gathered press photographers. She was back in the limelight where she belonged. Guy, her loyal publicist, hovered next to her, taking and interpreting the questions for his star client, making sure her best interests, not to mention his own, were being served by the assembled media. She didn't really need chaperoning, but Guy was keen to protect her from doing anything tacky and was keen also to get himself some publicity oxygen.

'Come on then, Carmen, what about it?' a photographer called out again.

It was the shot that they all wanted and had been repeatedly asking for. Carmen looked over to Guy for his expert guidance. He could sense the whole room was now waiting for him and he enjoyed the way it made him feel. Oh, what the hell . . . ? Guy nodded at his star client and Carmen popped the baby's dummy into her mouth and once again the flashlights and the whirring sound of cameras filled the room. To Guy's ears, it was like listening to Mozart.

Marcus was a deeply upset and troubled man. Conran's request for his ribs had taken him to the stress limit and dumped him out the other side. He didn't like sharing his ribs in a Chinese restaurant and so it was hardly surprising that he refused point-blank to give up any of his own. At first he'd thought that Conran might have been joking but it had soon become apparent that he wasn't. Conran had been highly disappointed with his friend's reaction, pointing out how much he'd done for Marcus in agreeing to the deal with the football club, not to mention the generosity he'd shown him over the years: the free holidays, the car loans, the use of his properties for extramarital activities.

'Yes, Conran, no question, you've been incredibly

generous, that is without doubt, but, for Christ's sake, my ribs?'

Needless to say, Marcus had returned to Manchester that night and on the train. The offer of the chauffeur had been hastily withdrawn but that had suited Marcus just fine. He didn't want to be any further in the man's debt for fear of what it might cost him.

After a two-day standoff, though, with no contact between them, Marcus had grown very concerned. Conran wasn't taking his calls and he had started to worry about the deal, which, on reflection, was more important to him than a couple of bones. He'd finally managed to get hold of Conran on his mobile but it hadn't been a pleasant conversation and certainly didn't have the outcome that Marcus had been looking for.

'. . . it's not like I've asked for your liver.'

Marcus shook his head in disbelief. Was he supposed to be grateful now?

'And, anyway, I've found out that it might not even work – me using your bone, I mean – but it hurts that you dismissed it out of hand. Like you wouldn't even consider it.'

'I'm sorry, but it was such a shock, and it's not every day—'

'So, it is still a no then . . .'

Marcus paused to think.

'. . . because I've been thinking about the club.'

'What do you mean?'

'What with all these clubs going bust, I might quite like the idea of trying to save Middleton. I used to play soccer, you know?'

It was another veiled fucking threat. Marcus felt his ribcage. God, how he hated being threatened.

'Yes, all right. Take my bloody ribs, and while you're at it, you might as well take a pound of flesh as well. Everyone else has.'

They had agreed in principle to explore the possibility at least, but Marcus would first need to satisfy himself that the operation was feasible and that the surgeon wasn't just some butcher with delusions of grandeur.

Marcus lay back on the hard bed while his GP read the blood pressure meter and finally deflated the clamp on his forearm.

'That certainly is a lot higher than I would like to see.'

Marcus was relieved to hear that there might be something wrong with him, something the doctor could at least address. He should have visited him long before now but what with his workload and man's natural reticence to admit to being stressed, he'd kept putting it off and was now paying the price. This morning, though, he had been on the phone demanding an emergency appointment because his new condition was nothing short of critical. He's woken up to find his bed full of hair – hair that when he'd fallen asleep the night before had been greying but still firmly attached to his head. He had looked in the mirror in utter disbelief. Huge clumps of hair were missing. Gingerly he touched his head and watched in horror as another clump fell down his face, and he began running about his bedroom screaming.

The doctor looked at Marcus's increasingly exposed scalp.

'I don't think this is caused by an infection. This is a psychosomatic reaction, most likely due to stress. Do you feel stressed?' the doctor asked.

Marcus just looked at him.

'Yes, I expect you are. Work OK?'

Marcus nodded slightly. No more sudden head movements for him.

'Can you think of anything that might be causing you any undue amounts of stress at the moment?'

How long have you got? 'No, not really.'

'Everything OK at home?'

'Can you make it grow back? Can you give me anything for it?'

'No, I'm afraid I can't.'

Bloody typical, Marcus thought. They've got drugs to reduce the size of veins when they're hanging out of your arse but nothing for when, one night, your fucking hair falls out.

'Will it grow back?'

'Oh yes, I would hope so.'

'You hope so?'

'Well, in most cases it does. It just depends on the individual. Now, I can give you something to bring your blood pressure down?'

'What about the hair? Is there anything at all you can give me for the hair?'

Only a hair net. 'No, I'm afraid not. Just try and relax, is the best advice I can give, although I can give you something for your nerves.'

'My nerves?'

'Yes, something to calm you down.'

'That would be good.'

'How's your sleep?'

'What sleep?'

'Right, well, that certainly won't be helping, so let's see if we can't do something about that too.'

Marcus left the surgery clutching his prescriptions and headed for the nearest pharmacy at high speed. If he got stopped by a copper, surely they'd understand that this was a life-or-death situation.

Jeremy was lonely and miserably holed up in his house with just his ringing phone and incessant doorbell to keep him company. The press were camped outside and they weren't going anywhere until they had what they wanted. Jeremy knew that he couldn't avoid them for ever; he didn't have enough food, for one thing. When he'd last shopped, he hadn't anticipated a siege. He'd gone through his cereals to the last powder bowls and was already reduced to scavenging in the back of his larder where tins lurked that hadn't seen the light of day for years.

Davina had called to explain that the story was about to break and that she wished him good luck in handling it all because she was resigning forthwith. He begged her not to but it was no use. He was all alone.

He peeped through his bedroom curtain. Outside, the press were still gathered like terriers around a rabbit warren, laughing and joking as if none of them had a care in the world. What would last longer – their resolve or his food supply? Perhaps he might starve himself to death. It certainly seemed a better alternative than leaving the house.

He couldn't see that there was any point in denying the story. He'd done enough lying already. Everything was unravelling. His trip to Israel had been called into question with no record of his journey on the dates when he'd claimed to have flown out of the country. No, the game was up. It was all over. As so many smirking columnists and television journalists had said *ad nauseam* over the last two days, his political career was in tatters.

For Jeremy that had been most apparent when his case was

brought up in the commons during PM's Questions. Jeremy had stared aghast as Mr Blair fumbled awkwardly with the odd sexual motivations of his 'honourable friend', the one he would never have to talk to again.

And an apology wouldn't suffice either. As far as most of the population was concerned, unless discussing gender, the two words 'baby' and 'sex' are mutually exclusive. He hadn't hurt anyone, but he would never be forgotten or forgiven.

Actually, this wasn't quite true either. The BMW that Molly Constantine had received in exchange for pretending to be his loving girlfriend now seemed to her paltry compensation for the indignity she was suffering. As quickly as she'd become an 'It' girl, she was now a 'twit' girl.

Jeremy's stomach rumbled loudly. He couldn't face another tin of mackerel in spicy chilli sauce, and stood in his hall ready to face the braying pack. He studied himself in his mirror and suddenly felt a sense of pride. Like a Christian about to be thrown to the lions. Pride because he hadn't done anything wrong and therefore had nothing to be ashamed of.

He took his hand off the door handle and gave himself a pep talk. Sure, his political career was over, but that didn't mean he should hang his head in shame and hide himself away. The press would get their story eventually and it had just occurred to him that he might as well make them earn it. After all, wasn't that what had motivated Carmen? Jeremy hastily retreated back to his dark lounge and picked up his mobile phone.

'Davina, hi, it's me.'

'Jeremy, please don't ask me to come back.'

'I'm not going to. If you'd listened to me in the first place, then none of this would have happened.'

His criticism hurt her. How dare he blame me? she thought.

'So, what do you want then?' You pervert freak.

'I need to get hold of one of these PR types, people who do deals with the press.'

'You're going to sell your story?'

'Yes, and why shouldn't I? It's my story and what else have I got left?'

A devious thought occurred to Davina. Her final two fingers to her old boss. 'Jeremy, hang on a second . . .'

For the first time in days, Jeremy felt a sense of relief, like a great weight had been lifted from his shoulders.

'Jeremy. There's a few people here, but the best person for you is a chap called Guy Vincent of Vincent, Handley Associates . . .'

Wednesday morning had been designated the best time to shoot the Ronaldo Mara video at the Middleton ground. Bill and George had assembled with Vippin's uncle Sunni, a few of the reserve team and a hundred or so lads from the town who would act as extras for the behind-the-goal scenes. Katherine had turned up as well with Tess, which pleased Bill, but given that she was dressed up to the nines, he had his suspicions that she was here for reasons other than to appear in the video.

Another of Ronnie's free kicks crashed into the wall again, flattening one lad from the bakery who had been coaxed along by Bill with the promise of a day off work. This was the second time that he'd been hit.

'Shit. Sorry, mate.'

'OK, OK, help him up. Ya all right, son?' Bill asked.

'Fockin' hell, Bill. Get one over, will ya?' the lad screamed at no one in particular. Nerves were fraying fast.

'OK, come on, lads, stop arguing now. Good lad, Ronnie,' Bill said, clapping his hands. 'Don't worry about it, lad, we'll get it, we'll get it. Have another go. Here, Smithy, get the bloody ball, will ya?'

Ronnie O'Mara was on a strictly need-to-know basis about his impending transfer and consequently knew nothing. He had no idea that he was now known as Ronaldo, that he was Brazilian, or that he was a bargain at possibly two million quid. It was fortunate that Ronnie was so gullible. All he'd been told was that they were shooting a promotional video of him for his agent to show to potential advertisers. That supposedly explained why Seth had encouraged him to dye his hair and plaster himself in fake tan. It would wash off, everyone assured him, but no one had actually checked.

It immediately became obvious to everyone present at the video shoot that replicating a football match wasn't an easy task. Even with Sunni in charge of proceedings, things were progressing very slowly indeed. One hour into filming and the only footage they had was the sort of stuff that only *You've Been Framed* would be willing to pay for, and they weren't going to pay enough for Middleton's currents needs. It was Vippin's suggestion that a set piece might be easier to capture on film and everyone hastily agreed. Seth had said that the video needed an impressive opening, anyway, and surely there couldn't be anything better than a thirty-five-yard screaming free kick.

'Everyone ready?' Vippin, the first assistant director, shouted with as much authority as he could muster. He stole a quick glance over at Katherine and was thrilled when she smiled back at him. '. . . And action'

The human wall braced itself as Ronnie began his short run up to take his umpteenth free kick that morning. So far, none of them had even forced a save. Most had hit the wall, gone well wide or over the bar. This one, however, did manage to clear the wall and began to dip just in time on its way towards the goal. Bill looked on hopefully as he followed its flight right into the top corner of the goal. He yelled for joy as if it were a real match. It was a screamer, an absolute beauty. Everything had been perfect apart from the reaction of the fans behind the goal and the goalkeeper himself. Indeed, none of them had reacted at all because they had become so thoroughly bored the goal had taken them all by surprise. Bill was fuming, silently waving his arms about, trying to get them to celebrate.

'Well, don't just fucking stand there. Celebrate, then.' It was all a bit late, though, and their subsequent jubilation now seemed a little forced and artificial.

'Keep rolling,' Sunnie called out. 'OK, OK, that'll do.'

'We'll have to do that again 'cos of you lot,' Bill moaned.

'No, Bill, it's OK. I can merge those shots. It will be fine,' Sunni explained, because he hadn't intended to spend his entire holiday making a video.

'But what about the keeper not moving? Bloody hell, Tommo, you could at least have tried the save the bloody thing.'

'I wasn't expecting it to come over, Bill.'

'No, don't worry, Bill, the keeper doesn't matter. He didn't react because he was so well beaten.'

Bill wasn't convinced but he was relieved that at least they now had something. It might give Ronnie an impetus for the next five goals they were hoping to film. Meanwhile, Smithy had arrived with big flasks of tea and stacks of buns and cakes.

George didn't look at all convinced by Ronnie's free kick and was about to say so.

'Don't say it, George, not unless you've got any better suggestions for raising money; don't say a word.'

George felt winded and Bill consulted his sheet with Sunni peering over his shoulder.

'Now we need Ronnie to bang in a few goals from the corners. You know, headers mostly, but if we get time, a few volleys and even an overhead kick would be great.'

Sunni frowned at him.

'All right, just headers then.'

With the rumours rife in Middleton that the council was about to approve the planning permission, Councillor O'Dowd was discovering that he was increasingly unpopular and that he had seriously misjudged the mood of the local people. He hated public meetings at the best of times but usually they were poorly attended and merely paid lip service to the idea of open government rather than functioning as a vehicle for people to have their opinions heard. This particular meeting, though, was packed and the townspeople were making their feelings resoundingly clear.

'. . . but can you confirm to us whether or not the plans are going to be approved?'

O'Dowd shook his head. 'Look, as I've said repeatedly, nothing has been decided as yet and—'

The crowd jeered loudly to register scepticism for what they obviously felt was a hollow answer.

'But if your Planning Department have already rejected the plans, why are you even considering them?'

O'Dowd pressed the tips of his fingers together and waited for the cheers to fade away before replying. It gave him time to think, at least. 'Well, first of all it is our duty to consider all plans put before council, and—'

'But we don't want them.'

'Yes, and you don't like parking restrictions and bus lanes either but they are there for the greater good,' O'Dowd sneered.

'And what greater good is being served by closing down our club?'

The room cheered again, forcing O'Dowd to shout if he wanted to be heard. '. . . and the points that the planners quite rightly objected to have already been addressed . . .' By now, O'Dowd was entirely drowned out, which suited him perfectly because he wasn't keen to finish his point anyway.

Martha tapped her microphone insistently and appealed for calm.

'Please, allow Councillor O'Dowd to finish.'

O'Dowd glared at her. He was delighted that Martha had a thing about power and, indeed, he was thoroughly enjoying their torrid affair, but on occasion, she did entirely the wrong thing.

'Does anyone have any more questions for Councillor O'Dowd?' Sean Mills asked slowly and very clearly.

It appeared that there were no other questions.

'Any other questions?' Mills asked again. O'Dowd glared at him and began to gather his files, assuming that the meeting was over.

'Yes, Mr Baxter.' Mills pointed at Bill, who had raised his hand. Bill had been biding his time.

O'Dowd's eyes narrowed. 'Yes, go on,' he huffed.

'You've agreed that the club offers a great deal to the town.'
'Yes.'

'Is, in fact, a key part of town life, and you've agreed that the loss of the club would be irrevocable.'

O'Dowd didn't appreciate being told what he had and hadn't agreed to. 'I hope your point here is more than just a sentimental one because if it isn't, then it's already been covered.'

'Sorry, I must have missed it,' Bill countered.

O'Dowd sighed. 'We the council cannot allow sentiment to play a part in business decisions.'

'Well, I think you should,' Bill answered quickly.

'Oh, you do? Well then, I suggest that you run for office.'

The room cheekily cheered the prospect of having Bill as head of their council.

'And anyway, Councillor, this isn't a business, it's a football club.'

'Which is exactly why it finds itself in such a parlous financial position today.'

'But it's more than just a football club,' Smithy yelled out from the back of the hall in support of his mate.

'Yes, although not an athletics one,' O'Dowd smiled, and was delighted that others seemed to enjoy his little joke also. In fact, O'Dowd was rather pleased at how his little debate with Middleton supporter number one was going. If he could flatten him, the others might all shut up and go home.

'I think my friend was referring to the youth team football opportunities offered by the club to hundreds of kids in the area.'

O'Dowd was about to answer Smithy, but Bill wouldn't let him.

'It's been stated in the plans that the land by the canal will be developed into a playing field for kids, but wouldn't it serve the council's purposes better to address the chronic housing shortages with this land? It wouldn't affect the traffic in the town and those hundreds of acres of brownfield site could be put to far better use than as a patch of grass for kids to run about on. Or is this land too polluted and expensive to clean up? Perhaps the developers have no intention of delivering on their promises, and this is just a scam to keep us quiet?'

The crowd burst into spontaneous applause. People looked at Bill with total admiration. What the hell was he doing working at Beatty's, and why indeed didn't he run for office?

But O'Dowd didn't appear to be too concerned by what Bill had said. It was empty and harmless rhetoric, although he didn't care for the command of the room that the bakery supervisor enjoyed.

'Yes, it might well be that the land by the canal could be developed for housing, but it is not council policy to make such suggestions and we can only advise on plans that are submitted before us.'

Bill shook his head and raised his arm once more. O'Dowd looked irritated but he gestured for him to continue.

'I'm sure that everything has been done to the letter of the law, but are you not worried that the club's land was sold for only two million pounds?'

O'Dowd didn't like the inference of Bill's words. 'Again, it is not my responsibility to determine values in commercial ventures.'

'Because surely the developed value of the land is worth a lot more than that. It's been said, perhaps twenty times as much. Doesn't it worry you that some individuals, completely unconnected with this area, will stand to make tens of millions of pounds from our club, from our town, and Middleton will be left with nothing?'

'I hardly think that a development like the one being proposed could be described as nothing.'

'What, luxury flats that none of us can afford? But that isn't my main point anyway.'

'Oh, and what is, then?'

'Do you not think that with such a huge amount of money

riding on this deal, the people taking these decisions might be influenced by it and how it might benefit them?'

O'Dowd's eyes widened. Quickly, he was out of his chair and making his way from the hall. Bill's suggestion was utterly contemptible and frankly beneath him and he wasn't going to dignify it with a response. As far as he was concerned, the meeting was over, and he left the room with howls of derision ringing in his ears.

The Radio 5 commentator was understandably very excited at the prospect of London's biggest derby match.

'Welcome to a sunny day here at Highbury on Radio Five Live, for the big London derby. Tottenham are the visitors today, but the big news is that Lee Robson is in the squad again and we've even heard that he might be starting the match.'

Lee was very nervous in the dressing room. A football cliché, granted, but this was truly a massive game for him. He had so much to prove to so many people, not least to his employers, Tottenham Hotspur PLC, who had insisted on offering Lee a pay-and-play contract, albeit with more money. Quite within their rights, they wanted Lee to demonstrate that he wasn't a commercial liability.

The atmosphere in the Tottenham dressing room before the match was tense. In normal circumstances, Lee could have expected to be ribbed mercilessly by his team-mates about what had happened to him, but on this occasion no one had dared. It was too risky. None of them wanted to get injured before the game had even started. Lee's troubles and colourful sex life were off limits then, but it was unlikely the thousands of Arsenal fans eagerly awaiting his appearance would see it that way.

A huge cheer greeted the two teams as they filed on to the pitch and peeled away to opposite ends of the stadium. Seth sat anxiously in the stand, his eyes locked on to his client, who was manically darting back and forth in order to warm himself up.

'Come on, Lee lad, you show 'em, son,' Seth breathed to himself.

They'd had a long chat before the game and discussed the inevitability that the fans would try to provoke him into losing his notorious temper. 'Focus' and 'get into the zone' had been Seth's advice to Lee. Seth had intended to get Lee seen by a sports psychologist until he found out what they charged, but he was now wishing that he had.

The Arsenal fans had never in their lives been so pleased to see a Tottenham player as they were to see Lee Robson, and beginning in the North Bank stand and making its way round the ground was a swelling rendition of 'Driving in my Car' by Madness. The lyrics had been adjusted accordingly, but no one was worried about copyright.

'I like driving in my car . . . it's not much and it ain't been far.'

Seth tensed up immediately, as soon as the little ditty reached his hypersensitive ears. It was soon unmistakable, many thousands of people were taking the piss out of his volcanic client. Seth prayed that Lee was already in his calm zone and that it had thick walls.

'Well, *we talked about this happening in the build-up, but it seems . . . actually it's quite funny, but the Arsenal fans are singing to Lee Robson "Driving in my Car". Now I just hope that Lee Robson will be able to ignore this . . .*'

Despite the array of sporting stars on the pitch, the television cameras were focused solely on one player. So far, so good. Lee put his head down and launched himself into a rampant and impressive burst of sprinting about the centre circle.

'Good lad, Lee. Ignore the bastards,' Seth urged quietly from a few hundred feet away.

The Arsenal DJ in the stadium took it upon himself to help things along and so for the first time since 1979, Highbury was treated to the Gary Numan classic 'Cars', much to the hilarity of everyone in the ground. Even the Tottenham fans conceded that it was quite funny. Lee, though, was a picture of concentration, leaping into the air and simulating the headed goals he was going to smash into the Arsenal net. That's shut the cunts up. Gary Numan isn't famous for his complicated lyrics and so even those in the ground too young to remember the song had got the hang of the words fairly quickly and by the time Gary had reached his second chorus, Highbury was like the biggest Gary Numan concert of all time.

'Here in my car, I feel safest of all, I can drive anywhere, 'cos I only want to be' and this was the point that at least thirty thousand people screamed at the top of their voices . . . "IN CARS".'

By now, Lee's concentration zone had cracks everywhere. Seth looked on in trepidation as Lee began for the first time looking directly into the offending stands.

'Please, no, Lee, don't do it.'

But it was too late. Lee began to snarl as he approached the North Bank End of Highbury with his fists clenched.

'Someone stop him,' Seth called out, but Lee was running now and stopped about five feet in front of the stand where he proceeded to wave his two fingers while mouthing slowly and clearly that they could all 'FUCK OFF'. The fans screamed their delight. Other than seeing their own team score, getting a rise out of an opposing team's player is the most fun football fans can ever have. Now sanctimonious jeers and boos echoed around the stadium as Lee began spinning around on the spot flicking the Vs at the entire stadium.

'This is what I was worried about. Lee Robson will have to be careful here, because the referee has seen it. I say the referee has seen it, how could he not? Robson's gesturing at the whole stadium.'

Seth held his head in his hands as the referee produced a yellow card. Lee had been booked and the game hadn't even started yet. What were the odds on him now completing even the first half?

The match kicked off without further incident and for the first five minutes or so it seemed that Lee might be left alone by the fans, but his first touch of the ball quickly put paid to that. Football fans might appear unruly but they can co-ordinate their efforts with military precision, and as soon as Lee touched the ball, 'BEEP BEEP' rang out around the ground. It wasn't long before the spectators wanted Lee Robson to get the ball because he was providing more entertainment than the game itself. This put Lee in an invidious position: he needed to get the ball, and yet when he did he was driven nearly blind with fury as 'BEEP BEEP' resonated in his ears. He began wandering out of position to retrieve the ball and eventually picked it up just outside the centre circle and started a run. The fans were ecstatic, a Robson dribble was just what they wanted and every yard he progressed, the 'BEEP BEEPS' got louder. It seemed even the Arsenal defence were finding it funny because they appeared unable to halt his progress.

'This is good football by Robson. He's beaten two players

and he's still going, and so, might I add, are the fans. Still Robson, he's thirty-five yards out and he shoots and . . . oh he's hit the bar. That was a magnificent strike . . .'

With the excitement of nearly scoring a wonder goal, a dose of pure adrenalin coursed through Lee's bloodstream, running red lights and making straight for his brain. When it arrived in his head, some kind of chemical fusion must have taken place because it caused Lee to lose whatever grip he still had on reality. A dark and malevolent force from within had now assumed control. Lee didn't hear the warm applause from all around the ground that his effort had brought. Instead he just wanted to ram his effort down the necks of all those who had dared to ridicule him. And so he continued his run on past the Arsenal goal and proceeded to scream obscenities at the fans, and then began beckoning them all to a fight, the way lads in Ben Sherman shirts do outside pubs to impress the female of the species. Football violence has long blighted the national game but in living memory, never has an entire stand of fans ever been threatened by a lone individual, let alone a player. The referee was on his way over, his hand already fumbling on his breast pocket. Two Tottenham players got there ahead of him and began trying to restrain their team-mate, but it was way beyond them. Lee was in a zone, all right: he was in a fury zone. Seth watched in horror as Lee began grappling with his own players who, if they could have spoken English, would have probably been saying 'Leave it, Lee. It ain't worth it.'

'These are quite extraordinary scenes here at Highbury. The referee is in there, all the Tottenham players and half the Arsenal players. Fans are over there too, trying to restrain Lee Robson who's already been sent off, but who's going to get him off the pitch? Oh, I say, a Tottenham player has gone

down clutching his face. I think Robson has hit him. I couldn't be sure of that but I do believe that Lee Robson has hit and injured one of his own team-mates.'

Seth stood up in sheer horror. His star client was being wrestled and pinned to the ground by most of the players on the pitch while a few policemen fluttered about and waved on the St Johns Ambulance crew to bring on a stretcher. One thing was beyond doubt, from the crowd's perspective: Lee was worth every penny of his pay-and-play fee. Sheer entertainment.

'In all my years as a commentator, I have never seen scenes quite like it, not even in South America. What a terrible sight. Lee Robson has been strapped to a stretcher because he wouldn't calm down and is being carried from the pitch by eight policemen. Here's one for John Motson: is Lee Robson the first player ever to be carried from the pitch who hasn't been injured?'

CHAPTER 19

The protracted and bizarre consequences of Bill's jam-less doughnut were once again dominating the newspapers, but this time on both front and back pages. Jeremy's decision to stand down as an MP was on the front and Lee's sacking from Tottenham on the back. It was a great day to be a newspaper editor.

Bill scanned his paper in Ernie's shop and shook his head in dismay.

'Did you see the game last night on telly?' Ernie asked.

Bill nodded, still looking at the picture of Lee being carried off the pitch.

'Unbelievable,' Bill said. 'I met him last week, you know. He looked fine, as well.'

'Inner rage they reckon.'

Bill tutted. 'What's he got to rage about, eh?'

'Never mind Lee Robson, what about the lad on the front?'

Bill turned the paper over to see a picture of Jeremy Davidson mocked up in a nappy.

'He gets bloody breast-fed, Bill.'

'Oh, don't, please. I've already heard about it on the radio.'

'These people, they have all this success – him an MP and him a footballer – and they go and do this sort of thing. What's the world coming to, Bill?'

It was too early in the morning and too big a question for

Bill to even consider answering but he wouldn't have known where to start. Lee Robson and this MP fellah, they lived a world apart from him, far removed from his simple life and, looking at the newspapers, Bill was grateful for it. He scanned the *Chronicle* too, which still led with the story of the town's football club and its impending closure. Inside were the results of a town survey commissioned by the paper, which showed eighty-four per cent of residents had expressed a resounding 'NO' to the plans.

'That's good, isn't it, Bill?'

'I don't know. Makes me wonder . . .'

'About what?'

'Who these other sixteen per cent are,' Bill laughed, as he made for the door.

Later that morning, O'Dowd didn't find the *Chronicle*'s leader quite so amusing and, after skimming the text, he hurled the paper across his kitchen. The copy didn't reflect him in a particularly good light and even suggested that he had ducked the questions in the public meeting last week. The deal was going to go through – he'd made sure of that – but he was now worried by the passionate opposition to the plans and how the fallout might affect him. Last night he'd been enjoying a curry in the New Delhi Restaurant, where he'd been eating for years, and a new waiter had served him warm lager, and stale poppadoms and then had the gall to challenge him about what a loss the club would be to the town. Indians don't even like football, O'Dowd had scowled to himself as he paid his bill without leaving a tip. It will die down eventually he assured himself. As soon as the development goes up and perhaps a Marks and Spencer hits town, everyone will have forgotten the bloody club.

He anxiously ran through the schedule in his head. The planning permission was due to be signed off on 15 April, a month before the end of the football season and therefore awful timing and a ridiculous notion. He didn't want to imagine the ill-feeling that would be levelled against him if Middleton were doomed even before their season had ended. It would be the ultimate humiliation for the town and the club, and one for which he might never be forgiven. It was out of the question: planning permission wouldn't be granted until the football season was over. O'Dowd immediately felt cheered by his decision and he would make sure that the *Chronicle* knew the delay had been his idea. It would seem as though he was listening to the people and that he was trying to do all he could. The cushion O'Dowd was aiming to land on had been plumped up a little, but he still felt there was more that he could do and he just had to keep looking.

Lee too was perusing the morning papers beneath the glare of his furious agent. The only good news so far was that the first inspection of the video footage had been inconclusive and it was unlikely that Lee was going to face another assault charge. However, Lee would almost certainly face an FA enquiry now, and Seth expected a huge fine at the very least.

But there were other more pressing worries for Seth at the moment. Shortly after the Arsenal game, which finished nil-nil – not that anyone had noticed – Tottenham announced curtly that Lee had played his last game for the club, which incidentally they were also refusing to pay him for.

'Well done, Lee. Good work yesterday. Remember we talked about the zone. How you were going to ignore the fans,' Seth hissed, his temper rumbling beneath the surface like molten lava looking for an opening.

'I know. I just lost it, didn't I?'

'Yes, you fucking did,' Seth screamed, lava spraying everywhere. 'Everyone saw that, Lee. You're all over the fucking telly and, once again, not for kicking a fucking football.'

'Yeah, alright, calm down.'

'Calm down? Calm down?' It would be a long time before Seth calmed down – if ever, in fact.

'It's no good, Lee, if you, a football player, can't play bloody football. No one's going to pay you for nothing.'

'I'll get another club.'

'Will you? And what about in the meantime? I've just spoken to your insurance company and they're refusing to pay out any more. It seems they don't cover psychosis.' This was a timely piece of inspiration on Seth's part and at least got him off one of the financial hooks he'd been dangling from. It had an immediate calming effect on him, despite his gambling debts and the fact that Lee wasn't earning and might never do so again. It was highly likely that Lee was finished and so Seth had to look elsewhere in his stable for a lifeline. Thank God for Ronnie O'Mara – or Ronaldo, as Seth now liked to call him.

Michael Abbott's desk intercom bleeped. He didn't have a meeting scheduled and so he figured this was an offer of coffee.

'Michael, Bill Baxter and a friend of his are here to see you.' Michael groaned.

Bill entered with his customary smile and Michael shook his hand warmly. Bill's enthusiasm was infectious but not when it involved him breaking the law.

'Michael, do you know young Harry here? Manager at the NatWest in Altrincham.'

'Assistant manager.'

'Yeah, whatever.'

'So, Bill, what now, stealing the crown jewels?' Michael half joked.

'Need some advice.'

'Don't bend over in the showers.'

'It's about the O'Mara thing.'

'Yes?'

'If it goes through but we still have a shortfall, we'll need to raise the money ourselves. And how long will we have?'

Michael sighed. 'How the money is raised isn't important, just so long as it's within the law.'

'And what about timing, then?'

'I'll have to check the documents again. May, I think. By the way, Bill, I haven't heard back from the Thorpe brothers yet.'

'What about any of the other companies?'

Michael shook his head. In truth, he hadn't bothered to write any letters. Not because he was lazy or didn't care about the club, but he hadn't known where to start and he wasn't comfortable with discussing some of the things that Bill was proposing.

'Harry here is working on some sort of loan for us,' Bill announced.

Harry looked more than a little awkward and immediately, Michael was concerned.

'Bill, tell me you're not hoping to secure any joint loans to purchase the club.'

Harry gritted his teeth. This was exactly what Bill had in mind. Harry's boss had been understandably unenthusiastic when Harry had raised the prospect of offering a loan to a co-operative of individuals to buy a football club in the current climate, particularly one saddled with huge debts and a paltry income, but Harry hadn't told Bill yet. He didn't have the heart.

'So, will you represent us if things do move ahead?' Bill asked.

'No, absolutely not.'

'Oh, come on, Michael. The ground's worth millions and we'll be getting it for a song,' Bill beamed.

Michael was flummoxed by Bill's sheer brass neck. Losing the club would be terrible but a greater tragedy would be if a few of his mates lost their liberty into the bargain.

'I'll give you legal advice, Bill, but that's it.'

Bill smiled. That was as good as a yes. Everything was coming together perfectly.

O'Dowd scanned the crowd around him before opening the door of Marcus's wife's old Mercedes and creeping in. They were meeting in the G-Mex multistorey car park. No swanky London hotel this time and they would probably be splitting the cost of the parking ticket. O'Dowd looked across at Marcus and, for a second, thought he might have got into the wrong car. But it was Marcus, all right, and looking at the state of him cheered O'Dowd up no end. Where had the handsome, athletic young-looking man disappeared to? Who was this bald bloke? O'Dowd's eyes were drawn upwards by reflex to Marcus's shiny dome. He couldn't help it.

'Don't ask. It's stress, fucking stress, which you haven't helped with.'

O'Dowd tried to look sympathetic but he wasn't sure that he'd managed it.

'Bloody girlfriend's gone and dumped me.'

'I thought you were married.'

'So? Anyway, I haven't got much time. What is it you want?' Marcus fumbled with a packet of cigarettes and quickly lit one with his trembling hand.

'I thought you were trying to give up,' O'Dowd said before he realised how facile he sounded. Marcus sucked furiously on the fag. This was a man who was suffering and now even O'Dowd felt a tinge of guilt because he was about to ask for more from a man who clearly had already given so much.

'Don't tell me you've got anything other than good news,' Marcus said, the smoke finally escaping with each word.

O'Dowd shook his head and gestured that he wasn't the bearer of any such thing. 'No, no, everything's fine.'

'You've had the plans back from the planners?'

'Yep, everything is going through.'

'Well, what then?'

'It seems I underestimated the feeling and strength of opposition to—'

Marcus smashed his fists on to the steering wheel and turned, snarling at O'Dowd. 'You greedy little fucker, do you remember what I said—'

'It's not that. I'm not making any more demands.' O'Dowd was now genuinely scared of his fellow Masonic brother and worried what he might do to him. They were alone in the car park and no one would see if he was hurled from the top of it. O'Dowd even considered abandoning his plans to ask for a month's extension. Facing the wrath of the town might be safer than facing Marcus.

'It's not going to affect the deal.'

'Well, what then?' Marcus appeared to calm down a little

at least, sufficient for O'Dowd to summon the courage to continue. Why should he become a pariah in his own back yard?

'There is an issue with timing, that's all.'

'It has to be this season.'

O'Dowd held up his hand. 'Precisely. This season. We have to give the fans their last complete season with the club.'

Marcus was immediately dismissive. 'Bollocks. Who gives a shit what they think?'

Me, I do, O'Dowd thought, but he didn't bother admitting as much.

'We have to be careful here, Marcus. The last thing we want is for them to take their appeal to the high court.'

'They won't do that. They can't afford to, especially after Spelthorne have bought it. They're not going to go up against a big PLC in court,' Marcus scoffed.

'But is that a gamble you want to take?'

'Yes, I think it is. I'll have sold it by then; it won't be my problem.'

O'Dowd wasn't making any headway and decided he needed to up the ante somewhat. 'Terrible PR for them, though. Spelthorne won't be happy with you.'

Marcus hated PR, always had. A non-profession if ever there was one.

'So what are you suggesting?'

'That we delay it for four weeks. Just until the end of the season. Same result, but we avoid any unnecessary nastiness. Everything can go through clean as a whistle.'

'You mean, you do.'

'Come on, look, it would be folly to shut them down with only four games to go. There'd be an outcry.'

Marcus blew out his hollow cheeks. Another month? With

all that he'd been through lately, another month wasn't going to kill him.

'And, there is one more thing . . .' This was going to be the hard bit. It had become clear to O'Dowd what the icing on the cake needed to be. If Middleton FC could get themselves relegated from the English Third Division, then this would make his decision to approve the planning permission on the land seem almost logical, or at least a little less callous. '. . . it would be much better all round if Middleton could also get relegated this season.'

'Why?'

'Again, it's politics. It just helps to smooth the passage. They go out of the league, you and Spelthorne look like you're doing the right thing.'

'Yeah, but what the hell can I do about them getting relegated?'

'Look, they probably will be anyway. I think they're second bottom at the moment, but if you could shove them in that direction . . .'

'What? How?'

O'Dowd shifted awkwardly. 'You know, encourage them to lose. Perhaps make it worth their while.'

Marcus held up a finger that was shaking with either nerves or fury, but probably a mixture of both. 'This deal is not costing me anything more.' His finger was now pointing at his bald head. 'Anyway, why don't you pay 'em off? You're the one who stands to gain.'

'Well, it would hardly look very good coming from me, would it?' O'Dowd answered.

'And anyway, Middleton aren't going to start throwing games. You said it yourself, how bloody proud they are.'

O'Dowd was worried by Marcus's obstinacy. 'Yes, the

club's proud, the morons supporting them are proud, but not the players. They just want the money.'

'Well, then, you sort it out.' Marcus glared at him. Here was a man who'd been pushed too far already and O'Dowd knew when to back off. For now at least.

CHAPTER 20

In the club bar, a crowd of nervous men huddled around a television for the first screening of *Ronaldo Mara: The Glory Year*, shot entirely on location at Middleton Edwardians Football Club. Seth was among them, having made his first trip to the club in honour of the screening. So much hinged on this short video – namely, Seth's life and the future of the football club – and, understandably, everyone in the room was anxious.

Vippin started the video and stood back a pace. It began with the Ronaldo free kick, the ball screaming thirty yards over the wall and past a hopelessly stranded keeper. Surely, no one could fail to be impressed by the beauty of its precision and power. Even the people watching the video were mightily impressed and they knew exactly how many times it had taken to get right. Other angles followed of the same wonder shot. Here was a football genius at work.

In fact, the real genius on display belonged to Sunni, Vippin's uncle. Surely Hollywood beckoned, because given what he'd had to work with, the end result was miraculous. The three-minute video wasn't altogether a work of fiction either. Of Ronnie's nine genuine goals this season, Sunni had decided that three were worth using and they were interspersed with a whole range of shots of Ronaldo magic that were less reflective of the lad's genuine ability. Vippin pushed the stop button when the tape had run its course and instantly the room erupted into applause.

'Bloody hell, who is that lad? 'Cos we want him,' Bill shouted, much to everyone's amusement. They were all delighted with what had been produced. Even George seemed to have been won over, and both he and Bill gave Vippin warm thanks to pass on to Sunni.

Thankfully, Seth too was equally delighted, awestruck even at how good his client was. The painful demise of Lee Robson was already forgotten.

'You've done a great job, lads. I'm impressed, I'm really impressed.'

'What'll we do now then?'

'Well, I've spoken to a few continental agents, sent over the cuttings and what have you, and so far not a lot has happened. It seems the Spanish clubs aren't looking at the moment but I still reckon Italy's the best possibility and this video's really going to help.'

'But aren't they even more bankrupt than us?' George asked. It hadn't taken long for his cynicism to resurface.

'Yes, they are, which is why they're on the lookout for bargains like our Brazilian genius here.'

George looked nervous. He hoped it wouldn't be a Milan or a Roma because Ronnie wouldn't last a training session with a big club without being found out.

'It's all done through agents nowadays. They'll know who's looking for what and how much people have got.'

'And then they'll come over to see him?' George asked.

'Yeah, but they won't necessarily be expecting goals like that.'

Good job, Bill thought.

'Hey, George, don't look so worried,' Seth continued. 'Stranger things have happened in football.'

'Let's hope so.'

Seth retrieved the video cassette from the machine and Vippin handed him another five copies.

'Seth, how's Lee Robson?' Bill asked. It was question everyone had been itching to ask all morning.

'Lee who?' Seth joked. 'Not too good. Shall we leave it at that? I really don't want to talk about it. I'm much happier trying to offload my Brazilian maestro here.'

Four days later, Middleton were playing a midweek fixture away at Peterborough United and it seemed that somehow young Ronnie knew that the club's dreams of survival were pinned on him. Perhaps his confidence was high, having seen his own video, or perhaps he just subconsciously knew what was needed from him, but his two goals couldn't have been more timely in boosting his value and securing three vital points for his struggling club. The win was welcome, if a little late in the season, but Bill was far happier in the knowledge that the scorer's name would be splashed large in the *Chronicle*. According to Ceefax, neither of his goals was spectacular, but that didn't matter. They were goals none the less, and much-needed currency that Bill was hoping could be exchanged for many, many millions of euros.

Bill settled back into his armchair, having just attended to Tess, who had been having one of her nightmares. Katherine was out again and Mary had gone to Bingo, leaving Bill on double baby-sitting duty.

All along, Bill hadn't really thought that the scam would actually work. It was the stuff of movies, a longer shot, in fact, than that free kick that opened the video. But the video did look bloody convincing and Seth had said himself that he felt confident, and now with Ronnie banging in two goals, his first double of the season, Bill was beginning to wonder what might come of their efforts.

The following day, O'Dowd was less heartened by the Peterborough result. He'd read that it was Middleton's first away win all bloody season and was furious with the timing of it all. He could see the horrendous scenario playing out before him in not-so-glorious Technicolor. The team somehow manage to avoid relegation with the whole town rallied behind them and he, the devil incarnate, steps in to seal their fate.

He studied the Division Three league table and roughly calculated the implications of Middleton's win on their position. By his calculation, Middleton remained second from bottom and, with three games to go, he worked out that they would have to win at least two of them. He cast an anxious eye over their season's form and assured himself that he needn't worry. Including the Peterborough game, they'd only won eight games all season. Darwin was right. Survival of the fittest was being played out and nature was taking its course.

Bill got home from work early and so was in a good mood.

'Mary, you in love?'

'She's upstairs, Dad.'

'Bloody hell, Katherine, I didn't recognise you, love.'

'Ya what?'

'I haven't seen you in ages,' Bill joked. He was referring to her numerous nights out of late with an, as yet, unnamed boyfriend and it seemed that tonight she was heading out again.

'You're not going out again, are ya?' he teased her. She decided it was best to ignore him.

Just then, Mary appeared in the living room, holding Tom, who was wearing the cardigan that she had finally finished knitting for him. Tom was very upset about something and Bill wanted to suggest that he might be protesting about the cardigan, but he didn't.

'It looks great on him, Mary.' Bill picked the child out of Mary's arms.

Mary also now doubted the colour of the cardie and, indeed, was wondering whether it had all been worth her effort.

'Bit warm for him now, though, int it?' Mary complained.

'Don't matter. It's plenty big enough for him; it'll last until next year.'

Tom suddenly puked up whatever Mary had given him for his tea.

'Or maybe not. Come here, lad. He'll make a perfect student, this one. Hey, Mary, plan ahead, love; get going on his university scarf.' Bill began taking off Tom's wet cardigan, in a deliberately cumbersome fashion in the hope that Mary might relieve him of the duty.

'Oh, Bill, you're useless. Give him here.'

Perfect. No sooner had Bill sat down than the doorbell rang and he shot up in a flash.

'I'll get that.'

'Bill, leave it.'

He winked at Mary mischievously before disappearing into the hall and just made it to the door ahead of a fast-approaching Katherine.

'Come in, Vippin lad,' Bill beamed. 'I thought as much. you're a dark horse, aren't ya?'

'Dad,' Katherine shouted. Vippin was equally embarrassed.

'Well, come in then, lad.'

'No, Dad, we're going straight out.'

'Bill, let them go.' Mary now squeezed herself into the doorway too, to get a look at Vippin as much as anything else. 'Hello, love.'

'Hello, Mrs Baxter.'

Mary was impressed. Handsome and polite.

'Hey, Katherine, you're doing well here. Champion pole vaulter, our Vippin.'

Vippin laughed but Katherine wasn't so amused as she pushed past her dad.

''Ere, Bill, good result at Peterborough or what?'

Bill was delighted that Vippin even knew the team had played.

'Did you go?' Vippin asked.

'No, working, weren't I?'

'Hey, and good for Ronnie getting two goals as well. Have you heard from wossisname?'

'No, not yet. So? Where are you two lovebirds going, then?'

'Dad!' Katherine screeched.

'Just out,' Vippin said shyly.

'Just out. Blimey, Vippin lad, you really know how to spoil a girl.'

As Vippin had predicted when they first met, Beatty's was only ever going to be a temporary job for him and, true to his word, he'd left the bakery a few weeks ago. Bill had been sad to see him go but pleased for the lad as well. Even if the video scam did fail, it wouldn't be a complete waste of time because Vippin was now hellbent on a career in television. He was even talking about going back to college. Who knew, he might even make it. Bill hoped so. He didn't want to see the lad spend his entire life in a bakery like he had. And he would need a good job anyway if this fledgeling romance with his daughter was going to blossom.

'Speaking of work, Bill, how's Beatty's?'

'Same old, same old. I haven't been on doughnuts since we met, though.'

Vippin laughed. 'Good job.'

'What about you – are you working?'

'Just at me uncle's restaurant for some beer money. You know, the New Delhi.'

'Oh, I'll have to pop in.'

'Yeah, do that. Oh, and I'm coming to the last game of the season.'

Bill sighed. 'What about Southend this Wednesday?'

'Is it a home game?' Vippin asked.

'Yeah.'

Katherine decided that she needed to take control of this situation. She pushed Vippin further into the street and followed him.

'Vippin, for God's sake, don't get him started on the Club. You're supposed to be taking me out.'

Bill laughed. 'Have a nice time, and, eh, Vippin, you have her back by half-past eleven now, please.'

Jeremy Davidson was finally absent from the front pages of the newspapers and was having to get used to the idea of long lonely years in obscurity. It wasn't a prospect he was looking forward to. His doctor had upped his dose of tranquillisers and he was getting through them like a box of chocolate raisins.

He sat in a ridiculously uncomfortable chair in Guy

Vincent's office. Guy had been wary when Jeremy had first approached him to handle his PR, but was soon delighted to welcome him to his illustrious client list. Jeremy didn't much care for Guy, but reasoned to himself that he was probably no worse than any other of his breed. It had, of course, been Davina's little joke putting them together and he hoped that she had enjoyed it.

Ever ambitious, Guy was now proposing something altogether different and much bigger than usual. He was asking Jeremy to take a big leap of faith with him on to the domestic C-list of celebritydom. Jeremy, though, didn't seem convinced or excited by Guy's proposition.

'For God's sake, Guy, a few weeks ago, I was a serious politician with a cabinet future.'

'And you've said it yourself, that is a career door that has now closed. But, as always, other, bigger doors are opening for you. This is something you'll be great at and think about the two fingers you'd be giving to the world, all those people who've been laughing at you.'

Jeremy didn't need to work – his trust fund made sure of that – and he was quite tempted by the glamour of what Guy had in mind. Besides, it would be a great way of getting his own back.

'And she's definitely interested?' Jeremy asked.

'Are you kidding? Of course she is. I've had two meetings with them and I can tell you now, they think it's a fantastic idea. Honestly, it's a green light. They just need you on board.'

Jeremy sighed. This bloke was a walking, talking cliché and yet it was he that Jeremy was now depending on for his future. How much lower could things sink?

Guy, though, could sense that Jeremy was slowly coming

round to the idea. This had been the most magnificent year of his professional life and if he could pull this off, he might as well retire.

Until the FA hearing, Lee Robson was a player Seth literally couldn't give away. Press speculation was rife about how lengthy a ban Lee could expect and some quarters were even calling for him to be banned for an entire season. It was hardly surprising, then, that Lee looked thoroughly miserable slumped in Seth's office. It was very late in the evening and Lee had popped in unannounced from a shopping trip that he could ill afford and that hadn't managed to cheer him up anyway.

Seth retrieved a sheet of paper from his printer and handed it to Lee for his signature.

'What's this?'

'It's your letter of apology to Tottenham.'

Lee discarded it immediately without saying anything and the letter floated wistfully on to the parquet floor.

Seth grimaced and tried to stare down his irksome client. 'Right fine, don't sign it.'

'I won't,' Lee said defiantly.

'OK then, don't. If playing football really means so little to you, because contrition is now the only thing between you and a ban.' Seth pointed his well-chewed Bic pen at Lee.

'Fine.'

'Fine,' Seth agreed. A stalemate then of infantile proportions.

Predictably, Lee was the first to buckle. Reluctantly, he retrieved the letter and began reading it. It was sickly apologetic and verbose and he couldn't have been more than halfway through before he got bored.

'Pen.'

Seth handed over his Bic. Like a juvenile, Lee scrawled his signature deliberately messily, as though he was making some kind of point. It wasn't lost on Seth that Lee hadn't actually read the letter and it occurred to him that he could probably get his client to sign a very useful contractual waiver if ever his debts threatened to consume him entirely.

'So, no clubs. What, none at all?' Lee pleaded, still unable to believe his status as unemployed football star.

Seth didn't bother to answer him. What was the point? The phone hadn't rung since Lee had been in his office, and so the answer was obviously still no.

'This is ridiculous. What no one?'

Seth nodded, and perversely found himself quite enjoying the moment.

'What am I going to live on?'

I don't know, sell some of your home movie rights, Seth wanted to suggest. He was tired of Lee now and wanted him to leave.

'Lee, I'm doing all I can to get you placed, hopefully with a club over the closed season, but I can't do it with you in my face.'

Lee still didn't know what he meant.

'Lee,' Seth implored, 'I've got calls to make.'

Urgently, Lee jumped to his feet. 'One thing, though: I ain't playing for a shitty club.'

You might have to, my old son. Lee gathered his bags of hideously expensive clothes and finally left the office. What a blessed relief. The call Seth desperately needed to make didn't concern Lee. An Italian agent had made contact since receiving the Ronaldo video. The first bite, Seth hoped. Inevitably though, Lee reappeared in his doorway.

'Lee, I'm on the phone.' Seth slammed the receiver down dramatically.

'Yeah, yeah. I wanted to ask you about those adverts.'

'Which adverts?' Seth stalled.

'What d'you mean, which ones? The Ford ones. The ones they ain't paid me for.'

Seth froze. 'Yeah, yeah, I'm on to that.'

'Well, you wanna be. I bet they wouldn't say no to me. Actually, that ain't a bad idea. Give us the number and I'll call 'em meself.'

Seth stood up in alarm. 'No, absolutely not.' He approached Lee, gesturing with his arms that he should leave.

'But if you're so busy . . .' Lee protested.

'Lee, given your recent display of personnel skills, I'll handle it, thank you. Now, come on, it's late. I'll call you in the morning.'

No sooner had his office door shut, than Seth was flicking his remote control to find the Middleton score on Teletext, hoping his little gold mine Ronaldo might have notched up his value with another goal or two.

'Come on, come on,' Seth urged the Teletext pages on.

'Shit.'

It was half-time and Middleton were already two-nil down.

O'Dowd was now in a much better mood, sitting comfortably in his office listening to the delightful radio commentary of the Middleton match being played out not four hundred yards from his office. O'Dowd was highly excited at the prospect that in forty-five minutes' time, it would be almost mathematically impossible for Middleton to remain in the

English football league. Relegation would be a near certainty and his plans a formality.

O'Dowd had screamed himself hoarse when Southend scored their second goal; never before had the Essex seaside town meant so much to him. During half time, he'd poured himself a large vintage brandy and had stubbornly considered the pile of paper that had been stacked neatly on his desk. It was the petition against Table Top's plans and was screaming for his attention, but O'Dowd hadn't bothered to look at it since it had been delivered. He'd long stopped opening his own mail and had instructed his staff to filter out any letters concerning the club. Now, though, feeling more confident, curiosity got the better of him and he casually sauntered over and picked up the top sheet.

'We, the undersigned, passionately oppose the planning proposals Q6102562 to close down Middleton Football Club and to develop the club and its surrounding land.'

The first of the twenty thousand signatures was Bill Baxter's, and O'Dowd sneered as he flicked through the wads of paper.

'What a waste of perfectly good trees,' he mumbled to himself, as he turned up the volume on his radio a notch for the start of the second half.

O'Dowd opened his window. In the distance, he could see the dilapidated Middleton stadium lit up by floodlights. He felt a slight pang of guilt, but it didn't last long. The ground was an eyesore anyway, and was about to fall down of its own volition, with or without his decision. Either way, it was a site that wouldn't blot his successor's view. He or she, but most likely he, would be able to peer down upon a multi-million-pound residential and retail park, a worthy legacy to his tenure in office, while soon he, O'Dowd himself, would be enjoying views of the Atlantic Ocean. His nostrils flared as he breathed in the evening air. This should all have been over by now, he thought as he drained his brandy. The team's struggle to avoid relegation had become inextricably linked with the survival of the club itself. It wouldn't make a jot of difference, but he didn't like the challenge that would almost certainly be laid at his door if the blasted team were to survive.

The whistle blew to get the second half underway and O'Dowd could hear a roar, the pointless energy of thousands of people urging their team on. He resented the whole town for the way it was making him work so damn hard for his retirement. Wasn't thirty-five years of service enough? Still, it seemed tonight that their fight might finally be wrung out of them. He looked at his watch. In a little over twenty minutes, Middleton Edwardians FC would be facing oblivion, and from there it was all downhill.

O'Dowd's self-satisfied grin was suddenly wiped from his face by a huge roar from the Middleton ground. He didn't need the radio commentary to know what had just happened. It was perfectly obvious that Middleton must have scored. The radio confirmed the bad news and O'Dowd paced his office nervously, frequently looking at his watch. They were still losing, everything was under control and so he didn't need to panic, but in that case, why *was* he?

'Come on, Southend, come on,' O'Dowd bellowed, almost to counter the frenzied and sustained volume urging Middleton to find the all-important equaliser. Even in the sanctuary of his own office, O'Dowd could feel the fans' fervour, and it was having far more effect than the petition they'd all signed. In more ordinary circumstances, O'Dowd would have been proud of such passion and might even have wanted to be a part of it. At the moment, though, from his perspective it wasn't awesome, it was bloody terrifying.

Middleton's team surged forward once again as the crowd roared unstinting support; players and fans were feeding off each other's energy. The stadium was draped with various banners and flags stating opposition to the plans such as 'Middleton, Here For Ever' and 'Middleton, Going Nowhere'. As it had been at the previous four or five home games, the ground was packed, and Bill couldn't ever remember it being as tense. The large clock at the Thorpe end began to dominate Bill's view of the pitch. Morris forced a corner and the crowd, becoming increasingly desperate, reacted as if Middleton had been awarded a penalty. Hysterically the entire ground launched into an old favourite of a football chant: 'Come on, Middleton. Come on, Middleton . . .' Hardly the work of a genius lyricist but effective and inspirational stuff all the same. Morris held his two arms aloft as he was about to take the corner and everyone hoped that meant he was about to produce something special. Bill bit his bottom lip as he followed the ball's flight into the penalty area. Southend's keeper parried it away with his fist but the ball bounced awkwardly on the edge of the area and O'Mara came charging down on the ball.

Ronnie didn't wait for the ball to bounce. He hit instinctively, the way only players worth millions of pounds seem to. The ball screamed back into the penalty area and ripped into the top right-hand corner of the goal, making a mockery of Ronnie's video performance, which surely now would need re-editing. It was a wonder goal, and the crowd was delirious.

Bill couldn't take it all in at first. They'd equalised. They'd salvaged a point. They were still alive. If they won their last two games they'd be safe and, what's more, Ronnie had scored again.

As the fans filed out of the ground, the pubs on Middleton High Street filled up with people debating the club's chances of avoiding the drop. Bill stood outside the club bar, trying to make himself heard as he spoke to Seth on his mobile phone. Passing fans continually congratulated him as though he'd scored the equaliser himself. Bill had thought that he was calling Seth with good news but it paled in comparison with Seth's announcement that an Italian agent was interested.

'That's unbelievable. I can't believe it, it's fantastic,' Bill squealed with delight.

'And he scored tonight?' Seth asked, although he already knew the answer. Seth was just pleased to be able to make somebody feel happy for a change.

'Yeah, it was an absolute screamer.'

'So I heard. I'm gonna tape it off cable tonight and send it straight out to the agent,' Seth explained.

'I'm starting to think that this might actually happen,' Bill said hopefully.

'Well, we'll see. I'm speaking to the agent again tomorrow. Can you fax me the match report? And make sure your lad plays him up a little. Nothing too much, like he did before.'

'And you reckon the deal could go through straight away?' Bill asked urgently.

'Only if they really want him, but they're likely to wait until the closed season to start negotiations now.'

'No, Seth, that's too late. It has to be this season.' Bill was panicking now. 'It has to be all done and dusted by the end of the season, otherwise there's no point.'

'OK, OK, well, that's what we'll work to, then. You get me the cutting, and I'll get the video of tonight's goal out to him.'

Bill hit the red button on his phone. Never mind overcoming a two-goal deficit, Bill hadn't been this excited since Mary popped Tom out.

'What is it?' George asked, sensing that he had some exciting news.

'You're not going to believe this,' Bill beamed.

'No . . .' Smithy and George shook their heads in anticipation.

'Some Italian agent. He loves the video and reckons that Foggia are desperately looking for a striker to get them back up to Serie A next season and they want to move quickly, before the season's out.'

Bill was right. Smithy couldn't believe it and George didn't want to believe it.

CHAPTER 21

Spelthorne PLC had requested a meeting for Conran and Marcus to explain the reasons for the delay in getting planning approval from the council. Marcus had done his best to allay their concerns over the phone, but they'd insisted on a meeting in person. It was just routine, and although Marcus had been expecting the call and was fully prepared for the meeting, that didn't necessarily mean it was going to be easy. As ever, Conran was under strict instructions to say nothing, but in fact he was now the least of Marcus's concerns.

Marcus considered wearing a wig but had decided that it might only make him look more ridiculous. However, he couldn't bring himself to explain that the hair loss was due to stress either; it simply wasn't something any self-respecting businessman could admit to. Inevitably, therefore, as soon as Marcus entered the boardroom, the planning permission delay was forgotten. All eyes were fixed firmly on Marcus's head, and the entire Spelthorne team was gagging to know what had happened to him.

'Saw an old man get hit by a bus.'

'Blimey. Was he . . . ?'

'Killed instantly. It was quite a shock but I prefer not to talk about it.'

After that, nobody felt they could dwell on the subject of his hair. The meeting had begun, and Marcus was away to a lying start.

The delay in achieving planning permission was actually a slightly more awkward subject to explain because Marcus didn't feel that his corrupt official's plight with the locals would go over too well. Although subterfuge and bribery are integral components of big business, most big businesses would still rather not know about such practices. And so Marcus played the game and spouted something about local planning clauses promising that the deal would be approved within the next twenty-eight days, thereby gifting Spelthorne with a piece of land worth many millions more than they were paying for it. They relaxed somewhat after hearing these assurances and Marcus realised perhaps for the first time what a façade the whole thing was. It was all bravado on their part, Marcus thought to himself as he looked across the table at the four executives, who, judging by their full heads of hair had never even heard of the word stress. This was Spelthorne flexing its muscles, to remind Marcus where he was in the pecking order, in case he got greedy and started looking for an extra ten million from another developer. Actually, the thought had crossed his mind, but that was before his hair had gone grey, let alone fallen out.

In the toilets after their meeting, Marcus paused to peer at himself in the mirror. He had crow's-feet now even before he smiled. He looked bloody terrible but assured himself that all was not lost. He was still a handsome man and, so far as he knew, stress had never accounted for a good bone structure. It was nothing that six months on a beach in Cuba couldn't put right. Recharge his batteries, sprout some hair and start spending the cash.

Conran joined him at the appropriately named vanity unit. Marcus watched as he zipped himself up and smiled warmly at his image in the mirror, as if imagining how it might look after Marcus's ribcage has been welded to his lower jaw. Marcus shuddered at the thought and threw his towel into the bin.

Bill sat anxiously at work, waiting for his mobile phone to ring. It had been two days since he'd spoken to Seth, and he had hoped to have heard something more by now.

The young chap who'd been bombarded in the wall during the filming of Ronnie's video pushed a carousel of ginger nut biscuits towards Bill.

''Ere, Bill, will you check me nuts for us?'

Bill laughed. 'OK, drop 'em.' It was remarkable, Bill had worked in the bakery all his adult life and yet sexual innuendo about crunchy nuts was still funny. He'd long stopped relating the jokes to Mary, though, because she hadn't laughed at them for years. Bill decided it was a bloke thing.

'You going tomorrow night, Bill?' the lad asked.

'Nah, working. Couldn't face it anyway.'

The following night would see Middleton's penultimate game of the season away to Rushden and Diamonds, a game they absolutely had to win.

Suddenly, Bill's mobile phone bleeped and he grabbed it, his heart sinking immediately.

'You all right, Smithy?'

'You heard anything yet or what?'

'No, I'd have called you, wouldn't I?' Bill snapped.

'All right, all right, I was only wondering.'

'Is that all you wanted?'

'Actually, I was going to ask if I could do anything for you.'

Bill smiled, feeling guilty. Good old Smithy. He'd done as

much as anyone for the club since the plans had been announced. 'Yeah, you can come and relieve me here,' Bill joked. Smithy wasn't due in for another two hours.

'I will if it'll help.'

'No, Smithy, I was only jokin'.'

'I don't mind. Not if you've got something on.'

Bill thought for a moment. He did want to go and see Michael, to find out if he'd had any responses from his letters and talk generally to him further about raising some bank finance.

'Well, I was—'

'You haven't got to say it. I'll be right over then,' Smithy said and he was gone.

Bill looked over at the Perspex apron, which Smithy would be bursting through in a minute or so, seeing as his little house wasn't a goal kick from the bakery.

O'Dowd's jaw muscles bulged in his cheeks as he considered the *Chronicle* and its latest leader in the smear campaign against him. How fucking dare they? In his career, O'Dowd had become skilled in manipulating the media, and he didn't much like being a recipient of its punch. Today's headline was the one he'd most feared: 'Councillor O'Dowd: The Decision is Yours'. He slammed his coffee cup down on the table and grappled for his mobile phone.

'Fucking thing. Why do they make them so small,' he raged. Finally, he managed to dial Marcus's number correctly but, infuriatingly, was put straight through to his answer phone.

'Marcus, it's me. Where the hell are you? We need to talk because I am getting hung out to dry here. I assume you've seen the *Chronicle* – well, I want to know what you're going to do about it and I hope you've got some fucking suggestions because this decision, the one that's all MINE, hasn't been ratified yet. So, I take it you understand what I'm saying and I'm sure you'll be in touch.'

Council leaks were to be expected as part of political life, but the *Chronicle* was evidently being fed information from within and generating sensationalist headlines. The goal posts had been moved, as it were, and now the *Chronicle* was suggesting that, such was O'Dowd's influence, it would be his decision alone to close the club rather than a Council one. This, of course, meant that in theory he also had the power to save the club, which was exactly what the *Chronicle* was calling upon him to do. O'Dowd was being forced to carry the can. The way he'd envisaged retiring, with a fanfare, the unveiling of a bronze bust and a ticker-tape parade was now looking increasingly remote. In a Sherman tank with his passport was the most likely option at the moment. Although he would retire an extraordinarily wealthy man, that wasn't the point. He'd lived in this area all his life and he wanted the people's gratitude. His assistant popped his head into the office.

'Ready, sir.'

O'Dowd ignored him.

'I've got some phone messages, sir.'

O'Dowd looked up from his desk and glared at the man. He glanced at the telephone receiver that he'd deliberately not replaced on its cradle. The *Chronicle* was urging its readers to call the Council to register their protests and had helpfully printed the number of O'Dowd's direct line. O'Dowd replaced the handset and looked at the young man quaking in the doorway. He held a finger up and gestured to the phone, which rang almost immediately. O'Dowd stood up angrily, sending his chair crashing against the wall. Grimacing, he picked up the phone and, with both hands, ripped it clean out of its socket, hurled it across his office and stormed out of the door.

O'Dowd was seething when he entered the boardroom for what he now hoped might be his last meeting as head of the Council. He looked around at the eighteen people already seated, suspicious of them all. One of these bastards was selling him out. This meeting had been specially convened to discuss the plans for the club as a direct result of the campaign launched by the scheming public. Of course, O'Dowd had tried to block it, arguing that it was a waste of time, but he'd been overruled by an all-powerful majority. O'Dowd was sick of politics, and democracy in particular. As far as he was concerned, Third World despots like Robert Mugabe didn't know how lucky they were. It seemed that some councillors were being won over by public opinion but O'Dowd wasn't unduly worried. The deal had been approved and there was absolutely no chance of it not going through. This meeting allowed the councillors to feel they were at least doing something to address public concern, but crucially without in fact doing anything. A meeting, then, designed to heal the conscience and little else.

Only a brave person would take on O'Dowd in this kind of mood, and he scowled at his assembled colleagues to emphasise this point.

'Welcome to this complete waste of time, a meeting that I oppose entirely, so I suggest whoever wanted it to take place should kick the bloody thing off.'

O'Dowd looked around the room as people shuffled awkwardly in their seats, but no one spoke.

'Well, if no one's got anything to say, I'm leaving to deal with the more important tasks waiting for me.'

He was on his way out, when Sean Mills piped up and plunged into the icy waters of O'Dowd's foul mood. He wouldn't have chosen to do so but Bill had got to him last night and spent an hour bending his ear with Michael's theory that O'Dowd was somehow in on the deal. Michael saw infinitely more mileage in trying to expose council corruption than in selling off bogus Brazilian football players.

'Erm . . . I've got a problem with the timetable of the whole thing.'

'What?'

Mills hesitated a fraction too long, allowing O'Dowd back in.

'Well, come on, spit it out.'

'It just all seems too rushed to me,' Mills offered, somewhat feebly.

'What does?' O'Dowd spat back instantly.

'The whole timetable. I mean, all in one season the club has been bought and sold on by an unknown chairman. If that isn't asset stripping—'

'But we've been through this,' O'Dowd shouted, taking everyone, including himself, by surprise.

'Yes I know that, but—'

'But what? We've all agreed the club isn't viable.'

'But that's not my point,' Mills argued bravely, although by now he was cursing Bill Baxter and his bloody crusade.

'Well then, what is it? Because I'm darned if I know.'

O'Dowd was an intimidating man and Mills swallowed hard, wishing that he'd kept his mouth shut.

'Well, come on, then, man, what do you mean?' O'Dowd boomed like the Wizard of Oz at the cowardly lion.

'It seems as though we've all been bamboozled into it. Why does it need to be decided so quickly?'

A blip appeared on O'Dowd's radar screen that he immediately considered as hostile, an accusation almost, and he knew that he had to meet it head on.

'And what exactly are you suggesting?' he asked.

'Nothing,' Mills quivered. 'Shouldn't we wait a while, to find out—'

'To find out what?' O'Dowd bellowed, keeping the pressure up.

'Well, if they stay up, for a start,' Martha chipped in, buoyed by Mill's startling courage and also keen to register the fact that she hated O'Dowd's guts, in case he didn't know that already. O'Dowd had been forced to call an end to their affair because within a month of his sleeping with her, Martha had been talking of them running off together.

O'Dowd eyed her angrily. 'This decision does not depend on football results. Whether they stay up, get relegated or win the bloody league is irrelevant. The club is not viable. We've seen the auditors' report. Jee-sus what more do we need, if we are to act responsibly in the best interest of the town?'

'Yes, but Middleton are—'

'are going bankrupt whether they stay up or not, look at bloody Leicester City,' O'Dowd interrupted, 'and this flurry of support in the town! Where was that when they needed it last season?'

No one could think of an answer.

'And where will it be even if they do survive?' O'Dowd pressed home his advantage.

'Well, we'll never know, will we, because there won't be a club,' Mills answered him facetiously.

'Yes there will. That's the whole fucking point,' O'Dowd seethed, noting the fear and disgust registering on the faces of several people at his use of the f-word in such a hallowed chamber. 'Please, excuse my language, but I am tired of gesture politics. This is nothing more than emotional horse-shit. Sorry, I'm sorry. This council will support a Middleton football club, but not at the expense of the town's development, and that is and must remain our decision and priority.'

Mills shook his head defiantly. The arrogant little shit, O'Dowd thought to himself, it was now abundantly clear who the council mole had been.

'Well, I still think we should delay it. Have a twelve-month cooling-off period.'

O'Dowd slammed his fist on to the table. 'And will you fund the legal bills when the developers sue us? How will that be serving our community? Hm?'

Finally, all arguments had been dealt with, even though it had taken a loss of temper for O'Dowd to prevail. He might be about to retire but not until he'd made sure Mills' career in local government was on its last legs.

Middleton High Street was busy and Bill was making slow progress. As he elbowed his way home, his mobile phone rang and vibrated and generally made it known that someone needed to speak to him. Bill hoped it was Seth.

'Hello.'

'Bill, it's Seth.'

'Yes, yes, go on.'

'Good news . . .'

'Yes.'

'The agent from Italy is coming over.'

'You're joking.'

'And he's bringing two people from Foggia with him.'

Bill hurriedly stepped in to Mr and Mrs Fernandez's convenience store. Mr Fernandez smiled and was about to say hello when he noticed that Bill was on the phone. Mr Fernandez gestured proudly to the 'Save our Club' banner that was hanging above his vegetable counter. Bill smiled back and gave him the thumbs-up, although when he looked at the brown mush that Mr Fernandez was hoping to pass off as bananas, it occurred to him that the shopkeeper had got his priorities wrong and a 'save our fresh produce' banner might have been more appropriate.

'Have they seen the video?'

'Yes, of course they have, why else do you think they're interested? They know all about English football and its money problems. All I've told them is that Middleton are struggling and that's why we're having to let the lad go cheap.'

Cheap at two million quid, Bill thought to himself. What had happened to football? 'When are they coming?' he asked.

'Friday, I think, for the Shrewsbury match. Now, can you organise things at your end?'

'OK, but what? I mean, I've never done this before.' Bill gulped.

'You know, hotels, picking them up from the airport, good seats at the ground, that sort of thing.'

Bill nodded as Seth reeled off the list. Good seats in the ground might be tricky. There weren't any.

'But you'll be coming?' Bill fretted.

'Of course, although I might not be able to get there until Saturday, so you'll need to look after them until I arrive.'

'Have you talked money yet?' Bill dared to ask.

'Only ballpark. They're more concerned about his wages than his fee, but don't worry about it, that's my area.'

'Anything up to two million.'

Seth ignored Bill. 'Now, about tonight's match?'

'What about it?'

'We can't afford for Ronnie to get injured, so is there any way we could leave him out? Give him a rest until Saturday.'

'But we need a win tonight, otherwise—'

'Yeah, I know that, but if Ronnie gets injured there'll be no sale this season either. Look, just think about it, that's all. Now, Bill, there's just one thing . . .'

'Go on.'

'These Italians, they can't know about the club going bust.'

'How do you mean?'

'Because they'll just stall the purchase until the club folds. Then the players are no longer bound by their contracts and the Italians can negotiate their own terms.'

Bill understood what Seth was saying but he was assessing how difficult it would be to conceal the club's plight from the Italian visitors. The Ronaldo Mara scam was supposed to be a secret, but secrets in towns like Middleton last no longer than a bunch of flowers from a garage forecourt. Someone always blabs, and at the game last week there had been a conspicuous number of fans wearing pirate Brazilian shirts with Ronaldo emblazoned across their shoulders. And then there was the town itself, festooned with banners and posters about saving the club. Even Mr Fernandez had a banner.

'And what about Ronnie? Will you tell him?' Bill asked.

'Leave Ronnie to me, I'll sort Ronnie out. I'll be in touch as soon as I know their travel arrangements.' Seth hung up. Bill was in a complete state of shock.

'Bill-ee, I hope we will win on Saturday, no,' Mr Fernandez beamed.

Bill's mind was racing, thinking about who he should call first and what exactly he should do.

'I dink two-nil to us.'

Bill hardly heard him as he walked past the counter, his mind still churning. Bill turned back as he got to the front door of the shop. 'Mr Fernandez, would you do me a favour?'

'Yes, of course.'

'Take that banner down, will ya?'

Bill thought he might as well start somewhere. It was highly unlikely that the three Italian footballing dignitaries would set foot in Mr Fernandez's shop, and certainly not for bananas, but Bill couldn't be too careful. Everything would have to come down.

Marcus finally returned O'Dowd's call and they arranged to meet in their Masonic lodge. Marcus took some solace in the fact that O'Dowd now looked remarkably stressed too but, as far as he could tell, the councillor's hair still seemed firmly attached to his head.

'So you see my predicament?' O'Dowd asked.

Marcus nodded warmly. 'Yes, I can, I can see your point exactly, but there's nothing I can do to help,' he replied. He noted with some joy the fear spreading across O'Dowd's face. His hair might fall out yet.

'But it would serve your purposes as well for them to be relegated,' O'Dowd argued.

'Yeah, and if they lose tonight, it'll be all over anyway,' Marcus replied nonchalantly.

O'Dowd breathed out heavily. He didn't want to leave

things to chance. Look what had happened earlier in the week when they were two-nil down.

'They have to get relegated, you know. Encourage them to lose.'

Marcus laughed. 'What, throw a game? No way. You've seen the town with all the banners and the blasted talk about saving the club. There's no way anyone's going to throw this game—'

'But we—'

'– and if we start trying to organise it, they'll smell a rat and we don't want that, do we?'

'Well, then, couldn't we injure one of their players?' O'Dowd blurted out. 'This O'Mara lad, the one who's suddenly become a footballing messiah, according to the *Chronicle* – and, by the way, have you seen what they've been saying about me?'

What, that you're a corrupt little worm? How dare they? Marcus thought. For the first time since he'd set this plan in motion, Marcus was enjoying himself. He stroked his bald head, feeling for any hairs that might suddenly have made a welcome break through his scalp.

'So, what do you think?' O'Dowd asked.

Marcus stared at him. 'Injure a player? Are you serious?'

'Yes, of course I am. I'm not talking about killing him, just whacking him on the knee or something.'

Marcus looked aghast. 'And who do you think is going to do this?'

O'Dowd suddenly realised the folly of what he was suggesting. He had no intention of doing such a thing. Not because it was morally wrong but rather because of the legal consequences should he get caught.

'Well, we can't just pray that they lose,' O'Dowd complained.

'I don't see what else we can do.'

'We could bribe the ref,' O'Dowd suggested. 'Look at Korea in the World Cup.'

Marcus chuckled. Surely the man's hair follicles couldn't withstand this kind of pressure much longer.

'Look, stop panicking. Whatever the results, it won't make any difference.'

'No, not to you it won't,' O'Dowd answered.

Exactly, thought Marcus.

'They're going bust anyway. Since Conran's owned them, I've made sure no bills have been paid. The VAT people alone will close them down. Your decision is the right one and people will come to understand that.'

O'Dowd didn't look convinced. 'Well then, can't we just wait a while, until they fold naturally? That way, we're all winners.'

'But then why would I need to be paying you so handsomely?' Marcus almost smiled.

'I'll have to move out of the area, you know that, don't you?'

'Well, there's always Portugal,' Marcus joked. He was beginning to feel in control again. The town's reaction wasn't his concern. O'Dowd and Spelthorne could worry about that.

As O'Dowd drove home, he tried to calm himself down.

'Things are going to work out just fine,' he assured himself, but he wasn't convinced. Indeed, if Middleton lost tonight at Rushden and Diamonds, then his problems would all be over.

'Come on, Rushden and Diamonds.' O'Dowd had never even heard of them before, but he was now praying they would win. However, he had an awful feeling they wouldn't and then everything would hinge on the last game of the season, next Saturday, at home to Shrewsbury Town. O'Dowd didn't even want to think about the possibilities of Middleton winning that match too but three hours later, that was exactly what O'Dowd was having to consider. He stared at his Ceefax screen in utter disbelief.

Rushden and Diamonds 1, Middleton Edwardians FC 2.

Even without their star striker, O'Mara, the bastards had somehow managed to win and O'Dowd was panicking more than ever. Sod leaving things to chance any more, he simply had to do something. Middleton could not be allowed to beat Shrewsbury next Saturday, it was as simple as that.

Suddenly, a thought occurred to O'Dowd: weakening the side wasn't the only way to affect the outcome of a match. What if he were to do it by strengthening the opposition? What if he made the Shrewsbury team unbeatable? It sounded like a preposterous notion but O'Dowd was suddenly energised. He didn't have a clue whether it could even be done, or exactly how he might go about it, but as O'Dowd had no other option at the moment and time was running out, he seized his last chance with alacrity.

CHAPTER 22

At the last minute, Smithy and Bill had decided to go to the Rushdens match after all. The long journey home had passed quickly as they discussed avoiding relegation, beating Shrewsbury on Saturday, selling Ronnie to the Italians and, of course, saving their club, on an almost continuous loop with just toilet and petrol breaks coming between them.

Bill's pie-in-the-sky idea of selling Ronnie to the Italian club Foggia had suddenly taken on a very real life and looked as though it might even come off, and so Bill desperately needed some advice. Three Italians were coming to see the lad play, for God's sake. What if they did want to buy him?

Without an appointment, Bill pushed his way into Michael Abbott's office on Monday and urgently blurted out an update on the Ronaldo Mara situation. Understandably, Michael was dumbstruck.

'They are actually coming to watch Ronnie play?'

Bill nodded sheepishly. It was his way of asking for help, but Michael looked even more anxious than Bill.

'What?' Bill asked.

Michael shook his head. 'Bill, as a lawyer, I'm telling you that this has gone quite far enough.'

'Michael, we need your help.'

'Yes, I can see that and I'm giving it to you. You simply have to renounce this ridiculous notion.'

'Why?'

'Because you'll go to gaol. That would be the main reason.'

Bill shook his head in blind denial. 'But, they'll only be buying what they see.'

'You've changed his name, and don't tell me it's a typo,' Michael scoffed.

'All right then, it's just a nickname. Come on, Michael, all players have nicknames.'

'Bill, you've said he's Brazilian.'

'No, we've let them come up with that on their own.' Bill clutched at another straw.

'Well, I'm not surprised. You've called him bloody Ronaldo.'

'Anyway,' Bill said, pressing on, 'we've looked back into Ronnie's family tree. Turns out that loads of his ancestors were missionaries. Went all over the world.'

'Missionaries?' Michael screeched.

'Yeah, and some of them went from Ireland to South America.'

'Catholic missionaries.'

'Yeah,' Bill answered, hoping he might be on to something.'

'Shit, Bill, they're priests?'

'So?' Bill nodded his head but without much conviction, suddenly realising that Catholic priests are not famous for laying down roots.

'Yeah, OK, Michael, I know it's not perfect. But no one else has come in, have they?'

Michael shook his head.

'We haven't heard from the sons, or any of those vulture capitalists or whatever they're called. So, desperate times require desperate measures, or whatever the saying is.'

Michael breathed out heavily, and retrieved a file from his

cabinet. 'It'd be better if you could find evidence of wrong-doing at the council. That's still the best way of getting a delay.'

'We've tried that,' Bill sighed.

'I just know that O'Dowd's involved. It's all too neat. Everything's glued together too neatly, and it's just before the bastard retires as well.'

'Yeah, but he's too clever to give himself away.'

'Oh, I don't doubt that. He's been at it for years.'

'Sean Mills had a go at getting a rise out of him.'

'And?'

'No, didn't get anything other than a ruined career.'

'Which is a small sacrifice compared to the risk that you're taking.'

'Ronnie's agent seems OK with it all.'

Michael tutted. 'A football agent! Oh great, Bill, because they're famous for their probity.'

Bill didn't really have any answers for Michael but his mind was made up anyway.

Michael began flicking through the file noisily to register his total disapproval at what his foolhardy friend was doing.

'Does Mary know about all this?'

'Course she does.'

'But does she know what might happen? Five years, Bill, that's the tariff; I've checked.'

Michael and Bill had reached stalemate and, with a heavy sigh and even heavier heart, Michael pulled out the deeds on the land that he had copied from the public records office. With a gloomy air of acceptance, he set about telling Bill what the next step should be in the unlikely event that the Italians did cough up the money for Ronnie.

'Right, so . . .' Michael mused as his index finger passed

over the text, '. . . sufficient funds need to be in place within twelve months of signature, but if a written agreement can be reached for funding, any original deal cannot proceed until subsequent funding has been proven unreliable, and this must take place within the twelve-month period also.'

Bill stared at Michael. 'Meaning?'

'Meaning, the club cannot be reassigned to anyone else if you have a written promise of funding, and those funds will need to be in place before . . .' Michael looked at another document, 'the thirty-first of May.'

'And how do I announce the funding, through you?' Bill asked.

Michael was aghast. 'No way! I'll be struck off, and besides, the Italians haven't made an offer yet.'

'No, but if they do?'

'We'll talk about that when it happens or if it happens.'

Guy Vincent cracked open the champagne as the ink dried on the contract that Carmen and Jeremy Davidson had just signed. The drink dutifully exploded over the top of the bottle and raised the obligatory laugh from everyone. Guy's office had been newly redesigned in tribute to his two new cash cows. Hanging on the wall behind his desk were the framed front-page exclusives enjoyed by both Jeremy and Carmen. Actually, at the time they hadn't enjoyed them at all, but Guy certainly had and, as far as he was concerned, that was the main thing. The only broadsheet framed was a *Daily Telegraph* front cover, the one that had brought Carmen and Jeremy back together. It held a very special place in Guy's heart. What a year it had been. Guy handed them each a flute of champagne.

'Can I just say, well done, the pair of you.'

'Thank you,' Jeremy said, although he wasn't entirely sure what he was thanking Guy for. In fact, he felt faintly ridiculous, standing there drinking champagne with the two people who had orchestrated his downfall. But what else was there for him? He might as well capitalise on his new-found, albeit somewhat embarrassing, celebrity. He was also feeling awkward because this was his first meeting with Carmen since their last 'professional' liaison. To say the least, things were a little strained, with neither of them knowing quite what to say. After all, the last time they'd met, Jeremy had been wearing a nappy.

They would have been sworn enemies but for the foresight of Guy Vincent, who could see mapped out ahead of them prosperous and successful careers. Carmen was on board from the word go, but Jeremy had been highly sceptical at first and had required some gentle coercion from Guy. Guy had drawn upon his years of PR experience, using eye contact, empathy, agreement, flattery, more eye contact, referring to Jeremy by name, win-win, more flattery, touching the shoulder, synergy, nodding, just a little bit more flattery and eventually Jeremy too had found himself clambering aboard. Jeremy had posed a high hurdle for Guy to clear, but he'd managed it easily and could have done so without underpants, his dangling groin waggling free of his own bullshit.

'I'm sorry about the papers and stuff,' Carmen offered sheepishly, unable to stand the tension any longer.

Jeremy shrugged. 'Don't worry about it. I suppose I always knew that it would come out one day.'

'Yes, I guess.'

'Better that it happened now, before I made the cabinet.'

Carmen wasn't sure what he meant and smiled nervously. 'Do you still . . . ?' she asked.

'Oh yes, I'm afraid so. It's the only thing that really does it for me and at least now I can finally talk about it freely. It's quite a relief actually. Been something of a burden, I have to say. I suppose I should be thanking you, really.'

Guy could have cried with delight. They were going to make a fantastic duo.

'Absolutely,' Guy butted in, refilling their glasses. 'Hard feelings only ever stifle opportunities, that's what I say. Every situation, every single situation, no matter how terrible it may seem at the time, always has an upside, a positive – and that, my friends, is what we're all about.'

Jeremy and Carmen half smiled. Understandably, it was still awkward for them.

'So, shall we get going? The good people of the press are waiting for you.'

O'Dowd was conscious that he didn't want to give too much away about his current situation and his sudden interest in football. He had decided that he couldn't even risk discussing it at his own lodge because of the strength of public feeling, and had therefore travelled all the way to Lincolnshire for a stupefyingly dull dinner with his fellow brethren. He'd engaged a group of gentlemen in a discussion about the ethics of affecting the outcome of a football match, and whether they believed match fixing ever took place. Everyone agreed that the most effective way to alter the outcome was by upping the number of goals that one side was capable of scoring.

'How do you mean?' O'Dowd had asked.

'Improve their strike force, of course.'

'Oh course, yes.'

That was it then. Simple. Shrewsbury needed a goal scorer, a player who would ensure that Middleton would concede more goals than they could score. Michael Owen would have been O'Dowd's first choice but clearly he was unavailable and more than a little out of O'Dowd's price range even if he had been.

'It could never be done, though – not really,' one man said of the hypothetical scenario that O'Dowd had placed before them.

'Why?'

'Because players are with clubs. They're contracted to clubs and they can't just leave, they have to be transferred.'

'And then there's the transfer deadline as well.'

'That's right, you'd have to wait until the end of the season at least.'

'But what if there were a great player who wasn't signed to a club,' O'Dowd asked, fumbling in the dark.

'Wouldn't happen.'

'Why?'

'Because great players are already assigned to clubs. And players without clubs aren't the sort of players who can affect the outcomes of games.'

O'Dowd drove back to Cheshire with an imponderable problem. What he needed was a top-class striker, who didn't have a club, and was equally desperate for a game as for the cash.

O'Dowd put his radio on.

'*This is Radio Five Live, Jim's on the line from Woking. Hello, Jim, what's your point?*'

'*I'd like to discuss the season that Lee Robson has just had . . .*'

Perhaps for the first time since he was born, Lee Robson was about to be considered perfect.

Seth hadn't been this busy since his days as a bookie on the Old Kent Road. What with the impending sale of Ronaldo Mara and now this ridiculously lucrative approach from Shrewsbury Town, Seth was quite overcome, and mopped his brow with an old handkerchief. His whole life had taken on a surreal quality.

O'Dowd had wasted no time when Jim from Woking via Radio 5 had appeared to him as an angel holding up a little figurine of Lee Robson, his potential saviour, his literal match winner. O'Dowd had feverishly raced through his Palm Pilot and it hadn't taken many phone calls to establish a mutual acquaintance with Leslie Rose, Chairman of Shrewsbury Town. O'Dowd called Mr Rose and briefly outlined his proposition and they had hastily arranged to meet the following day.

In strictest confidence O'Dowd briefed Rose over lunch in a pub alongside the A47. O'Dowd didn't elaborate on why he needed Shrewsbury to win or, more accurately, Middleton not to win, and Rose didn't care and nor should he. Basically, O'Dowd was offering to pay for the playing services of Lee Robson on behalf of Shrewsbury Town, an offer that Rose didn't feel he could miss out on.

Rose called his lawyer and sounded out the validity of O'Dowd's suggestion and the legal man agreed in principle, at least. Rose and O'Dowd reached a gentleman's agreement and Leslie Rose asked his PA to get Lee Robson's agents on the phone.

Now Seth scratched his head and mulled over the proposition in his mind. In his entire career, it was certainly the strangest request he had ever received and he was naturally suspicious. Could there be a catch? Was there something he wasn't seeing? He and Rose had agreed a thirty-thousand-pound playing fee for Lee, plus a further ten thousand pounds for each goal Lee scored, up to a maximum of forty thousand. Seth quickly calculated that it could mean seventy grand for a day's work. It would certainly solve a lot of problems.

Seth chewed what was left of his thumbnail as he considered all the permutations. Calling Bill with the news wouldn't be easy, that was for sure. Effectively he was condemning Middleton to a calamitous defeat. Quite right, Bill would go apeshit. But that wasn't what was worrying Seth. He was far more concerned about telling Lee that after his arduous search, he'd finally found him a club, in the Third Division. And if he survived that, somehow he had to think of a way of getting him to play.

CHAPTER 23

Seth's intercom buzzed. 'Seth, Lee's here to see you.

'OK.'

Quickly, Seth stretched his mouth the way luvvies do before going on stage, and rubbed his clammy palms on the back of his trousers. This wasn't going to be easy and Seth was wondering about the wisdom of inviting his psycho client in to hear the news in person. It would have been far safer telling him on the phone but Lee would have hung up before Seth could persuade him to sign. Seth wasn't a brave man and as his door handle turned, he felt he might be staring death in the face.

Lee breezed in wearing an immaculate suit, which he'd chosen to ruin with one of those hideous shirts most football players seem to favour.

'Lee, how are you?' Seth beamed, trying his best to create an atmosphere of happiness in the room.

'Been better.'

'Well, I've got some great news.'

Instantly Lee's eyes lit up. 'You've got a club?'

Seth breathed in. 'Yes . . .'

'Chelsea?'

'No.'

'West Ham?'

'Lee, listen, it's not a club with a future for you and I'm not expecting you to stay there—'

'Fuck me, not Man U?'

Seth was now panicking badly. 'Lee, listen to me. It's not a Premiership club.'

'Abroad then?' A thought occurred to Lee and he looked serious. 'I ain't going to Germany.'

'No, not abroad, it's in this country.'

Lee thought for a moment. If it wasn't abroad and it wasn't a Premiership club, then that meant . . . The realisation almost winded him.

'Jesus, Seth, Scotland . . . ?'

'Lee, no. Not Scotland. It's an English club . . .'

This was now even worse than a Scottish club. Lee stood up, pointing aggressively at Seth. 'Don't even mention a First Division club to me.'

Seth gulped. Don't worry, I'm not going to. How about a Third Division one instead?

'Lee, if you'd just let me finish and stop jumping to conclusions. This is a one-game deal, that's it, and it could be a right little earner. It's to get them out of a hole—'

'Who?'

Seth felt like a debut parachutist about to leave the plane. 'Shrewsbury Town.' There, he'd said it, he'd jumped and immediately began searching for the rip cord. Never mind this waiting-for-three-minutes bullshit.

Seth's desk almost lifted off the floor as Lee kicked it. Lee could so easily have injured himself in the process and obviously hadn't learnt anything from his past mistakes.

'Shrewsbury. Fucking Shrewsbury. I don't even know where it is.'

'It's near Chester.'

'I don't give a shit where it is. I was playing for England last year. I'll be a laughing stock. Don't you think I've had enough piss taken out of me for one season?'

'Lee, it's only one game, and they're paying you twenty-grand playing fee and five grand a goal. You could do forty grand in an afternoon.'

'I ain't playing for Shrewsbury.'

'Look, Lee, I can't get you a permanent club until your disciplinary hearing takes place. No one will touch you until then, and this is a golden opportunity.'

'You're supposed to be my agent.'

'I am.'

'And you think playing for Shrewsbury is a golden opportunity?'

'Damn right it is. You play the match and you show the panel that you haven't kicked anyone to death. That's the first thing. You also make a tidy sum, but, most importantly, you bang in a hatful of goals and show the bigger clubs that you're still shit hot. It'll be two fingers to Tottenham 'n' all.'

Lee shook his head defiantly, but was in fact thinking about it quite seriously. He didn't have anything else to do this Saturday. 'Forty grand?' he asked.

As O'Dowd drove down Middleton High Street something nagged at him and it wasn't his wife. Something was wrong, something had changed, but he couldn't quite work out what it was.

It wasn't until he reached Middleton's stadium that it finally struck him. All the banners had gone. Even the stadium was banner free. O'Dowd stopped his car outside the ground and looked intently at the row of terraced houses opposite and the parked cars outside them. There was not one poster or car sticker to be seen.

What the hell was going on? Had they capitulated? It certainly appeared so, but why, with just one game to go, when they still had a chance of staying up? O'Dowd was more confused than suspicious. Perhaps they'd finally realised it was all over, whatever the result on Saturday.

He shook his head. There was no way that they'd just give up like that and it would be bloody annoying if they had, because if they had, it meant he'd just wasted a potential seventy grand.

Vippin and Katherine were sitting in Bill's living room. Tess was stuffing something into the video and Bill was too pre-occupied to stop her. It hardly worked anyway. Bill was edgy and couldn't settle down.

'So, Katherine, they've got the best rooms, yeah?'

'Yes, Dad, and you can have 'em at normal rate.'

Vippin was struggling to hold Tom safely.

'Vippin, give him here, you'll break his neck.'

'Well, he won't stay still.'

Bill looked at his list again. 'And, Vip lad, you're on for the airport.'

'Yes, boss. Got me uncle's Mercedes all sorted.'

'Have ya now? You never told me that,' Katherine complained.

Vippin proudly dangled a car key from his index finger.

'In that case, tonight you're taking me out. Can you baby-sit, Dad?'

Bill grunted. He looked awkward and shifty, like he needed to break wind but couldn't.

'You've been in the car yet, Vip?'

'Yeah, drove it over, didn't I?'

'Not being rude, but, er . . .'

'What?'

There was no easy way of saying this. 'Look, don't give

out or nothing, but your uncle, being in the curry business and all that . . .'

Katherine and Vippin both stared at Bill.

'. . . well, you know.'

'Are ya askin' if it smells, Bill?'

'Dad.'

'I'm just saying . . .'

'Well, it doesn't,' Vippin said angrily, although he managed not to swear. He'd learnt very quickly that swearing was an absolute no-no in Mary's house.

Bill looked embarrassed and felt terrible for even suggesting it. 'I'm sorry, son.'

Mary came into the living room holding Bill's mobile phone. 'It's that bloke . . . from London.'

Bill's eyes widened as he held the phone. Seth was the only person he knew in London.

'Seth?'

'Yeah, hi Bill.'

'Hang on . . .'

Bill waited until he was outside in the garden before continuing his conversation. If Seth was calling with bad news, then he would need to call upon language that Mary wouldn't approve of. Given what Seth did have to say, it was a wise move.

'So we're still on for tomorrow.' Bill was delighted. He looked fondly at his rosebuds and noted that they could do with a spray.

'Yep, nothing has changed. Two o'clock, Manchester airport.'

'OK, good. My lad's picking them up and we've got them the best rooms in a lovely hotel.'

'Yeah, whatever,' Seth said. The state of their rooms and whether they had bidets or not didn't concern him.

'Now, we're a bit worried about what to say to them, so can you get here on the Friday?' Bill asked.

'I'll do my best, but I might not be able to.' That meant no and Bill knew it.

'About the match on Saturday, Bill, I'm afraid I've got some bad news.'

Bill had feared that he might. It had all been going too well. As Seth explained the situation, Bill's anxiety soon turned to confusion and then anger.

'Ya what? But they can't do that. They can't. The transfer deadline's gone.'

'It's not a transfer. Lee doesn't belong to a club, remember.'

Bill couldn't believe what he was hearing. How the hell could this be happening? Like everyone else in the country, he had enjoyed the demise of Lee Robson in the full glare of the public eye, but now the consequences of Bill's jamless doughnut were coming full circle and he was about to suffer for his own actions.

'You'll have to stop him from playing,' Bill protested.

'What? Why?'

'Why? Why? Because he'll bloody well put us down, that's why.' The young green fly didn't stand a chance as Bill rubbed a rosebud between his thumb and forefinger.

'Bill. I can't do that.'

'Why not?'

'How long have you got?'

Bill didn't say anything, his silence challenging Seth to make his case.

'Right, OK then. Because, one: Lee's a free agent and he does what he wants; two: he needs the money; three: he needs to show the FA that he can play without killing anyone; four—'

'Yeah, all right, all right. Doesn't seem fair, that's all.'

'Bill, I'm sorry, but this isn't about Middleton staying up. There's a much bigger picture here and it's about you remaining a football club.'

'Yeah, but it would be nice, though, wouldn't it?'

'What?'

'To remain in the bloody league if we do manage to survive. Who else have you got on your books for Shrewsbury to poach, Mara-fucking-dona?'

'Bill, come on now. Please calm down.'

'Calm down!' Bill shouted. 'Not getting relegated is all we've got to cling to. If we go down, it'll be a piece of piss for them to shut us down.'

'But not if the Mara deal goes through.'

Suddenly everything seemed quite hopeless to Bill. 'Oh yeah, and what are the chances of that? Everyone here reckons it's a load of bollocks.'

Seth was inclined to agree but, desperate as he was, he forced himself to sound hopeful.

'You let me worry about that. That's my job. I'm going to have a word with the young Ronnie; get him really fired up for the match.'

'You better bloody well had. And, anyway, how come Shrewsbury have suddenly come in for Robson?'

'No idea, just got a call. They need to stay up as well, you know.'

Seth didn't give two hoots about whose idea it was. Just as long as he was making on the deal.

*

O'Dowd was in another terrible mood. His dark moods seemed to merge into each other these days, overlapping every time something new pissed him off. Today's mood was caused by the painful transfer of twenty thousand pounds into a subsidiary account of Leslie Rose. Far from being happy that the deal for Robson was going through, he was furious that he'd had to commit his own hard-earned savings to the deal. Marcus had once again given him very short shrift when he'd been invited to contribute to the costs.

The press and any number of football pundits for hire had questioned the legality and ethics of Shrewsbury's new signing and agreed that Lee Robson was likely to banish Middleton from the professional football league by gorging himself on a goal feast. He better fucking had, O'Dowd scowled to himself. Even if he scored a hat trick, it would be worth it. Seventy grand for a peaceful life with his villa and a million quid. It wasn't a bad payoff, but O'Dowd was still incensed that Marcus hadn't agreed to cough up as well. If he hadn't been about to retire, he would have made the little shit come up with the lot.

O'Dowd's mood had darkened still further when Rose had made new demands of his own. When the honeypot is open, every one wants a scoop, and O'Dowd hated them all. His lawyer advised him that because Mr Rose was likely to receive some unfavourable press for procuring the service of Lee Robson for such a crucial game, it was deemed only fair that Mr Rose should be adequately compensated by Mr O'Dowd. Mr O'Dowd's face twitched with rage when he ended the call. It had just cost him another twenty grand.

*

Saturday would see the English football season draw to a close for the year 2002/2003. On Saturday, the Premiership title would be decided between the two leading foreign teams playing in England. No fewer than twenty English football clubs would commit everything they had to secure promotion or avoid relegation. Cups would be won and hearts broken, but the greater intrigue rested on the outcome of Middleton Edwardians versus Shrewsbury Town. Shrewsbury needed a draw. Middleton needed to win and with Lee Robson thrown into the frame at such a late hour, the whole country would be watching.

CHAPTER 24

Saturday finally arrived. The news that Lee Robson would be playing for Shrewsbury had sent a shudder through the town and, indeed, the whole nation. It was considered a scandal in some quarters, a brilliant piece of opportunism and ingenuity in others.

In Middleton, though, not surprisingly, it was considered a bloody travesty. Every football fan had an opinion and the matter had garnered huge press interest and so, once again, Lee Robson was front- and back-page news. The town of Middleton was weighted down with an expectation that only grew as the national journalists, photographers and news crews arrived, eager to capture the unfolding saga, which had everything from intrigue to scandal and romance. Middleton hadn't seen a day like this in anyone's living memory. It was the epicentre of something very big indeed and no one knew quite what was going to happen.

Vippin waited in the hotel for the Italian party. Katherine had called them in their rooms to let them know that their driver had arrived.

She looked at Vippin disapprovingly. 'Blimey, Vip, what are you wearing?'

Vippin grinned sheepishly, looking down at his trousers, which could best be described as slacks.

'I've got to look smart, haven't I?'

'I don't mean your clothes. I mean your bloody smelly stuff.'

Vippin rolled his eyes. 'Can you still smell it?'

'Not half.'

On reflection, Vippin had decided that his uncle's car was a little on the niffy side and so he'd emptied the remainder of his noxious Kouros aftershave into it rather than actually cleaning it out. It might have been because the cologne was nearly ten years old, but when mixed with garam masala, it produced a devastating combination not too far from nerve gas. Vippin began to laugh.

'I haven't even got any on, you know. This is from the car. It stinks.'

A fat, balding man called Alfonso Raldini appeared in reception with his two colleagues and instantly recognised Vippin as his driver.

'Ah no, it's the perfuma man again.'

Seth had travelled up north first thing to avoid the traffic. There was no way he was going to miss this game for anything. He'd spent most of his car journey trying to establish the best way of getting the performance of a lifetime out of his young client, Mr Ronaldo Mara. What would Sir Alex Ferguson say in such circumstances, he'd wondered.

Now that Seth was sitting in front of the young Ronnie, he realised exactly why he would never have made it in football management.

Ronnie didn't know what to make of it all. Until two weeks ago, he had hardly ever spoken to his agent, and now he couldn't get rid of him. First it was haircuts and false tans to make a video and now he was sitting in his lounge trying to give him a pep talk. Ronnie was terrified and on guard for a homosexual advance at any minute.

'Ronnie, I've always liked you, and what I need from you is simple—'

Ronnie flinched.

'Don't look so worried,' Seth reassured him, and was about to rest a hand on his player's knee. It was fortunate that he didn't. 'You and I Ronnie, we like each other, yeah?'

'Huh.'

'We work together as a team.'

'What sort of team?'

'And we have a great future together.'

Ronnie looked over to the door and thought about making a run for it.

'Because I'm not like other agents.'

'You're not?'

'No, I'm not in this for the money. I'm in this because I care about my clients. I care about you, Ronnie.'

Ronnie had heard enough. The video and the false tan was now all making sense.

'Listen, man, you've got me all wrong.'

'No, I haven't.'

'Yes you have.'

'Ronnie, today's a massive game for you.'

Ronnie slumped forward with relief. 'For the club, you mean.'

'Yeah for the club, but for you in particular.'

'What do you mean?'

Seth scratched his head and assessed how much information Ronnie needed to know.

'Is there another club interested?' Ronnie asked.

Seth thought about lying. The truth would either spur Ronnie on or terrify him. It was a close call.

'Yes. There's an Italian scout flying in for today's match with some officials from Foggia.'

'Blimey.'

Seth studied his client's face, looking for any signs of panic. He seemed a little surprised but otherwise OK. Seth reasoned that he should press on. Ronnie needed to know just how important it was that he had a blinder this afternoon.

'Ronnie, we're looking at two million quid, possibly more.'

Immediately Seth knew he'd made a mistake. Panic spread across Ronnie's face like a dark shadow and now he looked truly terrified. It was as if Seth had just unzipped his flies and produced a big tub of Vaseline.

Against the specific advice of Marcus, O'Dowd had decided that in fact he was going to attend the big game. He'd argued that if he stayed away, it might look like he had something to hide or, even worse, that he was scared. He also had a burning desire to see Middleton lose. He was sick of the way the campaign had singled him out and now he wanted to watch them burn. He wanted to witness at first-hand Lee Robson terrorising their defenders and banging the ball in from inconceivable angles. O'Dowd wanted his money's worth.

It was mid-morning and O'Dowd had just given a press conference at Loughton Hall Hotel about his own and the Council's position on the application for planning permission. The conference had gone rather well but, oddly, he was still feeling anxious. The hotel was unusually busy with the sudden influx of journalists eager to cover the story, which seemed to have an angle for everyone. O'Dowd felt more than a little excluded from it all, as if he wasn't welcome at the party because he was the only local person praying for a Middleton defeat.

He recognised the young Indian lad hanging about in the foyer as the rude waiter from the New Delhi Restaurant. The man greeted three Italian-looking men and headed off towards the revolving door to the car park. It wasn't a surprise to O'Dowd that he'd left the restaurant business. If there was any justice in the world, he'd been sacked.

Marcus and Conran were certainly not going to the game. Neither of their highly comprehensive medical insurance policies would cover them for that kind of folly. Marcus had no intention of ever setting foot in the ground again. Conran's one and only visit to the ground had given him the moronic idea of having a new chin built out of his partner's ribcage, and so now Marcus had an even greater desire to see the place vanish from the face of the earth. Whatever the result this afternoon, it would be the club's last match.

In actual fact, if Middleton did manage to win, it would make O'Dowd's life hell, and that idea was particularly appealing to Marcus. For the first time since his plan was conceived over a year ago, Marcus was rooting for Middleton. How ironic.

In his bathroom that morning, under his shaving light, Marcus had seen a light fuzz of hair covering his head. It was as welcome as his first pubic hairs had been all those years ago. His hair was making a comeback; the old Marcus was re-emerging.

Now, he sat calmly in his garden, still heavily dependent

on the happy pills, but with one hand gently stroking his fluffy dome. He could sense that everything was going to be fine.

Seth was having a busy morning. He needn't have bothered with a pep talk for Lee because by the time he'd arrived at his hotel room, the man was seriously pumped up.

'Remember, Lee, five grand a goal.'

Lee stopped his shadow boxing for a moment and, breathing hard, pointed at Seth. 'I am not here for the money, and I am not here for the goal bonuses.'

'No, I know that but—'

'I am here to show everyone that I am still a fucking fantastic football player.'

'Absolutely,' Seth agreed. 'That's right, and I want you to shove that right up their arses.'

'I will. Right up their arses. I'll make Tottenham's eyes water.'

Seth wished his speech with Ronnie earlier that morning had gone as well. He'd left him in a terrible state. Seth looked at his watch.

'Right, well, got to get on. Go easy on the boxing, Lee. Don't want to tire yourself out.'

'Fuck off, Seth.'

'OK then.'

Supply and demand is the only axiom of economics that everyone understands, and today was a classic example of it in action. Middleton's ground was too small for the number of people who wanted to see the game. Last games of the season are always special, but there was every likelihood this would be Middleton's last game ever. For an array of personal reasons, practically the whole town wanted to cram themselves into the tiny ground.

Bill and Mary walked down to the ground at a little after two o'clock. Katherine had offered to baby-sit but Mary hadn't wanted to watch the match. It wasn't her thing and, anyway, she feared the worst. Thousands of grown men in tears, no thank you very much.

'Have a good one, Bill,' she said as she kissed him goodbye. She squeezed his hand tightly, the way people do at funerals, which was entirely appropriate because, barring a miracle, the mood in the town would be funereal, come twenty to five.

CHAPTER 25

The police had decided that the match should be delayed for fifteen minutes to help quell the crush of fans as they were herded into Middleton's ground, and at twenty past three, in glorious sunshine, the referee finally got the game underway and the crowd roared its approval. Because the little stadium only had one thousand actual seats, many thousands were able to squeeze themselves into the ground and God only knew how many people were there. After the legal capacity of six thousand was reached, George had instructed his tellers to disengage the turnstiles and charge cash to get in. Should the club fold today, at least they would have enough money for a good sendoff.

The few Shrewsbury fans who'd managed to get in certainly wouldn't be heard because it seemed the entire population of Middleton was present to drown them out and urge the home team on. There was no repeat of the treatment Lee Robson had received that fateful day at Highbury. The Middleton fans had far more to worry about than singing silly car songs at the man.

In actual fact, five minutes into the game, Robson still hadn't touched the ball, which suited everyone just fine, proving the maxim, he can't score if he hasn't got the ball.

The ball deflected off a Middleton player and was retrieved by the star guest of the Shrewsbury side. The intake of breath around the ground was audible as Lee set off on a powerful run towards the Middleton goal.

'Tackle him', 'Bring him down', 'Have him', 'Have his legs', the fans screamed, but none of the Middleton players appeared to be listening as Lee made his inexorable way forward.

Bill winced, unable to look away, and Lee unleashed a fierce shot from the edge of the penalty area. Thousands of eyes watched the ball, willing it to miss its target, and thousands of voices screamed their delight to see it being met by their goalkeeper, Thomson, who'd flung himself in its way. The relief was palpable.

'What a save!'

Spontaneous applause rippled through the ground. Whether it was for the shot or the save, no one knew, but the danger hadn't yet passed because Shrewsbury still had a corner.

The ball was floated in very wide and was met by a rampant Robson on the full volley at the edge of the area. Once again, the ball careered towards the Middleton goal and this time Thomson was nowhere to be seen, but fortunately it merely clipped the top of the bar and went out for a goal kick. Lee Robson screamed his frustration into his hands. It had been another brilliant effort. The man was on fire.

Middleton fans looked on agog. How the hell were Middleton going to last another eighty minutes without this bloke scoring? Undeterred, the fans screamed at full voice, but no longer for their players. Now they were appealing directly to God for a miracle.

It soon became apparent to everyone watching that Middleton were having to survive off scraps. Lee Robson was utterly dominating the game. He was playing all over the pitch and seemed to be wherever the bloody ball landed. The goalkeeper, Thomson, was the only Middleton player who had distinguished himself so far, with an array of saves he probably hadn't thought he was capable of.

Thomson held the ball in his hands and, in the time-honoured tradition of a side that is struggling, he threw the ball ahead of himself and hoofed it high into the opponent's half. The ball bounced and should have been cleared by a Shrewsbury defender but he only managed to half clear, and the ball sat up like a beach ball for Ronnie O'Mara right in front of the Shrewsbury goal. Not six yards out with only the keeper to beat, the crowd willed him on. He had to score. It was one of those harder-to-miss-than-score opportunities.

A surge of excitement took hold of Seth. This was it. Signor Raldini, get your cheque book out, son.

Ronnie too knew that this might be a pivotal moment in his life. He was worth millions of pounds and here was his chance to prove it, but that wasn't going to be easy. It was as if everything in front of him suddenly slowed, apart from the goal, which shrank to resemble a croquet hoop and, similarly, the ball would need teeing up if it got any smaller. Still in slow motion, Ronnie panicked as he flailed at the ball. He managed to connect with it but could only release a hopeless effort. The ball bounced agonisingly off the cross bar.

He'd missed, he'd fucking missed. No one watching could quite believe it, including the Shrewsbury defender who had been racing back to help his goalkeeper, and had run straight into the flight of the ball, knocking it back into his own goal.

Back in real time for Ronnie, the place erupted as Ronaldo peeled away to celebrate the most dubious goal he'd ever scored in his career. When it comes to claiming goals, football players genuinely have no shame and the Middleton keeper had as much right to claim this one as Ronnie.

Signor Raldini made a little note in his notepad, and looked at Seth wryly. Seth was relieved the goal had been scored, but he wasn't best pleased by Ronnie's hand in it.

'How the hell could he have missed from where he was?' a fan standing directly behind Alfonso Raldini asked.

How indeed, Seth winced.

Bill wasn't exactly overwhelmed by Ronnie's effort either. It was great that Middleton had scored, but he would have felt much happier had it been a goal of genuine class. As it was, Ronnie had had a shocking game so far, with Middleton being totally outplayed by Shrewsbury, and by Lee Robson in particular. Bill didn't have a good feeling about what he was seeing from his team or from Ronnie. The Middleton goal seemed nothing other than a temporary reprieve.

O'Dowd looked at the clock and chewed his lip anxiously. Ten minutes to go until half time and Middleton, somewhat miraculously, were still ahead. But surely it couldn't remain that way. Lee Robson had done everything but score, which meant he'd done nothing. They might give points for assists in fantasy football leagues, but this wasn't a fantasy, this was real, and the only thing that mattered to O'Dowd was goals. So far, Lee had not only been denied by every inch of wood that made up the Middleton goal but also every inch of Thomson's body. The Middleton keeper was still having the game of his life.

Lee received the ball from a throw-in, leaving his attentive defender wondering where he'd gone, and in the blink of an eye, was within range of goal once more. O'Dowd had to muster all his self-composure not to let rip and roar the bastard on. He'd already been asked by several fans if he was cheering for Shrewsbury and he would dearly have liked to answer in the affirmative.

Lee dispatched the ball and it curled towards the goal. Defenders jumped up and turned their backs because they weren't paid enough to get hurt, but in any case, the ball avoided them all and sailed unhindered into the top corner.

Lee Robson had scored and it was the best ten grand O'Dowd had ever spent. He wanted to turn around and holler his delight at the fans who had been abusing him. He steadied himself and took a moment to internalise his joy. He closed his eyes and clenched his jaw as his entire body almost shuddered with sheer delight. Lee set off on his victory charge and O'Dowd wanted to join him.

Sensibly, the other Shrewsbury players waited for the right time to embrace their new colleague after his great goal. If any of them had tried to embrace Lee in the immediate aftermath they might have been killed because Lee was viciously punching his fists at the rank of photographers who were all snapping away at the demented player. These photos would guarantee Lee two things; his picture in tomorrow's newspapers and an aftermatch drugs test.

No one had yet noticed the linesman's flag nor the fact that the referee was on the way over to him. After a brief chat with his colleague, the referee ran towards the Middleton penalty area pointing that a foul had been committed on the Middleton goalkeeper. The goal was disallowed. A cheer of relief spread throughout the ground like a Mexican wave although it ended abruptly when it reached O'Dowd. Middleton were still winning.

Given whose goal was being disallowed, it was a brave

decision to make, and Seth held his breath, hoping that Lee would decide not to attack the referee. To his credit, though, Lee merely looked pensive. He didn't even seem bothered. He hadn't scored but he felt sure that he was going to. It was inevitable.

O'Dowd urgently consulted his match-day programme for the name of the bastard official who had just denied him the all-important equalising goal. Nigel Rees. A bloody taffy – he should have guessed.

Jeers spread through the crowd in anticipation of the half-time whistle. If Middleton could just hang on to their slim lead, Joe Burke would then need to give them the team talk of his life.

In contrast with Lee Robson's first-half display, Ronnie O'Mara had been quiet. Everyone assumed that he was over-awed by the occasion but Seth was cursing his early morning pep talk now more than ever. Middleton hadn't created many chances, but Ronnie hadn't looked good in possession of the ball, and certainly hadn't looked like a multi-million-pound bargain.

Signor Raldini had taken to talking in Italian with his colleagues every time Ronnie got the ball and Seth couldn't see that this was anything other than bad news.

Shrewsbury didn't want the first half to end because, for all their industry and effort, they wanted to be on equal terms at the interval. With that in mind, they pushed forward in numbers. No one was in the Shrewsbury half at all and so a quick-thinking Thomson saw the opportunity ahead and ran out to clear the ball, which sailed in to the Shrewsbury half with only Ronnie O'Mara bearing down on it. The crowd roared him on. Seth clenched his buttocks and joined them.

Shrewsbury's keeper, alert to the threat, charged out to

meet Ronnie, but he was never going to get there. Ronnie was known for his pace and he was always the favourite. The crowd roared again and Bill held his nose between both his hands.

This was exactly the position that Ronnie should have wanted to be in and it would have been had his agent not paid him that visit. What the hell was Seth doing, telling him they'd flown in specially to see him play? Why couldn't he have kept his mouth shut? If he had, the ball would have been buried in the goal by now and Ronnie would have been simulating sex with a corner flag. But as it was, in his eagerness to reach the ball, Ronnie had allowed his momentum to get ahead of himself. Immediately, his balance was gone, and now his main concern was to remain upright. He looked like a sprinter who's lunged too early and ends up crawling over the finishing line. Mirroring Seth in the crowd, Ronnie's head fell forward and got nearer and nearer to the ground as his legs hopelessly tried to catch up with his torso. His nose eventually touched the pitch and then it was all over because his legs, still pounding like steam pistons piled his face further along and into the dirt.

The Shrewsbury goalkeeper waited to retrieve the ball and idly kicked it upfield. Ronnie hadn't even managed to touch it.

Bill and Seth looked on aghast as people all around actually laughed. Seth felt most embarrassed of all – like a second-hand car salesman trying to explain why the steering wheel had just come away in the driver's hands.

The whistle blew for half time. A wave of relief rushed through the ground, but Bill's heart sank.

Seth turned awkwardly to his Italian guests.

Alfonso stared at Seth, waiting for some sort of explanation. He'd travelled all this way to watch a player who had just had a miserable first half and couldn't appear to run after a ball without falling over.

'Very uneven pitch, this, you know . . . not easy to keep your balance . . . I think he's nervous, his mum's not well ya know. Loves him mum, that lad.' Seth realised that he should shut up.

''Ee scored a great goal, though, no?' Alfonso joked. His colleagues laughed.

'Yeah, well, they all count, don't they?' Seth enthused.

'That lasta one. I could have scored myself,' Alfonso added with some amusement.

'Right, can I get anyone a drink. Coffees, teas?' Seth offered.

'That woulda be nice. Three coffees, please, er, espressos, no?'

Bill and Seth had arranged to meet at the tea hut at half time but neither of them had dreamt it would be in circumstances like these.

'I can't understand it. He seems nervous,' Bill said.

'Nervous? He's not nervous, he's bloody shit, that's his problem.'

'No he's not.'

'I said to him this morning, I'm bringing some important—'

'You what?' Bill glared at Seth.

'I gave him a pep talk, didn't I?'

'And you told the lad that they were coming?'

'Well, yeah.'

'Ah well, that's bloody well it then, int it, ya bloody moron.'

'Hang on.'

'You've put the frighteners on the poor lad.' Bill was now angry.

'Well then, how would you expect him to cope in Italy?'

'He'd 'ave been alright.'

'Three espressos,' the lady serving in the tea hut barked sarcastically.

The coffee came in prepacked cups, with or without sugar. Strength wasn't an option. Seth grabbed the lukewarm cups and chased after Bill, but it was no use, he was gone.

George pushed his way through the crowd towards Bill with the grim news that Joe had decided to substitute Ronnie for another defender. It made sense.

So much for the O'Mara deal, then, Bill thought to himself. He was resigned to defeat.

He looked at the thousands of people, all with their fingers metaphorically crossed, and he wondered what his dad would have made of the scene. He looked to the skies; perhaps he was watching. He'd probably be sad, as Bill was, not only for his team, but for football in general.

Appropriately enough, Lee was the first player to emerge for the second half and, worryingly, he looked even more pumped up than before.

As the teams took their positions, it was glaringly apparent that Middleton were looking not to concede any goals. Shrewsbury faced one goalkeeper and ten defenders.

The referee blew his whistle and the siege began. Inevitably the ball came to Lee Robson and the crowd groaned. Forty-five minutes to go.

Seth noticed that none of the Italians had touched their coffee, and who could blame them? It was fake coffee, and not the only thing in the Middleton stadium today that had been posing as Brazilian. It was highly unfortunate that Ronnie had been substituted and even more embarrassing that none of the Italians even seemed bothered. Ronnie hadn't been mentioned again and Seth wasn't sure whether he should bring the subject up.

'Ronaldo, he must have picked up an injury,' Seth ventured.

'Yes, per'aps 'ee broka his nose on the ground,' Alfonso joked.

'Yes.' Seth forced himself to smile.

'I don't think that we will be a signing this Ronaldo.'

'No.' Seth knew as much but still he was disappointed, as much for Bill as for himself.

'No, but this Robson. 'Ee's a good player, no?'

Seth admonished himself for being so stupid. What an absolute fool he'd been. It hadn't even occurred to him until now: never mind Ronaldo, what about Lee bloody Robson?

'Come on, Lee.' Seth screamed to himself with clenched fists. All was forgiven. Seth wanted Lee to score now more than ever.

Marcus was enjoying the radio commentary of the match enormously. Every time Robson was denied, he imagined the agony and anguish etched on the blubbery face of O'Dowd. However, with Shrewsbury being awarded a penalty, it seemed that O'Dowd's agonising wait might be finally over.

'*Lee Robson stands up to take the kick and you can hear the howls about the ground. The Middleton fans feel, and some would say quite rightly, that they have been cheated here by Shrewsbury recruiting Lee Robson's services just for this game. Well, whatever your opinion, although we might expect a player like Robson to shine in this kind of company, let me tell you, today he has been magnificent. Tottenham, please take note. So, Robson against Thomson. These two teams have been at it all afternoon for league survival . . . oh, and a fantastic save . . .'*

Marcus was jubilant. In fact, in all his life, he had never been quite as moved by a sporting occasion. At last, he could understand the passion these football fans felt.

'Conran, Conran, he's saved it.'

'What?'

As the stadium erupted with Thomson's save, O'Dowd felt sick. He might as well have given the money to a blasted charity. Not fifty feet from him, Bill was trying to calm Smithy down for fear that he might have a heart attack. By now, George had joined them for good and even he was leaping about the place and not because of the piles of cash sitting in his office. Bill too was finally caught up in the mania and the veins on his neck stood out like straws as he celebrated the preservation of Middleton's one-goal advantage.

Somehow, it felt as if everything was preordained. This was the club's defiant last stand, stubbornly refusing to die and forcing the Council to make a decision they would never be forgiven for.

With only ten minutes to go, Middleton's lead was still intact and the existence of a God was now beyond doubt, because divine intervention could be the only possible explanation for Lee Robson's lack of goals. His wonder headers, volleys, free kicks, half-volleys, chips and now even a penalty had all conspired against him, and the Middleton fans were fervently praying that it might continue.

Appropriately enough, throughout the entire game, renditions of 'We Shall not be Moved' had rung out, and as the game drew to a close, the chant seemed even more poignant as the clock counted down on the club. It was an emotional end, not lost on O'Dowd, who was now being jeered by all around him. It was time for him to leave.

The fourth official produced his board, indicating that two minutes of extra time had been added and, again, the volume of shouts from the crowd cranked up another notch. A famous victory was upon them, perhaps the club's most famous victory ever. To their credit, the Middleton players had run themselves ragged and the fans appreciated their efforts. The level of emotion in the stadium was almost palpable and incredibly intense.

Bill had seen nothing like it before and he had been coming here since he was a kid to watch his dad play. Middleton could do with his old man now, he thought. A tear formed in Bill's eye and he wished that Mary was beside him.

Lee Robson effortlessly controlled the ball after it spun at him awkwardly from a Middleton player, and from nowhere released a shot. It didn't look as if he had enough room to generate any power in his kick, but somehow he did, and the ball sliced through the air but it wasn't on target. However, God must have been having a rare lapse in concentration – either that or he had a sick sense of humour – because the ball deflected off an unsuspecting Middleton defender and was suddenly heading towards the goal like an exocet locked on to its target.

A dreadful sense of inevitability hung in the air, as the ball agonisingly by-passed a wrong-footed Thomson and hit the back of the net. This time there was no linesman's flag to save them. Shrewsbury had equalised. Middleton were finished.

O'Dowd almost ejaculated in that instant. He leapt to his

feet, desperate to get out of the ground. Mainly so that he could scream himself hoarse with delight but also to avoid being lynched.

'Yeah, you'd better go O'Dowd.'

O'Dowd ducked as he heard a man clear his throat and sprang down the steps to safety, almost skipping with glee. What a relief, and what a fantastic result. The more he thought about it, the more he realised how perfect the whole thing had turned out to be. Middleton hadn't won and Robson hadn't scored, it was the perfect and cheapest possible scenario.

O'Dowd noted that Robson had claimed the goal and no doubt his odious little agent would be invoicing him for the ten grand, but O'Dowd certainly wouldn't be paying it and he didn't expect them to argue about it either.

When the referee finally signalled full time, the Middleton players sank to their knees. The game was literally up on Middleton Edwardians FC and there wasn't a dry eye in the house. Over a hundred years of history and local culture had just ended with a hollow whistle. The Shrewsbury players were understandably delighted but their opponents and their fans were devastated. Everyone has seen the football news on the final day of the season and witnessed the agony etched on to the faces of various fans but no television camera could adequately capture the depth of sadness and despair in the Middleton stadium that afternoon. It wasn't merely due to the pain of relegation, it was grief at the loss of their club.

It was Bill's nightmare, what he had feared all along, that Middleton would be added to the growing list of honourable football clubs that were no more. Many people wept openly and no one moved an inch. Perhaps as many as eight thousand people stood with their arms raised above their heads, clapping their team, their club, themselves and their town. It was a good job O'Dowd had already left. A hand squeezed Bill's shoulder as he stared out at the pitch which, by the start of next season, would probably be a Japanese garden, or a gymnasium for fat people with too much time on their hands.

CHAPTER 26

O'Dowd telephoned Marcus and sounded ecstatically happy with himself, and even Marcus had to concede that he was privately pleased with the result. It made things easier all round and, although he hated to admit it, he admired O'Dowd's verve and cunning in recruiting Robson.

'I take it you'll owe Mr Robson a few bob now,' Marcus chirped.

'Let me tell ya, worth every penny, that lad,' O'Dowd laughed.

'So, you've got what you wanted. Where are we now then?'

'Full steam ahead. Decision will be ratified on the Friday and then you'll have your permission.'

Marcus smiled. This was music to his ears – 'Money Money Money' by Abba, most probably. This was what he'd worked his whole life to achieve.

Conran, who was sitting opposite, could sense it was good news and smiled back at him, somewhat ruining the moment.

Vippin's chauffeuring services were no longer required because Seth had decided he should drive his Italian guests back to the airport. They had many important things to discuss.

'Lee is definitely open to a move abroad, but it will depend on what you can offer, because there are so many clubs in the Premiership that want to sign him.'

'He issa not being banned, no?'

Seth smiled. 'No, that's just speculation. My lad Lee, he's a beauty.'

About an hour and a half after the game, the stadium was finally empty. Everyone had gone home including Bill.

Mary had given him a hug when he got in, but she hadn't said anything. What would have been the point, and what could she have said anyway?

Later that evening Bill was still sat in his chair, lost in thought. It had been an exhausting day for everyone, but especially for him. The television was on but he wasn't watching it.

Mary was flicking from channel to channel and stumbled across a stunningly crass show. It featured two presenters sitting in front of a garish and crude set, and faced by a studio audience that looked as if they were part of a medical experiment. It was one of those shows that was so bad, it had a car accident quality to it, in that it was utterly compelling but left the viewers with a rampant sense of guilt for wasting their Godgiven lives watching it. If this was a magazine show, then it was undoubtedly based on *Razzle* or *Horny Slut*, but without the budget. Mary recognised both presenters but couldn't work out from where.

''Ere, Bill, who's he?'

Bill looked at the posh-sounding presenter, who looked hopelessly out of place, and shook his head.

'Dunno, but I can see why they've cast her. Bloody hell . . .'

Mary threw a cushion at him. 'Isn't she the one from

the papers? The one who was going out with Lee Robson?'

Bill groaned at the very mention of the man's name.

'Sorry, love.'

'No, you're right. Carmen, isn't it? That's her name.'

Carmen and Jeremy had been saved from obscurity by Guy Vincent and the commissioning editor of Channel Four, who had made the most of their tabloid popularity by handing them their own live talk show. It was hastily put together and loosely bound by sex and titillation. It was perfect late-night television, and the Channel Four executives were patting themselves on the back for their opportunism and creative vision.

Carmen and Jeremy made a fascinating combination. She was good to look at while he had the credibility and novelty value. In fact, their combined inexperience and lack of any discernible talent made the show even more delectable. For their debut, the subject was prostitution and so both presenters were on safe ground. She'd been one, and he'd used her. What a hook, Guy had said when he'd sold in the concept.

Viewers were invited to phone in with their experiences, and, of course, the studio audience was encouraged to participate too. In addition to this, there was the usual array of relevant guests and one questionable 'celebrity' interview right at the very end of the show.

Jeremy was empathising with a man who'd called in from Chipping Norton to explain that he was forced to use prostitutes because his girlfriends wouldn't tolerate his fetish of being defecated on. The audience moaned, and the TV executives watching from the green room cheered.

'Bloody hell, Mary, turn this crap off, will ya?'

'Yeah, sorry.' She handed him the remote. 'I'll put the kettle on. Have you checked your numbers?'

Bill hadn't bothered and pointed his remote control at the television. He knew the number already. Page 315 on Ceefax. He waited for the page to appear as he retrieved his coupon from the drawer. The message flashed up on the screen: 'Dividend Very High. Players with more than twenty-four points should call . . .'

Bill huffed. He couldn't remember ever having twenty-four points on the football pools for as long as he'd played. It meant at least eight score draws, but as he did every week, he began checking them off.

When he had five score draws, Bill felt the first tinges of panic.

'Bill, do you want tea?' Mary called out again.

Blackburn 1, Liverpool 1. Six score draws and counting.

'Bill . . .'

'Hang on, love, hang on, I'm busy.'

By the time Mary got into the living room with his tea, Bill was sitting in front of the television screen and for the second time today, he had tears welling in his eyes.

'What is it?' Mary asked, panicking that he might have had a heart attack or something.

Bill couldn't speak. He tried to, but he couldn't. Mary was frantic now and sat down on her knees in front of him, grabbing at his wrist to feel for a pulse. He smiled at her.

'I've won,' he managed to say, gesturing to his coupon.

'What?'

'Love, I've won the bloody pools.'

Neither Bill nor Mary slept a wink that night. How could they? They had each checked the coupon independently until they were satisfied that they really had won. And they had. Remarkably Bill had twenty-six points but, most crucially, he had all eight score draws on the coupon, one of which just happened to be Middleton versus Shrewsbury Town.

'How much have we won, Bill?' Mary kept asking. It was a fair question but not one anyone could answer before Wednesday at least. It takes the pools company that long to establish how big the pool of money is and to verify how many winners will share it. The last day of the season is traditionally the biggest weekend for the pools and if Bill was the only person with the winning combination, he dreaded to think what he might have won.

By Monday afternoon, Bill still hadn't slept but he had thoroughly researched the history of the pools in a desperate attempt to determine what he might have won. He and Katherine had examined all the pools going back over ten years and had annoyed the hell out of the freephone pools telephonists in the process. Outside the family, Bill and Mary hadn't told anyone about their possible good fortune in case it really was a fortune. Bill clung to the fact that in February 1994, one gambler won £2.25 million from Littlewoods with a 60p bet on a winning combination and, coincidentally, that had also been with eight score draws. That amount would be enough for the club, and just thinking about it made Bill giddy.

Bill hadn't ticked the 'no publicity' box on his coupon but that didn't matter because everyone in Middleton would know exactly what he'd won if it were that kind of sum. But it was unlikely – in fact almost impossible – and, according to the library books that Bill had devoured on the subject, the odds were as much as four hundred thousand to one against.

'That's not bad, Bill,' Mary pointed out. 'Lottery's fourteen million to one.'

Bill agreed as he broke another of the complimentary poppadoms that Vippin had brought to their table in the New Delhi. Incredibly, Katherine had offered to baby-sit, probably because her parents might be on the verge of becoming very rich.

'Oh, I don't know, Mary, this waiting is bloody killing me. Why has it got to take so long?' Bill added loudly.

Vippin's uncle overheard Bill and frantically came rushing over.

'Are you still waiting for your drinks?'

'No, no, don't worry,' Bill laughed and Mary joined him.

Since Bill had discovered he had at least won something, he had become very superstitious. Everything seemed to be falling in to place perfectly. He had needed eight score draws and he got them, but who should have scored the goal in the last draw of Saturdays matches? Lee Robson. It was none other than Lee Robson's goal that had given Bill his last and all-important eighth score draw. At the time, it had broken his heart, but now it seemed a Godsend.

'Mary, I've gotta tell ya, I think it's going to be big, I really do.'

'Just calm down, Bill, just calm down. Two more bottles of Cobra, please,' she asked Vippin's uncle.

'What did Michael say?' she continued when they were alone again.

'He thinks I'm nuts. Mind you, he's relieved the Italian thing didn't happen.'

Mary frowned.

'First, I go to him with this crazy deal to sell Ronnie and now I'm telling him I've won the pools.'

'But what did he say?'

'Nothing he can say until we know how much it is. But if it's enough, we'll have eight days to invoke that clause.'

'And you'll buy back the club?' Mary asked.

Bill couldn't bring himself to say it. It was beyond contemplation.

'Sorry for the deelay. Two chicken masala . . .'

By Tuesday afternoon, Bill and Mary felt quite ill for the continued lack of sleep. Bill couldn't stand the secrecy any longer and had told Smithy and George, in the strictest confidence, of course. Mary had warned him against it but he hadn't been able to help himself. They'd noticed he was acting strangely anyway and had known something wasn't quite right. Mary had pointed out that the whole town would know within the hour and, of course, she was absolutely right. It wasn't long before their phone and front door bell started to ring.

'No, Marge, we haven't won a thing. It's all just a joke.' Mary put the phone down. 'That bloody Smithy, I'll kill him.'

Meanwhile, Bill had gone to answer the front door to another of his 'best' friends.

*

Marcus too had got wind of the worrying rumour that someone in Middleton had won millions of pounds in the National Lottery and was thinking about buying back the club. He phoned O'Dowd in a terrible panic and found the councillor wasn't too happy either because they both stood to lose everything if the rumour was true.

'Look I'm sure it's a load of horseshit. I'll check with the lottery people and get back to you. But don't worry, the *Chronicle* have been trying to get me to react for weeks and this sounds like more of the same.'

'So, you don't think it's true then?'

'I very much doubt it.'

'But what if it is?' Marcus whimpered.

'It isn't. I'll call you back.'

'Call me back right away. I'll wait by the phone.'

Marcus could easily have checked himself but simply couldn't bear to find out it was true. It would be too painful. It only took O'Dowd a minute or two to establish there had been no winners from this Saturday's draw. He laughed. Someone foiling their play by winning the National Lottery – he'd never heard anything so ridiculous.

He entered Marcus's number on his mobile and was about to hit the green button when he stopped to imagine Marcus anxiously waiting for the phone to ring. O'Dowd hit the red button instead. Marcus could wait a little longer yet.

By mid-morning on Wednesday, Bill's lounge was packed. George, Smithy, Vippin, Michael, Ernie, Millsie, Katherine, Joe, Reggie and many others had crammed in to hear the news. The doorbell rang again. Mary gave her husband a wry look and went to answer the door. Bill waited for her to return.

'Come on then, Burt,' Bill said. 'Squeeze yourself in.'

Bill dialled the freephone number, which was answered by a recorded message, asking him to hold the line. Bill imagined it would take an age to get through with all the winners phoning in to hear what they'd won.

'Hello, Pools claim line, can I help you?'

Bill was startled. 'Er, yes, I'd like to know what the dividend is please.'

'Do you have more than twenty-four points sir?'

'Yes, I do.'

'Can I take your reference number, please?' The young lady sounded as if she too was getting excited as Bill read out his number.

The line went quiet, as quiet as the atmosphere in Bill's lounge. No one dared even to breathe.

'Hello?' the lady chirped at Bill.

'Yes, hello.'

'Congratulations, sir. You are the only winner for of this week's pool and the pool fund currently stands at two point six million pounds.'

Bill stared directly ahead. Everyone stared back, aching to know whether it was good or bad news. From his reaction, it was either very, very big or very, very small. Bill dropped the receiver and burst out laughing but still people were none the wiser.

'What is it, Bill, good or bad?' Smithy blurted out.

Bill looked at all his family and friends. 'Two point six million. I've won two point six million quid.'

Baby Tom had just gone down for his morning nap and

was abruptly awoken by the deafening roar of twenty or so adults downstairs. Mary couldn't hear his cries but figured he must have been woken and so hastily went to retrieve him from his cot. He shouldn't be left out of the celebrations. After all, his dad had just become a multimillionaire.

CHAPTER 28

Michael had called in Conran Beaumont and Marcus Howell to tell them what they must already have heard by now. Bill's big win and what he was going to do with it was the talk of the town, and the *Chronicle* was already calling him Saint Bill, the 'Saviour of Middleton'. Michael hadn't expected it to be a pleasant meeting, especially for Mr Beaumont, because, after all, he had just lost out on tens of millions of pounds. Therefore, Michael was surprised on two fronts. First, because Conran Beaumont sat there impassively stroking his jawline and didn't seem to care a jot, but also because his lawyer, Marcus Howell, on the other hand looked like he'd just been given a month to live.

'You can't do this.' Marcus was shaking with the loss and pushed Conran away as he tried to comfort him. 'Get off me, don't you dare touch me,' he snarled, his eyes glistening with rage. 'OK, what does he want?'

'Who?'

'Oh, don't give me this shit. You know who – Baxter – how much does he want?'

Michael looked at him oddly. 'I'm afraid I'm not with you.'

'For the club,' Marcus screamed. 'He's just the same as all the others, nose in my bloody trough. How much does he want for the land?'

'You mean the club?'

'Whatever.'

'He doesn't want anything for it. He's buying it back from you.'

Marcus's eyes were now even more moist and he shook his head in utter frustration as his well-honed plan unravelled before him.

'Yes, I know that, and we're offering to buy it back from him,' Marcus spat, his face wet with perspiration, tears and saliva. He was becoming an embarrassment and Conran tried to interject.

'Marc—'

'Don't you say a word.'

'Marcus, listen—'

'Not a word. Do you understand?'

'I just—'

'Do you want my ribs?'

Michael was dumbfounded.

'Do you?' Marcus stared manically at his partner.

'Yes.' Now Conran was really embarrassed.

'Well, then, shut up.' Marcus turned his attention back to Michael. 'Five million.'

'I'm sorry?'

'You should be. All you bastards feeding off me, no wonder my bloody hair fell out. Five million for the club, put that to Baxter and let's get this fucking thing sorted out once and for all.'

Michael looked a little awkward, not really knowing how he should respond.

'Well, go on, get him on the phone. Five million quid.'

'Mr Baxter has no intention of selling his club.'

Marcus's vision was blurred by his tears. 'But, why?' He suddenly broke down, sobbing as Conran began shuffling him towards the door. 'Please, oh, please. You have no idea . . .'

'Pull yourself together, for God's sake.' Conran opened the door. 'I'm dreadfully sorry about all of this.'

'No, it's OK. Er, Mr Howell, before you go . . .' Michael called out.

Marcus wiped his face and looked earnestly at Michael.

'Six million,' Marcus offered desperately.

Michael shook his head slowly. 'No, you misunderstand. You said that my client was "the same as all the others", something about noses in your trough.'

'Parasites, the lot of them.'

'Might I ask who they were?' Michael prayed his long-held suspicions about O'Dowd were about to be confirmed.

O'Dowd shuddered at what might have been. He looked around his office for the last time. His retirement plans were shattered and so was he. Last night, his colleagues had thrown a surprise leaving party for him, the surprise being how stingy they'd all been in clubbing together for his sendoff. A few vol-au-vents, sparkling wine and a new golf bag. He'd been expecting a golf villa and had ended up with a bag.

The timing of the whole thing could not have been worse either. Because he'd already granted planning permission on the land, he had officially taken on leper status, but before Baxter's win it had been worth it. Now, though, it was all for nothing. Shamefully, he had been prepared to sell out the club and that was how he was going to be remembered.

In fact, O'Dowd was actually down on the whole deal. Leslie Rose and Seth Meyer had insisted on being paid in full at the threat of exposing him, and Marcus once again had refused to chip in. Naturally, O'Dowd had tried to argue that his villa and cash were also due on the basis that he'd delivered on what he'd promised, but Marcus counter-threatened him with death and, given his state of mind, O'Dowd had taken him at his word and quickly backed off. His life might be shit, but he wanted it to continue, which it wouldn't if his true involvement in the deal ever came to light. He told himself he should feel lucky that it hadn't, but it felt like a particularly hollow victory and probably always would.

Bill had always been a popular person in Middleton, but now he was enjoying a new status of town hero. The news that he'd turned down offers from Conran Beaumont and subsequently from Spelthorne only increased his cachet, and Mary realised that her husband had been a long-term investment after all, and that she would never have to knit Tom another cardigan again.

Michael had quickly drafted in a team of experts to advise Bill, and their message had been quite clear and a little foreboding. Even under the fond ownership of Bill Baxter, the future for Middleton Edwardians FC was certainly not a rosy one. They were still saddled with debt and most people were agreed that they simply could not survive as a professional football club, but this didn't worry Bill at all. Tragically, more than half the teams in the hallowed Premiership would face similar problems eventually, and that would be football's loss. If Middleton reverted to an amateur football club for the surrounding community, then that suited Bill perfectly. After all, that was why the club and football had been founded, and Bill was excited at the prospect of another hundred years of the same.

Three weeks after that momentous last Saturday of the season when Middleton Edwardians had been saved by the late goal of Lee Robson, Bill and Mary laughed as he signed the deeds of purchase in Michael's office.

There was no trouble in getting witnesses for the signature. An excited posse had gathered around Michael's desk and they all cheered and clapped as Bill scrawled his name. Bill smiled for the camera, another front page of the *Chronicle* no doubt. Champagne corks were popped and a little impromptu party got underway.

Bill, slightly the worse for wear, arrived at the bakery half an hour late but no one minded, least of all Smithy, who Bill was relieving. Bill had every intention of leaving Beatty's but didn't feel he could do so until they'd recruited his successor because he didn't like to leave Smithy in the lurch.

'All done then, Bill?' Smithy asked.

Bill smiled and they hugged each other.

'Well done, mate, you're a bloody top man,' Smithy whispered into his ear.

'How's it all going here, then?' Bill asked, looking around at the old place.

Smithy frowned. 'Got a surprise for you, mate.'

Bill smiled, expecting some elaborate commemorative loaf to be wheeled out before him, but he was wrong. Smithy simply began to gather his belongings. Bill was bemused.

'What is it then?'

'Well, you know that you're a millionaire club owner and all that?'

'No, I'm a club owner, but I'm not a millionaire any more.'

'Yeah, whatever. But you're still loaded, though.'

Bill grinned.

'Well, the good news is that we've got a new supervisor.'

'Have we?'

'Yes, Gerald from Beatty's in Chorley is coming over, so

you can leave, and this, Billy boy, is your last day at work.'

The whole bakery team had now gathered round and everyone clapped and cheered. Bill was very touched. He'd worked at Beatty's since he was sixteen and he had grown to love the place.

'Is that the surprise?' Bill asked.

'No.'

'Well, what is it then?'

'For your last shift, you're on jam doughnuts,' Smithy announced.

Everyone shrieked their approval and Bill began to laugh too. He thanked everyone and, after many hugs and cuddles, Bill was still laughing as he made his way over to the station. There waiting for him was a massive commemorative Middleton FC loaf of bread beside a parcel wrapped in black and yellow paper.

Bill gingerly pulled at the wrapping paper and was absolutely choked to see a wonderful oil painting that brilliantly captured a Bill-like figure standing proudly outside Middleton's football ground.

'Blimey. This is an Austin Moseley. Smithy, how did you know?'

Smithy couldn't speak for the lump in his throat and instead opted to hug his dear friend. In fact, Mary had organised the present but Smithy had insisted that he and the lads should stump up the cash for Mr Moseley's commission.

'Thank you everyone, thank you so much. I love it.'

Now Bill too could hardly speak. For the last time the doughnuts were waiting for him and Bill was going to fill these ones so that they were fit to burst.

The Thorpe brothers had in fact received Smithy and Michael's letter asking for their help and, struck by a sudden surge of altruism, they declared their intention of saving the club and town that had given them so much. However, by the time they had sobered up enough to make their intentions known, Bill had already saved the club. Fortunately, though, they still wanted to help and the club's debts were wiped clean by their generous donation.

Marcus decided to go ahead with the operation and accepted Conran's generous offer of one million pounds per rib. He would at last become a wealthy man, if at some considerable personal cost. Conran, though, had eased the pain further by giving Marcus O'Dowd's villa, in which Marcus was currently convalescing. His new-found wealth would allow him to retire and also afford him the luxury of exposing O'Dowd, which would give him as much pleasure as his views of the Atlantic.

Conran was informed that the bone graft had been a success and in two months' time he would be in possession of a chin for the first time in his life. He was still heavily bandaged and was keeping the pain at bay by flicking through men's fashion magazines to pick out for himself the ideal jawline.

*

O'Dowd was a ruined man. He twisted and turned, lied and denied, but he was only delaying the inevitable, and corruption charges loomed. His intention was to plead insanity, which by now wasn't too far from the truth but wouldn't be sufficient to keep him out of jail.

Lee Robson signed for Foggia for one million pounds on a 'buttons' salary of five thousand pounds a week. In a hushed-up, out-of-court settlement, Lee was also awarded three hundred thousand pounds by Tottenham Hotspur for unfair dismissal, but that money was kept by his agent, Seth Meyer, who used it to clear some of his debts.

PC Waddle was no longer observing any diets at all. Having met a beautiful young woman at Weight Watchers, he'd fallen hopelessly in love and promptly left with her. Now, neither of them watched what they ate and nor did they care. They were much heavier for it, but blissfully happy.

Jeremy and Carmen continued to enjoy huge success with their television show, which ran for six series. Jeremy is currently dating a German fetish queen, and Carmen is considering whether to announce to the world that she is in fact a lesbian. She isn't, but Guy considers it would add another dimension to her tabloid currency.

Vippin was accepted on to a film course at Manchester Technical College. He and Katherine are still going out and as soon as Katherine's divorce is finalised, they intend to get engaged.

*

Daryl the wheel clamper is busy writing a novel about the calamitous repercussions of clamping a legally parked car. It is to be called *The Ripple Effect*, and Hodder and Stoughton won an auction to publish it and paid Daryl a handsome advance.

A businessman, Reuben Van Horst, dressed in an immaculate suit, stood outside the offices of Marshall Cavendish Burns PLC ahead of the biggest meeting of his life. Years of planning and many hundreds of millions of dollars hinged on the next hour. He looked at his watch, it was five minutes to ten. He'd just flown in on the red eye from Brussels and needed a quick sugar fix before he went into battle. He opened his bag, looked at his jam doughnut and took a large bite. Jam squirted out from the dough ball. His suit was ruined . . .

DOMINIC HOLLAND

Only in America

'An LA to London love story to rival Notting Hill' *Heat*

'A hilarious modern day fairytale' *Hello*

'The characterisation is warm, the dialogue is witty, and the plot – a friendly, feelgood fantasy' *Guardian*

How does a film script by an unknown writer get to be read by a Hollywood studio boss? What happens if he loves it? And what do his people do if they have no idea who wrote it?

Stuck in workaday London, rejected by the literary elite, wannabe scriptwriter Milly has no idea of the pandemonium her script is causing Stateside. And so it falls to LA movie executive Mitch to cut through the Hollywood madness, save his own job, and rescue Milly from obscurity. All he has to do is find her.

So begins a breathless romantic hunt, and a hilarious modern day fairytale from a sensational new voice in contemporary comic fiction.

FLAME
Hodder & Stoughton

MIL MILLINGTON

Things My Girlfriend and I Have Argued About

'A brilliantly written comedy. A novel that manages to be both funny and affectionate' *Guardian*

'There is little to say about coupledom that is not wittily and often movingly explored here. Sharply-written, brilliantly observed and absolutely hilarious' Wendy Holden, *Daily Mail*

'With his tear-inducing humour, Millington has tapped into the zeitgeist' *Vogue*

Pel Dalton leads an uneventful life. His days are spent bluffing his way through an IT job in the university library, pillow-fighting with his two sons, surviving family outings to the supermarket, and finding new things to argue about with Ursula, his German girl-friend. But things for Pel are about to change . . .

In this rupturingly funny tale of love, fatherhood, Anglo-German relations and being in all the wrong places at the wrong times, Pel discovers that sometimes the things that drive you crazy can be the only things that keep you sane.

FLAME
Hodder & Stoughton

DAVID NICHOLLS

Starter for Ten

'The funniest book of the year . . . trust us, you'll love it!' *Arena*

'There have been many pretenders to the throne of Hornby: David Nicholls is his legitimate heir' Mike Bullen, creator of *Cold Feet*

'*Starter for Ten* is the funniest book I've read in years' Emily Barr, author of *Backpack* and *Cuban Heels*

It's 1985 and Brian Jackson has arrived at university with a burning ambition – to make it onto TV's foremost general knowledge quiz. But no sooner has he embarked on 'The Challenge' than he finds himself falling hopelessly in love with his teammate, the beautiful and charismatic would-be actress Alice Harbinson.

When Alice fails to fall for his slightly over-eager charms, Brian comes up with a foolproof plan to capture her heart once and for all. He's going to win the game, at any cost, because – after all – everyone knows that what a woman really wants from a man is a comprehensive grasp of general knowledge . . .

Starter for Ten is a comedy about love, class, growing-up, and the all-important difference between knowledge and wisdom.

Are you up to the challenge of the funniest novel in years?

FLAME
Hodder & Stoughton

FAITH BLEASDALE

Deranged Marriage

'The perfect tonic . . . hilarious' *OK!*

'Juicy' *Heat*

'Riotously funny' *Company*

Would you ever consider a marriage pact? Holly did. In a heart-broken and drunken haze, it all seemed to make perfect sense. George was her best friend, would always be her best friend and, if they both found themselves single at the age of thirty, well, why not?

But when, a decade later, a man Holly hasn't seen for years says she's signed a contract and has to marry him, she realises exactly why not. Forget the fact that her career is going places, forget that she's head-over-heels in love with a gorgeous boyfriend, George wants the pact fulfilled and will stop at nothing to get his way.

Can I do become I don't? Or will it all end horribly ever after? Watch the confetti fly in this fabulous new novel from the bitingly funny Faith Bleasdale.

FLAME
Hodder & Stoughton